FATHERLY LOVE

"Daddy!" she cried as he rushed toward her. There was a demented leer on his drunken face. "No!"

His shadow fell across her like a swooping bird of prey. But before he could reach her something happened. Slowly at first, his feet began to twist. Before he knew it he was spinning.

"Stop it!" Ginny cried. "You're scaring *me!"*

But he continued to spin, looking like a disjointed puppet on a twisted string.

Suddenly he stopped and hung there limply, as though loosely suspended from a puppeteer's rack.

Ginny knew the pose at once. She had seen it in the stained glass window behind the altar of her father's church: arms stretched out wide, palms opened, head hung loosely to one side, and one bare foot planted firmly over the instep of the other. It made her stomach twist.

"I am the Lord, thy God," he whispered in a raspy voice that was dark and unfamiliar. "Suffer not . . ."

He did not finish. He toppled to the floor in a jumbled heap.

HOCUS-POCUS

HOCUS-POCUS

JACK SCAPARRO

ZEBRA BOOKS
KENSINGTON PUBLISHING CORP.

For Susan Hester and Bob Brier, who began it all with tales of snakes and sorcerers. And to the memory of Adrian Boshier, who handled the deadliest of snakes, and was not harmed.

ZEBRA BOOKS

are published by

Kensington Publishing Corp.
475 Park Avenue South
New York, NY 10016

First printing: February, 1988

Printed in the United States of America

PROLOGUE

Maybe it was because she had been working up there all alone, or that the fumes from the small campfire she had built in the cave were finally getting to her. But she now heard a peculiar hissing sound coming from the dank walls of the eerie cave. It was as though the array of fierce serpents that had been painted on them in red ochre, centuries and centuries before anyone could remember, had come to life.

The setting sun sent long ribbons of dusty light sailing across the barren floor of the never-ending landscape below the mountain cave as the woman tried to block the hissing noise from her mind and complete the sketches of the vipers she had traveled so far to obtain. Far below the craggy steep where she hurriedly made her pen and ink drawings, her guides moved about a tiny cluster of flapping tents and prepared the evening meal. One of them looked up from the flames of his cooking-fire. He thought he might have heard something and lifted his eyes to the winding trail that led to the forbidden mountain range. In the rapidly diminishing light, he could barely make out the sliver of firelight that emanated from the twisted opening of the cave where the young white woman had gone to do her work. If he lived to be a thousand, he would never know from where she mustered the courage to go up there all alone.

And she knew she should not have been up there alone. It was no place for a woman in her condition to be. She had been back and forth, from camp to cave, over a dozen times that week, and never once had there been the slightest hint that the child she carried in her womb would choose to be born so early—months before its time! She clutched her abdomen. She had been working so intently that she had not noticed the pains at first, had not thought to time them. She did so now and realized she'd never be able to make it back to the camp—where the native guides, who had brought her to this godforsaken place, had remained behind, too afraid to accompany her up the rocky trail that led to the forbidden caves.

If she could only hold it off a bit longer, she urged herself. If only the hissing noise—which she now knew to be coming from the pressure in her own head—would only stop, she could get the work done. By morning, if she did not return to camp, the guides would surely come to find her, she thought. They had to! They couldn't simply let her die up there all alone like that—with a newborn child! What would they tell her husband back at the mission?

Her water broke and the stain of it now spread across her sand-colored bush skirt in the image of something grotesque—something that resembled the horrible ochre-colored vipers that crowded and closed in on her from the wavering shadows. The hissing noise that had earlier filled her head, had filled the *cave,* now stopped when she looked down at herself and gasped.

She was in the cave of some unknown evil. According to her guides, a "man of evil magic" had once lived and perished there, more centuries ago than anyone could imagine. It was said that he had painted the demonic-looking serpents that crowded the cave's walls, and that he had a power to make them live again. But he was long dead. Fragments of his skull and bones were scattered to the far reaches of the cave as though it were a defiled graveyard. She placed her knuckles between her teeth and began to cry. Tears spilled freely from the slits of her tightly closed eyes and tumbled to the dusty floor of the cave like salted crystals. Not here, she thought. Not now. At the mission hospital she had helped her husband deliver children for the local natives. Now she would have to be midwife to herself. The thought terrified her.

Something suddenly made her open her eyes and focus on the cave's eerie paintings in a new and different way. The crimson glow of her fire made the monstrous serpents appear to move—as though they were alive. The thought was so bizarre she forget her pain for a moment and laughed. But when the hissing sound of the vipers loudly resumed, and poured into every awakened pore of her consciousness, her feeble laughter instantly transformed itself into a chilling screech of terror. And in that moment of total horror, her child began to slither down the darkened channel of her blood-drenched womb. Her cries took on the anguish of the victim of a sacrificial slaughter.

When all grew still again, and the dense blackness of night swallowed the earth, it appeared as though the only living thing beneath the vast canopy of shimmering stars was that lonely flicker of firelight that came from the twisted mouth of the cave. The agonized shrieks that had earlier cascaded down the mountainside had been followed by the quiet wail of a newborn child. To the guides who came out of their tents to hear it, it had sounded like the cry of death itself.

PART I

CHAPTER ONE

He would have liked very much not to be doing the thing he was about to do. He had done it too many times before. It was bad for the girl. She was only twelve. His only daughter. His only child.

He knelt beside her bed as quietly as he could and looked down at her. A wash of moonlight played across her well-scrubbed face as though it were a translucent gem. She reminded him of his wife, her dead mother.

Through the open window the early spring sounds of crickets and toads clashed with his unnatural desire. He wanted her, his own daughter, the same way he had wanted her mother. And he was a minister of the Lord. A man of God!

Reverend Watkins bit into the knuckles of his prayer-locked hands and almost wept as he lowered his eyes to the rest of his daughter's body. The pale light that filtered in through the window made her young body appear to float on the softness of the rumpled sheets that had been kicked off in her sleep. Her slightly parted lips glistened.

It was a warm night and the thin nightdress Ginny wore clung to her developing breasts like a pair of cupped hands. It heaved as gently as the swell of her breath, as quietly as the fragrant breeze that billowed the white summer curtains into the room.

Watkins had finished a full bottle of claret at dinner, and several snifters of brandy after his daughter had gone to bed. And now this, he thought. Again! He didn't seem able to control himself. It made his mouth go dry.

"Oh, Lord," he mumbled to himself, sounding like the whimpering of a frightened animal. "Deliver me from evil . . . from temptation . . . from every form of sin."

The words grated in his throat like lumps of burning sand. He knew they were useless. The Lord couldn't help him. Not anymore. He was lost. He knew it. But, somehow, it didn't seem to matter anymore.

He unlocked his hands and reached out to touch her. In his whirling mind it wasn't the top of his daughter's nightgown he was awkwardly attempting to undo, but that of his dead wife—the mother Ginny had never known. How seductive she had been! He could see her face before him in the darkness now. It held a beauty that was as fragile as her youth. Her soft blond hair fell, when it was loosened from its knot at the back of her head, across her thin shoulders and made her look like a Botticelli Venus. And her eyes! They were like pools of light through which the inner glow of her dazzling intelligence gleamed. Looking into them had brought him peace—a peace that had ended when she died while giving birth to Ginny in that godawful cave in Africa.

The sensation of his cold hands on his daughter's breasts wove itself into the fabric of a dream she was having. She was listening to the rocks that were strewn about a bare and barren range. They sang sweetly. Yet the meaning of their song escaped her. She lifted a phallic stone into the air and brought it down into a worn depression in a stone slab upon which she sat with her legs crossed. Stone upon stone. The air filled with its sound, a vibrating harmony that hummed along the barrenness of the strange landscape as clearly as a church bell. She circled her fingers tightly about the blunted stone and struck it again, and again, and again—until the earth itself began to throb with the feel of it. The song was good, sweet. Yet it told her nothing. Off in the distance stood the savages, as dark as the night itself. Their bodies were slick with sweat. They didn't like the song of the rocks. They made angry gestures on the horizon of her heat-filled dream and charged at her through the rocky slopes. But it didn't stop her song. She raised and lowered the blunted stone in her hand, striking it repeatedly into the hollow depression between her crossed legs. The throb shivered up her body, causing her insides to feel light and tingly. It felt good. She knew what she was doing was bad. Yet she never wanted it to stop—even if the dark savages caught up to her, even if they tore the flesh from her body.

Ginny suddenly cried out and bolted upright in the bed. Her father's perspiring face hung beside her like a shiny blue mask in the moonlit room. She screamed.

Watkins leaned back on the heels of his loose slippers, startled. He licked his hand out at her like a snake. It caught her on the forearm and knocked her back against the headboard of the bed.

"Daddy!" she cried, rubbing the arm she had raised

to protect herself. "What did I do!?"

He swiftly rose to his feet and yanked her from the bed. With his hands clutched firmly about her shoulders he then shoved her out of the room and into the hall. She knew what he wanted.

"Please," she pleaded. "I can't." She covered her face with her hands and began to cry. "Not tonight."

He grappled with her for a moment when she resisted and pushed her down the narrow passageway that led to the attic. Her nightgown came off in his hands. He tossed it aside like a sticky spiderweb and followed her. "Go!" he commanded. And she ran up the creaking wooden staircase without looking back.

The dangling overhead light bulb was already swiched on, indicating that he had been up there earlier. The old leather-covered steamer trunk at the far end of the dim attic had already been opened, too. She felt more humiliated and hateful than ever before as she slowly approached the trunk and waited for him, naked, crying herself sick as she focused on the contents of it. The sound of her father's scuffling slippered feet approached from behind.

"Put it on," he said.

When she turned to face him a spark of light caught the edge of his gold-rimmed glasses like a shooting star. The small white patch, framed on either side by the black neckband of his clergyman's shirt, was ice smooth. Above it, his adam's apple jerked nervously.

It's a dream, she thought. A very bad dream.

That was what he had trained her to believe ever since she was a very small child. But now that she was old enough to ask questions, the answer was always the same—a bewildered stare. With it he seemed to be saying: What's wrong with you? Don't you *enjoy* our little game?

"Put it on," he repeated evenly. His shadow darkened her blood-flushed face as he took a step closer.

She raised her hands to protect herself and saw a bruise that had already begun to ripen on the arm she had earlier raised in the bedroom. He took a step away from her. He seemed confused.

"I never hit you," he said. "I couldn't have."

It wasn't the lie that upset her. It wasn't even that he was drunker that she had ever seen him before. It was something else. Something was very different about him tonight. There was also something very different about *her.* Thinking of it made her shiver. She tried to cover her nakedness.

Without warning he suddenly turned away and stumbled toward a darkened corner of the attic where there was an old leather-covered armchair. An empty bottle of claret rested on the bare wooden floor beside it. Stoop-shouldered, he collapsed into the bulky chair and caused its ball-and-claw feet to grate on the naked floorboards. He sat there, perfectly still, as the hanging light bulb he had brushed against swung in a shallow arc. It created a vortex of false shadows. In the child's mind her father appeared to be suspended in a murky void, a void that was feathered-in at the edges with cobwebs and the disused remains of a shattered life. And when he finally jerked his body forward, so that he could reach for an old photo album that was lying on a crate, it startled her. He did not notice how his abrupt movement had made her jump.

The girl's hand closed about the raised lid of the trunk as her father open the book across his thin knees. She began to walk her fingers down the lid of the trunk until they touched the thing he wanted her to wear. Her eyes never left him as she reached blindly into the trunk.

Watkins slowly turned the brittle pages of the velvet-covered photo album in his lap. He turned past pictures he had taken a long time ago—of zebras and rhinos and elephants, and of the small group of grinning blacks who had once worked beside him to build the mission he had established in the remoteness of the African veldt. He paid no attention to the sound of Ginny's rummaging through the contents of the old trunk. It was as though she were no longer there, as though *he* were no longer there. He had to find the picture, the one he cherished above all others—the one he often cursed. It was of his young bride on their wedding day. He had taken it himself.

Ginny swept her soft blond hair back into a knot and fastened it there with a tortoiseshell comb she had drawn from the trunk. She knew what her father expected of her—knew it all too well. The dark secret showed in her moist blue eyes like a searing scar. She hated herself for what she was doing, and, now that she was growing up, was beginning to hate her father even more. She wondered if she could kill him—kill him in such a way that no one would ever know she was responsible. Like the way she childishly believed she had once killed her own pet hamster. She was much younger then, and was thinking how much fun it would be to see just how fast it could travel the wheel of its cage. *Faster-faster-faster!* she had repeated to herself at the time. And it did just that, spinning the wheel until the cage grew warm in her hands. Then it died, right there in the wheel. She would never forget feeling responsible for having somehow killed the little creature.

The musty fragrance from the trunk reached him at the same moment he found the picture he had been looking for. His young bride stared out at him from the glossy print as though she were still alive. Behind her was the simple whitewashed mission where they had been married.

Staring at the picture made it all suddenly feel like home: the veldt, the sublime darkness of a noble night, and the several billion stars that punctuated the black velvet sky above the mission roof—where they had first made love. She had been a virgin. He had, too. He closed his eyes for a moment and imagined that he could detect the scent of that sweat-soaked, first night of love. He was positive it was on that night that Ginny had been conceived.

God save me from myself, he thought, brushing his fingers across the worn photo. Deliver me from the beast that has grown within my soul. Allow it not to have its will of me.

As though in response to his fervent plea, Ginny pushed the heavy lid of the trunk closed with a startling thud. It shook the floor, causing wispy puffs of dust to shoot up from the cracks between the wide floorboards.

Watkins looked up. His steel-grey eyes came from far away and lit up when he finally focused them on his daughter. As he had desired, she now stood on top of the trunk's lid, dressed in her dead mother's old wedding gown—the same one as in the photograph.

Ginny could hear the breath rush into her father's

lungs at the sight of her. In spite of her uneasy feelings, the quiet sound of that first gasp sent particles of electric current shooting though her flesh. It was a secret joy—as though she had some sort of power over *him*. She couldn't help herself. Her eyes brightened as she fanned the pleats of the wedding dress between her fingertips.

The gown, far too large for her slender body, hung loosely from her shoulders and cascaded down her body until it pooled in gentle eddies about the trunk on which she stood. A full-length oval mirror on an oak stand stood slightly to the side behind her. As the light from the single suspended light bulb passed through the gown's lacework, her nakedness was reflected in it.

Her father's eyes told her nothing. She had often seen that vacant gaze in church, just before he was about to denounce the sinners of the world from the pulpit. Her knees began to loosen.

"Turn, my darling," he finally said, leaning forward in the chair. His voice surprised her, it was so calm. "Turn," he repeated.

Her long hair fell from its knot and covered her pale shoulders as she began a studied pirouette. Raised up on the ball of one foot she pushed with the toes of the other, making the leather sheathing of the trunk squeak beneath her feet as she turned. For many moments it was the only sound that filled the room.

When she completed one full revolution she resumed a neutral position facing him. His eyes maintained the same blank gaze. It was as though he were centuries away. It chilled her to guess what he might be thinking.

"Can I put it away now and go back to bed?" she asked. "I have to get up and go to school tomorrow." It was a lie. The next day was Saturday. She risked it because she saw how lost he was; how totally far away his mind had wandered. She had never seen him that way before.

Without responding, he lowered his eyes back to the photograph. "Amelia," he said softly, as though beckoning his bride back from the grave. *"Why?"*

It was the way he said it that chilled her. The tone he used was different from anything she had ever heard before, as though a stranger were speaking. His face changed. The blood drained from his cheeks. His knuckles whitened as he balled his fists in the air.

"You slut!" he hissed at the picture. "You heathen slut!"

His fists came down upon the album, splitting its fragile spine in two. The pieces flew from his lap and spiraled into the dark pools of emptiness beneath the slanting attic roof.

Ginny's breath caught.

"I have to get up early tomorrow," she said rapidly. "I have some homework to finish before going to school."

He rose from his chair like a shot.

"Jezebel!" he screamed. "Whore of Babylon! The fall of man lies at your feet!"

Ginny wanted to turn and run as he started toward her, but there was no place to go. He blocked the only way out.

"Daddy!" she cried as he rushed toward her. There was a demented leer on his drunken face. "No!"

His shadow fell across her like a swooping bird of prey. But before he could reach her something happened. He froze in the middle of the attic with his arms stretched out wide on either side of him, as though they were tied to an invisible rod that ran across the tops of his shoulders. He was as puzzled as the child. A quirky smile played on the edges of his thin white lips. He looked at her as though she might somehow be responsible for what was happening, and then stared at each of his outstretched arms as though they didn't belong to him. He couldn't figure it out. Then, slowly at first, his feet began to twist. Before he knew it, he was spinning. One of his hands brushed against the suspended light bulb and it almost hit the rafter from which it hung. Shadows raced across the floor and slanted roof. He began to mumble gibberish.

"Stop it!" Ginny cried. "You're *scaring* me!"

But he continued to spin, looking to her more and more like a disjointed puppet on a twisted string. It was like something at the heart of a very bad dream, and she wondered for a moment if she might be dreaming it, after all. She tried to scream for help—someone might hear and come running—but no sound left her lips. A hot bubble of nausea blocked her throat.

Her father's feet were now moving so swiftly on the floor that his slippers flew off and scuttled along the boards until they disappeared into the darkness beneath the eaves of the attic's low-pitched roof. Dust twisted up from the floorboards and gathered like wispy ropes about his legs. Then, just as abruptly as he had begun to spin, he stopped and hung there limply, as though loosely suspended from a puppeteer's rack.

Ginny knew the pose at once. She had seen it in the

stained glass window behind the altar of her father's church: arms stretched out wide, palms opened, head hung loosely to one side, and one bare foot planted firmly over the instep of the other. It made her stomach twist.

"I am the Lord, thy God," he whispered in a raspy voice that was dark and unfamiliar. "Suffer not. . . ."

He did not finish. He toppled to the floor in a jumbled heap.

Ginny clutched the hem of the gown in her cold hands and leaped from the trunk. When her feet touched the floor she froze. Something made her stand there, looking down at her father's contorted body. He was breathing, that much she could tell. But what rooted her to the spot was that he reminded her of something—something that was just as bizarre as the thought she'd had earlier of having once been responsible for the death of her own pet hamster. Her father looked just like the puppet she always kept hanging from one of the posts at the foot of her bed.

As she stood there, swallowing hard to find her breath, something cold and terribly swift seemed to race into the attic behind her. She turned. There was nothing. But whatever it was, it swept right through her bones and made the flossy hairs in the curve of her spine stand out and prickle.

Ginny bolted and headed straight for the stairwell, knocking against the light bulb as she fled. It exploded against the rafter in a shower of sparks that danced along the boards of the attic until they all died out. Then it was dark—blacker than black. She couldn't see to find her way out. She flailed her arms about wildly, as though the darkness had substance, as though she could somehow slide her hands along its emptiness to find her way out.

It was then that something in the cold darkness of that deep-black attic laughed! It didn't sound like anything she had ever heard before.

CHAPTER TWO

Sara Garrett didn't like waking up with the dark feeling she had. Something in the night had worked on her in the most unexpected way. It was probably a dream, she thought. If only she could remember it. They always told her so much. She wondered if the long plane trip from Africa the day before had anything to do with it.

She closed her eyes for a moment and tried to recall the dream. Nothing. The dark feeling wasn't as strong, but it was still there. It even managed to work itself into the reality of the early morning light that was beginning to come in through the opened window beside her bed. Its soft glow shimmered on the ceiling above her like a handful of silver coins falling out of the sky.

The dream, she thought, attempting to remember. There was this . . . bird, and it . . . no, he. . . . It all abruptly faded with a yawn, back into the void from which it came. She really didn't have the time to go into it anyway, she thought. In another couple of hours she was scheduled to present a paper before the National Parapsychological Association. There was a partially completed draft of the talk on the night table beside her. It was the first time the association had ever asked an anthropologist to read at the annual one-day conference, and she wasn't as ready as she would have liked to be. Thank God it was going to be a closed presentation, she thought. Less stress, much more informal. The thought made her feel more comfortable, but she still had a lot of polishing to do on it before the paper could be presented without a hitch.

She sat up and swung her shapely tanned legs over the edge of the bed. When her bare feet touched the small rug on the floor she yanked them back, as sharply as if she had stepped into a bucket of live scorpions. For the past two years she had awakened each morning in a canvas tent. Stepping on a live scorpion or a poisonous snake was always a real possibility. She smiled and lowered her feet back down and raked her long toes through the shaggy pile of the rug. It felt good. It helped dispel the remaining darkness of the nagging dream. So too, did the unexpected view from her window.

Wilston College in southeastern Texas had provided her with a small cottage that overlooked the hilly campus. One of its windows faced the sprawling lawns for which the college was famous. So green, she thought. So lush. So different from the parched landscape she had so quickly grown accustomed to.

She rose and sunk her hands into the deep pockets of the loose-fitting pajamas she liked to wear and walked toward the window on the other side of the cottage, where there was a writing desk. Having arrived in total darkness the night before, she was curious to see where she was. There were no curtains on the window behind the desk, and through it she could see the outskirt of the small town of Wilston itself. She didn't know why, but it reminded her of some of the New England towns she had grown up in. There was even a white church spire spiking up into the brilliant blue sky, but there were no green mountains or rapidly gushing brooks. Yet, to her, it had the feel of a small New Hampshire town. Maybe she had been away too long, she thought.

She was about to turn and go to the small kitchenette she had passed on her way to the window, to fix herself a cup of coffee, when something in the distance suddenly drew her attention. About a half mile down the hill upon which the cottage stood, toward the town, the rising sun caught on something that shone like silver through a stand of trees. She attempted to identify what that might be, running so brightly through the middle of all that cool-looking greenery. A lake? she thought. No. Although it did have the size of a small lake, it didn't seem to have the character of one. Probably a pond, she thought. A very large one.

She hadn't seen a pond in years. The part of Africa where she had been doing research had rivers and lakes—where there were no deserts—never ponds. She made a mental note to take a stroll in that direction before she left the town. Although she couldn't swim a stroke, it might be fun.

The kitchenette was no larger than a closet, yet it had everything. A two-burner electric stove rested on the top of a half refrigerator. To the side of it was a small stainless steel sink with a set of unmatched dishes, cups and saucers on a shelf above it. No window. Beside the sink there was a small low cupboard. She opened it. Empty. And she was hungry, too! In the bush she had grown accustomed to a full breakfast. A roasted lizard that had been caught by one of the tribesmen wasn't bad. It would hold her all day, until dark when she began to get hungry again.

She stooped down and opened the refrigerator. A can of coffee, a fresh carton of milk and a loaf of white bread. She wrinkled her nose. Coffee would be fine. No milk. No bread. She had a problem figuring out how to use the electric coffee pot—a Silex. She had seen one before, but had never used one. It had a pot on top, and one on the bottom, too, which looked as though it would boil the water. That was good enough for her. She removed the top part and set it aside. Into the bottom half she poured some water from the sink and plugged its cord into the wall outlet. When the water boiled, she emptied half a can of Folgers into it. When it had boiled for fifteen minutes she found a juice strainer, lined it with a paper napkin, and poured herself a cup. Perfect! she told herself. And the aroma that filled the cottage was almost the same as her mornings in the veldt. She then walked wit the coffee, and the draft of her paper, to the small writing table in front of the window.

Now that the sun was higher in the sky, and no longer in a position to reflect itself off the water, the pond, or whatever it was, had vanished into the spreading brightness of the day. All she could see from the window was the small stand of trees that appeared to start where the town ended.

After arranging a pile of note cards next to her unfinished draft, she took a sip of the delicious coffee and leaned back in the chair. There was a V in the soft flesh between her eyebrows. She had always been considered beautiful, but since having spent so much time in the stress-free environment of the bush, immersed in the studies she felt so driven to pursue, she had become lovelier; her chisled features softer, more translucent. There was even greater depth in her vibrant green eyes, suggesting a cultivated intelligence. She would sometimes blush when she met someone who appeared able to read what was in them. She was almost thirty-six, yet looked no more than twenty-five.

As she allowed the sun from the window to fall on her face for a moment before beginning to work, she wondered, probably for the fiftieth time in the past two days, what she was doing there. Why had she accepted the invitation to speak at this particular conference? Was it the topic?

She did have more than a passing interest in parapsychology—in things that appeared to go beyond the ordinary laws of physics. Before going to Africa with a research grant, she had even considered becoming a parapsychologist herself. The conference might be just the place for her to gather information that might complement her own studies.

She unscrewed the top of the old-fashioned fountain pen she always used for making notes in red ink and looked at the blank index cards she had placed beside her written draft. She thought of opening her talk with a direct quote from Carlos Castaneda, the famed anthropologist. Although most people by now realized that the sorcerer he had written about, don Juan, did not actually exist, Castaneda had once stunned the world with the introduction of a concept of separate realities. If a man thinks he flew, he *flew!* For him there was no other reality.

As she leaned forward and touched the gold nib of her pen to the note card, something in the distance outside her window caught her attention. She looked up and saw a light. It danced in her eyes as a cool breeze entered the window and scattered her note cards. She focused on the distant trees, where the pulsating light appeared to be coming from. The pond! It was glittering like a burnished strip of precious metal.

That's odd, she thought. It was almost as though the sun had decided to go back to the position it had been in when she first woke up. Its light now flickered off the water and darted up the hill to where she sat.

Something began to happen to her. She looked down at the pen in her hand. It was clutched so tightly that the tips of her fingers were white. At first she didn't know what was happening. It had been such a long time since. . . .

Oh, God! She suddenly realized what it was. The light. She shouldn't have. . . .

But it was too late. The last thing she remembered before losing consciousness was the note card she had been about to write on. Red ink poured across it from the tip of her pen like a pool of blood.

CHAPTER THREE

When Ginny woke up everything was so quiet in the house that she could hear old Miss Lettie whispering a song to herself as she fixed breakfast downstairs in the kitchen. But why was everything so dark?

Then she knew. She had spent the night in the closet, the way she always did whenever she was frightened—all balled up on a pile of loose clothing. The door was locked with a wire hanger she had twisted about the knob and then fastened to a hook on the wall beside it. She undid the hanger and slipped it off the hook. The door opened a crack and she peeked out without opening it any further.

A band of light from the window across the room striped her face with a thin white line. It followed the graceful curve of her forehead, rolled down the bridge of her nose, crossed her lips like a finger and finally spilled from her chin down to her naked body. She was cold.

At the foot of her bed, dangling from one of the posts, was the string puppet she now remembered playing with before going to sleep. She froze. Maybe it was a dream, she thought. She was always having scary dreams about her father touching her, beating her, forcing her to. . . .

But when she lifted her arm to open the door a bit wider, the light caught the fresh bruise on her arm. And with it came the full memory of the night before—the blow that had caused the bruise, being pushed and shoved up to the attic, being made to wear her dead mother's old wedding dress, and . . . and the spinning her father had done in the center of the attic!

She thought of her dead hamster, the way she once believed she had willed it to run the wheel until it collapsed and died. Then she studied her puppet. It was a hobo doll, dressed in baggy pants and a tattered vest over a blue checkered shirt. Its face was painted to look sad and in need of a shave. Its shoes had been lost a long time ago. She slowly walked to it.

Six strings ran down from the crisscrossed control sticks to where they were attached to the puppet's flexible body: two to the ears, which made the head move any way you wanted; two to the hands, which were loosely attached to its wrists, so that its hands, arms, and shoulders could move any which way; and two to the knees, which could make the thing dance if you wanted it to.

A breeze came in through the open window and made the puppet slowly roll from side to side. Its outstretched wooden hands tapped hollowly against the footboard of the bed. Ginny held her breath as she watched it twist. In her mind she had been repeating the word *move,* over and over, just to see if she could do it—as she thought she had done with the hamster, as she thought she might have done with her own father in the attic.

Her heart was pounding strongly as she approached and gingerly lifted the puppet from the post. She didn't want to have anything to do with it again and hurled it into the closet where she had spent the night. It landed there, in a disjointed heap, just as her father had landed on the attic floor the night before. She ran to the door and closed it. It had to be a dream! she told herself. It just *had* to be!

She caught sight of herself in the mirror above the dresser across the room. Her eyes widened at her nakedness. She shivered, though the room was as warm as summer. On a chair next to the closet there was a robe. She quickly put it on and left the room, quietly, so as not to draw attention to herself. On tiptoe she headed down the hallway for the attic stairs. She wanted to be certain that last night had not been just a dream.

It hadn't. The first thing she saw was her own torn nightdress near the bottom of the landing; further up, her mother's old wedding gown. It dangled from a banister post at the top of the stairs. She sucked in her breath, remembering how it got there; how she had ripped herself out of it after it had caught on the post. Everything was beginning to come back to her now.

The steps beneath her bare feet creaked as she climbed higher. The sound sent shivers through her scalp. Everything within her cried out for her to leave, at once, but she couldn't. Something seemed to be calling to her from above, drawing her farther and farther up the cold wooden steps. She drew in her breath and told herself she wouldn't go all the way up into the attic—no matter what.

With her eyes tightly shut, she took one more step and stopped. Her head protruded above the line of the stairwell opening and into the darkened attic like a bubble coming to the surface of a calm grey sea, her closed eyes remaining level with the line of the dusty wooden floor. When she finally screwed up enough courage to do so, she opened her eyes—wide, but only for a fleeting moment.

The images she took in with that hasty peek now began to develop like a photograph in the darkness behind her once again closed eyes: the smashed light bulb came up first, then the trunk, the old leather armchair . . . the rest, the most important, was not clear. She would have to open her eyes again.

Her teeth were pressed so tightly together that the nerves at her temples twitched. Her eyes opened slowly. She kept them wide until they grew accustomed to the dim light that filtered in through the heavily shaded window.

The area in the center of the attic—the area in which her father had spun so wildly—was empty. She had half expected he'd still be there, in that mad heap he had made of himself. But he wasn't. That fact, and the comforting aroma of Lettie's sage muffins drifting up to her from the kitchen, made her feel, for one hurried instant, that the whole thing might possibly have been a terrible dream, after all. But she knew it hadn't been, no matter how hard she tried to make herself believe it had.

The light bulb. It *was* smashed. Wasn't it? She checked. It was. And for further confirmation, she slowly rotated her eyes to the side, as far as they would go, to see if her mother's old wedding dress was still hanging from the banister post. It was. The tattered hem of it hung like a wispy ghost at the level of her cornered eyes.

Then something suddenly came back to her, something she couldn't imagine having forgotten—the thing that had made her lose all caution and caused her to bolt through the darkness of the attic last night. That laugh! That cold and unfamiliar . . .

GINNY!

She didn't know where the voice was coming from. Her eyes darted to the dark corners of the attic from which it echoed.

GINNY! it called again.

There was a sudden noise on the steps behind her. A chill sliced through her scalp like a surgeon's knife.

"Ginny. What are you doing up *here,* of all places?"

It was her father.

She backed away from him. She didn't know how to explain it. He looked so . . . innocent. How could he have forgotten!? Or was he simply pretending? He stood there in his freshly starched clergyman's shirt, looking for all the world like a saint. She almost wished she could fall into his arms and sob the whole thing out, as she used to do before she grew to understand what he was really doing to her. Yet, at times like this. . . .

As though he could read his daughter's thoughts, he gently reached out and circled her shoulder in one arm; with his other hand, he stroked her disheveled hair. "There, there, my little pumpkin pie. What's wrong?" he cooed. "Did you have another one of those bad dreams of yours?" His voice was caring, full of soothing calm. Yet there was a coldness to it that chilled the girl right down to the base of her soul.

He held her away from him for a moment and studied her eyes. They blinked rapidly, avoiding his.

"Why don't we just go downstairs and get us some of Miss Lettie's hot muffins," he finally said, with rolling waves of cheer in his voice. "You know how she comes over every Saturday just to fix 'em for us."

The hot tears that had built up in Ginny's eyes stung like fire. He *knows* about last night! she thought. Why doesn't he die! Why doesn't he just die and go straight to hell!

But when her father leaned down and pressed his lips soothingly to her forehead, the tears she had been struggling to hold back suddenly gushed out. He carefully wiped them away with a handkerchief from his pocket, never once offering her the opportunity to tell him why she was so upset.

"It's going to be a glorious day!" he went on to say as he led her down the stairs with one arm still about her shoulder. "And I'm going to be performing a wedding ceremony in a little while. I want you to come to church with me and watch." His voice had gone up at the announcement like someone offering sweets to a hurt child.

"No," Ginny said. "I . . . I can't . . . I. . . ."

His cold glare immediately silenced her.

"I'll tell you exactly what you can or cannot do," he said in a low, controlled voice. "And in a little while, after you've had some of the breakfast that Miss Lettie is putting up for us, you'll get yourself dressed and come on over to the church with me. It's not up for debate. Do you understand?"

Ginny looked down as he tugged her closer to his side. Her heart hammered like a trapped bird, thrashing its wings against the frail cage of her ribs.

CHAPTER FOUR

When Sara Garrett opened her eyes she was on the floor. The chair on which she had been sitting was toppled over next to her.

The light from the pond, she thought. That flickering! She shouldn't have stared at it.

Sara Garrett was epileptic. Flickering light sometimes triggered a seizure. Having been free of seizures for many years, she had almost forgotten about it.

According to the clock in the kitchenette, she could not have been unconscious for more than a minute. It seemed more like a year. It had been a very long time since she had had such a total blackout. If she were back in the Transvaal a flock of witch doctors would have come out of the bush and gathered about her by now. There would be the inevitable string of questions: Revelations? Omens? What?

The lifelong condition had unexpectedly provided her with a special calling card into the ancient cult. Anyone who had such spontaneous seizures was accorded special treatment, not only out of respect for the victim, but to the spirits they felt produced such events. Sara didn't believe any of that—and had made her feelings known to everyone—but she finally allowed herself to be initiated into the cult because of the unique opportunity to further her studies of cultural myths.

Her mouth was dry and she felt ravenously hungry, the way she always did after a seizure. Although she would have preferred the succulently roasted malangano lizard she had developed a taste for, she'd have to settle for whatever the college had provided in the larder. She rose and quickly went to the refrigerator. Opening it, she removed the loaf of white bread. She undid the wrapping and hurriedly pulled a swatch of softness from its core. It was quick and it was filling; just what she needed. She then washed it down with a gulp of cold milk and almost retched. Cow's milk! She hadn't had any in years; hadn't even realized how fond she had grown of the tepid goat's milk that she now craved and preferred. She arched an eyebrow. Maybe she was getting to be a true witch doctor after all.

She walked back to where she had fallen over and picked up the chair and set it beside the small writing table in front of the window. The light on the pond was gone. Nothing down the hill in the distant greenery moved.

Uneasy, uneasy thoughts. Abstract furies fluttered through the hazy vault of her unconscious like a flurry of dark-winged birds. She tried not to focus.

She sat back down at the writing table and examined the ruined note card. If she were taking a Rorschach test, she would have sworn that the red inkblot stain resembled a viper's head. The gaping jaws of the "serpent" even seemed to reveal a healthy set of sharp fangs, dripping blood!

She frowned and laid the card to one side and picked up her fountain pen to examine it. She didn't like the way the ink had decided to run out of it like that. Neither did she like the chilling image it had formed on the blank card.

Sara lifted the pen to the light and studied the point carefully. It was clean. Not a drop of red ink could be seen anywhere on its gold nib. She then rotated the pen between her pointing finger and thumb so that the light from the window raked across it at a sharp angle. Further up from the nib, just past the curvature of the finger grip, she noticed a thin line of red that circled the base of the stem that housed the rubber ink-bladder. She carefully unscrewed it and smiled. The rubber had gone brittle and ruptured. That was all, she told herself. An ordinary event. No magic. Just an accident.

She was about to reach for a pencil when a sharp chill swept into the room behind her. It felt as though some angry thing now stood beside her. She could almost feel it touching her. She turned. There was nothing there.

She looked back down at the stained note card in her hand. The image of the "serpent" appeared to have grown . . . *angry.* She dropped the card.

Whatever it was that troubled her, it now began to slither along the threads of her consciousness, like beads of ice. She wanted to stop everything right then and there to think it all out—the way her analytical mind always prompted her to do. But there was no time. The clock across the room indicated she had only another hour before the conference began.

She picked up her pencil again and reached for a

new note card. An old chant came to her mind. It was one she had heard the Sotho witch doctors use whenever they encountered the unknown. She smiled to herself and began to hum it. She had never done anything like that before.

CHAPTER FIVE

As Ginny and her father sat at the breakfast table, Lettie busied herself at the kitchen sink, doing up the pans she had used to fix the sage muffins that the girl and the reverend liked so much. Her soft brown eyes moved across the view outside the window before her. It was early June, and the backyard lawn still showed signs of the rich lushness of spring she loved so much. The pinkness of her face glowed as brightly as the day. She had been going to the reverend's house almost every Saturday morning for the past ten years, ever since he and Ginny first moved to town. The girl had been no more than two years old when they'd arrived, and there were times when the kind old woman had been called on to take care of Ginny when she was ill, and though she was now almost eighty three years old herself, Lettie still didn't mind the extra doing for others. She had no family of her own, not right nearby, and being with good folks was something that gave to *her* more than she could give herself. She had a special feeling for Ginny, too. Lettie had held and rocked her comfortingly in her arms many a time, though there seemed to be less and less need of that these days. The old woman knew it had to do with growing up—the way young girls get as they near becoming a woman.

Something happens to them when the monthly bleeding begins, like she knew it would be starting any day now for Ginny. She could tell. Little girls no longer wanted to be held, nor did they care to share the secrets of their inner thoughts with others. And these days Ginny seemed to be far more drawn into her own self, too! Lettie noticed how the girl even acted strangely toward her own father. Well, it would pass, she thought. The girl will grow out it.

At the breakfast table Ginny couldn't take her eyes off her father. He casually munched on one of Lettie's sage and cornbread muffins as though he was entirely at peace with himself. Ginny again wondered if he had really forgotten about last night, or if he was pretending. She knew that when her father had had too much to drink he'd forget anything—even a familiar passage of scripture in the middle of a sermon. But how could he have forgotten about hitting her like that? She hated him, hated him more than she ever had in her whole life.

Lettie was bothered by something, too; not by the fresh bruise on Ginny's arm—for it was hidden by the sleeve of the child's robe—but by something in Ginny's eyes. The old woman was never one to speculate about the goings-on in a child's mind. That was private territory. She knew that a child could live in two—maybe three—different worlds before it all got braided together somehow to form the life that others see. But why, she wondered, was Ginny looking at her father as though he might be some sort of criminal? And he seemed not to be noticing it, either! She knew the reverend had a cold side to him, but he wasn't a bad man.

The old woman patted a few stray strands of grey hair into the bun behind her head with one hand, and with the other she carried to the table a bowl of fresh-made muffins that had been kept warm in the oven.

"Ginny," she said softly. "You haven't touched a single muffin yet." She wanted to ask if there was something wrong, but knew that this was not the right time. "Have some of these," she finally said, offering the bowl to the girl. "They're hot, right from the oven. Just the way you like them."

It was as though the old woman hadn't spoken. The girl's eyes did not move. They were locked to the motion of her father's fingers as he held and buttered another muffin from his plate. He suddenly stopped, butter knife in one hand, opened muffin steaming in the other.

"Miss Lettie's talking to you, sweet lady," he said to Ginny. "Why don't you say something?" He leaned forward. The girl knew it was not a question.

"Yes, ma'am," she replied quickly. She even tried a quick smile with her eyes as she reached out for a muffin in the bowl that Lettie was still holding for her. The old woman blinked when the sleeve of Ginny's robe slid back and revealed the bruise. The girl was quick to yank the sleeve back down to her wrist after placing the muffin on her plate. Her eyes instantly darted back to Lettie's, before quickly returning to her own plate.

"Now don't tell me you went and fell out of another tree?" the old woman asked good-naturedly. The warm smile on her face tried to make it all seem a natural thing for her to have asked. But she didn't wait for a reply. She could tell by the way that the girl's eyes had gone blank that wasn't going to get one, and she was a bit curious to note that the reverend hadn't prompted the girl to answer, as he would normally have done.

Lettie thought it best to let things go and placed the bowl on the table between Ginny and her father. She then went to the counter by the sink to get a pitcher of milk. "Never seen such bump'n and thump'n being done to one's own self," she muttered in a teasing tone, just barely loud enough for them to hear. The reverend's eyebrows arched, ever so slightly, but she saw it. He had even stopped his buttering for a moment.

Ginny saw Lettie's eyes go squinty. "Trees are tall," she said, attempting to draw the old woman's attention in a tease-back. "And I do fall."

Her father smiled. So did Lettie.

The reverend's hands resumed the rhythm of his buttering. "Told you many times before," he said in a fatherly tone. "Young ladies don't climb trees. Do they, Miss Lettie?"

The old woman looked at him with a slight knot in her brow. He winked at her, but she wasn't going to go against the girl—not this morning, not with that frightened look in those large blue eyes of hers.

"Why, sometimes I get the urge to go up a tree myself," she said to the reverend. "Used to do it all the time when I was Ginny's age. Even tried it once or twice when I was older. Nothing like a good tall tree to make you want to climb up in it and get away from things—is there Ginny?"

The girl looked at the old woman and silently broke open the muffin in her hands. Vapor rose from the core of it like mist off an herb garden. "Mmm . . ." she hummed, deliberately drawing the conversation to a turn. Her nostrils flared as she inhaled the savory aroma. "Smells just like heaven," she said.

Lettie smiled, going along with the child's diversion. "Now, that's what I like to hear," she said, bringing her hands down smoothly over the apron tied about her waist. "That's worth the whole trip over here every Saturday," she said. "Just so I can fix them for you."

The old woman removed a pair of wire-rimmed eyeglasses from the pocket of her apron and looped them over her ears. She picked up Ginny's empty milk glass, quickly refilled it from a pitcher and handed the glass back to the child in a seemingly absent-minded way. Ginny had to reach for it in a hurry to keep it from falling to the floor. With her eyeglasses now on, Lettie had a better look at the fresh bruise the child was trying to hide up the sleeve of her bathrobe. From where she stood, it looked like a small purple mouse. She decided that as soon as they were alone she would talk to Ginny and try to find out how it really got there. She just knew the girl hadn't been climbing in any trees lately. There was something in Ginny's eyes that settled in Lettie's intuition like a chunk of something scratchy. She couldn't remain at the table. She was afraid she might say something—something she could hardly believe she was thinking.

At the sink, pretending to wash an already washed muffin pan, the old woman received confirmation that something was indeed wrong. Reflected in the window before her, she observed a scene that hurriedly took place behind her back: the reverend motioned to Ginny with his chin and placed a stiff finger across his tightly pursed lips—a gesture that clearly indicated the child had better remain quiet about something. The girl reacted as though she had been struck across the face. She quickly lowered her head and stared into her plate.

Lettie's shoulders stiffened. Whatever it was that the reverend didn't want Ginny to talk about, she thought, she was going to find out *anyway*—just as soon as she and the child could have a moment alone.

After Ginny and her father left for the wedding ceremony at the small white frame church down the street, Lettie sat alone at the oak breakfast table in the kitchen. The coffee she had poured for herself had gone cold before she touched it. She didn't know how long she had been sitting there.

That bruise on Ginny's arm, she thought. Her soft brown eyes squinted as she tried to visualize it. And all that trouble in those sad eyes of hers, too! What was going on? She wondered at the gesture of silence that she had seen reflected in the kitchen window. What was the reverend trying to keep Ginny silent about? She hadn't been able to get anything out of the child when she was alone with her in the girl's bedroom helping her get ready for church. She shook her head when Ginny had decided to wear a long-sleeved dress; thought it was too warm for that. But the girl had insisted on wearing it, anyway. Lettie knew it was to hide the bruise.

The old woman knew the reverend drank a bit; everyone knew that. He was a man alone, who never had gotten over the death of his pretty young wife. But no one had ever seen him drunk, and no one had ever seen or heard of his having been anything but a good and loving father to his daughter. What, then, was wrong?

Lettie sighed. No, she told herself. She had to be mistaken about what she was thinking. Reverend Watkins was a good man. He would never raise his hand against his own child. Not Ginny. The girl did everything she was told; never caused a particle of trouble for anyone. Why, there was no reason on God's good earth why a child like that should ever be beaten.

She rose with the cup of cold coffee in one hand and with the other pushed the ladderback chair into place against the table. At the sink she emptied the coffee down the drain and washed the cup. When she set it in the rack beside the sink to drain, she felt something brush across her back. It was as though someone had come up from behind and momentarily placed ice-cold hands on her shoulders. She spun about so quickly that the saucer she was about to rinse smashed against the chrome faucet of the sink. There was no one there.

"Yea, though I walk through the valley of the shadow of death," she hurriedly whispered, half to herself, "I shall fear no evil."

Her heart was twisting so that she thought she might have to sit down for a moment and catch her breath. Instead, as though nothing had happened, she forced herself to turn back to the sink where she picked up the pieces of the broken saucer. After placing them in a heavy paper bag beneath the sink, she examined her hands to see if she was cut, and thanked the Lord she was not.

Spirits, she thought, rubbing an icy chill from her arms. She had heard about such things. But the peculiar part of it was that she thought it had been

Ginny, somehow reaching out to her, stroking her kindly, telling her that she loved her more than she could ever say. But the feel of it was so cold!

Now don't go and let your imagination run away, she told herself. Just because you feel a little coolness on a warm spring day, it doesn't mean a spirit's rubbing up against you. She half chuckled, pleased with herself for taking the matter so lightly. Why, it was almost as though such a thing happened to her every day!

She looked at the clock on the kitchen wall beside the oven. It was almost noon. She knew that Ginny would be sitting all alone in the partially empty church as her father prepared for the wedding service. If she hurried upstairs and got the beds all made, she might be able to get there in time to keep the girl company—and see the wedding, too. Never having been married herself, Lettie loved a good old-fashioned wedding.

CHAPTER SIX

". . . . Somewhere in his writings, Carlos Castaneda is told by his sorcerer, don Juan, that there is a part of us for which there is no description, no words, no names, no feelings, and no knowledge."

Sara Garrett lifted her eyes from the paper she was reading and quickly scanned the faces about her. Including herself, there were only nine participants in the richly paneled room. They all sat about a long, highly polished, table—except for the recorder. She sat off to one side at a smaller table and taped the proceedings on an old reel-to-reel Wollensak. The tapes of the one-day conference would later be transcribed and published in the Annual Research Journal of the National Parapsychological Association.

Each member of the conference came from a different discipline—each a facet of the complex science of the paranormal. They ranged from a well-dressed elderly mathematician who tested ESP at the roulette wheels of Las Vegas to a NASA scientist who had developed a phschic training center for certain sensitive astronauts. Each participant was burrowed deeply into the narrow band of his or her own particular area of research and were eager to share some of their findings with others. They had drawn by lots—scraps of papers with numbers penciled on them—and Sara was the first to speak. After her last statement, most of the members leaned forward in anticipation as she continued.

"The Sotho witch doctors I've studied and lived with for the past two years would agree with Castaneda's sorcerer. It is a part of their cultural myth that there is indeed a part of everyone for which there can be no description, no name, and no knowledge. It is simply there. And most sorcerers pray that it will remain buried within, where it can do no harm to themselves or to others."

Sara Garrett's words caught in her throat. She had once eaten a bat, had lived on lizards, and she knew how to snatch prey from a lion. Yet nothing was as cold as the dark feeling that now, so unexpectedly, began to pour into her blood. It was as though something deep within her had suddenly decided to make a mockery of her. The feeling scuttled through the cortex of her thoughts like something echoing in an abandoned cave. It blocked her mind. She attempted to go on with her talk, but couldn't. A great weight had descended upon her, forcing her down, heavily, into her chair. She sat there with such stiffness that those closest to her thought she might be having a heart attack.

"Don't do that!" she suddenly screamed, clasping her hands to either side of her head. "Leave me alone!" She had no way of knowing what she had just said.

The elderly mathematician sitting beside her sprang to his feet. His alarmed face was ashen. "What is it? What's wrong?" he asked. "Can we get you anything?"

Her paper spilled loosely to the floor. Her eyes were

wild—as though some unnamed thing lived just behind their icy glare. Her body became rigid. It appeared she had even stopped breathing.

Everyone's words suddenly ran together in a chorus of commotion.

"Get a doctor! Call the infirmary! She needs oxygen!"

Then, without any warning, her body loosened. Air rushed back into her lungs and her chest expanded. Color returned to her cheeks. The eyes were the last to clear, becoming warm and beautiful again. The panic that had almost swept the conferees subsided. There was as much relief in their eyes as in the warm smile that now brightened Sara Garrett's face.

She didn't ask, Where am I? or, What happened? She appeared to know.

Two men arrived with a stretcher from the infirmary and hastily approached the table where she sat.

"No," she said brightly, rising to her feet. "I'm all right. It was jet lag—fatigue or something. I just need some air and I'll be fine."

There was only one thing she knew for certain, and that was that she had to stop what she had been doing and get out of that room as quickly as possible—which, to everyone's amazement, was exactly what she did.

CHAPTER SEVEN

The sound of the organ rumbled down into the soft earth beneath the small wooden church and spread out in every direction until it reached the edge of town. Inside the church people stood in the painted white pews, waiting for the bride. They could feel the organ in their feet. If they touched the backs of the pews in front of them the vibrations traveled up their arms and tickled their ears. Only the kids liked doing that, and some of them did. Even Ginny.

Lettie had helped the girl dress in a summer-yellow dress that was soft and puffed at the shoulders, with sleeves that ended in flared ruffles of lace about her slender wrists. In her hands she clutched a prayer book, which was closed on the crook of her pointing finger, as though she had wanted to keep her place in the missal. She had been reading psalms before the organist started to play an improvised prelude to the "Wedding March."

Ginny stood like everyone else and faced the vestibule, where some last-minute activity was taking place. Beyond it, the large white doors of the church were opened wide, letting in a breeze. It filled the church with the fragrance of fresh-cut flowers and rose to cool the exposed wooden rafters that supported the roof. They sporadically creaked in the heat, sounding like the timbers of an old-fashioned schooner.

Outside, the light was golden. Through the doors Ginny watched its shimmer spread across a sea-green field of tall grasses that ran down a gently sloping hill to where the large pond was. A cross-breeze made the grasses roll, like a gently undulating sea. And when the tall blades parted in a certain way, Ginny could see all the way down to the pond at the bottom of the hill. The shimmer of it appeared and disappeared with the sway and fall of the wind-tossed green. The sight made the tightness in her shoulders loosen a bit. There was something reassuring about the dappled glitter of the water's surface. She wished she could leave the church and go there at once. But no one ever went to the pond anymore, not since it had been taken over by the deadly water moccasins. Yet, for some curious reason, the pond had always seemed a safe and comfortable place for her to go. Maybe it had something to do with all the wonderful snake stories Lettie had told her when she was a little girl.

Lettie's father had raised poisonous snakes for a living, and as a little girl Lettie had helped to milk them of their venom, which her father then sold to research hospitals all over the country. The old woman had a lot of good stories about those days, and maybe, Ginny now thought, that was why she had never been afraid of the water snakes, as all the rest of the children in town were. Lettie had even told her the story of how she had once *trained* some of her father's vipers to come to her whenever she called out the names she had given them—just like they were pet puppies. Lettie always claimed that snakes were far more intelligent that most folks ever gave them credit for.

Ginny recalled how she herself had once *taught* a water moccasin to do figure eights on the surface of the pond. It was after school one day, before the pond had become totally infested with the moccasins and declared off-limits by the town selectmen—who in their directive had called the pond, which had never had a name before, "Snake Pond." It was a name that stuck. She had gone there by herself that day, and had pulled her shoes and socks off before wading out up to her knees in the cool, dark water. She never went any farther than that because she had not yet learned to swim—that, she did later, in the town swimming pool that had been built for the children just as soon as the pond was no longer a safe place to go. While she stood there in the water, watching it lap in ripples about a long twig she had carried in her hand, a thick black moccasin had glided lazily across the surface toward her. She hadn't seen it until it was right up close. Her first reaction had been to bolt away from there in a hurry, but she'd remembered how Miss Lettie had always told her not to panic if she ever happened to come upon a snake. They'd strike at anything that moved right up close to them. So Ginny just stood there with the twig in her hand and slowly trailed it back and forth before her, making Vs and Ss on the smooth surface of the water. It was as though the snake's sudden appearance was as natural as anything in the world. She was only seven or eight at the time, she couldn't remember, but she knew it was about the same age that Miss Lettie had been when she used to raise snakes with her father. She thought she might be able to teach the snake to do something, just like Miss Lettie had when *she* was a child. As it circled about her, Ginny reached out with the twig—as far as she could stretch herself without disturbing the viper—and began to incise figure eights on the surface of the pond. "It's easy," she had said to the moccasin, after repeating the eights a few more times. "Now you do it."

And it had! Yet she had forgotten all about it until that very moment.

Something suddenly drew her attention to a side chapel where there was an ornately carved marble baptismal fountain. The church had at one time been Catholic. When their numbers had decreased, it had been taken over by the Deacons of the Presbyterian Church, of which her father was the minister. Only two signs of the previous religion remained: a stained glass window above the altar, depicting the crucified Christ, and the intricately carved baptismal font. It depicted a scene of Adam and Eve being tempted by the Serpent in the Garden of Eden. Ginny looked at it now as if she had never seen it before.

The serpent was magnificent! Its sleekly carved body coiled gracefully about a tree as its forked tongue licked close to Eve's ear. The figures were smooth and polished from having been rubbed against over the years. Eve looked interested in what the serpent had to say. Beside her stood Adam. His expression was blank and lifeless. But it was the serpent that had so unexpectedly drawn Ginny's attention. For some reason, it looked so alive!

She was still staring at the baptismal fountain when Lettie stepped briskly into the vestibule of the church. Ginny turned immediately, as though the old woman had called her name. There was trouble in Lettie's eyes—more trouble than she had ever seen before. Ginny's fingers instinctively sought the ruffles on the sleeve of her dress and she tugged them down. She lost the place in her psalm book as she did so.

Lettie forced herself to smile, and even managed to put some light in her eyes as she nodded to the girl and made her way into the church. She didn't want to draw attention to herself—everyone was standing and facing the vestibule, waiting for the bride, who was about to move down the center aisle with her attendants—so she chose a half-empty pew at the back. From a dozen rows away, toward the front of the church, Ginny saw the light go out of the old woman's eyes.

Ginny turned away and faced the front where her father now stood. He choked a small black wedding book in his tight hands and looked down at his shoes, the way he always did whenever he was far away in thought. But once the "Wedding March" began he quickly looked up and arched his eyebrows toward the groom. He stood a few paces in front, and to the side, of him. His grey eyes then lifted above the gold rims of his glasses to the bride's retinue, which had begun to move down the center aisle of the sparsely filled church.

Ever since his wife had died he had lost the joy of performing such rites. It was as though something inside had dried up and left him empty. Everyone seemed to know it but him.

Ginny's insides twisted as the bride passed her pew. It was too real . . . the gown . . . her father. The memory of the night before rushed at her like a hot wind. She had to grip the back of the pew in front of her to keep from falling.

She had never spoken to anyone about what took place when her father drank too much. He had threatened her with severe punishments if she ever did. But last night was different. All that spinning he had done, those strange words he'd muttered—and that chilling laughter that had rung out of the darkness at her! It now reverberated in her heart like the rumble of the thundering organ. Then, as though to highlight the inner turmoil she was feeling, the sun suddenly filled the stained glass window that was above and behind the alabaster altar. The image of the crucified Christ back-lit her father in a blazing hue of iridescent light. The sight of it caused a blackness to swell inside of her. By the time the organ stopped, and her father began to recite the service, her insides were squeezed as tight as a drum.

Lettie saw the child's shoulders trembling and quietly made her way out of the back pew and went to stand beside the girl. She knew what was wrong; had figured it out the moment she had gone upstairs that morning to make the beds. She saw the girl's torn nightgown at the bottom of the attic stairs and went up to investigate. When she saw the old wedding gown, and the recently emptied bottle of claret by the minister's chair, it told her something she should have suspected a long time ago. She cursed herself for having been so stupid, so blind!

CHAPTER EIGHT

No one saw them leave the pond and travel up the hill, pushing themselves through the tall grasses toward the church. Maybe it was how the organ had disturbed the calm of the water. It was an imperceptible disturbance, of course, but they felt it and lifted their noses out of the water and darted their forked tongues in the direction of the church.

Their cold bodies left faint creases in the sweet-smelling grass, which quickly disappeared as the gentle breezes waved the green like a lazy quilt. There were three of them in all; a family, one would suppose, if such things were possible. Although they were of a common mother, they didn't think of themselves as a family. They didn't have the capacity to think. Yet they *knew* something. It wasn't only the vibration in the earth that had roused them; they had felt such things before. It was something else. The confusion showed in their small, steel-black eyes. They should have been spending the day as they always did, at the pond, basking on a warm rock, dipping into the clear water whenever they felt like it—lunching on small snap-fish and terrapins. Instead, something was driving them up the hill, hundreds and hundreds of yards away from their home at the pond. There was no turning back. Their will belonged to something else.

When they arrived near the back of the church they approached an old shade tree. Its long branches reached out in all directions. One of its twisted arms stretched a good distance from the rest and leaned out over the church's wood-shingled roof. At the base of the tree the water moccasins paused and coiled about one another in a knot as they studied the limb that protruded over the roof of the church. It would be a chancy thing. One would have to go alone while the other two remained below, watching, guarding, ready to take the place of the first if it failed. Even though no one was about, they couldn't afford to take any chances on being interfered with. Something unusual was working at them today, something they hadn't ever felt before. It had to be obeyed. There was no choice.

The youngest of them was chosen. Without question it left the other two and began to work its body about a gnarled protrusion at the base of the old shade tree. It had no trouble working its belly scales on the rough bark. It even helped that the whole tree was inclined toward the roof of the church. The going would be less difficult.

At the top, the serpent slithered out on the overhanging branch and curled its head toward the bottom so it could examine the fall. It would have to drop almost three times its own length before it landed on the shingled roof. Its glossy black eyes clouded. It had never done anything like that before.

Below, the other two felt the fall; a faint plop as the one above landed on the roof. They lifted their heads and waited as it slowly made its way toward the gabled peak at the back of the church. There, just above the stained glass window of the crucified Christ, there was a louvered vent. High above, the other two saw the younger snake poke its head out beyond the roofline and gaze down at it. It flicked its tongue out and tasted the thin wire mesh that covered the vent. Something within the viper assessed the risk, weighed the next move, and . . . and suddenly it drew itself back. Something was wrong. Its head shot up like a sprung coil.

A black doberman came around the side of the church and sniffed for a place to do its business. Too bad it decided to use that particular tree. The two waiting serpents struck and clung to its neck. The doberman never knew what hit it. It shot into the air like a startled colt, legs as stiff as rods of iron. Clutched to its throat, the water moccasins emptied their venom into its jugular. The dog didn't even have a chance to yelp. In a matter of moments it had just enough life left in it to jog, with an awkward, bouncy gait, off to the woods behind the church. If anyone had seen it they would have wondered why such a healthy-looking doberman was staggering about like that, and wetting all over itself, too.

It didn't take very long for the dog to topple down a scrubby ravine and die. It was only then that the cottonmouths loosened themselves from about its throat and glided back to the base of the tree where they had been standing guard. They looked up at the younger one and waved their tongues between their bloodstained fangs. The young one could proceed. They watched as it once again lowered its head beyond the roofline and began to chew at the mesh that covered the louvered vent. Pearls of blood splattered against the white clapboards of the church as the viper chewed and pushed farther and farther through the wire.

It was against their basic instinct, against all of nature, that the three of them should be there that day, far from their home at the pond.

CHAPTER NINE

". . . Wilt thou take this woman, here present before you, as thy lawfully wedded wife, according to the sacred rite of our Holy Church?"

"I will."

Reverend Watkins noted that the groom had responded quickly, clearly, without reservation. He then turned to the bride. She was tall and buxom, wearing a white gown that was not unlike the one his own bride had worn on their wedding day. Its high lacy bodice revealed the young bride's ample cleavage. A pocket of phlegm gathered in his throat. It had to be cleared before he could go on.

"And wilt thou take. . . ."

The sound was so faint, so distant, and so high up toward the rear of the church that no one would have heard it, even if Watkins's throat-clearing cough at that precise moment hadn't completely obscured it. Besides, a snake tearing through a mesh screen was not the type of sound most people would be familiar with. Nor were their eyes sharp enough to notice the slithering motion along an exposed electric wire that ran to one side of the roof's hand-chopped ridge beam, just below the thick cross-rafters that came together like the widely spread fingers of a pair of praying hands.

Both bride and groom spoke in unison as the vows were exchanged. Their voices were as soft as the light that filtered into the hushed church.

". . . to have and to hold, from this day forward, for better or for worse, for richer or poorer, in sickness and in health . . . until death do us part."

Watkins had performed the ritual so many times that he thought he would, by now, have overcome the curious sense of anger he felt over the loss of his own bride. She had been so young—had promised to fill so many of those empty spaces in his life. He would probably never get over it, he thought.

His hands were like ice, and he noticed how one of them trembled as he extended it above the joined hands of the bride and groom. For a moment, the concluding pronouncement of the rite escaped him. It came back slowly.

"Look with favor, we beseech Thee, O Lord, upon these Thy servants. . . ."

Ginny spotted it. God knows why she looked up there. At first she thought the electric wire had somehow come loose from the roof beam and was bowed out. But it was too shiny, too . . . *alive.*

The movement seemed to have stopped the moment she spotted it. But now, as she studied it more closely, she saw what it was—a snake, high above her father's head. If it dropped it would probably land right on him! Her first reaction was to shout a warning to everyone gathered at the altar. But something held her back. What if the snake *did* come down upon her father?

Even though the thought terrified her for a moment, and she couldn't imagine herself wishing such a dreadful thing, Ginny held her breath and concentrated with everything she had. The snake felt it. She could tell. It curled back in a loop along the wire, just as she had willed it to. Then she brought it forward again. Still, just to make sure she was actually doing it, she tried it all over again. It did exactly as she wished—almost the same as that water moccasin with those figure eights at the pond.

She shot a quick glance at the old woman beside her. Lettie seemed to be all wrapped up in a faraway thought as she coldly stared at the altar—right at Ginny's father. There was something in her eyes that looked like death itself. Deep within Ginny something whispered a dark and sinister thing. All her humiliation and fear at what her father had done to her boiled up within her.

At the top of the church, the snake opened its cotton-white mouth, as though it were responding to the resolve that had come about within the girl. There was blood on its fangs, and Ginny lifted the back of her hand to her lips. It was hurt. She didn't like that. A bead of red fell from the snake's mouth and landed somewhere in front of the bride. Ginny could tell by the slight change of expression in her father's eyes that he had seen it.

Reverend Watkins saw a dot of blood land on the bride's lacework bodice. He wondered if the bride was having a nosebleed in all the excitement that comes with a church wedding. He hurried to conclude the service.

"Protect the institution which Thou has established for the increase of the human race, O Lord, that those who are made one according to Thy will, may be safeguarded by Thy protection."

Another drop of blood. This time the bride noticed it, too. She glanced down at herself and then quickly turned her face toward the beams of the church. She jerked her head aside as another splotch of blood landed on the side of her face like a red gash.

Watkins, too, now glanced up toward the roof, but saw nothing . . . saw nothing until the slithering black thing dropped to of the rafters and landed on him. Then the screams began. The horror. The shocked commotion.

The snake coiled itself about Watkins's neck like a streak of black lightning and struck. It kept hitting at one spot beneath his right ear until it opened a wound. Then it buried its fangs deeply into the spot and didn't let go. Watkins fell as he tried to pull it off. The backs of his feet hammered the floor so violently that the bones in his heels shattered. Chaos erupted in the church.

Ginny and Lettie were the only two in the midst of all the pandemonium whose eyes never blinked. It was as though they had been engrossed in the events of some make-believe late-night horror show on TV. When Watkins's body finally stopped twisting and went limp, they knew he was dead.

Lettie was the only one to see the snake shoot up the center aisle of the church and go right out through the front doors. She had never known a water moccasin to travel as fast as the one that had just zipped out of the church.

This is crazy! the old woman thought. Topsy-turvy! A water moccasin this far from the pond, in such a high and dry place? Water snakes simply don't do things like that!

She looked at Ginny. The girl's eyes were wide and unblinking. Behind them was a mix of terror and confusion. She placed her arms about the child's trembling shoulders and held her tightly as she led her through the clamor toward the exit of the church.

Ginny turned as they left, not to look at her father's body at the altar, but to look at the baptismal fountain in the side chapel. It glowed in a dusty ribbon of sunlight like a translucent chunk of finely carved alabaster. There was something about it that now gave her a sense of peace, made her momentarily put aside the terror and confusion she felt about having called the snake down upon her father. It was a newfound power. A terrible power! Deep down inside she loved her father. How could she possibly have done such a thing?

Ginny looked back at the baptismal fountain as Lettie led her outside. It somehow made her think of the pond—Snake Pond. Outside, from the steps of the church, she now looked across the road and down the hill to the pond itself. Something within her whispered as softly as a kiss when the sweet-smelling breeze parted the grasses so she could see the water clearly. It seemed alive, as though something deep within it rejoiced at her ungodly triumph.

CHAPTER TEN

When Sara Garrett left the conference in the middle of her presentation, she didn't know where she was going, or why. All she knew was that she had to stop what she was doing and get out of there—fast.

She now stared at the expansive slope of waving green that led down to the pond. It was about a half mile from where she stood. As best she could, she attempted to empty her mind of all thought.

A cracking sound in a nearby tree caught her attention. When she turned she saw that the end of a twisted branch had snapped off and landed in the grass. It was over three feet long. She squinted at the part of the branch that had remained attached to the tree. There was a gash of raw whiteness at the break. Sap oozed from the wound. The jagged opening of the break reminded her of a snake's gaping mouth, just like the ink blot on her note card that morning. She took a step closer to study it more carefully. The part of the branch that was still in the tree looked uncannily like a viper about to strike. She shifted her position to get a better look at it, and her foot pushed against the part of the branch that had fallen to the ground. It seemed to jerk up and poke at her lower leg. She jumped, as though having been struck by a snake.

I must have snakes on the brain, she thought. Her eyes widened as she watched a crease form in the grass where the branch should have been. The v-shaped indentation glided rapidly away from her and headed down the hill toward the pond. She watched until the crease disappeared into the stand of trees that surrounded the pond.

Could the wind have done a thing like that? There certainly was a strong breeze. A curious stillness spread itself into the afternoon. Was she seeing things, feeling things, that weren't there? She didn't remember exactly what had happened at the conference, but she knew it hadn't been another seizure. The feel of it was entirely different . . . or was it?

The only thing that drew her from her thoughts was a sudden, almost mocking, cross-breeze. It made herringbone patterns in the grasses about her. The effect reminded her of the v-shaped creases she'd seen, or had thought she'd seen, a moment before. A distant sound rolled down the hill toward her from the edge of town. A church bell! She hadn't heard one in a country setting in years. How . . .

How beautiful, she was about to conclude the thought. But another sound had mixed with it—the discordant bark of a police siren.

She frowned as she looked toward the town. The sound of the police siren and the pealing of the church bell hammered pathetically against each other. They seemed to reflect the inner turmoil of her own troubled thoughts. And it was almost in a trance that she then began to walk up the hill toward the church.

CHAPTER ELEVEN

When Sheriff Loren Mitchell pulled up to the church in his own 1964 Peugeot, he was expecting to be of some assistance to the victim of a snake bite. It being a Saturday, he had been doing what he did most Saturdays—working on his old car. He had brought it right up to the porch behind the house and left his police radio going, just in case. He had hardly put his wrench to the nut that held the housing of the permanent oil filter, when he heard a call go in to the hospital for an ambulance. It seemed that someone over at the church had been bitten by a water moccasin. He had hoped it wasn't a child. Kids often teased a snake when they saw one, and sometimes they'd get chased. Never once, that he could remember, had there been a fatality. It made them think twice before they'd go poking a stick at a water moccasin again, just for the fun of it. But what was a water moccasin doing all the way up at the church? The pond was almost three-quarters of a mile away.

There was a first-aid kit in the trunk of the car, and he knew that he could get to the church a lot faster than the ambulance, which had to come from three counties away. He returned the wrench to the tool box on the porch and wiped his hands clean with a rag.

After carefully lowering the hood—it had a tricky latch and would sometimes fly up while he was driving—he placed the flashing red bulb on the roof and climbed in behind the wheel. When he pressed the starter button the engine turned over like a charm, the way it always did. He loved that car the same way some men might love their wives, he thought. But he didn't really know for sure. Somehow he had managed to be forty-one and had never met the right woman. He was beginning to believe he never would.

He had hardly got his foot out of the car and onto the gravel driveway of the church when folks came at him from all over.

"He's dead! Killed!"

He was taller than most of the people who gathered about him, slimmer, too. And his gentle brown eyes seemed to do two things: first they blazed into you as though he could read what was going on in your mind, and then they opened you up—like you just had to tell him everything, even secret things.

"Who's dead?" he asked softly.

He hadn't spoken to anyone in particular. From the moment he stepped out of the car he had been staring toward the church. Ginny was there, chalk-white. Old Miss Lettie was there, too, holding on to the girl as though they had been welded together. Reverend Watkins was nowhere in sight.

As Mitchell moved through the crowd several parishioners nervously offered him what they had seen: a water moccasin had attacked the reverend in the middle of the wedding service. It had dropped on him from the rafters. He was dead.

Mitchell almost broke stride. He had never heard of a water moccasin's attacking anyone indoors before, not unless it somehow got into your house and you happened to step right on it. They must be imagining things, he thought. But everyone seemed to have the same story.

He knew Watkins, had had dinner with him once about ten years ago—just about the time the reverend had first come to town with his little girl. He'd never known the wife; she had supposedly died while giving birth to Ginny somewhere in Africa, where Watkins was doing missionary work. Yet there was something about the man that he didn't much care for. He hadn't spoken to him, except in passing, since that first and only time at dinner.

He lowered his eyes as he climbed the steps of the church. No one followed. The crowd remained behind on the graveled driveway.

Mitchell walked up to Lettie and Ginny at the door of the church. Ginny's eyes had a blankness to them that he knew appeared when one was close to shock, if not already in it.

"You go on over with Miss Lettie to her house for a while," he said to the girl. "I'll be right over to see you just as soon as I can."

"Okay," the girl said quietly. Her voice was clear. There were no tears in her eyes.

Something made Mitchell look at Lettie. It seemed she wanted to say something before starting off with the girl, but the words simply would not leave her pale lips. This was not the time to press, he told himself. Time enough for that later on, just as soon as he had a chance to sort out what had happened. He stood back and watched the crowd at the foot of the church steps open up to let the old woman and the child pass through.

Lettie placed her arm about Ginny's tiny waist and gently tugged at her in a way that was filled with love. Behind the horror and death of the child's own father, the old woman felt a surge of something cool and bright pass into her heart. She clutched Ginny even tighter as they reached the bottom of the steps. Ever since she could remember, Lettie had wanted a child of her own, but that had never come about. Now, there being no family left for the girl, who else was better qualified to take care of her? Hadn't she practically been a grandmother to the girl ever since she and her widowed father had first moved to town? Lettie had to keep her lips pressed firmly together, lest she would show the curious joy she was feeling.

At first Mitchell thought the church was empty. Even the wedding couple and their entourage were gathered outside with everyone else. But, as he went further down the center aisle, closer to the body of the reverend at the foot of the altar, he saw that someone was leaning over the corpse. A woman. A stranger. What struck him most was how close she was to Watkins's body, and the expression he saw in her eyes when he finally reached the altar and knelt down opposite her. It was as though the woman was attempting to decipher the bite wounds in the minister's neck; as if the marks might have formed some arcane script. He couldn't help but lower his own eyes to the jagged

He had never seen anything like it. Watkins's jugular had been torn to pieces. It looked as though the snake had pulled a part of the reverend's neck inside out through a hole the size of a half dollar. He didn't like the smell of it, either. A lot of blood had been lost before the reverend's heart had stopped pumping it out all over the place. It smelled like the raw insides of a charnel house. Mitchell's stomach tightened. He had seen more dead bodies than most anyone around. Vietnam did that. Maybe that was why he was able to stand it without retching. But what about the woman—the stranger?

He looked back up at her. "Who are you?" he asked. "Are you a relative?"

"What?" she asked.

Her eyes dazzled him, as did her graceful beauty. She shook her head as though the suggestion bewildered her.

"No, I was just passing by when. . . ."

Mitchell stood up. "I'm afraid I'll have to ask you to leave," he said. "If there's anything you have to say, I can talk to you later, outside." He didn't know why he was rushing her like that, and sounding so darn official about it, too.

Her eyes sparkled like a set of perfectly matched emeralds for a moment before she finally lowered them. She rose from Watkins's body and faced him, eye-to-eye. She was as tall as he was.

He couldn't help himself; he smiled. It had been a long time since he had seen an attractive woman as tall as himself. He suddenly became aware of his appearance. He was only wearing a T-shirt, a pair of old khaki pants, and sneakers without socks. He didn't have his gun, he didn't have his police shield, and, as a matter of fact, he thought, he didn't even have his driver's license with him. He had left the house in such haste that he'd forgotten to pick up his official credentials. He wondered how he was going to introduce himself.

"Police?" she asked.

It was now his turn to squint incredulously into her alert eyes.

"Yes," he responded. "Sheriff Loren Mitchell. I cover Perry, Wayne, and Tylor counties."

She lifted her chin slightly. "I'm Sara Garrett," she said. "I'm staying up at the college. I'll be there for another day or so if you need me. I'm not sure I know how to say this," she added in an uneven tone that was both formal and familiar at the same time, "But . . ."

He stared at her for a moment. She abruptly turned and began to make her way up the center aisle of the empty church. The way the afternoon sunlight filled the opened doors, he could see her shapely legs silhouetted through the summer dress she wore.

He shook his head. Women had always been a puzzle to him. That was part of their charm. But what could she possibly have wanted to say?

He once again knelt beside the reverend's body to reexamine the puncture wound in his neck. A chill crawled through the roots of his hair.

What am I looking for? he wondered. Watkins was killed by a snake . . . a freak accident . . . what else could it have been?

He looked up to the top of the church, followed the center beam that supported the roof rafters, and finally focused on the screening that had covered the louvered vent at the gabled end of the roof's peak. Something had chewed through it and pushed it aside. He had never known snakes could do that.

He slowly rose to his feet. His hands were shaking, something they hadn't done since he had faced combat in Vietnam.

PART TWO

CHAPTER TWELVE

Winkie Bols owned and operated The Bols General Store right in the center of Wilston. It had everything, from Marlboro cigarettes in a hard pack to one of those screw-in plugs that fits into the drain hole near the bottom of a galvanized watering trough for cattle—just in case someone happened to have a pressing need for one—and it would only cost two or three times what he himself had paid for it almost thirty years ago, when he first opened the store; which would bring the price of that little plug up to somewhere, about . . . "Oh, maybe fifteen cents," Winkie would say when the time came to sell it to someone, and there would be a genuine note of surprise in his tone of voice, and an honest raising of his eyebrows as he pronounced the cost. "Inflation," he would say. "Could get a dozen plugs back then for the price you pay for one today." He'd pause thoughtfully for a moment, and he'd then place the plug in a tiny brown paper bag and say, "Yessir, things sure seem to be headed in the wrong way."

And for the small, stout, red-complexioned Winkie Bols, things certainly did seem to be headed down the hill. He used to be one of the most respected and influential town selectman around, but lately he hadn't been able to get a single recommendation of his passed. He was the oldest of the group, and it seemed his fellow selectmen, had, for reasons of their youth, he rationalized, chosen to ignore his ideas. They were polite about it, that was for sure, but it looked like he was soon to bite the dust in the next election, just as the other, more mature, members of the select committee had over the past couple of years. It seemed the only reason Winkie was able to hold on to the position at all was because of the store. It had always been a good platform to test any idea he thought worthy of pushing for, from a new road to declaring the town pond off limits to children because of the snakes. But times had changed. There were shopping malls, and hardly anyone stopped by anymore. Most folks now chose to travel the twenty or so miles to the newest shopping center that was just the other side of Perry County, going toward Wayne to the east. He shopped there himself sometimes, just so he could have himself a good laugh at the fancy prices they charged for the most ordinary things—like a dollar and forty-nine cents for twenty-five finishing nails in a small see-through plastic box. "Shoo!" he would say out loud to anyone who happened to be within earshot. "For that kind of money you could get a bagful back at my place in Wilston." Folks who knew him would smile, knowing that he probably had a nip or two in him. Ever since his wife passed away about a half-dozen years ago he had taken to having a few too many on occasion.

Winkie wasn't his real name. That was Oscar. Oscar Bols. Folks just called him Winkie because, when he got to thinking deep thoughts, his right eyelid began moving quicker than his left, and he appeared to be winking at you. He'd been winking for close to a whole week now, ever since Reverend Watkins had been killed by that water moccasin in church. Watkins wasn't cold in the ground before Winkie called an emergency meeting of the town selectmen. In the back room of the grange hall, which was over a three-table billiard parlor in the center of town—and across the street from Estelle Whidden's funeral home—he introduced a proposal for doing something about that snake-infested pond, once and for all. It was something quite drastic, and he was overwhelmingly voted down. The meeting had broken up a few minutes later. The memory of the laughter that his fellow selectmen had greeted his proposal with haunted him all the rest of that night, haunted him more than some of the greater hardships he had had to endure during his entire life, and he was soon going to be sixty-eight years old! After a sleepless night, and half a bottle of Jim Beam, he fixed his mind to do something about it on his own—with one or two other like-minded cronies, if he could get them to agree.

Winkie now rubbed his hand across his smooth-shaven chin and looked out through the beveled glass pane in the front door of his store. Through it, in the blazing light of near-noon, he could see Judd Winslow, the former fire marshal, headed toward the store. A hundred feet behind him, hobbling as fast as he could on his bad leg, was Jerry Knox. Winkie smiled. They were both right on time.

"Howdy," Winkie greeted Judd as he came into the store. There was an expression on the retired fire marshal's face that told Winkie he would be receptive to what the storekeeper had talked to him about on the phone earlier that morning. Winkie's right eyelid almost returned to its normal beat for a moment or two, but speeded up again when Jerry Knox finally limped into the store.

"Close the door and turn the sign over," Winkie said to Jerry. "We can go on out back and take an early lunch while we discuss what we talked about on the phone this morning."

Jerry Knox was the youngest of the three men, but he had had to retire early from farming because he'd slipped into a bailing rig a few years back. He spun awkwardly about to turn the sign. "Out To Lunch," the worn, hand-lettered cardboard read. "Will Be Right Back." Jerry smiled at that. He remembered the "lunch" they all had had a few weeks back that had lasted several days. It had taken them another couple of days after that to get all the liquor out of their systems. He wondered if this was going to be another such "lunch." He wouldn't mind it in the least.

Out in back of the store there was a long wooden shed with a corrugated tin roof. Winkie had built it himself over a quarter of a century before to warehouse goods for the store. In those days there hadn't been the need to lock it in any special way. Now, after it had been broken into a dozen or so times by some local teenagers, he didn't bother keeping much in there anymore. Besides, there wasn't that much need to warehouse supplies for the store since most people had begun to use the shopping malls.

On the bare dirt floor inside the shed, there was a simple wooden table. Its top was made of old barn boards that were nailed to a number of rickety wooden crates beneath them. As one crate wore out and collapsed, Winkie, over the years, had simply shoved in another of approximately the same height and nailed it in place. They were arranged in such a jumble beneath the table top that there was no telling how many crates had been jammed in there. But that didn't matter to any of the three men. What did matter was now glittering in a shaft of pencil-thin light that shot at it from a nail hole in the rusted tin roof. On the table was a brand new unopened bottle of Jim Beam. Jerry Knox's adam's apple started to jerk the moment he saw it, and Winkie Bols knew he was halfway home.

Each of them selected a seat from an untidy arrangement of rickety old bentwood chairs that lined either side of the table. Winkie pulled three plastic glasses from a pack of them that he had carried into the shed and got the Jim Beam opened and poured all around.

"What'd you all think of what I had to say on the phone this morning? Why don't we talk about it a little," Winkie suggested after they had all downed the first drink as though a fire was waiting to be put out. "We don't have to decide anything right now," he said, even though he considered his proposal to pour gasoline into the town pond and set it afire to be worthy of the swiftest possible action. It was the one sure way that he knew of to get rid of the water moccasins that infested it—and had now gone so far as to attack and kill one of the townspeople, the Reverend Watkins, and he was way up at his own church, too, nowhere near the pond. *Burn the filthy vipers out and give the pond back to the children!* he had pleaded at the selectmen's meeting last night. *It's not natural that snakes should attack people who aren't bothering them. And what about Bobby Jennings's doberman? Anyone ever hear of a dog being killed by a snake before? I tell you something's gotten into the slithering devils, making them do unnatural things. Maybe it's pollution, maybe it's magnetic storms. Whatever it is, it doesn't matter. What does matter is that we should have done something to get rid of them blasted mocs a long time ago! Most of the folks in these parts learned to swim there, had their first picnics there. Some of us even kissed the girls who later became our wives there. And now no one can go there anymore. We've allowed the snakes to breed and multiply. We have to put an end to it now, before they cause any more harm. Before they begin to infest the whole dag-blasted town!*

It was an old argument, most of the selectmen there had heard it before. Winkie just wanted to have a good ol' time, and now that his close friend, the Reverend Watkins, had met with an unusual accident, he wanted to capitalize on it. Some saw it as Winkie's last hurrah, others thought it a possible bid for his reelection to the selectmen committee—if what he proposed turned out to be successful.

"I think it's some kind of chemicals that makes creatures do things they're not likely to do otherwise," Jerry Knox now said, stretching his twisted leg out to the side of the table because there was no room for it to be comfortable beneath it. "You hear of the government dumping all sorts of waste and whatnot all over; maybe something like that's gotten over this way."

Winkie poured another round and remained silent.

"Waste's got nothing to do with it," Judd put in after downing his drink. "I don't think it has anything to do with anything."

"Then what do you think it was?" Winkie asked. He

was beginning to feel the back part of his mouth go numb, the way it always did whenever he took his first drink of the day. Over the past few years, the sensation had come to feel as comfortable and friendly as a trusted companion.

"Freak accident," Judd shot back. "Simple as that."

Winkie's right eyelid danced, but he knew Judd just as sure as he knew the inside of his own mind. He smiled across the table, and nodded his head, as though the fire marshal might be right—all while he extended the bottle across the table and poured another drink of Mr. Beam's best into Judd's empty glass.

"Besides," Judd said after another quick swallow, "if you go and light the pond with fire you might burn the whole town down. The grass is tall this time of year, and winds can come up at any time. Then there's those willows close to the water." His eyes grew misty for a moment as he remembered something from long ago. When he spoke again, it was as though his voice came from another man—a man who was reliving a tragedy from the past. "I once saw six hundred and thirty acres and three houses go up in less time then it would take for a fly to land on a piece of overripe fruit," he said, finishing what was left in his glass.

No one smiled, they knew what he was talking about. He had lost two of his best firemen in that holocaust—men who'd left behind wives and little children, to say nothing of the families that had lost all they had ever owned in the whole world. He stared off to one end of the shed as though he was examining the uneven ridges that grooved the bare dirt floor. The lazy sound of insects being noisy in the sunlight outside did not comfort him as it usually did. Twisted shafts of light filtered in through cracks in the old barn-board siding of the dusty shed. When a breeze came up it caused some of the looser boards to shift, and ribbons of sunlight moved across the ridges in the floor to create the illusion in his mind that the dusty floor was alive with snakes and fire. He didn't say a word. He just held his glass out in the direction of the bottle of Jim Beam. Winkie obliged and poured another round for everyone.

"I think I know how we can do it," Judd said, breaking the silence. "But first . . ." and he looked up for the first time since seeing the snakes twisting in that smoldering fire on the floor of the shed. The other two men were holding their glasses up to him in a toast. They didn't know why, but it was obvious to Winkie Bols and Jerry Knox that Judd Winslow, their former fire marshal, had come to some sort of a decision, one that was soon going to be turned into a plan of action.

"Sheet," Judd said, clicking his glass to theirs. "It's going to be a piece of cake." A boyish grin swept across his face. It blazed in the eyes of his smiling compatriots like coals of fire.

CHAPTER THIRTEEN

His name was Mr. Ocean, but all the kids at school called him *the big drip*. There was obviously nothing vast or deep about him. Even the children could see that.

Harvey Ocean was the guidance counselor at Ginny's school. It was a common concern among the teachers that he sometimes caused more harm than he did good. And lately, ever since he had begun to have trouble with his childless marriage, most thought he shouldn't be in the guidance office at all. But there was no other choice. He was the only board-certified guidance counselor in the entire three-county district—which meant he had passed a state-regulated test, not that he was qualified to hold the job.

He had been awake most of the previous night, after a number of unsuccessful attempts to engage his wife in "a simple act of love," as he called it, and for some curious reason, this morning, felt it his pressing duty to speak with the little girl whose father had recently been killed by a water moccasin. He was sure he could help her with any problems she might be having in adjusting to that tragedy—after all, he told himself, what was he being paid for?

When Ginny was called to his office, Mrs. Peabody, the girl's homeroom teacher, had a strong urge to ignore the summons and tell the guidance counselor that Ginny was too busy with preparations for the sixth-grade play that was coming up. But she knew that Mr. Ocean—she called him a drip herself—would take that as an invitation and saunter down the corridor to her classroom, where he would discover that the children weren't preparing for the play at all. Mrs. Peabody hadn't expected to get into that for another half hour or so. What the children were doing, as was their custom after having had lunch, was to have a free period—which meant they could wander about the room, in an orderly fashion, talk quietly with their classmates if they chose to do so, read a book or magazine from the rack she had herself constructed, or ask any questions of her that they might have about the schoolwork.

When the summons to the guidance counselor's office had arrived, Ginny had been sitting off to the side of everyone else, staring out the window—the same as she had been doing ever since she'd returned to school after her father's funeral. Mrs. Peabody hadn't been able to engage her in any sort of a conversation since then, and she was beginning to wonder if it might be a good thing for someone else to try to bring the girl out—even if it was Harvey Ocean. So, almost against her better judgment, she allowed Ginny to go and see the guidance counselor.

Even though Ginny had never been to Mr. Ocean's

office before, she visibly winced when Mrs. Peabody called her up to the front of the room and wrote out the necessary pass for her.

"Do I have to?" Ginny asked.

"It will only be for a few minutes," Mrs. Peabody assured her.

Ginny now sat in Mr. Ocean's office listening to him speak as though his words were disconnected sounds, unattached to any meaning. Yet they stirred her deeply: *father . . . death . . . harmless snake . . . old Miss Lettie* (she noticed how the word *old* was stressed) *state regulations . . . you must feel . . . I mean, really feel, deep down . . . you can come to me anytime . . . adoption . . . orphanage* . . . The counselor's words formed abstractions in her mind. Their value and meaning meant nothing. The only word that clicked for her was *orphanage.* It caused the most damage. It was as though, if she wasn't a good girl, that was where she would wind up. Hadn't her own father told her the same thing—about what would happen to her if. . . .

Ginny looked up at the guidance counselor for the first time. His eyes reminded her of her father's—cold and gray. A shiver leaked down her spine and tightened her abdomen.

Thirty-six-year-old Harvey Ocean, dressed in his usual brown three-piece summer suit, looked at the child seated across the room from him—where he had a good view of her—and thought there were question marks in Ginny's beautiful blue eyes. He cleared his throat and attempted to respond to them.

"That doesn't mean that anyone's going to come right in and take you away from Miss Lettie," he began. "It's just that there's a state regulation and it seems that she's simply too old to qualify. . . ." His voice trailed off at the sight of the tears that suddenly began to well up in the girl's eyes. He didn't know how to handle it. The lovely child had filled his mind with uneasy thoughts from the first moment she'd entered the room.

If it weren't for those kiddy magazines he had secretly purchased while he was out of town at a guidance convention last fall—the ones that had started all the trouble when his wife discovered them in his closet—he might not be having such thoughts. He would then have no trouble in going over to the child and holding her in his arms in an attempt to comfort her. He might even stroke her long blond hair with his hands, or even kiss her soft, unblemished cheeks. Never for a moment did he think he might comfort her with words.

His necktie suddenly became tight and he began to perspire. He realized that Ginny looked very much like some of the little girls in those magazines he had come to like so much. His face reddened to the color of a cooked beet.

Ginny felt uncomfortable. Something made her tug on the short blue skirt she wore so that the hem would cover her knees. It wouldn't reach. The guidance counselor was staring at her legs the same way her father sometimes had before he'd asked her to remove all her clothes.

"Can I go back to my room now?" she asked softly, averting her eyes from his. "There's some work I have to finish before going home today."

The guidance counselor's face partially returned to its normal ashen color, but his breathing was choppy.

He sucked in deeply to fill his lungs with whatever stagnant air was left in the room. Earlier, right after the girl had arrived, something had made him close the door. He hardly ever did that, but was now glad he had. The only problem was that the oscillating fan didn't help once the cubiclelike room was sealed up like that. The air-conditioning in his room wasn't working as it should, and as for the one window, before which there was a small collection of cactuses, succulents, and a half-dead aloe vera in a parched sand box, it had been nailed shut—the custodian's answer to security precautions after a burglar made off with a slide projector one night.

Harvey Ocean now stood up and slowly walked around his desk toward the girl. She could tell there was something working on his thoughts in a bad way. He had that same glazed expression in his eyes that her father sometimes had had. He now stood so close to her that she could smell him—all sweaty. That, too, was like her father.

He hesitated before her for a moment as though he was about to say something, but when his lips moved nothing came out. Then, awkwardly, he slowly reached out to touch her cheek. She quickly recoiled from his hand before it got there, as though it belonged to a slimy science-fiction monster.

"Don't," she said. But within her something else said, *let him.* Then it showed her one frame of a mind-picture that revealed what would happen if he touched her. It was worse than what had happened to her own father. That unknown part of her that had been screaming in and out of her thoughts for the past ten days, ever since her father's death, somehow compelled her to bring her cheek closer to the palm of his sweaty hand. And when it finally touched her, that inner voice—that wasn't really a voice, but more of a dark feeling—laughed inside of her. It sounded just like the laughter that had echoed through the attic the night her father forced her dress in her dead mother's old wedding gown—for the very last time. She suddenly jerked herself away from the guidance counselor's clammy hand.

Although he had been dreaming about caressing such a sweetly innocent child as Ginny for years, Harvey Ocean couldn't imagine what had possesed him to do such a risky thing. He hadn't planned to touch her at all, he had simply wanted to . . . wanted to. . . .

His leg brushed against her as she tried to rise from the chair, and he was suddenly lost in a sea of churning lust. He held her down by the shoulders and stared into her shiny, well-scrubbed face. "I'm not going to hurt you," he said.

From where he stood he could see right down into the front of her dress. Her tiny breasts were heaving erratically, matching his own choppy breathing. He had never done anything like this before. He wanted to stop. But something had pushed him over the edge. It was too late. She was the most beautiful child he had ever seen. He imagined what she would look like without her clothing. He saw her in furs and lace, naked on a silken couch. There were sparkling pearls about her throat and she wore long black stockings. She stared temptingly, innocently, out at him from the recesses of his lust-filled imagination—just like a photograph from one of his forbidden magazines.

"Don't!" Ginny shouted. "You're hurting me!" She was about to add that her father would come to school and have him fired. But that was worse. He was dead, and she was *happy* about that! That only made matters worse. Her body began to shiver. "Please," she said, sobbing. *"Please!"*

The guidance counselor reddened brighter than before. To him it seemed the child actually *wanted* to be held and comforted. He swallowed his adam's apple and tightened his arms about her quivering shoulders, lifting her from the chair and bracing her head against his hammering chest. He thought his heart would burst as she continued sobbing into his breast. Then, very gradually, he let his hand slip down her back. When she felt it there, and what it was doing, she turned her head upward and stared into his face as though she were seeing him for the first time. Bewilderment was etched deeply into her sparkling blue eyes. He thought it was an invitation; that she wanted him to kiss her—but the mind-pictures that were unreeling in Ginny's thoughts were like nothing he could possibly have imagined. She saw snakes slithering in and out of his empty eye sockets. The vipers chewed and gnawed at his putrid, decaying brain. Their fangs dug deeply into his throat, reminding her of how her father had been killed by the water moccasin she herself had called down upon him.

Ginny pushed herself away. There was a scream in her eyes, but nothing emerged from her lips. It was the silence of it that went into Harvey Ocean in a way that was more disturbing than anything he had ever experienced.

"I just wanted to help you," he finally managed to

mutter. "That's all." He was as aroused as any teenage boy. The girl could see it; indeed, as he had held her in his arms, she had even felt it.

Without saying a word, Ginny opened the door to his stagnant office and left. The sound of her leather heels clicking down the corridor as she went back to her classroom sounded in his ears like the ticking of an old-fashioned alarm clock, each tick growing fainter and fainter, until he stood there in absolute silence, in absolute fear. There was no doubt in his mind that he had passed over into another realm of reality. He was a moth, and the child a blazing flame.

He straightened up. A curious surge of energy jolted his thoughts. It was as though he had suddenly been liberated from all the bonds that had formerly held him to the straight and narrow for the better part of his entire life. He wanted to surrender himself to the passion that touched him every time he opened one of those magazines and saw the picture of a naked little girl: fur, lace, lipstick, dangling earrings, and pearls about her delicate throat.

The moth and the flame, Harvey Ocean thought. So far, he had managed to avoid its incandescent trap. Now, it suddenly didn't seem to matter anymore. He could always rationalize what had just transpired in his office. If Ginny ever told anyone about it, he could say that the girl didn't know what she was talking about; that he had merely tried to comfort her in his arms when she began to cry over the loss of her father. There were deep-rooted feelings that the child had yet to deal with. Guilt was always a good one to use. Most kids are guilty, to one extent or another, over the death of a parent. Ginny was no exception. Why, he might even make a home visit, right now. Talk to the girl's temporary guardian, Miss Lettie. Wouldn't that show his innocence? Wouldn't that show that he was doing his job? Wouldn't that *prove* he was the best-meaning guidance counselor the school district had ever had?

CHAPTER FOURTEEN

Those "snakes" that had been slithering in and out of the dusty shadows of the former fire marshal's mind now almost looked like the real thing. Out of the corner of one eye, Judd Winslow caught some sun-striped movement on the dusty dirt floor of Winkie Bols's shed. He jerked his leg up in a hurry, as though something had been coming at him. Then he laughed. So, too, did Jerry Knox, who wouldn't have been able to get his foot up so fast because of his leg having been bent out of shape by that hay bailer a few years back. And Winkie, well Winkie didn't know what he was laughing at. Ever since the three of them had emptied most of the bottle of Jim Beam, he had been having himself a good ol' time. Judd Winslow had agreed to help burn down the pond, and Winkie was happy about everything—even the sight of the lazy batch of flies circling about the plastic glasses on the barn-board table made him smile.

"So it's settled then," Winkie said, shooing the flies away from his drink with an unsteady sweep of his arm. "Tonight's the night?"

Judd Winslow stiffened his back against the bentwood chair. "We'd better have a good look at the place before we come to any . . . any. . . ." And for the life of him, he couldn't think of the word he wanted to finish with.

"Decision?" Jerry Knox filled in for him. "Come to a decision, you mean?"

"Yes, that's right," Judd answered, as though it were the most natural thing in the world for Jerry Knox to be finishing his sentences for him. "But there's that problem of the fire spreading," he said. He blew his breath out between his front teeth. "If we're not careful the whole town could go up." His bleary eyes went wide with the horror of such a thing happening.

"That's why I wanted you in on it, Judd. You know about fires. Jerry and I don't. Least we don't have the experience you have."

Judd jutted out his chin, like he'd once seen John Wayne do in a movie. He used to be able to do it better when he was twenty years younger. Now, there were two or three too many chins under his face for him to look like anything other than ol' Judd Winslow—*drunk* ol' Judd Winslow.

Winkie and Jerry looked at each other. "Man's drunk," Winkie said of Judd. "Don't I know it," Jerry responded.

Judd stretched his empty glass out in the direction of the bottle. "Put another one right in there and I'll show you who's . . . who's. . . ."

"Drunk?" Jerry Knox finished, smiling at Winkie who was already pouring the rest of the bottle out into the three empty glasses.

"Right!" Judd shot back. "Just one more and we'll get ourselves down there'n figure the how and the when of it."

When so much Jim Beam hits the back of your gullet in such a short space of time, it does funny things to your mind—and your body, too. Jerry found that out when he thought both his legs still matched each other, like they did before the accident. He stood straight up from the chair to make a toast . . . to whoever it was who, once upon a time, had driven the snakes out of . . . of. . . .

"Tennessee!" Judd shouted, jokingly completing the sentence for Jerry this time.

"Timberrrrr!" Winkie called out as Jerry fell over on his uneven legs, just as gracefully as a slow-motion tree-fall in the forest.

And before Jerry could hit the floor, Judd snatched the glass from the falling man's hand. Not a drop was lost.

"There," Judd said, proclaiming his prowess to Winkie Bols. "Told ya I wasn't drunk!" They laughed. Even Jerry rolled and convulsed in gleeful circles on the dusty dirt floor. It was all so funny that the three men had to get out of there in a hurry, just so they could pee before they lost control of their bursting bladders.

It was a shame, Judd Winslow quietly remarked as they all stood there splattering away, trying to keep the wind from carrying their streams onto each other's shoes or pants legs; he thought it was such a beautiful day outside that they should have brought their drinks along with them. Without missing a beat, and without pausing in the act of relieving himself, Winkie Bols drew from the pockets of his pants and jacket three separate pint bottles of Jim Beam. He handed them around, proudly. "Jezzus!" Judd said, almost splattering himself as he removed his bottle from Winkie's hand. "Do I have to think of everything!?" he jested. They all laughed at that, just like a bunch of schoolboys playing hookey in the springtime.

CHAPTER FIFTEEN

When Ginny returned to her classroom she didn't tell anyone about what had just taken place in Mr. Ocean's guidance office. She wouldn't have known how to explain it. One part of her had *wanted* him to touch her, so that he could be punished for it—as the mind-pictures showed; while another part of her was repulsed by what he had done with his hands, and the hardness of his body as he'd pressed himself up against her. It was too much like some of the things her father used to do.

Her face was red and her eyes lowered as she returned to her seat at the side of the room, next to a row of windows. The girl in the seat next to her, Betty Bird Johnson, looked across at her slyly and giggled, as though she knew all about what had happened.

"What'd he say?" Betty Bird asked in a confidential whisper. There was a suggestiveness to her tone that Ginny found difficult to handle. Did she *know?* Ginny wondered. She felt herself begin to go on the verge of tears again. She abruptly turned her head toward the window as though something outside had caught her attention. She'd never liked Betty Bird. She was just a nosy busybody.

Behind her back she could hear another of Betty Bird's quiet giggles. It sounded like the noise air bubbles make in a bathtub. Ginny knew, without turning back to see, that Betty Bird had wiggled her shoulders in exaggerated annoyance at her refusal to answer her question.

All this took place in the few moments that Ginny had been back in the room—back from the humiliation she'd felt at Mr. Ocean's hands and the reawakening of the memory of the dreaded things her father used to do. It was enough for her to hate snooty Betty Bird forever—enough for her to hate everyone.

"Ginny," Mrs. Peabody called from the front of the room, when she saw the distracted expression on the girl's face. "We're about to go over the story of the play again. Pay attention to the chalkboard."

On the front board, Mrs. Peabody had created a sprawling plan of the school's gymnasium, where the sixth-grade play was to be held. She had used different colored chalks to indicate the various players, and, with dotted lines—in the appropriate color of each player—indicated the path they would travel as they spoke their lines. The scenery, which the children had already made out of papier-maché, and painted, was also chalked in. There were trees, rocks, bushes, and—although it was only indicated as a long curved line on the bird's-eye view of the set (with the word "backdrop" pointing to it with an arrow)—mountains and sky. The children knew what it was. They had all had a hand in painting the mountains (with a flowing waterfall) and the sky (with clouds and brightly colored birds) that served as the backdrop to the whole set.

As Mrs. Peabody began the story, she stood before the chalkboard with a long pointer and indicated the action as it progressed—reminding some of the children, especially the boys, of the way a football coach on TV outlined his plays.

The story was an African folk tale called "The Spear." It was about a great warrior-king. One day, while out hunting for his family, he was eaten by a lion. Soon, his family forgot all about him—until the child his wife had carried at the time of his death was born. When the child grew old enough to speak, the first words he uttered were: "Where is my father?" To everyone's dismay, they realized that they had forgotten him. So they went out searching and soon discovered his bones. As they wept, their tears fell onto the remains of the king, and he momentarily came back to life so he could bestow his spear, which was the symbol of his authority, upon one of his sons. There were five of them gathered about the temporarily resurrected king, including his wife and the newly born child she had carried along in her arms.

Several weeks ago, when Mrs. Peabody first read the story to the class, she had paused at that point and asked: "Who do you think he gave the spear to?" Everyone guessed that it was the eldest son upon whom the great warrior wished to bequeath his authority. But it was not. The warrior left his kingdom to the last-born child, for it was *he* who had been the only one to ask for his father—and in his kingdom, a man was not dead until he was forgotten.

If Ginny had not heard the story before she wouldn't have been able to follow it. It came at her in bits and pieces. Abstractions of her father's death, of the guidance counselor's hands, of the feel of his body—or was it her father's body? She felt herself to be an observer and a participant at the same time. Events were taking place in the play, in the classroom, in the guidance counselor's office, and in the dreaded cold of her father's attic—all at once. Forget, she told herself over and over again. Forget . . . forget . . . forget. And then it cleared. The sun was shining on a mountain range more beautiful than the play's backdrop. There were birds in the dazzling blue sky and the sounds of animals roaming about through the bushes. It made her close her eyes more tightly—to imagine them more vividly. Zebras, water buffalo, gazelles . . . it was as though the girl had been transported back through time to a place of magic. And she was a part of that magic. She killed and tortured for the sheer joy of it. Her father, Betty Bird Johnson, and the puny guidance counselor were ground like squirming insects beneath her feet. And as she trampled them into the dust, mountains and valleys were created in her footsteps. Nothing could stop her!

When Mrs. Peabody finished she looked up and noticed Ginny. The girl's eyes were closed and an inner glow spread itself across her cheeks, making them appear smooth and lustrous. The teacher was pleased. Even though Ginny had refused to take a major speaking part in the play—she had accepted a part in a group dance instead—the teacher was sure that the story had somehow touched her—touched her in a way that was, perhaps, far more profound than its effect on any of the other children. Mrs. Peabody liked that.

CHAPTER SIXTEEN

Harvey Ocean sat at the large round oak table in the center of Lettie's well-kept kitchen, staring at the cup of tea that the old woman had just placed before him. She was now at the kitchen counter, opening the tin of cookies she had made for Ginny's after-school snack. The aroma of them being baked that same afternoon still scented the kitchen. The guidance counselor found himself beginning to perspire. He had arrived and greeted Lettie well enough, he thought. But, he now realized, he shouldn't have pushed his luck by coming here. What had he hoped the visit would accomplish? That by coming here on some piece of business, he could assuage his own guilt for having touched Ginny in his office, convince the old woman of his innocence in case the girl told her about what he had done? He didn't know where to begin. There was a musty coldness crawling about in the heat of his worried mind. He tried to keep it from showing on his face.

Lettie returned to the table with some cookies in a

dish and offered them to the guidance counselor. She hardly knew him. He seemed like a man who could never relax, always twitching and tightening his lips as though he was about to say something. It was almost as though he was on the brink of a nervous breakdown. There must be a bundle of dumb things going on his muddled mind, she thought. And she wondered what he wanted.

She slipped the loops of her wire-rimmed eyeglasses over her ears and looked at him squarely. It was an invitation for him to plainly state his business, and leave—although she had been as polite about it as anyone could possibly be. There was just something about the man that she did not like, that she was not entirely comfortable with; and it had nothing at all to do with the rumors that he was having trouble with his marriage. Lots of people these days were having trouble with that, Lettie thought. And she wondered, not without a touch of humor spilling over into her eyes, at now many men she had saved from going miserable by not marrying any of them herself.

"So," she finally said, breaking the silence that had settled over the guidance counselor like a sudden gloom, "What can I help you with?"

The hot tea stung Ocean's palate. Had he been at home he would have gone to the sink and spat it out to keep it from peeling the membrane off the roof of his mouth. Instead, he gulped it down, as quickly as possible to avoid any further damage, and almost choked.

"Goodness!" Lettie exclaimed, watching him go red

in the face. "I guess I should have warned you it was hot," she said, although she saw no good reason to warn a full-grown man of the fact that when steam is lifting off a cup of freshly poured tea, it's hot! "Can I get you a glass of water?"

Harvey Ocean looked up at her through watery eyes and motioned *no* by shaking his head. He would be all right, his raised hand—palm facing her—seemed to indicate.

Lettie arched her eyebrows and leaned back into her caned ladderback chair. It creaked with age, but it suited her fine.

When Ocean finished his sputtering, he looked up at her and said, "I just wanted to come over here this afternoon and discuss something with you before Ginny got home." He pulled a scrap of paper from the inside pocket of his suit and laid it on the table, beside the cup of tea, and rubbed his hand across it to iron out the wrinkles.

Lettie could hardly belive what the man then began to tell her. From the paper, he quoted a statute that he had scribbled out of a state service manual. It all boiled down to the fact that Lettie could not keep Ginny, she would have to turn the child over to the authorities, who would then begin adoption procedures; Lettie couldn't hope to adopt Ginny herself because she was too old. "Eighty-three hardly seems the age to be starting a family," he concluded with a nervous chuckle.

If ever anyone wanted to kill an old woman with words, that was what he almost did. Lettie felt her heart stop for longer than it should have, but her composed—but wrinkled—face showed no sign of it. Instead, something resembling a thin snarl of contempt planted itself across her tightly pursed lips.

"Now, tell me," she began softly, after the breath went back into her lungs, and the beat of her heart had returned. "Who's going to make me give her up?" It was not only a question, it was a challenge. Harvey Ocean hadn't expected that.

"Why . . ." he searched for some way to respond. "I'm mandated by law to inform the proper authorities. It's part of the child abuse laws."

Lettie's eyes bored into him like drills of cold-tempered steel. "And if you should happen to fall down a deep hole and disappear from the face of the earth, as you were on your way home for supper tonight, who else do you suppose would be stupid enough to do such a darn fool thing as that!?"

Ocean squirmed, and with the crook of his pointing finger, unstuck the starched color from his dank neck. "Why . . ." he said nervously. "Any school official, or even the police . . . Loren Mitchell, the county sheriff. They're *mandated* to." He pointed to the sheet of paper beside his teacup as though it was the Bible itself. "There's no other choice."

Lettie sucked in a breath of air before responding. The tiny yellow buttercups that were printed into her pale blue housedress appeared to swell and ripen. "Mister," she began, obviously on the point of boiling over, "I'm going to tell you something about your fancy mandate. Before you were ever on this earth, there were farmers here. Life was a whole lot harder than anything you might care to imagine. When babies died at birth, and there were a good number of them—just you go up and check in the cemetery—their parents would just go up there and dig a hole and bury them. Sometimes, if they had enough money to buy one, they'd have a stone placed on the spot. Ever see those stones up at the graveyard, the ones that are marked with one word: *Baby?* Well, that's what those are, in case you didn't know. There must be a dozen of them up there on the godforsaken hill, and. . . ."

Lettie caught herself. Maybe it was the way she had been feeling fulfilled ever since the sheriff had let Ginny come and live with her, but she was about to tell the guidance counselor about the nameless child she herself had buried there over sixty years ago. Well over half a century, and she could still remember it as though it had happened that very same afternoon! The smell of the earth. That cold moonless night. She had buried it herself, in an agony of pain, long before she was able to afford a stone to mark the place. Six months later, she carried the small stone there herself—cradled in a shawl as though it were a child itself. There was only one word cut into the stone. It read: BABY, and in her mind she remembered how she had traced one of her fingers through every crease and curve of it. It was the finger on which a wedding band should have been, but was not.

Harvey Ocean didn't know how to regain his footing. The old woman was obviously on a course to roll him as flat as a worn-out dime.

"Well," she came back to where she was in a flash, speaking quicker, lest those faraway memories began to leak back into her thoughts. "There wasn't any *statute* in those days, telling decent folks that they couldn't do this 'n that when the Lord decided He would take their children on Home with Him. And when *parents* died, leaving no one behind to raise and care for their children, there was no *mandate* that prevented a good neighbor from taking a child or two into their own home and caring for it, if there were no relatives who could." She played her eyes over the guidance counselor as though he was something considerably less than when he had first entered her kitchen. She felt like scatting him out of there with a broom, like some detestable thing that had crawled through a hole and gotten itself loose in her kitchen.

"Besides," she continued in the face of his cowed silence, "I've been taking care of Ginny ever since she first came to town. That was *ten* years ago. Her father was alone and didn't know too much about how to do such things. Ginny thinks of me as family. Where will the state put her? In some orphanage somewhere, where she'll have to stay until she's old enough to leave on her own—put a few dollars in her pocket, pat her on the back: *Go out into the world, young lady, you'll make it. And if you don't, well, there's a whole system of welfare to support you for the rest of your life!*"

"Someone will adopt her," he offered in the feeble tone of a person who had been whipped.

"Oh, bull!" Lettie exploded. "Folks these days adopt infants, not twelve-year-olds. Don't you read the papers?" She waved the back of her hand in his direction as though she was shooing flies off the table. "Besides," she went on without taking the time to catch her breath, "Ginny's happy here."

Harvey Ocean looked down at his hands without really seeing them. His eyes were worried. He had a feeling he should leave her alone, but he couldn't help himself. "What if something should happen to you?" he asked in a tone that was close to a whisper.

Lettie sat back at that. She hadn't thought that far, but she wasn't going to let him know. "I've already been to a lawyer," she lied, "about having my will changed to favor the child. If anything happens to me. . . ."

The thought clouded the old woman's mind like fog coming off her baby's grave marker at dawn. A lump of dryness swelled in her throat and she began to swallow hard, trying all the while not to show it. When she got her breathing back she stood up sharply, almost toppling the ladderback chair behind her.

"Nothing's going to happen to *me,*" she said in a cold and even voice. "But one thing's for sure. And that is if you stay here one more minute, something's going to happen to you!" She hadn't lost her temper in . . . she didn't remember how long, and here she was losing it at the fool before her. She felt like cursing herself. No wonder the kids at school called him a *drip.* There certainly was no question that he was.

As he quickly departed, relief flooded back into Harvey Ocean's mind like a tide of breezes in the deep heat of a summer's day. In a sense he had won. How could he ever be accused of having attempted to molest the little girl in his office, when he had boldly walked into her house that same afternoon and got her guardian all riled over a point of law that was clearly in his favor? He was only trying to be helpful, he told himself, sauntering down the flagstone walk that led to the street. Yes, he thought, bracing his back stiffly, he was only trying to be helpful. Doing his job. One call to the state authorities and he would be as helpful as all get-out. And innocent, too!

CHAPTER SEVENTEEN

Something made Ginny stray in the direction of the pond after school that day. She knew she should have gone straight home, as Lettie had asked her to, but the feeling she had—the one that urged her further on in the direction of the pond—was too compelling. She couldn't imagine intentionally disregarding anything Lettie had asked her to do, like getting herself right home after school—where there would be a batch of freshly baked cookies and milk ready for her—but here she was doing it, anyway! It was as though something inside of her had taken over, and all her best intentions couldn't keep her feet to the path that led back to the old woman's house.

Most of the children had already gone their separate ways, and Ginny was alone. She had been a loner ever since the year before, when she had been taken ill with a series of high fevers and had lost a half year of school. The doctors hadn't known what it was, but it had seemed to leave her somewhat *different* from the other children. She had suddenly grown taller, and, when she had to repeat the sixth grade because of the excessive absence caused by the mysterious illness, it made her stand out as a more mature child among her classmates. There had been talk that she might jump to her normal grade, which would be the seventh, but the problem with that had been that the seventh grade was the start of junior high—and that was housed in a building in the unified school district of Wayne County, which was close to thirty miles away and involved complicated busing—busing that was too risky, so her father had said, for a child just getting over some unknown type of illness. Better she should repeat the entire sixth grade, right where she was within walking distance of home, and wait for her to skip ahead once she got to the junior high. Only Lettie and a small handful of teachers had understood the emotional debasement such a thing would cause the girl, but Ginny's father would hear none of it.

Almost every girl in the entire sixth grade, which was composed of three classes, didn't like Ginny. She looked like she belonged in junior high, and it made them feel smaller than they actually were. As it turned out, Ginny didn't much care for them, either—not because she was taller and developing better than any other girl in the grade, but because they occasionally forgot their manners and said mean things to her; like right after school that day, Betty Bird Johnson had come right up and told her that her parents thought Ginny shouldn't be wearing bright ribbons in her hair because it was too soon after her father's death. Ginny didn't say a word. She simply turned away and headed toward the pond. In her head, the thought *I'll fix that snip!* played like a litany against the sound of her feet as she hurried away. But what did going to the pond have to do with anything? she thought. Was it the water moccasins?

Ginny stood with her back to the church where her father had been killed and gazed down the hill toward the pond. The afternoon sun was beginning to dip and the shadows were long. It wasn't the way she usually went back to Lettie's house after school, but there was still a chance for her to do so. If she turned to the right, she'd be headed back toward the center of town, and to Lettie. If she walked straight ahead, she'd be walking down the hill through the tall grasses toward the pond. She headed down the hill, remembering that long-ago afternoon when she was just a little girl—when she had taken her shoes and socks off and waded out into the cool water up to her knees. She remembered, too, the moccasin she had "taught" to make figure eights on the surface of the water.

It suddenly occurred to her that she knew why she was going there. If she could really get a water moccasin to do what she wanted, leaving no doubt in her mind that she had actually controlled it, then she would know for sure that she had caused her father's death in the church that afternoon. The thought almost halted her steps. Suddenly she wasn't so sure she wanted to be so certain about such a thing. What would she do if it turned out she could really do it? What then?

Kill Betty Bird! something whispered in her heart. And the thought rooted her to the spot, not because it was such a horrible thought to imagine, but because the image of Betty Bird Johnson, struggling to keep a water moccasin from gliding down her throat and tearing her wicked tongue out, brought her a surge of joy. She even caught herself smiling. The thought was as good as anything she had felt since her father's death!

She started to walk again, with greater purpose. She seemed to be aware, for the very first time in her life, that there appeared to be two parts to her: one told her she was just dreaming everything up, and the other caused her to rejoice at the evil mind-pictures that had, more and more lately, begun to flash into her thoughts—like the one she just had of the snake tearing out Betty Bird's tongue, and the one she had had earlier of the snakes twisting in and out of the guidance counselor's skull-like head.

When Ginny reached the pond, she deposited her books beside her and sat down on a broad, flat outcropping of rock that overlooked the water. A gentle breeze came up as she gazed off toward its opposite shore. A stand of mature willow trees bent gracefully toward the water and trailed the tips of their branches into it, like sets of long elegant fingers playing across the strings of a harp. Tall grasses spread out from the water's edge in every direction and raced toward the rolling hills on the horizon. The further the grasses receded from the pond, the dryer and more golden they looked in the afternoon sun. There were other trees, too, and when Ginny turned her head, she could see all the way up the hill she had just descended. The spire of her father's white clapboard church loomed up above the treetops. In the opposite direction, away from the town, she could see the campus of Wilston College. She would go there one day, she told herself. Lettie had told her of the book her mother had been working on when she had died in Africa, where Ginny knew she herself had been born. Maybe that was why she had so many dreams that seemed to be about Africa, she thought. Maybe that was why she didn't want to take a speaking role in the school play, but instead had decided to be one of the dancers. For some reason, she was afraid of the speaking lines, afraid that something other than what was written would come out of her mouth—like the fear she had of ever seeing her mother's manuscript, which was in the college library. Reading it might do something to her!

School would be out for the summer in another couple of weeks, and Ginny dreamed of how wonderful it would be if she could only pitch a tent on that outcropping where she now sat and spend the rest of her life there. It was so peaceful and quiet that the inner turmoil that had earlier driven her to the spot appeared to vanish. She felt like taking off her clothes and diving off the rock into the water—the way she had heard children used to do before the snakes took over. She leaned forward, drew her knees up into her arms, and looked across the smooth surface of the pond again—this time, attempting to see if she could sight a water moccasin. There wasn't a single one around. Disappointment circled down into the pit of her heart. How was she going to find out if she could get a snake to do what she wanted, if there weren't any around to practice on? The thought that she should be as afraid as everyone else of the poisonous moccasins never entered her mind. She sighed and let her breath out as she leaned back on the palms of her outstretched hands. Feeling the warmth of the sun on her closed eyelids, and the heat of the day that had been stored up in the smooth soapstone rock, made her feel good.

After a while she opened her eyes a tiny slit to look back out over the calm, undisturbed surface of the pond. Still, not a water moccasin in sight. She didn't know distances that well, but folks said the pond was one of the largest spring-fed ponds in the state; some called it a lake. Its irregularly shaped shoreline was close to one mile around—which didn't mean the pond was that *long*, Ginny's teacher had once explained, it only meant that if you ran a string all around the edge of it, and then took that same string and stretched it out straight, *that* would then measure a mile. Mrs. Peabody, who had once been to New York City, said that the pond was about the same size as the model sailboat pond they have in Central Park, and she showed pictures of it, too.

Ginny didn't know how long she had been lying there on the warm outcropping that overlooked the pond, but when she opened her eyes again, it was as though she were waking from a dream. She was sitting upright, without a stitch of clothing on, and in each of her two hands she held a stone. Her clothes were in a neat pile beside her school books. The bright yellow ribbon she had worn in her hair rested on top of the pile.

Maybe it had been the sound of the stones being struck against the stone slab on which she had been lying, or the sound they now made as she struck them gently against each other, she didn't know; but when she looked down at her feet, there were three nestling water moccasins, looking as though they wanted to curl up and snuggle as close to her as possible.

Ginny didn't know how the rocks had gotten into her hands. She didn't care. All she knew was that this was the moment she had been waiting for, the moment in which she would decide, once and for all, whether or not she could really control the creatures. She wiggled her toes and the snakes moved closer, winding sideways up to her and stopping just short of making contact with them. She knew if she wiggled her toes one more time the snakes would come right up and touch her feet with their cold noses. She held her breath and tried. They did! Not only that, but over the edge of the outcropping there appeared the heads of other moccasins who seemed to want to do the same thing. Where did they all come from? Ginny thought. A moment ago there were none. Now, there were dozens of them!

She looked at the stones in her hands and wrinkled her brow. Then, slowly, she began to strike them against each other. It was suddenly like the dream she had had the night her father had pulled her from her bed and forced her up into the attic:

She was listening to the rocks that were strewn about a wasted landscape. They sang sweetly as she struck stone upon stone. There were those who didn't like the song—the vibrating harmony that she caused to hum along the barrenness of the strange landscape in which she found herself. Yet, she couldn't stop herself. She didn't care to stop herself. She hammered the blunted stone into the depression of the rock on which she sat until the earth itself began to throb with the feel of it. It shivered up her body and made her insides go soft and tingly, like falling weightlessly through the sky.

She knew what she was doing was bad. But she now remembered how good the dream had made her feel, and how she had not wanted it to end. It was then that she had awakened to find her father's cold hands on her breasts. The memory of it made her strike the stones more firmly against each other. And this caused more and more snakes to gather about her. At last she really knew that she had some sort of control over them, that they seemed to *want* her to control them—to give them deeds to do. It was as though they had been waiting all their lives for her to come along.

"Go!" she said. And they vanished, departing as rapidly as a dog chasing after a tossed stick. The afternoon was suddenly as still as it had been before she woke to find herself striking the stones together. There was not a single snake in sight.

Ginny was about to see if she could call the snakes back to her, when she heard voices tumbling down the hill toward the pond. She quickly gathered up her clothing and school books and scampered off the soapstone slab to hide beneath it. There was a cavelike opening there, created by the overhanging rock. In the shaded coolness of it she quickly wrestled her clothing back on. When she was fully dressed, the yellow ribbon neatly back in her smoothed hair, she cautiously stole a look through the bushes that surrounded the opening of the false cave.

Three men stood in a clearing that was about a hundred yards from where she was. She couldn't hear what they were saying, but could clearly make out who they were: Winkie Bols, one of her father's friends, Judd Winslow, who used to be a fireman, and Jerry Knox. All but Jerry Knox, probably because of his bad leg, had been pallbearers at her father's funeral. They were all dead drunk. She could tell that much by the way they could hardly stand up. They swayed and wavered about as much as the wavering waist-high grasses that seemed to engulf them. It looked as though they would fall flat at any moment.

Ginny continued to watch as Judd Winslow waved his arms in the air. Then he held one hand down, palm parallel to the ground, and ran it back and forth as though he was rubbing it across a highly polished piece of furniture. With the other hand, he made tornado-like motions in the air above his head. Winkie then placed his hands out toward the pond and drew them back and forth with soft pushing motions, as though he thought whatever Judd had been talking about was all wrong—that whatever it was Judd thought would be spreading like a tornado from the pond could easily be held back. Jerry just stood there swaying, agreeing with whoever at that moment happened to be speaking. Ginny wondered if they were planning to do something about the snakes. She had once overheard Winkie Bols saying something to her father about it. She wished she could remember what it was.

Something made her look down at her feet. On the floor of the cavelike shelter in which she was hiding, a small number of water moccasins slithered about her feet like kittens. They rubbed against her shoes and slid their heads across her ankles.

She stooped down and picked one up. When it caused her no harm, she picked up several more. They coiled lazily about her wrists like trained pets. If they were kittens they would have purred. "Okay," she whispered, and her small voice echoed darkly in the cool shadows of the cavelike grotto. "This is what I want you to do." After she told them, she gently placed them back on the ground, and watched as they shot off in the direction of the three men who, at that moment, happened to be relieving themselves in the tall grasses.

Ginny laughed. The sound of it reminded her of the laughter that had rung out of the darkness of the attic that night her father spun like a top in the center of it.

CHAPTER EIGHTEEN

Sara Garrett had been taken ill with an unusual fever and had requested to remain on at the college for another week until it passed. She would then be visiting friends and family in New England before returning to finish her work in America. The curious illness had unexpectedly provided her with a much needed rest; also, with a new friend, Edna Malikoff—the wife of Sir James Malikoff, the college's visiting professor of astronomy.

Sara and Edna were having early tea in the astronomy lab—where Edna's husband had what he presumed to be the only decent electric tea kettle in all of Africa. And since he was a man who had been knighted by the queen for his scientific achievements, his opinions were not to be dismissed lightly—which his wife always did, of course. That was why he loved her. Even she could never figure that one out.

In the absence of her knighted husband, Edna had suggested tea in the lab because of the tea kettle. She knew it would please Sir Jimmy, as she had playfully nicknamed him. That had been almost a quarter of a century ago, the very night he was knighted. They had celebrated the event by spending a full thirty-six hours in a four-poster bed at Claridge's in the heart ot London, doing what he later said were "naughty things." They had both been, at the time, over fifty years old, and had been married since they were eighteen. They had come a long way together, and now, at seventy six years each, they fit each other like a remarkably matched set of finely crafted silver spoons.

Sara, feeling much better now—largely because of the wonderful care and concern administered to her by the wiry Edna Malikoff (who had insisted on nursing her back to full health with honeyed tea and vodka)—looked about the astronomy lab and sipped her tea. The Smirnoff gave it a flavor that Sara thought she might possibly manage to get used to. She smiled at Edna, and wondered, out loud, why Edna hadn't been invited to participate in the parapsychological research conference herself. She had published in the field in England, and even Sara had heard of her work when she was herself thinking of venturing into the mysteries of the paranormal.

"Pshaw!" Edna said lightheartedly, rattling her cup about in the saucer to keep it balanced. "I gave that up years and years ago." Then—maybe it was the tea, the pleasant warmth of the afternoon sun slanting in through the opened metal shutters of the tall and narrow windows, or maybe it was simply because she had grown so irresistibly fond of Sara, who reminded her of her own daughter, the one who had run off with a Tibetan and never been heard of since—something compelled her to add, "Gave it all up after I saw something that frightened me half to death." She had never mentioned what that something was to anyone, except, of course, Sir Jimmy, who never listened too carefully to anything she had to say anyway—and that was why *she* loved *him.* It was a pity, she thought, that he was not there with them now. Astronomers! she thought. They sleep all day so they can stay up all night, gazing at the stars.

Sara placed her tea on the slate-topped workbench beside her and looked intently into Edna's bright hazel-colored eyes. "What do you mean?" she asked. "What was it that frightened you?"

Edna toyed with the eyepiece of a polished brass spotting scope that was being fitted with a mounting device. It belonged to the much larger telescope that was poised to poke through the dome of the lab that night. So, she thought, it's out with it. And after all these years! Whatever hesitation she felt melted away as she began to speak. It was as though she had told the story a thousand times before.

"Ever hear of the events at Wilderness School, in Wiltshire, just outside of London?"

Sara shrugged, and shook her head. "No," she said. "I'm afraid not."

"Well, 'The War Was On,' as we used to say in those days—and that probably accounts for its not having been given wider coverage. It was a classic poltergeist phenomenon. After it took place, even Scotland Yard was called in, with no better results than I could achieve. . . ."

At the word *poltergeist,* Sara sat up straighter. It was the area in which she had once been most interested. It showed in her eyes.

". . . . In those days, children went about collecting chunks of metal that were left over from the bombings; *shrapnel*, I believe it was called. Well, every child had his or her own collection. One day, Anna Freud, daughter of you-know-who, visited. She was preparing a book on the effects of war on children—it's now a classic." Edna's eyebrows arched as she reached for the tea kettle and poured for Sara, doing the same for herself when she was through.

"Well, Anna took one look at those lumps of jagged metal and, quick as a flash, thought of a game the children could play; a game in which they could unburden themselves of the psychologically hidden traumas they no doubt possessed when, each and every night, the Germans flew over and bombed everything they possibly could. She saw, immediately, that the collecting of the metal scraps—some as large as American baseballs—was a means by which the children themselves had unconsciously sought to lessen the trauma of the war upon themselves—by inventing a sort of game—so she merely pushed it a step further. In the play yard, she had noticed a tree with a ladder leading up to a platform of boards that the children had put together. It was some five or six meters from the ground, about fifteen of your American feet. She climbed up with about a dozen children, boys and girls between the ages of eleven and thirteen, and suggested what should happen next: they should *bomb* the earth with their pieces of metal, imitating the Germans, and in so doing lessen the terror, or the psychological trauma of the thing—similar to stroking a cat in order to overcome your fear of it. Well, the game went *smashingly,* in no uncertain use of the word. No sooner had the game begun, than it ended, in a horror of blood and death."

Sara gulped her tea, audibly. "What?" she asked, setting the cup carefully back into the saucer on her knee. Her eyes were as large as an inquisitive child's. "What happened?" she urged.

Edna was warming to the story, its events playing in her mind as though they had happened only the day before. She tipped the vodka bottle toward Sara's cup, then also poured some for herself before going on.

"That's when I came in, right after Anna, and before Scotland Yard. The headmistress of the school, Sylvia Beach, was an old classmate of mine from Bath, and she called me—almost before she contacted the authorities. She, of course, knew of my work in parapsychology and asked me over to have a look-see. By the time I arrived—in those days, travel from one part of the country to the other was very difficult, no petrol and things like that—the children who had been killed in the incident had been buried, and the blood, along with pieces of their bodies, had been washed from the side of the schoolhouse (the side facing the play yard) as best as could be expected. But as for the holes that had been bored through the side of the building, there was no washing *those* away! The wall resembled a bloodstained slab of Swiss cheese. It was immediately apparent that no child could ever have hurled a lump of metal with such force as to penetrate the side of the schoolhouse—even if it was only wood-framed. I tried to replicate the act, but barely managed to chip the paint off the siding! It was then that

Sylvia told me the story of what had happened:

"Anna and the children had been bombarding the earth for about fifteen minutes, when one of the chunks of metal *bounced* back up at one of the children."

"*Bounced* back?" Sara questioned. "Is that possible?"

"It isn't!" Edna said, drawing in her breath. "When I tried to do the same thing, from the same platform, the piece of metal I hurled merely went *plunk*, and lay there on the ground as though it had roots. It didn't even roll!"

"Then, what caused it to . . . *bounce?*"

Edna's eyebrows twitched. "Not only did it bounce back up at the child," Edna continued as though Sara hadn't spoken, "but it put a hole right through his head, splattering everyone in the tree with bits of his brain."

Sara sat back, almost upsetting the cup and saucer on her knee. She couldn't speak.

"Of course," Edna went on, "right after that the children began to scream and attempted to scamper down the tree. Some fell out, some jumped, as did Miss Freud, and ran for cover—you see, the scraps of metal that the children had been playing with had all begun to hurl themselves about of their own accord. Some went through the wall of school building causing no more damage than the gaping holes I described, but others. . . ." Her voice trailed off, as though it wasn't necessary for her to finish.

"It was a bloodbath," she said after a brief pause. "Eighteen children were killed. Anna narrowly escaped with her own life, and by the time Scotland Yard was through with the investigation, they had everyone believing that some sort of an air raid had occurred and wasn't recognized as such. A ouija board might have provided more accurate information than the report they filed!"

Sara studied her for a moment. It was obvious that a surge of something uneasy was struggling with Edna's thoughts. "But that was what you had been told," Sara said, careful to avoid making her words sound like a challenge. "What was it that you actually *saw?* The thing that made you give up your work?"

Edna Malikoff let the breath go out of her lungs as though a balloon had collapsed within her breast. Her frail shoulders rounded as she reached for the bottle of vodka and poured another half ounce into each of their cups. Then she added the honey and more hot tea from the electric kettle. "What I *saw,*" she began softly, after replacing the kettle on its stand, "was this:

"I arrived several days after the incident had occurred. By then, as I said before, the children had been buried and things cleaned up a bit. Of course, the authorities had closed the school and transferred the surviving children to other districts." Her eyes narrowed, as though attempting to recall everything in the minutest detail. "I remember sitting at a student-desk in a classroom, all by myself, and staring out through the holes that had been driven through the wall. The violence of it all worked into me somehow, and I began to wonder if it might have been some sort of an air raid after all. According to the headmistress, the children had been so worked up when the incident occurred, that she herself, when she went to the window to investigate the screams, had first turned her face toward the sky, expecting to see German planes dropping bombs. But there had been none, and there were no sirens warning of such an attack. It was also daytime, and the Germans never attacked before dark. Yet, I thought: *hysteria* . . . you know. War, children screaming, shrapnel hurtling about, nightly bombings—it all seemed to add up, if you asked me.

"But while I was sitting there, wondering about what had happened, I noticed a movement out of the corner of my eye. All the shrapnel in question had been carefully collected and placed in a coal bucket that was on the teacher's desk, at the front of the room. Scotland Yard was coming by that day to pick it up for analysis—or some such thing. Didn't matter, of course, because it never got there."

Edna took a swallow of tea to clear her throat, and her mind, before going on. Sara's eyes were riveted to her.

"When I turned to see what had moved in front of the room, I saw nothing—but I *felt* something. It brushed past the top of my head and made my hair stand up. No sooner had I felt that, than I heard a loud report behind me. It sounded like two wooden planks being smacked together with great force. I turned to see what it was, and saw that there was now a hole in the opposite wall. There hadn't been one there before, of that I was sure—since when I first entered the room I took note that the only wall with holes in it was the exterior wall, beyond which was the play yard. It took a moment for me to realize that the thing I had just felt zip across the top of my head, and that one particular hole in the wall, had a connection.

I immediately spun about to face the coal bucket at the front of the room. No sooner done, than another chunk of shrapnel came sizzling right at me. I threw myself to the floor and clung flat to its boards. I heard the bucket go over at that point, and the whistling sound made by the shards of jagged metal as they whizzed over my head and smashed through the opposite wall and into the room beyond—a room I later discovered to be the office of my friend, Sylvia Beach, the headmistress. She had been killed," Edna concluded without offering any detail beyond which she already had. "And I never even heard her scream."

Although the afternoon sun was pouring in through the windows and falling direction on Sara, she found that she was shivering with cold. It was nothing external. It was the cold that comes from within.

Beginning slowly, Sara asked, "How did you discover it was a poltergeist event?"

Edna Malikoff's throat had gone dry, too. She swallowed against it before answering. "Just before the shrapnel started to fly from the coal bucket," she said, "I thought I saw a child standing outside in the play yard, looking at me through one of the many holes in the wall. She was off to the side, which led me to suspect she was peeking in at me and didn't want to be discovered. That's when the shrapnel started to fly. It was only when everything had quieted down, that the child approached. I must have fainted or some such thing, but as I finally managed to lift myself from the floor, there she was, right in the classroom with me. I'll never forget those tragic eyes of hers—large as saucers and curiously apologetic. 'I'm sorry,' she said. 'I thought you were. . .' and she didn't go any further. Her eyes simply moved to the recently perforated wall, beyond which was the grotesquely mutilated body of Sylvia Beach. I had to sit down heavily after that. I knew it was the child, the poltergeist, and that she was responsible for everything that had occurred."

There was a pause in the afternoon, a pause in which the beat of the universe could be felt in the silent sheets of golden sunlight that streamed in through the tall windows of the hushed lab. Edna Malikoff drew the edges of her lips in tightly and let her breath out before continuing to speak again.

"I had observed poltergeist activity before," Edna said quietly, as though she were responding to Sara's unvoiced question. "It occurs mostly in adolescent girls, and appears to be nothing more than a bundle of repressed emotions, projected outward." She looked down at the backs of her sun-spotted hands in her lap. "No one knows what triggers it off," she said, looking up again. "But abused children or those in foster homes appear to be the one who produce such events most frequently. The appearance of puberty, especially in young girls, somehow releases an . . . an *aberration,* for want of a better word. It seems that some dark force, lying dormant within the child, comes to birth with alarming speed—as though to mark the significant change from childhood to adulthood. In a young girl, that time appears to be just prior to her first menstruation—after which the phenomenon usually disappears—as was the case with Melissa, the child I met for the first time in that dreadful classroom."

Sara already knew much of what the textbooks had

to say regarding such phenomena. What she didn't understand was the familiar manner in which Edna had pronounced the child's name.

"Melissa?" she asked.

Edna's eyes moved as though she were reading something printed in the air just to the side of Sara's questioning eyes. It seemed as though she were considering whether or not to go on. When her eyes stopped moving, Sara knew she was ready.

"The child had lost her entire family in a bombing, just weeks before the incident at the school had occurred. She had been living off rubble heaps, on any scraps of food she could find. But she went to school each day, *pretending* that nothing out of the ordinary had happened. It didn't take long for her to grow scruffy in appearance, and the children at school teased her. It got the attention of the headmistress, and an informal investigation into the situation was soon to be launched. That's when it all happened. As she later told me, she had simply wanted the bombings to stop; and as for the headmistress, she had simply not wanted her to find out that her family had been killed—she didn't want to have to go to the city and live in the underground, as she had been told happened to little children without a family to look after them."

Then, as incongruously as a sunburst in the middle of the darkest night, Edna Malikoff grinned. "I adopted her," she said. "Sir Jimmy and I. Our only child."

The warmth and simplicity of the statement brought a broad grin to Sara's face, as well.

"And where is she now?" Sara asked. "What does she

do?"

Edna shrugged. "We haven't seen her since she was seventeen," she answered without drama. "She ran off with some Tibetan Chinaman. Last we heard, all she wanted of us was to send her a plastic bathtub—to Tibet!" She chuckled gayly. "Can you imagine?" she asked, not really intending to be answered. "I have a daughter out there somewhere—and God only knows how many grandchildren—with the biggest, bluest plastic bathtub in all of Tibet, or China—or whatever it is these days!"

Edna's thoughts wandered off as she took another sip of tea. It was obvious to Sara that she had been locked onto the image of her daughter and that bathtub for many, many years. She knew Edna would rather imagine her alive and well than damn her for running off like that—running off to do the same thing that Edna would probably have done herself, had she only been in her daughter's shoes at the time.

Sara remained behind to rinse the teacups after Edna left. Had she looked up from the slate-stone sink, and glanced out the window above it, she would have seen an extraordinary scene. . . .

Down the hill, toward the pond, it appeared that some men were playing a very spirited game of soccer. But there were only three of them, and such a game was impossible to play in such a mix of tall grasses. Whatever it was they were kicking at with such a frenzy, they soon gave it up and raced for a footpath that led up the hill toward town. A long black snake corkscrewed into the air and sailed at one of the men like a whip. Had it not been for the fact that the man limped badly, stumbled on a rock, and almost fell, it would have gotten him right in the neck. The other two men hooked their arms beneath either side of his shoulders and heaved him along, up to a point where the trail disappeared behind a thicket of waving greenery—and Sara wouldn't have been able to see what had happened after that, even if she had been looking. But what she did see, when she finally did look up, was a little girl with a bright yellow ribbon in her hair, skipping and dancing up the hill, just as merrily as though something had infused her with a boundless joy.

CHAPTER NINETEEN

The minute the guidance counselor left Lettie's house, the old woman reached for the telephone and called Loren Mitchell, the county sheriff who had "temporarily" placed Ginny in her care. In doing so, he knew he had taken it upon himself to circumvent certain state regulations for the sake of doing what he considered to be the better thing for the child. If anyone was to have custody of Ginny, it should certainly be Lettie, he had thought. There was no one else better qualified to do the job. The little girl had no other family, and he knew she loved the old woman as much as any child would love her own grandmother. So, when Lettie called to tell him what Harvey Ocean had just said about having Ginny taken away from her, he was quite concerned.

"That guidance counselor has his nose in the wrong place," he tried to assure her over the telephone. "Why don't I stop by in a while and see if there's anything we can do," he said, even though he knew there was nothing that he, or she, could ever do to stop Harvey Ocean, once he put the whole of his pea-sized brain to it!

Lettie felt better after the call. Loren Mitchell was a good man. He'd do anything in his power to see that the right thing was done—not the right thing according to what a piece of paper had to say, but the right thing according to the law of common sense. Yes, she felt better, and even managed to smile at the boldness she had mustered in bluffing the guidance counselor out of the house. She had no more been in contact with any lawyer about having her last will changed than a blue cow has wings! She didn't even have a will, or a lawyer, for that matter; she didn't believe in the need for either of them.

She had managed to get herself so worked up over the matter that she didn't notice that Ginny was late in getting home from school. It was only after eliminating the presence of Harvey Ocean from her kitchen—washing the teacup he had used and getting it put away, and sweeping up the mess of cookie crumbs that had fallen from his thin little mouth when she threatened to clobber him—that she settled herself down at the old oak table in the kitchen with a cup of herb tea to steady her nerves. It was then that she glanced at the pendulum shelf clock across the room and saw that Ginny was late by almost an hour.

It was unusual for the girl to be that late. But the thought of Harvey Ocean's taking Ginny away from her pushed the child's tardiness out of her mind.

She took a swallow of freshly brewed tea and glanced over her shoulder at the clock again. Another dreadful thought entered her mind. She knew that some of the children at school, especially the girls, sometimes picked on Ginny because she was older than they were. Taller and more developed, too. She hoped that it wasn't because of anything like that that Ginny was late. The girl had once confided in her that the teasing had caused her to go wandering off after school one day—in the direction of the *pond*, of all places! Lettie wasn't afraid of snakes; never had been, not since her father had taught her how not to be attacked by one. But, even though she had taught Ginny some of the same things, she knew it was no longer safe for anyone to be going there. From what Winkie Bols had been talking about at town meetings, it seemed that the snake population had been increasing in a way that was not in accordance with the laws of nature. She didn't know why such a thing should be possible, but she wondered—what with all one heard on the radio and television these days—if some sort of toxic waste, or acid rains, or some other thing had managed to find its way into the pond and caused the snakes to multiply unnaturally. And to go loco in the process.

A coldness touched the side of her throat as she sat there and continued to worry herself over the notion that the child had been teased and had wandered off to the pond. She placed one of her hands—warm from holding the teacup—against the spot of cold that was just above the shoulder and below the ear. It was the same spot that the snake had struck Ginny's father, but she leaned herself into it anyway. The warmth of her hand was soothing, but not as soothing as the sound of Ginny's footsteps approaching the house. The girl bounced lightly up the wooden steps of the back porch and opened the kitchen door.

"Goodness!" Lettie said as the child entered and set her books on one of the kitchen counters. The old woman was about to question her lateness, but the brightness of the child's steps, and the mirth that glowed in her eyes, stopped her. She hadn't seen Ginny that happy in . . . well, she didn't know how long.

"I guess you had to stay after school today, to work things."

The girl didn't respond to what the old woman said, but rather told her about what Betty Bird Johnson had told her; about how her parents thought that Ginny shouldn't be wearing bright ribbons in her hair so soon after her father's death.

"Oh, you never mind that," Lettie said. "Your father would have wanted you to wear them. He always liked the way they looked in your hair." She paused a beat, then asked, "Is that what kept you so long from coming home after school? That little Betty Bird?"

Ginny shrugged. "Did you make cookies today?" she asked. "I sure would like to have one if you did."

Lettie wasn't fooled. But she wasn't going to press the issue, not right now. She'd get back to that later, she thought—if the child doesn't first come out with it herself.

"You'll find some fresh cookies in the tin on the counter," she said to the girl. "I'll get you some milk to go with them." And she started to rise from the table.

"You sit there," Ginny said. "I can fix it for myself." She looked at Lettie's empty teacup, and then at the counter, on which the pot was keeping warm beneath a quilted tea cozy that was shaped like a big yellow hen. "Can I have some tea, too?" she asked. "I feel like having something more grown-up today."

Lettie laughed. There was no harm in it, she thought. "I'll have myself another cup, too," she said to the child, who was already reaching into the cabinet where the cups were kept. "There should be enough left in the pot for another cup each." Lettie always made three cups of tea when she fixed a fresh pot for herself—two cups for herself and one for the pot. It was wasteful, she knew. But ever since she was a child, that was how it had been made. Her father had taught it to her that way, and that was probably the way it was going to be until the Good Lord decided to call her home.

When everything was all settled at the table, Ginny sat down opposite the old woman. She was silent for a while. Then, "Do snakes hear?" she finally asked, snapping her front teeth into a ginger-scented cookie. "I mean, do they have ears or anything?"

"Gracious no," Lettie answered. "They can't hear a thing."

Ginny chewed with tiny bites, her brow knitted. "Then, how come . . . you know, that story you told me a long time ago . . . how come you were able to *call* one of your father's snakes by name, and it would come to you like a puppy dog?"

The smile went off Lettie's lips. "Well," she said, "while snakes can't hear, they can feel. Snakes don't have ears, or eardrums. So they can't hear sounds that travel through the air. What happens is, they have a bone attached to the inside of their jaw, and that carries vibrations to an inner ear. So it's *vibrations* that a snake hears, and not sound. It was the particular vibrations of my tone of voice that one snake caught on to. Calling out the name I had given him, a dozen or so times a day, must have produced the same vibrations. When he felt them, he came. Guess the vibrations felt friendly to him."

When Lettie finished, she casually took a sip of tea. "What makes you ask such a thing today? It's been years and years since I first told you that story."

Ginny fiddled with her teacup. "I learned something about vibrations in science once—but I don't remember it too clear—can hammering on stones make vibrations, the kind that snakes can feel?"

"Everything makes vibrations," Lettie responded. "From a herd of stampeding cattle to the tiniest spider tiptoeing across its web. I saw on TV not too long ago, how *thinking* even causes vibrations. I didn't understand it too good, but they showed some person with wires pasted on his forehead. When he thought something up, it made an ink-pen move across a sheet of rolled paper with lines on it."

Ginny tried to restrain the swell of interest that suddenly swept right through her. If thoughts could be felt, like vibrations, then maybe that was how she had made the snake in church drop on her father, and the others chase after Winkie Bols and his two friends that afternoon!

"It's some kind of electro-something that people's brains give off when they think," Lettie responded, trying to recall exactly what it was that the TV announcer had said. She finally gave up, spreading her hands to indicate her confusion. "I don't much understand it, I'm afraid."

"And thinking can make an ink-pen move on paper?"

"So the man on the TV said."

Lettie looked at the child over the rims of her wire-frame eyeglasses. The girl didn't look half as confused about what she had just said as she herself felt after saying it.

Lettie moistened her lips, as though she were relishing the taste of the herb tea she had just sipped from her cup. "Did you see a snake today?" she asked cautiously.

"Will a snake ever harm you if you like it?" Ginny asked ignoring Lettie's question for the third time.

Lettie drew the edge of her lower lip into the corner of her mouth. "The only time I ever knew a snake to go after me," she began, "was when I *disappointed* it. It was the same snake I had trained to come when I called it by name." Something like a chill shot across her arms at the memory and she rubbed them with her hands. "I didn't know it at the time, but I must have been thinking resentful thoughts—deep down inside of me—when I called it to come to me. My dad, well . . . my dad didn't always understand that I was a little girl and had to have some time to myself. I had certain chores and they were supposed to be done, no matter what. So, one day, when I wasn't feeling too much like doing chores, but knew I had to, 'or else,' as parents used to tell their children in those days, I went into the pen where the snakes were kept and called to them like usual. They came, all right. Right at me, winding and curling and ready to strike. I did something like a backward flip over the top of the meshed-wire pen and landed outside. If it wasn't for that, I'd have been killed. When I looked back in at them, they were striking the mesh as though they wanted to get out at me. I stood there for a long time and wondered at that. I guessed, even way back then, that it must have been something like what those TV doctors said on that program I was telling you about. It was like the snakes had picked up my thoughts, my vibrations, about my not wanting to do my chores that day. Guess they felt disappointed in me, that I was somehow being disloyal and had betrayed them, or something."

Ginny lowered her eyes, hiding from Lettie the secret excitement she felt.

CHAPTER TWENTY

Loren Mitchell was about to leave the county sheriff's office and head on over to see Lettie, when Winkie Bols, Judd Wilson, and Jerry Knox exploded in through the door and began to gabble like a flock of scattered geese. They even waved their arms as though they had wings. All Mitchell could make out, when he focused real hard, were a few isolated words that ran together from their blurting lips in a gasping chorus of garbled speech.

"Snakes!"

"Pond!"

"Pond!"

"Almost got . . ."

"Killed!"

"One chased . . ."

"Him!"

"Him . . . Jerry."

Winkie Bols and Judd Winslow ended up pointing to Jerry Knox, who had somehow broken loose from the two men who had dragged him up the hill and clear across the center of town to Loren Mitchell's office—a distance somewhat greater than a country mile. They were huffing and puffing like a pack of steam engines chugging up a steep grade, and Jerry, who had enjoyed the luxury of the "free ride" up from the pond, was not in any better shape. He limped about the office on his bad leg and tried to catch up with his own breath, too.

Loren sat back in the swivel chair at his desk and stared at them. "Slow down," he said. "I can't make sense of anything you're trying to say. Did somebody get hurt?"

Jerry Knox, who had most of the air back into him by now, was the first to speak. "We wuz down the pond," he said. " 'n then there wuz this big black water snake. If I didn't slip on my bad leg getting outta there, it would've got me in the neck!"

Mitchell stopped swiveling in his chair. He remembered the hole in Reverend Watkins's neck. "What were you all doing down at the pond?" he asked with a frown. "You know better that to go anywhere near the place." He looked at Winkie. "You, more than anyone, from all the talk you let out at town meetings, should know better than that."

Winkie stood there like a scolded schoolboy, winking his right eye down at his shoes. The top of his head, beneath his thinning hair, was the color of canned beets in a jar.

"We were . . ." he began, but couldn't finish.

"Winkie," Judd Winslow said. "Why don't you just

out and tell him."

There was silence after that.

"Tell me what?" Mitchell asked. "What have you boys been up to this time?" He was only just beginning to see how drunk they really were. When they'd first arrived, he could smell that had been drinking. But that wasn't unusual. Winkie and his cronies had a few every day. What did look unusual was the staggering Mitchell observed now they they were all quieted down. They looked as though they were about to fall over like sacks of loose potatoes.

"Why don't we go into the other room," Mitchell offered. "Where we can all sit down."

"Oh, no!" Winkie came to life. "You can't do that. We didn't do anything wrong."

The only other room in the place was the jail cell. It had two bunk beds, a table between them, and a tin can for those who smoked. There was also a small corner sink with a johnny to the side of it. Everyone of the three men had spent at least one night in that cell for having been drunk and somewhat disorderly. But none of them had a violent bone in his body and Mitchell had never booked them for anything. He had always let them go in the morning with a warning that next time he'd have to book them fully, and ship them on over to the real jail in Wayne County—the one that held twelve prisoners.

"I don't mean to lock anyone up," Mitchell reassured them. "It just looks as though you boys have to get yourselves seated before you fall down."

They looked at one another, and all of them saw

more than the one person they were looking at. There were two, and sometimes three, of everything they happened to look at. Winkie had the advantage, of course, because his right eye was winking so fast that it was almost like being closed—a condition under which he could focus better than his two friends.

"All right," he said, as though someone had appointed him to be the spokesman. "But it's just so we can sit a while," he said. "Right?"

"That's all," Mitchell responded. "I don't want anyone of you catching a heart attack."

They laughed at that, like comrades coming home from an invigorating hunt, patting one another on the shoulders as they slowly ambled into the windowless cell and spread themselves out on the lower cots that faced each other; Winkie sat beside Judd and faced Jerry, who, because of his twisted leg, needed most of the other cot for himself. Loren pulled himself up on the table between them.

"So tell me," he began in an easy voice, as though he had all the time in the world, "what happened down at the pond?"

Winkie spoke for a full quarter of an hour, telling how they had gone to the pond after having a few drinks—just to see the place again. Like in the good old days, when folks could take a picnic lunch and spend a pleasant spring day being friendly. He stayed clean away from the business of why they had really gone there. By the time he was through, Jerry Knox had cocked his crooked leg up on the cot and had fallen asleep. He was now beginning to buzz in a quiet snore.

Mitchell looked at the rate Winkie's eye was blinking and knew he was lying about something. One look at Judd Winslow—who was doing a good job of keeping his eyes focused on a scrap of manure that was caught on the worn-down heel of one of Jerry Knox's shoes—and Mitchell knew what it was all about.

"Don't tell me you boys were planning to set the pond on fire. Like the plan you couldn't get the selectmen to approve?" He stared Winkie down with a look that told the store owner he had better not lie in responding.

Winkie jutted his chin forward and scratched the loose flesh on his neck with an up and down motion of the three middle fingers of his right hand.

Mitchell looked at his wrist watch. "Tell you what," he said, rising to his feet. "I have a piece of business to attend. Might take me an hour or so. Why don't you all stay put in here until I get back."

Winkie noticed that there was no question mark at the end of the sheriff's last statement. He was telling them to stay. Maybe, if they complied without protest, they would be free by the end of the evening to go and finish up what Winkie knew had to be done. So he didn't complain.

"Yessir," Winkie said. "That'll be just fine. Won't it, Judd?" But when he turned to face the former fire marshal, who was sitting beside him on the cot, he discovered that Judd had fallen asleep, too, just like Jerry Knox, who was now in a full snore on the cot across from them. "Judas Priest!" he exclaimed. "Guess

I'll get me a nap, too."

And when Mitchell left the cell, he made sure to lock it. He didn't want to see any of them doing anything foolish. As soon as he got back from seeing Lettie, he'd let them go—as long as they had a chance to sleep off whatever it was they had had in mind to do at the pond that afternoon.

CHAPTER TWENTY-ONE

It was as though something had sparked and ignited a flame within her. She was aglow in the darkness of her thoughts. Lettie's story of how snakes "hear" had confirmed her power, a power she had always known existed within her, but had never tested.

Ginny slid lower into the tub until the water touched her chin. She smiled, remembering the helter skelter of Winkie Bols and his two friends scampering and scraping themselves up the hill that afternoon. The warm water rippled across her like a coating of glass. The scented bath oil that Lettie had bought especially for her—because she was so grown-up now—made the water feel smooth and silky against her skin. She let her hands wander down across her body, to her nipples, then to her lower abdomen—where she thought she could already feel the pangs of the first period that the old woman told her would be coming anytime now. Lettie had even purchased a small box of sanitary pads for the girl, and had told her all about what they were for and why things like that happened to women and not to men.

Ginny loved her. Being with Lettie was far better than being back at home. Although she knew that could never happen again, because her father was dead, her hatred went all the way back to the house itself. After moving her things out and settling herself into Lettie's guest room, she had no desire ever to go back there again. The attic, where her father had forced her to do those terrible things, was the most despised place in the house. She wished something would come along and burn it to the ground!

Ginny stood up and began to soap her body. There was a full-length mirror attached to the back of the door opposite the side of the bathtub. She looked into it as though seeing herself for the first time. There was something different about her. It had nothing to do with the bright pink tone that the hot bath had lent to her flesh. It was something else. She couldn't figure it out for a moment. Then it came into focus, slowly. Her body was shiny and smooth from the bath oil, but it wasn't only that. It had to do with the feel of her hands on her breasts as she soaped herself. When she cupped them in the palms of her hands—the same way her father used to—she felt. . . .

Ginny wasn't able to get to the point where she knew exactly what it was she was feeling. That was something much too complicated. All she understood, as she stood there, cupping her budding breasts in her hands, was that she missed her father; that while his touching her had always disgusted and humiliated her, she had also loved him.

That unwieldy flood of abstract emotion came to her without image or form. It had simply thrust itself upon her like a knot of throbbing darkness at the core of her inner being. It made her choke; made her sit back down in the tub and cover her face with her hands. How could she love her father when she hated him so much? And that was when she began to cry. It was the first time she had done so since he had died. She didn't know what was wrong with her.

Downstairs in the kitchen, which was directly beneath the bathroom in which Ginny muffled her sobs into a washcloth, Lettie bustled about, preparing to get ready for the simple cold supper she intended to serve. The sounds rose up through the pipes that ran from the back of the kitchen sink to the water taps at the foot of the bathtub. Ginny could hear everything that was happening below, and that somehow managed to pull her back and quiet her sobbing. The emptiness she felt receded, as if it had been nothing more than a horrible dream.

Ginny straightened her shoulders and set the washcloth aside. She lifted her chin to the image of herself reflected in the mirror, and was about to rise and finish her bath when she heard Mitchell being greeted into the kitchen below. She sat back down, wondering if his visit had anything to do with what had happened in Mr. Ocean's guidance office that afternoon. Had someone seen!? Had someone told!?

As Mitchell began to speak, Ginny focused her eyes on the two stones she had carried home from the pond. They were resting on the low windowsill above the bathtub, like a pair of innocent doves.

Lettie laughed, almost exploded, when Mitchell told her why he was late in arriving. Tears almost sprang to her soft grey eyes. "My word!" she said. "That Winkie is going to get himself in real trouble someday. Judd and Jerry are no better." She dabbed at the corners of her eyes with the ruffled edge of the cotton apron she had tied about her waist before starting to prepare for supper. "And you say they had been down at the pond?" she asked, this time without the laughter in her voice.

Upstairs, Ginny froze when the pond was mentioned.

"So they said," Mitchell answered. "They said something about being chased by a water moccasin. It *flew* at Jerry Knox and would have gotten him in the neck if it wasn't for the fact that he had stumbled on his bad leg while they were running away."

"What do you suppose they were doing way down there?"

"That's what I intend to find out just as soon as they have a chance to sleep it off. When I left, Judd and Jerry were snoring, and Winkie was lying back getting ready to do the same thing. A good snooze for an hour or so will do them a world of good."

Lettie didn't say anything for a while; she didn't have to. As the old shelf-clock's pendulum ticked off a full minute, both of them felt the silence of it. And both of them knew what was pressing on the other's mind.

"So, what exactly did Harvey Ocean have to say?" Mitchell began. "Did it sound as though he was actually going to do something about having Ginny taken away from you?"

Ginny gasped. The water in the tub suddenly felt very cold.

Lettie's former mirth over the circumstances of Winkie Bols and his two friends was gone from her eyes. She had been looking down at the pattern of yellow buttercups printed on her pale blue dress. They were so bright they showed through the thin white fabric of her tie-around apron. She finally knotted her hands in her lap and looked up and told Mitchell everything the guidance counselor had said—about how he was mandated to report the fact of Ginny's being orphaned to the authorities, and about how he'd said Lettie was too old to qualify for legal guardianship.

Ginny had grasped the knobs of the water taps tightly in her hands as Lettie had begun to answer Mitchell's question. It was as though, by connecting herself to them, she would somehow hear more clearly what was being said downstairs—like Lettie said that snakes could "hear" vibrations. She was doing the same thing. She felt the old woman's words come up through the water pipes, and they now made her insides shake with rage.

"He's a fool, Lettie. I'll have a talk with him, see if I can persuade him not to do anything stupid."

"The trouble with fools," Lettie retorted, "is that they can't be persuaded to change what's already in their little minds!" She let her hand come down on the table with a loud report. It stung the palm of her hand and made it hot.

Mitchel didn't know what he could say to comfort her. Telling her that she was the only one on earth best suited to take care of the child would only make matters worse. She already knew that; so did everyone else in town. "If only he wasn't here," he said, absentmindedly. "No one else 'round these parts would ever file such a report with any authorities. Even a snake has better sense."

Ginny looked at the stones on the windowsill, but kept her hands tightly gripped to the water taps. She didn't want to miss a word.

"I hope he falls into a deep hole on his way home to supper tonight," Lettie said, a sparkle of mirth returning to her voice. "Maybe it should be a big hole filled with snakes!" She didn't know why she ever said a thing like that, but the thought pulled a thin smile across her tight lips. "Yessir, I hope it with all my heart," she concluded in a tone of resignation.

"Well," Mitchell tried, "maybe you can work on him. Treat him nice, fix him some of that cornbread fried chicken of yours. Maybe that'll soften him."

Lettie appreciated the thought, but she knew, as well as did Mitchell, that once she got to disrespecting someone, there was no treating them good—especially with her own cornbread fried chicken. What was going to be, was going to be, she told herself—and she wasn't about to interfere with what the Lord was going to see get done anyhow! She was too old and self-respecting to butter up to a fool. Never did it before in her entire life, and she wasn't about to start doing it now.

An idea suddenly shot across the old woman's thoughts like an apple falling up a tree, instead of down. She knew it was a foolish notion, but she'd pitch it out anyway. "I may be too old for the state to approve my being Ginny's legal guardian, but if you had a wife, then. . . ."

The old woman's words faded into thin air at Mitchell's broad smile. "Lettie," he said, grinning brightly, "that wouldn't be a proposal I'm hearing, would it?"

Lettie guffawed. "When I think of all the men I could have made perfectly miserable by marrying any that asked. . . ."

The smile and mirth momentarily vanished from

her mind, but not her face, as she recalled the first man who had ever asked for her hand. He had been the father of the baby she had buried up in the graveyard. He had gotten stepped on by a bull while crossing a pasture on his way to see her one day. The question had been asked, and the answer not yet given when he'd died, right there in that pasture, of a crushed spine. He'd never known Lettie was carrying his child. And, at the time, neither had she. He was twenty-four, and she was only seventeen.

Lettie looked up quickly and tried to put the smile and sparkle back into her mind before she got too lost in the misery of that long-ago sun-filled pasture, just a stone's throw from where her father's dooryard used to be.

"You're too sensible to be getting yourself hitched to an ol' grandma like myself," she said, with just enough light in her eyes to let Mitchell know she appreciated his jest about her proposing to him—and she being almost eighty-three years old! "But you should try it sometime, you know. You might get to like it. Some folks do."

And out of nowhere, the image of Sara Garrett entered his mind—as it had several times that week. He wondered if she was still at the college. He slowly rose to leave.

"Least you can do," Lettie said, looking up at him, "is stay and have some supper with us. Ginny's upstairs finishing her bath and will be down soon. There's some cold ham, and all I have to do is get the light going under a pot of already-cooked greens. Cornbread takes only two minutes to make fresh up. What do you say?"

Mitchell looked as though he would like nothing better, but he told her he should be getting back to the jailhouse to see if Winkie and the boys had come to by now. He wanted to settle the matter of what it was, exactly, that they had been doing down at the pond that afternoon, and he hoped it didn't have anything to do with Winkie's foolish plan to burn the place down to get rid of the snakes.

Ginny came out of the bathroom once Mitchell had left, and called down to Lettie to say she didn't feel the need for supper—that the tea and cookies she had had earlier had filled her so that she couldn't eat another scrap.

The old woman understood that. She didn't feel the need for supper that night, either. And when Ginny mentioned that she had some homework to get started, she let it go at that. It was a night when Lettie was getting to feel the need of being alone with her own thoughts, too. All those memories coming back to her now, of things that had taken place fifty and sixty years ago, just as fresh and vivid as though they had happened that same afternoon. Maybe she *was* too old to be taking care of the child, she thought. But she wasn't going to give her up—not without a good old-fashioned fight!

That night, wrapped in a long robe, with her feet tucked up beneath her, Ginny sat in an overstuffed sofa chair by the window of her bedroom. Moonlight slanted in through the parted lace curtains and washed across her well-scrubbed face. She looked like an ivory carving. Her eyes were closed, and in each hand she held one of the stones she had carried home from the pond. As she thought of the guidance counselor she gently tapped them against each other. She didn't know how long she had been sitting there, doing that.

Outside, crickets sang while moths met their sudden death in a sputter of electric-blue light. Every home in town had at least one bug zapper. And into the almost subliminal glitch of that intermittent zap, another sound wove itself through the crickets' song and into the night like a thread being cautiously pushed through the warp of some dark tapestry. It slithered along on the darkness with a grace and ease that went unnoticed—except for the water moccasins at the pond, who understood the meaning of its cryptic call. Ginny herself could feel the vibrations caused by the stones being struck together in her hands. The sensation of it traveled through her arms and into her body, like the flow of the rumbling organ that afternoon her father was killed in church. Thoughts of the guidance counselor being torn apart by vipers pulsated through her mind like beads of light shooting out into the deepest part of the night. The mind-pictures were aided in their flight by the constant tap-tap-tapping of the stones in her delicate hands. She wanted Harvey Ocean dead. Without him she could live with Lettie forever. No one would ever take her away. But that wasn't the only reason she was sitting there in the stillness of that moonlit night, doing what she was doing. Even she knew that. She was also doing it for the simple joy of it—the same joy she had felt when her own father was attacked and killed. Something within her wanted more of that, and she gladly gave herself to its dark call.

She felt something stir inside of her and smiled into the alabaster softness of the light that fell upon her gleaming face. Her thoughts had gone out and traveled along the narrow threads of darkness that twisted into the night. They had woven themselves across fields of grassland and through country streets and past houses that were dark with sleep. When they reached the end of town they tumbled like silken fibers down the hill and caused imperceptible ripples to dance across the tight surface of the mirrored pond. And now there came a response. Her body shook, convulsed with a forbidden pleasure when she felt its vibrations humming along the tendrils of her consciousness like a stifled earthquake.

We are yours, the water moccasins seemed to respond. *You are one of us.*

CHAPTER TWENTY-TWO

The moonlight was on the surface of the rippling pond. Gathered about the exposed root of a willow—from which a portion of the pond's bank had fallen away and left the long twisted root protruding into the water—nine of them clung to it with their jaws. Holding themselves to the root with the same cautionary delicacy that a jeweler might hold a precious gem in a cushioned vise, they felt the young girl's call. It caught in the antennalike branches of the wispy willow and vibrated along its groaning trunk until it reached the root—where they "heard." They knew it was the girl who had sunned herself on the rock ledge that afternoon, just as they often did themselves. She wasn't afraid of them, for there was a bond between them. And now she was calling on them to kill again, the same way her mind had called on them through the rumble of the organ music that very first time. Their jaws tightened on the willow's root. Their eyes gleamed in the moonlight like unnatural sets of dazzling black diamonds.

She had left a note that she would not be home for dinner, and in it, somehow, he had read the notion that she would not be coming home at all, ever again. That didn't surprise him—if indeed that was what she had intended. And he didn't care. The only thing he had ever really cared for in his marriage was the sex. He hadn't known that at first, of course, but now that there hadn't been any sex in his marriage for close to a year, he had come to understand, all too clearly, what it was that he had wanted most out of being married to her. Sex, pure and simple, he told himself—and now he wasn't getting any at all, except for the simple pleasure he gave himself once his wife was asleep and he was able to steal from the bedroom and go to his study for those forbidden magazines of his; the ones that had started all the trouble in the first place.

So the note she had left for him on the kitchen table, where there normally would have been a place setting for his supper, led him to suspect she had finally left him—as she had often said she would. He looked about the kitchen. The stove and counters indicated she had not been anywhere near them since breakfast. He reasoned that she must have left shortly after he had gone to school that day. For a moment, it seemed to matter; in the next, his mind dismissed it as though her leaving was no more annoying than a pesky fly buzzing too close to his head. He swatted it away with a thought of his own, and it was gone. It no longer seemed to matter. All that remained in his mind was the thought that helped to shoo away that momentary uneasiness he felt at the possibility of never seeing her again. He didn't even bother to see if she had packed a bag, but went directly to his study and removed the envelope that contained a half dozen of his most cherished magazines from its hiding place at the back of the bottom drawer of his file cabinet, to which he had the only key. He wanted to check something—something that had been pressing on his mind ever since that little Ginny Watkins left his office that afternoon.

They came in through a cellar window. It had been left open and the screen that covered it had a tear at one of its corners and all they had to do was push their way through it. By the time all nine of them had entered, the hole was as big as the fattest of them, which entered last.

They landed, one at a time, like lengths of thick black rubber hoses being plopped on top of a disused workbench beneath the window.

She hadn't left her husband after all, although when she woke up that morning—after another one of those long and tedious nights of having him paw at her and beg for a moment's worth of her body—Nancy Ocean had fully intended to leave him, this time for good. But right after she had packed a small bag and written the note saying she would not be home for dinner, she had become ill—throwing up everything that was in her stomach. Had her husband gone to the bathroom, he would have seen the remains of what she had been too weak to flush away.

She was asleep in the bedroom when he first arrived. It was only when he walked briskly past the closed bedroom door that she opened one eye and focused it on the bedside clock. Her head was still spinning from the earlier intestinal siege, and she feebly called out his name while still half dazed and having almost forgotten about her intentions to run away. But he did not hear.

She let her head carefully back down into the pillow and lowered one hand to the floor beside the bed. There, right where she had left it, was the small bag she had packed that morning. She pushed at it in a series of weak shoves until it finally disappeared beneath the bed. It had taken everything she had left to do it. She didn't want him to know she was leaving until she was well beyond his reach. He had a violent temper.

A cellar is much easier to get into than to get out of. They searched in the darkness for a way. There were wires pulled through holes that had been bored in the hardwood floor above their probing heads, and there were pipes that ran through larger holes. They separated and slithered along the wooden sill at the top of the poured concrete foundation walls, and where the floor joists came in at right angles to cross their paths, they skillfully looped themselves down and up beneath each one that blocked their path. When one of the cottonmouths found what they had all been searching for, the other eight turned their heads in its direction and let their tongues dart out. When they pulled them back in and pushed the forks of their tongues up into the hollow pockets at the roofs of their mouths—to analyze the information that was carried to them on thousands of microscopic particles of cellar dust—they shot from where they were and raced to the spot where an opening had been found—a spot that was closest to the man they had been sent to find.

She must have dozed, for when she opened her eyes again the sky outside had grown darker. She couldn't see the clock and was reaching for the bed lamp when she heard a crashing noise. She sat up, her head still wobbly, and listened in the darkness. From her husband's study down the hall, she heard a scream that bolted her fully awake. Her hand carefully sought the switch at the base of the bed lamp on the table beside her, and she twisted it. She squinted in the light. She saw little swirly things that made her feel all woozy again. She didn't like the sight of herself reflected in the bureau mirror either. She had gone to bed with all her clothes on, and now they were badly wrinkled. She switched the lamp off. Darkness was better than light. As for the crashing noise she had heard? Let the fool kill himself, she thought—and imagined her husband in a sleek, shiny black coffin. The thought was a comfort to her and she fell back to sleep.

Had Nancy Ocean been better able to focus her eyes before falling asleep, and had she taken the trouble to look more carefully into the darkness that lurked at the foot of her bed, she would have seen something that might have caused her heartbeat to quicken. There, looped up over the footboard, was the head of one of the vipers. Its tongue licked out and almost touched her toes.

Harvey Ocean was sitting in his favorite high-backed wooden chair. It was only less ornately carved than a pope's throne. Elegantly long flutes radiated from a setting sun at the back of his head, while naked cherubs romped and wrestled, using fluffy clouds as their rests. He had bought it at a summer auction when he was still in college. He couldn't resist it, either then or now. There was something about the image he had of himself sitting in it that gave him a sense . . . a sense of the eternal.

The back of the chair creaked as he hurriedly flipped through the pages of his magazines. He was looking for the child that he thought reminded him so much of little Ginny Watkins when the moccasins poured into the room through a disused register in the floor. They collected themselves beneath the desk.

When Harvey Ocean found the picture of the child he had been looking for, he set the magazine down across the blotter on his desk and gazed at it for a moment. The child had smiled directly into the camera, as though posing for a birthday picture—but not so innocently. She was naked, except for the lace thing she wore about her slender waist and the strand of pearls that graced her neck. He noticed, for the first time, that the dangling earrings the child wore matched the necklace. The little girl, about the same age as Ginny, reclined on a throw of downy fur that had been spread atop the sloping end of a chaise longue. Her lips were succulently moist.

Harvey reached for a pencil and leaned forward, resting his weight on his feet as the rear legs of the chair came slightly away from the floor. With pencil in hand, it was as though he was about to grade an examination paper. But that wasn't it. He had taken to writing stories across the naked bodies of the children who were depicted in his magazines. And across the budding breasts of the little girl who looked up at him so longingly, so he thought, he wrote the name "Ginny," then leaned back to gather an opening line for the story he would now compose for her. When the rear legs of his chair touched the floor behind him, he thought he heard a scraping noise at the door, and he turned. But there was no one there. Behind his back the door was closed. The house was still. He dismissed it as a house-noise and turned his attention back to the magazine on the desk.

The two vipers that had made the scraping noise against the hardwood floor as they slithered away to escape the descending legs of his chair now picked up where they had left off and began to inch their way up the rear of it. The others watched and waited in the shadows beneath his desk. When he leaned forward with his pencil again, the two vipers knotted themselves to a rung of his ornately carved chair, just beneath the rear of the cushioned seat. If they had poked their heads up a bit further, and darted their tongues out, they'd have been able to taste the fabric of the seat of his pants.

As he began to pencil in the first line of the story, beneath the bare breasts of the child in the magazine, his lust became so profound that he did not feel a second pair of vipers glide across the tops of his shoes and loosely loop his ankles to the front legs of the chair with their bodies; and while that was being done, the pair at the back of the chair coiled up past the red velvet seat and twisted themselves about the two end rails at either side of the chair's high back. With those four in place, another moccasin glided smoothly out from beneath the desk and made its way toward the rear of the chair. It was quicker than the rest had been, surer of its mission—and it was up to the top rail of the high-backed chair in less time than it had taken the rest to get themselves in place. And there it dangled loosely by its tail, just beneath the elegantly carved rays of the setting sun. Even the cherubs, romping through the billowed clouds, seemed to halt in their play as the viper patiently poised itself for the attack.

Having successfully composed the first line of his story, Harvey Ocean smiled and leaned way back in his chair, the better to contemplate what the second, and perhaps the third lines should be.

And that was when it happened.

That was when Nancy Ocean had heard the crash from her husband's study and went back to sleep. But now there was another noise that startled her awake. It sounded like the muffled scream of some wild animal. She sat up in the darkness of her room and tried to determine if she had been having some sort of a nightmare. She must have been, she told herself. Her body was drenched in perspiration and she was trembling badly. For a moment she thought she might throw up again, and was lifting herself up from the damp bedspread when she touched something—something that was cold and alive. She screamed.

"Harvey!" she cried, hurling herself from the bed like a small boat cut loose in a raging storm. "Help me!" She would do anything for him now, even the terrible little nasty things that repulsed her so much, if only he would come and rescue her!

She was out the door of the bedroom and ricocheting off the walls of the narrow corridor that led to her husband's study—in such a frenzy that she didn't realize that two vipers clung about each of her arms like a matched set of Egyptian arm-bracelets. And when she threw herself at the study door and it heaved open before her, her face froze in a grotesque mask of horror. Had her husband still been alive to see, he would not have recognized her. Her hair was as wild as her eyes. The vipers about her raised arms twisted tightly as she stood at the doorway, gasping for breath and trying to scream. But nothing would come out.

Her husband was obviously dead. Yet he was standing, tied to his favorite high-backed wooden chair by vipers coiled about his arms and feet. Another moccasin was looped about his throat and had apparently squeezed him so hard against the back of the chair that his mouth was still agape . . . and from it there emerged another viper. It was covered with bits and pieces of her husband's intestines, as though it had been eating its way right through him. And where her husband's eyes should have been, the tips of two pointy black things wiggled from its sockets. It only took one horror-filled moment for her to realize that they were the tails of the moccasins that had, judging from what was oozing down across his colorless cheeks, eaten his brains out!

She retched dryly. It was only when she leaned on the walls, to brace herself against falling, that she saw the vipers coiled about her arms. A soft whisper came from deep within her at that point. It was so faint that it sounded like air leaking from a tire. She knew she was about to die, and it didn't matter. She almost welcomed the viper's sting at the side of her throat.

The force of her hitting the hardwood floor made her husband's body sway off its precarious balance and fall backward. The chair's high back cracked when he hit the floor, and somehow, one of the snakes that had bound his body to it landed on the opened magazine atop the desk behind him. If it had had the ability to read, it could have read Harvey Ocean's opening line of the story he had been composing, *dedicating,* to young Ginny Watkins. It began: "Once upon a time. . . ."

Harvey Ocean had always wanted to start a story with a line like that.

CHAPTER TWENTY-THREE

That night Ginny dreamed she was swimming—swimming out into the center of an enormously large baptismal fountain made of cool white alabaster, just like the one in church. About it, in high relief, were carved a multitude of rejoicing serpents, thick and translucent in the rays of a glorious sunlight. She felt the coolness of the water enter through every pore of her body, as though it were a refreshing breeze. She swallowed it, and the water was the wind that gave her life, flowing in through her lips and nostrils like the nourishment of a mythical goddess. Her body felt as free and as at one with the water as if she had been born to it, never having known another element in which to exist.

She moved upon the crystal surface of the water with a speed that was remarkable, and when she desired to, darted below where she moved with equal grace, along the underside of the tight skin of light that was the shimmering surface of the fountain's baptismal waters. There were twists and turns with every stroke she made, and when she chose to glide beneath the surface, she drew her arms in tightly to her sides and propelled herself along with twisting gyrations of her entire body, as though she had no limbs.

And then, as in dreams, there was a shift that seemed natural and real. It was as though she could see herself from high above the fountain—which now became the pond. Its surface was aglow with moonlight, and she was swimming out into the center of its endless inky darkness. When the cottonmouths came to investigate the disturbance of the water that smoothly rippled in her wake, it was as though she were one of them, one who had somehow gone astray and was now returning home. At that moment, in her dream, she felt a fulfillment that was staggering. She could abandon everything and go on living with them in that pond forever. She was one of them, and they accepted her fully—as fully as they would their leader, their princess, their queen!

CHAPTER TWENTY-FOUR

At her age, there were three things Lettie cherished most about waking up in the morning: the first thing was that she hadn't died during the night; the second, after slowly rising from her bed, was to find that the *rumor*-tism—as she called it, because so many of the older folks she knew were always *talking* about it—hadn't worsened while she slept; and the third thing was breakfast. She always liked a good breakfast. But before going downstairs to the kitchen, she would first look in on Ginny. Since the girl had been with her, looking in while the child was still asleep was quickly becoming one more thing she cherished about waking up in the morning.

Lettie tightened the robe about her waist as she stood before Ginny's door. Then she grasped the knob snugly in her palm, so it wouldn't rattle noisily, and twisted it while gently pushing on the door with her other hand. There was no sense waking the child, she thought as the door silently swung opened. It was going to be another two hours before school began anyway.

Ginny was sleeping soundly beneath a thin crazy-quilt that the old woman had made when her fingers were still good enough to sew with, which was long before the girl was ever born. Lettie's face registered delight as she studied the child. Ginny's face seemed to glow with an inner radiance that matched the light of dawn outside the window. She was about to close the door and head downstairs when something made her pause and cautiously swing the door open again. The room, she thought. Something about it was . . . *different.* It took several moments for her to figure out what that difference was.

The furniture! It was all disarranged—not *re*-arranged, but pushed about in almost every which-way one could imagine. A chair was away from the wall at an awkward angle. She quietly entered the room and slid it back into place. Beside it, an old bureau with a mirror had done the same thing. That, too, she noiselessly backed into its former position, flush against the wall. Every picture hanging on each of the four walls was tilted. Even a small rug at the foot of Ginny's bed had gone askew.

Lettie didn't know what had happened, but she went about silently, straightening things out. It was when she finally approached the sofa chair at the window—she had been saving it for last because she was afraid that moving the clumsy old thing might wake the girl—that she was again startled. There were scratches on the wide wooden floorboards beneath its claw-and-ball feet; not the kind that were caused by getting up and sitting down again over the years. Those old scratches and dents were there, too. It was the sight of the other, newer marks that caused her brow to wrinkle up like a washboard. The new scratches ran right through the four old rub marks, where the legs met the floor, as though someone had drawn a circle through four dots on a piece of paper. It left little doubt that the old sofa chair had been spinning in a circle!

How on earth . . . *why* on earth . . . would Ginny ever do such a thing as that? And moving all the other furniture about, too?

Well, Lettie wasn't going to let it worry her; neither was she going to ask the child about it—not unless it happened again. Every child is allowed to have a fit or two in their time, she thought, especially after all that's happened to Ginny. And if doing all this made the girl feel as good as the glowing expression on her sleeping face seemed to indicate, then the old woman had no argument with it. None at all. As a child she could remember pitching a fit once or twice herself. Small price to pay, she thought, quietly sliding the heavy sofa chair around until its feet once again covered the original four spots on which the chair had been resting for the better part of a half century. Some wax on a cloth will smooth those scratches away in no time, she thought.

As soon as Lettie left the room, Ginny's eyes flickered open, as though she was awakening from a pleasant dream. She didn't know that the old woman had been in the room, but could now hear her ambling down the creaky wooden stairs toward the kitchen. Ginny hunched her back and stretched her arms straight out in front of her. She knew breakfast would be good, and that she had about another hour to be lazy in bed before she'd have to get up and go down to it. And there was something else, too . . . something that made her feel as though anything in the world were possible. Mr. Ocean would never be a problem to her again. She closed her eyes and smiled sleepily as the familiar sounds and scents of breakfast being fixed began to filter up through the floorboards to her. She smiled again.

Less than an hour later Ginny appeared at the round oak table in the center of the old-fashioned kitchen and sat down to a breakfast of sage-and-buttermilk muffins, scrambled eggs, fresh-squeezed grapefruit juice (with chunks of pulp floating in it—just the way she liked it), and an assortment of preserves that Lettie had put up herself (apricot, persimmon, and strawberry) along with a tall, cool glass of milk to wash it all down.

"Smelled the muffins cooking all the way upstairs," she said to Lettie as she spread a cloth napkin across the lap of her newly washed and ironed skirt. "Made me hungry to get up."

When Lettie smiled it was like being inside a comfortable cocoon, a secret place where you were loved and cherished above anything else in the whole world. Ginny had been feeling the loving force of the old woman's smile for all of her life. And now that Mr. Ocean was out of the way, it was good to know that nothing was going to change.

Lettie balanced a nickel-sized portion of scrambled eggs on the tines of her fork before she quickly flicked it into her mouth and swallowed—all in one absent-minded motion. For the past ten years or so, what Lettie enjoyed most about food was the cooking and preparing of it, not so much the eating of it. That was something that was better done quickly, without relish, so she could get on with all it was that had to be done.

As the old woman quickly finished her food, she thought of all the furniture that had been moved about in Ginny's room during the night, and wondered if she should somehow bring it into the conversation. The girl appeared relaxed and happy enough to cope with anything this morning. She decided to try—the long way around: "You going into interior decorating, or something like that, when you grow up?" she asked, setting her fork down beside her plate.

Ginny looked at her while spreading a patch of persimmon preserve across the crusty top of an unopened sage muffin. "What's that?" she asked.

"Oh," Lettie responded, attempting to choose her words with care. "Things like . . . like rearranging house furniture, changing the way things look by giving them a little shove here and there so things seem . . . *different.* More to the way of one's own liking." She hurried with the rest. "Because if you are, you can start with your room upstairs and go ahead and . . . and rearrange all the furniture if you like."

Ginny shook her head as though she had bitten into a wedge of lemon. "No," she said. "I like the way everything is, especially that big old sofa chair by the window. Last night I sat there and watched the sky until the stars came out."

The look in Ginny's eyes had been so genuine as she spoke that Lettie knew the girl had no idea of what she had been trying to draw out of her. She now whisked another morsel of egg into her mouth and chewed it.

Just then the wall-phone across the kitchen rang, sparing her the feeling of dread that was beginning to spread down her back.

As she lifted the receiver from its hook she glanced at the old shelf-clock. Somehow the simple and familiar click of its swinging pendulum helped to bring the warmth back into her soul. Who on earth would be calling her so early in the morning? she wondered, now centering her full attention on the phone. It was only seven-thirty.

The call was from Loren Mitchell. He had a special favor to ask of Lettie. Would she be willing to make a breakfast for the three hungry men—Winkie Bols, Judd Winslow, and Jerry Knox—he had locked up for drunk and disorderly last night?

"What's the matter?" Lettie asked. "Couldn't you wake them up to go home last night?" As she listened, Mitchell's answer brought the smile off her face in a hurry. He told her he had been about to send the men home last night when something had happened over at the Oceans' house. And when he told her what that was, her eyes swelled with astonishment.

"Snakes?" she asked, unable to control herself—unable to draw the word back in through her quivering lips before Ginny heard it and looked up with questioning eyes.

Lettie turned her back to the child as she continued to listen. The county sheriff told her he was still at the guidance counselor's house, and that the key to the jail cell, in which the three men were probably still asleep, was in the top drawer of his rolltop desk—just in case Lettie was able to make the breakfast he had asked her to. It was, sort of, an apology to the men for having had to spend the night there. When he got the call that there was some sort of a disturbance going on over at the guidance counselor's house, he'd thought it was just another one of those loud squabbles they had taken to getting themselves into lately. He'd just go on over there, as he had once or twice before, and cool them down a bit. Then he'd get on back to the jail and let the three men go home. That was what he told them before leaving for the Oceans'. He'd had no way of knowing the tragedy that awaited him there. He had been there ever since.

When Lettie got back to the table, where Ginny was finishing her eggs—wiping the plate clean with what was left of a warm muffin—there was no color to her face, and the paleness spread down into the opening of her housedress and out along her arms. Her hands were chalk-white, too.

The girl looked at her. "What's the matter?" she asked. "You feeling okay?" She rose and walked to the other side of the table to be closer to the old woman. "Can I get you something?"

Lettie drew in a deep breath. "Gracious, no," she said. "Just have to catch my breath a bit. That's all." She shook her head back and forth as though her thoughts had suddenly gone off somewhere. Doing so made her natural color return. She rubbed her hands and arms as though they were cold.

"What happened?" Ginny asked. "What was that you said on the phone about *snakes?*"

Lettie looked up. Her eyes were level with the child's. She reached out and circled her waist with one of her arms. "There's been an . . . an accident at the home of Mr. and Mrs. Ocean," she told the girl. "And . . . and they're both dead."

"Mrs. Ocean, too?" Ginny asked.

Lettie was so wrapped up in the turmoil of having to tell Ginny the news straight out—she never lied about things to anyone—that the girl's question didn't register as it should have. *Mrs. Ocean too?* somehow implied that the knowledge of Mr. Ocean's death had already been assumed.

"Yes," Lettie merely replied, "Mrs. Ocean, too."

"And they were killed by *snakes!?*"

Lettie looked at the child and in her eyes saw the horror of her father being killed by that moccasin in church. She couldn't at first respond. Then, slowly, as she held the child tightly in her arms, she nodded her head up and down. "Yes," she finally said, as though the word had been whispered through a lump of something dry and gritty lodged in her throat. "Sheriff Mitchell said it was snakes."

CHAPTER TWENTY-FIVE

Loren Mitchell stood in the middle of Harvey Ocean's study. The bodies of the guidance counselor and his wife had been taken to Estelle Whidden's funeral home to await the coroner for a report. Every room of the house had already been swept for clues, even though none were needed. Mitchell knew what had happened the moment he saw the bodies. They had been killed by snakes, pure and simple. The sidewinding marks through the pools of blood surrounding the bodies had told him that much. He had seen such an example in the church the afternoon that Reverend Watkins was killed. Besides, even if he wasn't sure—he told himself—there was the clear print of a snake's belly scales across the opened magazine that the guidance counselor had had on his desk—it, and the rest of the kiddie magazines had already been removed and marked for "evidence," in case there was ever a need for such a thing in court.

Up until the moment he had laid eyes on the pictures in the guidance counselor's magazines, Mitchell had had no real idea what the term *kiddie porn* actually meant. He'd had no idea how vile and low the guidance counselor had been, and he hoped that his perversion hadn't crossed over into actuality with any of the schoolchildren he had been in daily contact with.

"You can't try snakes for murder," Loren Mitchell had said to the state's homicide man after he had arrived from Austin. They had both stood there in Ocean's study, numbly staring down at the imprint of blood that the snake had left across the photograph with the *once upon a time* "story" the guidance counselor had been in the process of composing when the water moccasins had struck. The man from the state capital had simply shrugged, and continued to bag up and label things as though it were an ordinary homicide he had been called in on. The situation was so bizarre, it was the only thing he could think of doing.

While Loren Mitchell knew what had killed Mr. and Mrs. Ocean, he didn't know why. Water moccasins just don't do things like that, he thought.

It was when the mortuary men were gone, and all the neighbors had been cleared out of the house, that Mitchell remained behind and called Lettie about fixing breakfast for the three men in jail. After that, he wandered about the empty house, attempting to piece things together.

He found where the snakes had entered the cellar through the opened window. They had dropped to a dusty workbench beneath it and then worked their way back up to the flat wooden sill at the top of the foundation wall—by wedging themselves between the concrete wall and an electrical conduit that ran to a light switch beside the bench; all the cobwebs and dust had been disturbed. He wondered how many of them there had been as he pulled a stepladder over to the wall to see if he could find more tracks. He did, and they puzzled him more than anything. It appeared as though the water moccasins had separated and gone in different directions—as though they had been scouting something out, possibly an opening through which they could gain access to the upper rooms.

It didn't take long for Mitchell to find that opening. There was a small gas floor furnace that some of the older houses, like the one he was in, still used to heat certain rooms during the winter. Where the heated air above the burners rose through the grilles of an ornate cast-iron floor register, he found the unmistakable signs he had been looking for—blood. If the snakes had left the house the same way they had entered, there had to be traces of blood marking the escape route. He reached into his pocket and pulled out a small searchlight, snapped it on, and trailed its beam across the top of the wooden sill that the snakes had used. Yes, had he used the light before, he would have seen the faint rubbings of blood there, too.

Mitchell played the beam of the light above his head to the ornate cast-iron floor register. Through it he could see the bottom webbing of the carpet that covered it. There was a sliver of light coming down from a corner of it, too. He knew it was the guidance counselor's study. When he had first found the bodies, he had seen winding swipes of blood that led to a small oriental rug at the far end of the room. Two things had immediately struck him about it. First, the rug, no more than two feet by three, looked off center and out of balance with the rest of the room—something that seemed to be out of character with the fastidious nature of the prissy guidance counselor. Not many people would place a small rug like that against a wall in one faroff corner of the room. The second thing that had struck him about it was the winding trails of blood that led to it, and then apparently disappeared beneath the rug. He had thought of checking that out, but had lost sight of it when he got caught up in shooing the neighbors out of the room and making all the necessary calls to the state emergency units for assistance.

Climbing down off the ladder now, he knew what had happened: the water moccasins had pushed themselves in through a slit in the screening of the low and narrow cellar window, made their way into the guidance counselor's study by way of the hot air register, and left the same way they had come in. But knowing that didn't help much. It only brought him back to the same place he had been hours before, when he had first discovered the bodies: he knew what had happened, but he didn't know why—why the water moccasins had suddenly appeared to have gone against the very fiber of their nature and were now beginning to attack people in their own homes, in their own churches, and so very far away from the pond.

It wasn't the first time he had thought of Sara Garrett in the past few hours. Ever since he'd first realized that snakes had been responsible for the deaths of the guidance counselor and his wife, he had had a strong desire to talk to her. It was as though she might be able to help him with something he was not capable of understanding. He remembered his feeling, after speaking to her at the church the afternoon Reverend Watkins was killed, that she might be some sort of a snake expert. But that wasn't all—he also remembered how those emerald-colored eyes of hers had bored into his, as though a vast and uncharted world was locked behind their sparkling brilliance.

He didn't know if she was still up at the college, or even if he really *wanted* to see her again. There was a part of him that had never felt comfortable in the presence of a woman he could not completely read, and he had a feeling that Sara Garrett was the kind of woman who knew much more than she would ever say.

CHAPTER TWENTY-SIX

When Lettie arrived at the jail with two wicker basketsful of breakfast for the three men, they were still asleep. She set the hampers of food on a table near the window and quickly began to unpack: paper plates, napkins, knives, forks, and spoons. There were coffee cups, too (the nice big ones she kept on the top shelf of the kitchen cabinet for special company), and juice glasses. The food came out next: a dozen scrambled eggs in a Tupper Ware container (still steaming hot), tomato juice (ice cold in an insulated jug and laced with some Lee and Perrins Worcestershire sauce—to help absorb the liquor they probably had not yet been able to sleep off), homemade muffins, biscuits, and cornbread, and half a leg of cob-smoked ham (which she knew they couldn't possibly eat all by themselves but had brought along to save the time of hacking slices out of it. Besides, she knew how good it would look sitting up there on the table, all in one piece like it was.) A three-quart bowl that was covered with foil was laid out next. And when it was uncovered, it revealed a great mound of grits with melted butter oozing down into its core like a pool of liquid gold in the center of a smoldering snow-capped volcano. There was also more fresh-brewed coffee in a large thermos jug than she knew they could possibly drink.

When the picnic hampers were all emptied out, Lettie fanned herself with one of the paper plates before setting it back down in its place on the table. In all, after she saw Ginny off to school, it had taken her almost two hours get the breakfast prepared and over to the men. She was winded from the rush of it, and from having carried the two large baskets down the steps of her house to her car, then from the car up the steps and into the jail. But she was happy to do it. It helped her forget what Mitchell had said on the telephone earlier that morning—about how Harvey Ocean and his wife had been killed. Water moccasins! The notion made the back of her scalp crawl.

"Hello in there, you three sops. Wake up! Breakfast is here." Lettie had taken the heavy cell key from Mitchell's desk drawer and now hammered it back and forth between the cell's bars as though she were ringing a chuck wagon bell. "Come and get it!" she said in an exaggerated tone while unlocking the door.

Winkie Bols was the first to pop his eyes open. He jumped to his feet as though the place was on fire. "What . . . ?" he gasped, staggering in a small circle in the center of the cell, not knowing at first where he was. Then he placed one hand on the top of his head as though it was about to split. "Jeez!" he winced. "Jesus H. *Christ!*"

Lettie couldn't help but laugh. "Wake those other two varmints," she said, pointing her finger at Judd Wilson and Jerry Knox. They were snoring like they were going to swallow their tongues. "Food's getting cold!"

Winkie looked at the table of food through the opened door of the cell and . . . well, he *almost* smiled. It felt like his face was going to crack apart if he tried any harder. It was the tomato juice, raising beads of moisture on the outside of the sparkling glass, that had caught his immediate attention. He began to walk toward it as though he was dreaming.

"You just get yourself back in there and wake your two cronies," Lettie said as she blocked his exit with the palm of her raised hand. "And wash yourselves all up, too. You smell like something that's died beneath a heap of cow dung!" She wrinkled up her nose to punctuate exactly what she meant.

Winkie took one last look at the tomato juice and started to kick at the heels of his two sleeping friends. His throat was as dry as a cotton field in Georgia, and he could hardly talk. "Wake up," he said hoarsely. "Miss Lettie's fixed us some food."

Once the other two men stumbled to their feet and saw the table that Lettie had prepared for them, it didn't take long for them to make themselves presentable. There were no toothbrushes, of course, nor were there any washcloths, but the cold tap water—brought up in the palms of their cupped hands and splashed all over their heads and faces—helped considerably. Jerry Knox, for he had the most hair left, even had a pocket comb to share around. They had grins on their faces by the time Lettie nodded, with a mocked sternness, that they were presentable enough now to come out of the cell and sit down to the breakfast she had prepared for them.

As the men filed out, with their eyes fixed firmly on the food, Lettie switched on a small transistor radio that Mitchell always kept on the windowsill beside his desk. She thought it would be a nice touch to have some music going. But Mitchell had the station fixed to the local news. And when the men heard the familiar drone of the announcer, Bobby Jennings—the man whose doberman had been killed behind the church the same afternoon that Reverend Watkins met a similar fate—they froze. The last time Bobby Jennings had come on the air that early in the morning was when Judd Winslow lost some of his men in the fire that destroyed over six hundred acres of land and three houses.

"What's he doing on so early?" Winkie wondered out loud, looking at the electric wall clock to verify the earliness of the hour. It was only ten A.M., and Jennings didn't usually come on with the local news until four in the afternoon. "Must be something's happened," Winkie concluded with squinty eyes.

Lettie made a quick motion to change the station, but the men protested: "No!" they said, all in one voice. And Lettie thought: Well, they're going to learn it just as soon as they get out of here, anyway. So she let her hand come away from the radio and listened along with the three men as Bobby Jennings told of what had happened during the night to Harvey Ocean and his wife. Then, without saying a word, Lettie reached over and turned the radio's dial until she found some quiet music. This time the men did not protest.

"That's it," Winkie said, softly, almost to himself. "Something's gotta be done, and soon!"

The three men looked at one another and nodded. Their lips were tight, as though they were agreeing to something they did not care to expand upon in Lettie's presence. Something was going to be done, and there wasn't going to be any more talk about it. But first, the food. On that they were in complete agreement. Without another word, they sat and began to eat.

It was only when they were halfway through with breakfast that their tongues began to loosen a bit. Lettie frowned, and wanted to know what, if anything, they were talking about. It seemed to her, from the bits and scraps of their elusive, almost grunted, conversation that the men had some sort of a notion about what had to be done about ridding the town of snakes.

Winkie quickly responded with the story of why they had had to spend the night in jail. They had gone to Mitchell the evening before because they had been chased by a pack of water moccasins at the pond. Instead of trying to do something about it, Winkie went on, Mitchell had just given them short shrift and had decided to lock them up for drunk and disorderly.

"Phooey!" Lettie said. "You were all as drunk as skunks. Besides, he never meant for you to be locked up the whole night. Trouble was, he thought he was just going over to the Oceans' to calm them down. Neighbors reported they were quarreling loud again." Lettie wasn't going to let them even begin to badmouth Mitchell—not if she had anything to do with it.

"And another thing," she said, raising her finger in the air as though she had just remembered something, "what, in the name of all that's precious, were you boys doing down at the pond, of all places?"

Judd and Jerry looked at Winkie. His right eye was flickering as fast as the blades of a harvester going through tall wheat, he was thinking that fast. He was about to stutter something out, something he was sure would be only half-baked, when a different thought lifted like a wavering phantom from the dusty box of his remembrances.

"Didn't you used to know a fellow, once," Winkie began, addressing Lettie, as though he was reaching as far back into his memory as a man with a severe hangover could possibly go, "who used to be one of those West Virginia snake handlers?" he asked.

Lettie let her shoulderblades hit the back of her chair. "You never mind about anything like that," she said. "He's gone to his reward, a long time ago," she concluded. It was, and then again, it *wasn't* a lie. She strongly suspected that Jeremie Sorter had probably passed away ages ago. If he were still alive, he'd be . . . he'd be something like . . . oh, ninety-three by now, she figured. No, he was surely dead—as surely as she was sitting there before the three mischievous rascals who sometimes let the drink get the better of them.

Then it came back to her. It came back to her as strongly as the sunlight that was coming in through the window and spilling across the table they were all sitting at. The thought was that *Ginny* might have been to the pond yesterday, too! She shook her head as though the men weren't there, mulling over a private matter.

"What's the matter," Jerry Knox began to ask, sliding his crooked leg more comfortably beneath him, "that man from West Virginia get bit by a snake or something?"

Lettie didn't like the slyness of the probe, and the fire it caused showed in her soft brown eyes. "I'll tell you all one thing," she began, ignoring the question

Jerry Knox had just asked and turning her attention to Winkie Bols, "and it's simply this: if you go ahead with that fool notion you've been trying to pass by the select board, about setting fire to the pond, I'm going to personally drag you all back here and lock you up myself—for good!" She had been about to add that snakes would never bother anyone if folks just went and left them alone, but she swallowed her words when she thought of Reverend Watkins, Bobby Jennings's doberman dog, and now, Harvey Ocean and his wife, Nancy. She really *was* confused!

It was Judd Winslow who spoke next. "Lettie," he said, spilling the oil of his gentle voice into the sunlight. He had been born and raised on a farm in Alabama, and the rich tone of his drawl matched anything a master cellist could produce with a bow on the strings of his instrument. "I'm sure I don't only speak for myself when I say that this was one of the finest breakfasts I ever in my whole life have had."

Winkie and Jerry quickly nodded their heads in agreement. "Finest," they said in unison.

"The absolute best," Judd picked up again. "And God would have blessed the world if He had only been wise enough to have placed a few more of you on this great green earth of His."

Lettie leaned back in her chair with a sly smirk on her lips. She knew better when she heard it—but she liked it all the same. There was a warmth and coziness about it that she hadn't heard from a gentleman in a long, long time. She folded her arms across her breast and slowly tilted her head to the side. "You boys," she said quietly, lowering her eyes away from their mirthful stares. "You boys . . ." she repeated, and ended it there because there was nothing else she could think of to say.

It surprised the daylights out of her that such a buttery, bold-faced compliment such as she had just been paid could still bring a touch of rosiness to her cheeks. And she being an ol' octogenarian, too!

CHAPTER TWENTY-SEVEN

She closed her eyes and she could see . . . she could . . . *feel* the warm platform of fractured rock that overlooked a section of the veldt she loved so dearly. In that flat expanse of sun-baked basalt there had been a depression, deep enough for her to sit in with her legs stretched out fully; the sides of it were as high as her shoulders, and if she leaned her head way back and rested it on the sculpted edge of the angular crater, the sun would caress her face with a magic that was, for her, mythical. And when the rains would sometimes come to fill the depression on one of those rare days of endless heat, it became a sparkling pool that appeared to float in the sky, with an endless stretch of barren plains going all the way out to the horizon beneath it.

Sitting naked in the irregular cavity after it had been filled with rainwater was one of the single most luxurious feelings Sara Garrett had ever experienced in her entire life. And now, in the bathtub of the cottage that the college had provided for her, she "luxuriated" in the porcelain thing as best she could.

But even with her eyes closed and the sound of morning birds squabbling about in the warm sunlight for the scraps of bread she had placed on the sill outside her open window, it was no match for that magic rock-pool high above the African veldt.

She must have dozed for a moment, with her head tilted back and resting on the washcloth that was draped over the rim of the tub. The sunlight falling on her face from the window, the sounds of the birds, the gentle fragrant breeze. . . .

She felt a soft vibration stir the water of the seductively smooth pool of warm basalt in which she basked. It felt as though someone was hammering on the surrounding rock-ledge with something hard—like another stone. That was what it felt like: stone on stone. She didn't want to open her eyes. It would embarrass the witch doctors to find her there like that, lying naked in a crystal-clear pool of rainwater. They wouldn't know what to make of it. So she just slipped herself deeper . . . deeper . . . deeper. . . .

"WHAT?!" she shouted.

Water gushed out of the bathtub in great splashes as she bolted upright. Her hands were grasped tightly to the tub's cold rims on either side of her. She was still confused. The hammering she had heard, had *felt*, in her dream continued. "What!?" she cried out again.

And a voice came to her. It sounded far away, as though, as though. . . .

"Miss Garrett?" it called again. It was a man.

Her whole body relaxed when she finally realized what it was. Someone was knocking at the front door of the cottage. It was probably the dean, who had said he was going to stop by that morning to wish her farewell.

Sara quickly climbed out of the tub, dripping even greater puddles on the tiled floor than had already been deposited there when she'd bolted upright out of her sleep. She found a terrycloth bath sheet in a closet and wrapped it about herself. "I'm coming," she said, aiming her voice in the general direction of the cottage's front door. "Just a minute."

Before she opened the door she paused a moment to look at herself in the full-length mirror that was in the tiny alcove of the vestibule. She had begun to lose the rich tan she had acquired in Africa, but the yellow terrycloth in which she was now swathed, from her armpits to her calves, highlighted what was left of it. Her hair was a mess, but that didn't matter. The more frightful and distracted she looked, the less time the dean would be spending on his good-bye. She still had some packing to finish and was already running late.

When she finally opened the door, her lips froze wordlessly about the greeting she was suddenly unable to utter. It wasn't the dean outside her cottage door, it was Loren Mitchell, the sheriff. It took her a second to regain the use of her vocal cords, but it proved unnecessary. It was he who spoke first.

"I'm sorry," he said. He had the feeling that she had expected someone else and didn't want to embarrass her by allowing his eyes to stray across her towel-wrapped body, so he locked his eyes directly to hers as he continued. "I can come back later if. . . ."

"Oh, no," she said quickly. "Please come in. I can be

with you in a minute."

As she hurriedly put her clothes on in the bathroom, she couldn't imagine what he had come to see her about. It had been about two weeks since she had first seen him at the church. She quickly buttoned her blouse. The church, she thought. The minister who was killed by a water moccasin!

She had meant to ask in the town for any information that might have come out about it, but had been taken sick with the fever before she could. She was only now beginning to feel well, well enough to pick up the thread of her planned itinerary and visit her friends in New Hampshire before returning to Africa. She had almost forgotten about the minister, and about Loren Mitchell, too.

"What can I do for you?" she asked, emerging from the bathroom after she had patted down the stray wisps of lose hair at the nape of her neck. She liked to wear her long blond hair in a bun whenever she found herself in an academic setting. But she would much rather have had her hair down, and be dressed in her old loose-fitting bush clothes, rather than in the white blouse and pleated yellow summer skirt she had pulled from one of the half-packed suitcases on the bed.

Mitchell had been sitting at the small writing desk at the window, periodically gazing down the hill toward the pond, while she was getting out of her towel. He now turned and stood up as she reentered the room, and pointed with an apologetic gesture to the disarray of suitcases and clothing on the bed. What he had to say suddenly seemed hardly worth going into now that she was about to leave. "I didn't know," he said, still pointing to the suitcases; and he let his arm fall back down to his side without finishing his statement.

Sara looked at him. It seemed as though he had been up all night. He needed a shave, his khaki pants were all wrinkled, his sneakers—she saw bloodstains on them! "Is everything okay?" she hurriedly asked.

And in the silent pause that followed her question, she knew everything was *not* okay. "What happened?" she asked. "Has someone else been killed by a snake?"

His eyes widened. "You heard?" he asked.

"Heard what?"

Her question was followed by another silent pause that brought with it a confirmation of her most dreaded fear.

"Has someone else been killed by a snake?" she repeated.

Mitchell told her about the guidance counselor and his wife. As he spoke, Sara's brilliant green eyes grew larger and larger. She didn't say a word when he finished, but went to the bed and pushed a suitcase aside so she could sit down.

"That's incredible," she finally said. "Absolutely incredible."

They both sat in silence for a while, Mitchell at the small writing desk by the window, and Sara at the foot of the bed, opposite him. Sara's eyes were averted in thought, as though she were focused on an emptiness from which an answer would magically emerge. It did not.

Another moment passed before she felt Mitchell's

weighty presence in the room. "Why did you come here to tell *me* about it?" she asked, focusing on his deep brown eyes, liking their velvety quality as they darted from side to side, appearing to be searching for an answer to her question. There was a direct honesty in them, too.

"I don't really know," he finally said. "I guess I had the feeling you knew something about snakes. Something about the way you were looking so carefully at Reverend Watkins's body at the church that afternoon. It looked to me as though you almost understood what had happened."

Sara shook her head. "If I knew that," she said, "I'd be a magician. I was merely curious—curious because I had never heard of a snake's doing such a thing before. And now you say a *couple* of snakes got into a house and killed a man and his wife?"

"The best I could judge, from the tracks they made in the blood, was that there were at least five of them—maybe more."

Sara was bewildered. Snakes didn't pack. They were independent creatures. Maybe a male and female might jointly commit an act—an act that was usually intended to protect themselves—but certainly five, or more, of them would never enter a house for the purpose of attacking an innocent couple. She was willing to concede that what had happened to the minister in the church might have been a freak accident of some sort, but she could hardly believe that a group of snakes had banded together for a unified action. And she told Lorten Mitchell just that.

He knew she was right. Lettie had already told him the same thing on the telephone earlier that morning. He wished there was something more he could say, something that would keep her in town for a few more days. It wasn't that he thought she could solve the mystery of the snakes' puzzling behavior, it was something else—something he hadn't felt for a woman in a very long time.

"Sorry to have troubled you," he said. "I better be getting myself back to town."

When he was at the door, Sara followed. "Wait a minute," she said. "I might be able to help."

He turned and looked at her. "How?" he asked.

She shrugged and crossed her arms in front of her, holding her elbows in the cups of her hands. "I'm a good researcher," she responded. "The library here is one of the best I've ever seen in a college of this size. Maybe I can find something that might help explain what's going on. Have you ever thought of acid rains, pollution, contaminants, or things like that?"

"I've heard the argument," he said.

"Well, if such things can affect human behavior, they might also affect the behavior of snakes."

And for no apparent reason, they both turned their attention to the open window by the desk. Through it they caught a glimpse of the sparkling pond. It was difficult to imagine that something so clean and fresh-looking could be contaminated by anything that would cause the snakes to have gone berserk. Besides, if they had, why was it that they weren't up in everyone's house right now, killing people, as they had the guidance counselor and his wife last night? No, Mitchell thought. It's not like anything related to pollution at all—and he told her so.

Sara appeared to take his rejection of her idea in a matter-of-fact way, but inwardly she raced. "It's just that . . . that I thought I'd be staying on for a few days more and. . . ." She stopped when his eyes moved to the suitcases on the bed. Her shoulders sagged. "A lie," she said. "I had no such intention of staying. I just said that."

Mitchell let his hand slip from the doorknob. Little wrinkles spread out like fans in the corners of his eyes. "I don't understand," he said.

"Neither do I," Sara responded, audibly drawing in her breath. Her eyes showed no intention of lowering themselves away from his puzzled stare. "It's just that . . . it's. . . ." And once again she couldn't finish—couldn't let loose of the great abstractions that fluttered through her mind like cracking whips of vicious serpents. She finally took a deep breath and shrugged. "I guess it's simply the feeling I have that I can be helpful," she finally said. "But I haven't the slightest notion of what it is I can do."

The corners of Mitchell's eyes loosened and the fans disappeared. "Well," he said. "You might start with what you said before. Maybe there *is* something in the library that might be useful." He really didn't think there was, and had been about to say so, but he didn't want to extinguish the light that suddenly came into her eyes when he hadn't tried to dissuade her from staying. He liked that. Liked that very much.

As Mitchell walked away from the cottage he tried to figure out what had caused the sudden turnaround in Sara's apparent plan to leave. But he got nowhere with it. Every time he had ever tried to figure out what went on in the mind of a woman, he always drew a blank. So why should this time be any different? he asked himself. She was staying, and for the moment, that was all that seemed to matter.

CHAPTER TWENTY-EIGHT

It was almost lunchtime, and Mrs. Peabody thought it would be a good idea if she told the children as much as she knew and had already verified about what had happened to Mr. Ocean and his wife last night. She knew if her pupils were allowed out into the schoolyard, where rumor and half-truth ran as wildly as the kids at play, they might get to believing that sea serpents had dropped out of the sky and were about to devour the town. So she told her class, straight out, as much as she thought they could handle—which turned out to be as much as she knew—barring the gory details.

"Yikes!" one little girl said, covering her mouth with her hand. "Holy cow!" said a boy with dark, thick-rimmed eyeglasses. "Yucko!" said someone else from the back of the room.

Almost every child had something to say, except Ginny. She just sat there silently for a while. Then, when things quieted down, she raised her hand to ask a question.

"How can snakes get into a house like that?" she asked.

Mrs. Peabody thought Ginny probably meant: *How can a snake get into a church?* She knew the girl's recent trauma had not been forgotten.

"I don't really know," Mrs. Peabody responded. "Must be there was a hole someplace for them to sneak in through."

Many of the children said, *"Oooooooo,"* imagining all the gaping holes that probably existed in their own homes, too.

Betty Bird Johnson, the class busybody who always had something contrary to say about anything, said, rather gleefully, "There are no holes in my house!" And a boy, who was never identified because he quickly ducked his head when he spoke, said, "Only the hole in your head!" Which caused the class to erupt in laughter.

To regain control, Mrs. Peabody placed her hands out over the top of her desk like a conductor cuing a great symphony orchestra. It wasn't even necessary for her to stand. She had been using the same gesture for restoring order to a classroom for more years than she could remember: With the palms of her hands held out parallel to the desktop, she cleared her throat and slowly began to lower them. The closer to the desk her hands came, the quieter the children became. By the time her hands touched the green desk blotter, the room was dead silent. It was a conditioned response she had worked on with every class she had ever had. "There'll be no more of that," she finally said. And the tone, though not in the least bit sinister or threatening, told the children that she meant business.

Ginny raised her hand again. "That's not what I meant," she said. Her eyes moved rapidly back and forth, searching the space in front of her as though she were reshaping her thoughts. "What I really meant to ask was, how . . . *why* would a snake want to do a thing like that?"

She glanced at Betty Bird Johnson, who sat beside her giggling behind her hands at something she thought was funny. Ginny flicked her tongue out over her lips and moistened them before returning her attention to Mrs. Peabody. The gesture reminded her of a snake flicking its tongue out to test the air. Was she turning into a snake? she wondered. It was such an amusing notion, and so silly too, that Ginny almost smiled. She checked herself from doing so because Mrs. Peabody was now looking directly at her as she answered the question.

"Why a snake, or any other creature, would do a thing like that, is a . . ." She broke off and went to the chalkboard to write the word *mystery,* before finishing her sentence out loud. ". . . . mystery." She underlined the word.

"All we can do is pray, pray that nothing like this will ever happen again," Mrs. Peabody concluded as the dismissal bell for lunch rang. She looked at Ginny. Although she couldn't be sure—for all the fuss that the children were making as they jogged and jostled while preparing to leave for lunch—it looked as though Ginny was smiling. Such a strong child, Mrs. Peabody thought. And she wondered, in the face of the fact that Ginny's father had only recently died, where she derived such inner strength.

There were shade trees in the schoolyard, and picnic tables at which the children who brought their own lunches could sit. A weathered split-rail fence surrounded the expanse of yard, separating a set of swings and a small baseball diamond from the stretch of grass and trees that ran off toward the end of town. Some of the children milled about playfully, while others read from comics or school books; still others played ball or pushed themselves into small knots of dust as they wrestled in line for the next available swing.

Ginny sat off to the side, at one of the tables, and took small bites from the edges of an egg salad sandwich that Lettie had packed for her. In the opened lunch box before her there was also a small thermos of cold apple juice, and a candy bar for dessert. It was not unusual for her to be sitting alone. Ever since she could remember, there had seemed to be a space that separated her from other children. She had once overheard Lettie telling her father that her wanting to be alone most of the time might have something to do with the fact that she was the daughter of a minister, or that she had never known her mother. But it didn't matter much to Ginny. She preferred being alone. Whenever another child her own age made an attempt to be friendly, Ginny was usually evasive—but always polite—and she always erected a cautious barrier between herself and anyone else. It wasn't only that it had something to do with the shameful things her father sometimes did to her, it was because . . . because there was something different about her—something that the recent deaths she had caused was now beginning to make clear. But how could she ever tell anyone about it? she wondered. And why . . . why would she ever *want* to tell anyone?

From where she sat she could see the spire of her

father's church protruding above the tops of the tall green trees that surrounded it. The sky was a perfect, brilliant blue, and the air was shimmering with the comfortable warmth of a season that would last but for a short while before it became unbearably hot. Ginny's mind wandered as she unscrewed the top of her thermos and poured some apple juice into the plastic cover. Snips of mind-pictures flipped themselves into her thoughts like a stack of movie stills, one frame at a time. The images quickly dissolved back into the dark nothingness from where they sprang, like a spoonful of sugar dissolving in a steaming cup of tea. But one of the pictures had held itself in her mind a little longer than the rest. In it she saw her fellow classmates huddled together and screaming their heads off—as they were now doing in the schoolyard before her; only in her mind there was much more terror to it; as though the children were being attacked by . . . *by the snakes from the pond.*

Ginny doubled over in a sudden fit of quiet laughter.

She was going to be late in getting home from school again, but she didn't care. She had to go to the pond to think.

She took off all her clothes and spread herself facedown at the edge of the smooth, almost silky, soapstone rock that overlooked the pond. Her eyes searched the expanse of water from end to end. There wasn't a snake in sight. But the warmth of the broad stone slab beneath her, and the seductive caress of the sun on her back, made her disappointment fade. She stretched herself out lazily beside her clothes and tried to increase her body weight by pressing herself as tightly to the rock as gravity would allow. She wanted the flesh along the outer edges of her extended arms and body to flatten out and hug the stone, the way a snake's body would. She even tried to imagine she had scales beneath her, and contracted the muscles in her arms, torso, abdomen, and legs to see if she could propel herself like a snake. It was only when she pulled her arms along the stone, and simultaneously wiggled herself into a series of graceful S's that she began to move. It was nothing like a snake. She knew that. But it caused a feeling inside of her that was so intense she couldn't help but doing it again and again, until she had finally covered the entire area of the silky flat rock.

The exercise exhilarated her, and she needed to rest a while. She drew herself near the edge of the rock again and propped her chin up in the crook of her crossed arms and faced the water. The branches of the willows about the pond whispered softly in the gentle breeze that swept across the surface of the water. It was hypnotic. She closed her eyes and basked in the quietude of insect sounds from the tall grasses that now raced up the hill like a summer quilt flying in the wind.

It felt so good to be there, lying naked in the sun. She wished she could remain there forever. But when she rolled over on her back and began to massage the soreness she felt in her breasts from having "slithered" about on the face of the rock, a dark shadow fell across her body and she bolted up in terror. She had almost felt the shadow gliding along the rock before it fell upon her. It injected her with a jolt of fear. She shielded her eyes with one hand and lifted her face to the sky to see what it was. A hawk! She didn't know why a hawk would cause such terror to course through her body. It floated gracefully on a thermal updraft high above the pond. Then she saw the cause of her terror. In the hawk's talons, there dangled a twisting water moccasin.

Ginny sprang to her feet. The terror she felt was unique. She had never experienced anything like it. Her body was frightened, not her mind. Her body wanted to run and hide, not her mind. Her body held a chill that caused it to shiver in the warm sun. But not her mind. And as she stood there in the terror of her flesh, something whispered to her in the language of darkness she had once heard uttered in a dream—the dream she was having the night her father had pulled her from the bed and forced her up into the attic. The words hurried at her from across a barren landscape of rippling heat. She didn't know what the words meant, but it was as though some inner thing had risen to the surface of her being and was standing right there in her own flesh. She abandoned herself to its moment of ecstasy. And when the thing finally receded, dissolving back into the darkness from which it had so unexpectedly leaped, Ginny looked up and saw that the hawk had dropped the snake from its beak and was itself tumbling out of the sky, already dead. The hawk hit the water like a rock falling from the stars.

In her husband's laboratory at the college, Edna Malikoff drew her eye away from the brass spotting scope that was aimed out the window toward the pond. Through the trees, she had seen something moving along the flat rock that jutted out over the water. When she took a closer look, through the telescope, she was at first amused to see a child slithering naked along the shiny face of the rock. The amusement quickly disappeared when the dead hawk tumbled out of the sky. She was trembling now, trembling as badly as she had over fifty years before, when the events at the Wilderness School outside of London had caused her early withdrawal from any further study of the paranormal.

CHAPTER TWENTY-NINE

It was after supper, and Lettie could plainly see that Ginny was unsettled about something—had been unsettled ever since she'd arrived home late from school again. She had tried in every way she knew to draw from the child whatever it was that appeared to be bothering her, but got nowhere. And as to the cause of Ginny's lateness, she also came up empty-handed. She hadn't even been able to draw a simple conversation from the girl about it. Lettie stared at the girl sitting beside her at the round oak table in the kitchen.

All Ginny could think about was how the hawk had frightened her at the pond, and how it had tumbled out of the sky, dead. Ever since she'd arrived home, there was the feeling deep within her that something else was threatening to harm the snakes at the pond. It wasn't a hawk, either. She wasn't sure what it was. It seemed to be threatening her, too.

"Can I go to bed now?" Ginny asked. "I'm awfully tired tonight."

Those were the first coherent words the girl had

come out with all night. Must be she's wanted to go to bed all along, Lettie thought.

"Ginny," Lettie said. "Have you been sitting there all the while, half-sleeping in your mind?" She didn't wait for an answer. " 'Cause if you have, there's been no need of it. When you're tired, just come out and say so. You can go to bed anytime you want. No need pretending about things like that."

Ginny smiled. "Guess I just didn't know how tired I really was," she said with a yawn, and stretched her arms out wide.

Lettie leaned over and placed her arm about the girl. "You just get on upstairs now, and get all the rest you need." And she kissed her gently on the cheek.

Ginny snuggled into the old woman's embrace as though she had never been held with affection before. It felt good in Lettie's arms, but she couldn't shake the unexpected feeling of dread that clutched her heart—just as the hawk's talons had clutched the water moccasin at the pond. She gently twisted herself from the old woman's arms and began to leave the kitchen. "I know you think I must be feeling poorly," she said, facing Lettie before turning the corner and heading for the stairs. "But don't worry, I'll be all right," she said with a convincing smile. "It's just that I think the period is close. I've been getting those cramps, like you said I would." And without waiting for a response, Ginny left.

Lettie stared after her with deeply etched furrows in her brow. She knew that a girl's first period could make her go all funny for a while. Maybe that *was* the cause of it all, she thought. But there was still the nagging feeling that Ginny had been going to the pond after school, and she didn't know the reason of it. There was also the business of the moved furniture in the girl's room. She didn't know the *why* of that, either.

The old woman thought she could live with those questions. But when she thought of the future, she shuddered, as if a cold hand had touched her.

CHAPTER THIRTY

Winkie Bols and Jerry Knox stood in the darkness behind the county storage shed—where the road crew and volunteer fire department kept its machinery and equipment—and watched while Judd Winslow dug deeply through his pockets in search of the duplicate key that he, as the former fire marshal, had neglected to hand in upon his retirement. They all hoped it would still open the "belly" lock in the middle of the small side door. The entire strategy they had worked out depended on it.

Two pickups, one belonging to Winkie and the other to Jerry Knox—who could still drive, with the help of a built-up clutch pedal for his crooked leg—were pulled up close to the large overhead door, which was around to the side of where all three men now stood. The tailgates of the trucks were already lowered and almost touching the fold-up door, so that once Judd got himself inside and pressed the button, the door would roll up on its track and allow Winkie and Jerry to back their pickups right in. The reason they were not still seated in the cabs of their pickups, ready to back right in, was that they suspected something had gone wrong. Judd had been taking entirely too long on the other side of the shed. So they had left the pickups where they were and walked around to the side of the shed to find out if something had gone wrong. If the key didn't work, they wanted to get the heck out of there before anyone drove past the service road out back and spotted them—which was highly unlikely—because most of the town was asleep by now. But having just spent one night in jail they had no desire to repeat the experience—no matter how good the breakfast had been that morning.

"Judas Priest, Judd! Where'n hell did you put that key?" Winkie stage-whispered as he played his flashlight across the pockets of Judd's pants and jacket, and wherever else Judd's flailing hands happened to land on himself. "We ain't got all night, ya know." The edge of Winkie's exasperation was softened by the liquor that was percolating through his blood. They had all had a couple of stiff ones before starting out, but not so much as the night before. Just enough, so they told themselves, to get them into the proper frame of mind for what was now at hand.

"Praise the Lord," Jerry Knox said when Judd finally fished the key out of the inside pocket of his jacket and dangled it by its tagged ring in the beam of Winkie's flashlight. "See if it still works," Winkie urged.

Judd Winslow had never before done anything like what he was about to do. The closest he had ever come to stealing anything was when he had once brought home a one-dollar-and-sixty-two-cent soda and acid refill for the class "A" fire extinguisher he kept in the basement of his home. A whole box of them had been donated to the fire company for distribution to the schools, churches, and other community buildings in the area. That done, there were still over seventy-five of them left. So he'd pinched one, just like every one else who had a soda and acid extinguisher had—which amounted to only four other men. But, somehow, that had never sat too good with him, and the memory of it haunted him like a bad dream might haunt someone else. The only thought that consoled him at the moment was that he was not *stealing* anything from the fire company and road crew, but was only *borrowing* a few things—and it was all for the sake of saving the town from being overrun by snakes.

Judd's hands were shaking so badly that to get the key into the keyhole without its rattling and scraping all over the door he had to place one finger on the keyhole itself and bring the key to the finger with his other hand. There, he steadied it on the keyhole finger and guided it to the lock. The key finally slid right in like a hot knife in a block of butter. But it wasn't until he had twisted it, two full turns to the right, and the men heard the thick steel bars being turned out of the bracket slots on either side of the inside door jamb, that they all sighed with relief.

"Key's still good," Judd said, a touch of pride in his voice. "You boys can get on back to your pickups now. It'll just take me a minute to get inside and open the door."

Ginny's eyes flickered and opened, but she was still asleep. Her throat stiffened and her tongue whipped out between her lips and rapidly licked at the air as though to taste it. The lace curtains at the window billowed in and cast mottled shadows across her moonlit face. In her sleep she had kicked off her blanket and was now lying in her thin nightdress in the crumpled wake of her sheets. It looked as though she were floating on a choppy sea of soft grey shadows. Only her skin glowed.

Her tongue now stilled itself and came to rest, protruding slightly like a bulb of pink chewing gum from between her lips. A taste of something bitter rested on her moistened lips, and she drew it in, tasted it . . . tested it . . . and digested it. The night air had carried a warning to her. There was a threat, a threat that only she could thwart.

Still asleep, Ginny rose from her bed. She raised her arms as high as they would go above her head and pressed the palms of her hands snugly together. Her shoulders and hips moved in the undulating movement of a serpent as she slipped her feet across the bare wooden floor in a sliding shuffle that made her appear to float along. As she approached a small round table with a reading lamp, it glided gracefully out of her way. So, too, did the wooden chair that was next to it. She twisted and turned through the parted furniture like a viper churning through a sea of moonlit shadows.

Ginny had no waking sense of what was taking place. There was only the threat—a threat that only she could deal with. Something was after the water moccasins at the pond, something was going to cause them harm. A cool breeze pushed at her from the open window and her body turned to it. There, before the flowing curtains, was the comfortable old sofa chair she had sat in the night before, when the guidance counselor and his wife were killed. She wove herself through the dimness and began to make her way toward it. A hissing sound escaped from deep within her throat as she darted her tongue out and licked at the cool night air. A shoe that had been left at the foot of the bed moved away as she was about to step on it. So, too, did the bed itself, just before she was going to crash her kneecap against it. By the time she reached the overstuffed old chair at the window, almost every piece of furniture in the room had quietly shifted out of her way.

After having "borrowed" all they needed from the county storage shed, Winkie Bols and Jerry Knox left in the two pickups—which were now loaded up with ladders and ropes, saws and shovels, picks, and a dozen army surplus jerry cans filled with five gallons of gasoline apiece. And since he was the only one who knew how to operate it, Judd Winslow led the procession away from the shed on the town's only backhoe. It would have been a grim sight for anyone to behold—three drunken men, swerving about in the middle of the night on vehicles where there was no road, without their headlights on, and a flock of jerry cans tumbling about like lead dominos in the bed of each pickup—but no one saw.

Silhouetted against the moonlight that raked across the ridge of a hill, the vehicles skirted the edge of the sleeping town and headed for the pond. Judd's backhoe looked like some prehistoric monster riding in a coat of flapping armor. In order to muffle the rough sound of the engine, he had draped several heavy Red Cross blankets over its hood. It didn't help much, but it was probably enough to disguise the sound. In case it did wake anyone up, they wouldn't know what it was and they'd go right back to sleep.

As the backhoe dipped over the ridge of the hill that led down to the pond, it was swallowed by the darkness. The two pickups following it almost jammed into each another as they slowed for it. The gasoline cans jumped in the small trucks like a pack of Mexican jumping beans—rolling and tumbling all over the place. Winkie's shoulders hunched as he gripped the steering wheel tightly. He half expected the cans to come bouncing right through the wall of the pickup's cab in a fiery blast. And he wasn't far wrong in thinking such a thought. Behind him, Jerry Knox saw a loose shovel pitch up on its working end and scrape along the bed of Winkie's pickup, as though it was a match being dragged along the striking surface of a matchbook. Cherry-red sparks hopped and rolled all over the place. "Jee-*zus!*" Jerry gasped out in the cab of his own pickup. He held his breath and watched every last spark hop about and finally go out. We'd better be more careful, he thought, and sat back with a sigh of relief in his parched throat once Winkie's eyes grew accustomed to the dark on the other side of the hill, and the procession started up again. They didn't have far to go.

There was a noise, a sound she remembered from way back when she was a little girl. Lettie opened her eyes in the darkness of her bedroom and listened for the sound to repeat itself. It didn't. What it had sounded like, she thought, was the rubbing-thumping noise her father used to make with a glass of water. He would lie in bed, all propped up high with pillows at his back, holding whatever he happened to be reading in one hand, and absent-mindedly rubbing and gently thumping a half-filled water glass back and forth across the corner of the old wooden table beside his bed.

Lettie closed her eyes, and in the velvety blackness behind them, could almost see the marks that had been left on the old pinewood table. It was the same table she now used at her own bedside. Without opening her eyes, she reached out to touch it. The first thing she felt were her wire-rimmed eyeglasses, resting atop the prayer book she always read a few lines from each night before turning off the light. She carefully slid them aside to uncover the corner where she knew the rub marks to be. The wood was rubbed smooth with age, and her fingertips glided across its cool surface like a set of ballroom dancers, gracefully trailing along the many scratches and bruises that the table had suffered in its lifetime. Her fingers stopped when she thought she could still distinguish the precise markings that her father had left behind with his water glass. A comfortable smile played across her lips. It was almost like being a little girl again, sleeping across the hall from him during the final years of his life. He had died in her arms after dinner one night, after telling her how much he had enjoyed the meal she had prepared for him, but he didn't think he'd have time for the dessert, which she had just brought into the living room where he preferred to take it. The dessert had been homemade rice pudding with fresh cream and raisins—one of his favorites. And that was as far as she could ever carry the memory. He had died a few minutes later, in agonizing pain. And that was the part she could never remember, the pain. A story she had once read in a newspaper had explained that bit of unusual forgetfulness to her. It told how the human mind will sometimes block from memory whatever it can't accept, whatever is too horrible for it to deal with. And the pain, which she knew her father had to have suffered, was such a thing she could never deal with—even to this day. The article had called the blocking by some long psychological name she had never heard of before, and couldn't, if her life now depended on it, remember, either. Some things are best left unremembered, she thought, turning over to go back to sleep. There was a warm tear in the corner of each of her tightly closed eyes.

The comfortable smile was still on her lips when she heard the noise again. This time it didn't sound the same as before. It could have been anything: a hollow knocking of one's knuckles on the bare wooden floor, an old beam settling itself inside a wall, a mouse dropping from a closet shelf. . . .

She had almost put herself back to sleep with the ever expanding list of things that might have caused the noise when she suddenly turned over on her back and sat upright in the bed. Her heart was racing. Ginny! she thought. All that furniture that had been moved in her room last night! Was the girl doing it again?

Lettie held her breath and listened to the darkness. Unlike the girl, who kept her window shades rolled up all the way to the top so that the moonlight could come streaming into her bedroom, the old woman preferred total darkness, or as close to it as she could possibly get. That meant her shades were always pulled down all the way to the bottom, and the drapes shut tightly across them. That way, she thought—for more years than she cared to remember—if anything was out there in the darkness she couldn't see it; and if you couldn't see it, it couldn't bother you. It was only the things people *saw* in the dark that got to them!

And so it was that Lettie sat there in her bed with her eyes closed, and her ears opened. But she didn't hear anything that matched that curious hollow-knocking sound that had set her heart racing in the first place. There wasn't a single middle-of-the-night sound that now came to her that she could not identify as being perfectly natural for the age of the wood-frame house in which she lived. And it was with a feeling of relief that she settled her head back down into the soft pillow and fell asleep.

This time, there was no comfortable smile on her lips.

They had it all laid out and planned as carefully as a military maneuver, or so they thought. Tree branches had been trimmed, tall grass cut back, and a broad trench dug with backhoe, pick, and shovel, so that the fire they were going to build at the pond would not spread up the hill toward the town.

"You sure the gasoline is going to float on top of the water?" Jerry Knox asked Winkie Bols as they lugged the jerry cans out of the beds of their pickups.

"Ask Judd, if you don't believe me," Winkie responded, out of breath from having done almost two hours' worth of digging with a hand shovel. "He knows all about fire."

Jerry turned to Judd, who was climbing down off the seat of the backhoe. The Red Cross blankets that had been draped across its hood to muffle the roar of the engine were smoking, but none of the men paid attention to it. "It's true?" Jerry asked. "That you can build a fire on top of water with gasoline?"

Judd took out a handkerchief and mopped his brow. It was glistening with sweat in the moonlight. "We've been over that, Jerry. It's not a problem. Gas is lighter than water; and it floats. The wind will help spread it across the whole surface of the pond once it's lit. Then we get the heck out of here. By morning all that's gonna be left of the water moccasins will be a fried-up pile of dead snakes." He let his eyes scan the inky stillness of the pond as though he were studying the moon and stars that were reflected in its surface. "We'll lose a few of the willows that are up close to the water," he said. "But, if the wind keeps pushing at our backs, like it is now, that's all we'll lose—that, and them . . ." He was going to use a curse word, but caught himself. He didn't have much respect for folks who swore, and he had always kept his own tongue in check when he felt a bad word coming. ". . . . them mocs!" he concluded.

Jerry Knox was having pain in his twisted leg, but he worked right along with Winkie, unloading the gasoline and matching him one-for-one. He didn't know, figuring from the heft of the jerry cans, how gasoline was *lighter* than water. He imagined that when it was spilled into the water, it would sink right to the bottom. But if the former fire marshal said it would float, well, he guessed it would probably do just that. But that didn't make him like it any better.

"Let's sit a short spell and catch our breaths," Winkie said after the gasoline was all unloaded from the beds of the two pickups. "And maybe have ourselves another taste of ol' Mr. Beam."

The three men settled themselves on the tailgate of Winkie's pickup and passed the bottle of bourbon from one to the other. The two pickups were parked with their tailgates facing each other at an angle—like a V—and the blanket-covered backhoe was facing them to form the lower leg that made it all look like a Y. All three vehicles were parked so close together that they almost touched. In the triangular space formed by the backs of the pickups and the front of the backhoe—and at the feet of the three men—were the twelve five-gallon jerry cans of gasoline. Some of cans had leaky tops from all the jostling about they received on the short journey from the county storage shed. The fumes were strong, but the men didn't notice.

"We'd better get ourselves started," Judd said, after taking a deep swig of bourbon from the bottle. He scraped his bottom on the bed of the pickup as he stood up and handed the near-empty bottle back to Winkie. His back ached, so he stretched his arms out above his head and moved his fingers as though he was turning a pair of invisible radio dials in the air. The other two men laughed as he brought his hands back down with a grunt. They were all feeling the soreness of the night's work. "We ain't a bunch of spring chickens anymore," Judd concluded, twisting his shoulders from side to side.

Winkie and Jerry laughed again as they scraped

their own bottoms off the tailgate of the pickup as they stood up. They knew exactly what he meant, especially Jerry. Ever since the time he got his leg tangled in the bailer, he had not known a single day without pain. Yet he never complained, and always tried to pull his fair share of things when things needed to be done. "I can carry two at a time," he said, stooping over and curling his fingers through the handles of a couple of jerry cans. "It'll save us some time that way."

"Save us some time, that's for sure," Winkie said. "But it's over a hundred yards down to the pond from here. By the time we make ourselves . . ." he thought for a moment and calculated, ". . . a couple of round trips, we won't have what we need to get ourselves out of here once the fire gets going."

Jerry was about to protest that if Winkie couldn't deal with two cans at a time, *he* certainly could. But Judd Winslow cut in, as though he could read what Jerry had been about to say. "Winkie's right," he said. "Why don't we do it this way. . . ." And he explained how they could carry the cans, one at a time, to the crescent-shaped trench he had dug. From where they stood, the trench was halfway to the pond. It could be used as a staging point where they could rest up a bit before continuing to carry the cans the rest of the way down to the water.

Winkie agreed; so did Jerry—but he sucked the teeth at the side of his mouth in a way that signified he thought they were a bunch of sissies. Winkie and Judd just looked at each other and mocked a chuckle when Jerry turned his back to pick up the first can.

The crescent-shaped gash that Judd had cut into the earth to stop the accidental spread of fire toward the town looked like a giant moustache drooping down the hill. It was over a hundred feet on either side, and where the "nose" of the "moustache" would be was where the men agreed to store the jerry cans once they carried them down the hill—in the four trips Winkie had calculated. Once all the cans were there, they could take a breather before going on.

There was a soft perimeter of slippery soil that had been turned out of the pit by the backhoe. It ran like a miniature mountain range along the edge of the crescent-shaped trench—which was about three feet deep and just as wide. The men had to climb over the heap of soil to deposit the cans in the trench. Winkie got there first and slipped into the hole, as did Jerry and Judd right after him. Some of the gas splashed on their shirts, but they just stood the cans back up in the trench and examined themselves. No one had been hurt, and that was the most important consideration at the moment.

There were smiles on their faces as they climbed out of the trench and dusted themselves off before heading back up the roadless hill. They couldn't help but remark to one another about how good the fresh-turned earth of the trench smelled. They had all been raised on farms, and the scent was reassuring and familiar. And as they walked the rest of the way in silence, the fragrance flooded their minds with snatches of long-forgotten memories—of parents and family, of children and loved ones, springtime fairs, first kisses, and holiday picnics. Not a single man among them was able to conjure up a memory that was not a happy one.

On returning from their second trip, Jerry was glad

that Judd had come up with the idea of using the trench as a staging point. He was as winded as anyone else by the time they got back to the vehicles to pick up another can apiece for their third trip down. But he tried, anyway. "We could carry two each this time and call it quits for this part of it," he offered.

Winkie and Judd hardly paid any attention to him. "You can carry all you want to," Judd said. "And mine, too," Winkie added. They stood there looking at one another in the moonlight. They were huffing and puffing like old-fashioned steam engines. Jerry Knox got the point and picked up his one can. "I was only foolin'," he said with a weak smile. His leg was killing him, yet he walked on down the hill straighter than he had since his accident.

"Hold on there, Jerry," Winkie called after him. "Stop tryin' to make us look like a couple of old farts."

"Which we are," Judd chimed in and laughed.

They were three of a kind, they each thought, and had been so for a long time. It felt good to have a friend who could read your mind and make you smile when you needed it—and to drink with, too. That was important. It was no use getting drunk with someone you didn't like.

After they had deposited their load and headed back up the hill for their final trip to the vehicles, one of the jerry cans fell over in the trench. Gasoline seeped out at first, then gushed more strongly down one side of the sloping "moustache." The can had been set down on something uneven. It wasn't a rock. And judging by the way another can was now about to topple over, it was certainly something that was alive and moving.

A water moccasin looped itself into a figure eight

between the handle and the cap of the can, and rhythmically contracted and relaxed its belly muscles until the scales caught on the gnarled rim of the cap and loosened it—while beneath the can a knot of water moccasins swelled and caused it, too, to topple over. Its contents spilled down the other side of the sloping "moustache." Then another and another and another of the cans fell over the same way.

The men were approaching the trench for the first time before pausing to rest. Because the wind was at their backs, rolling down the hill from the town to the pond, they didn't catch the extra-strong stench of the spilled gasoline until they were standing on the slippery mound of turned-out soil above the trench.

"What in the name of. . . ." Judd began as they all stared incredulously into the trench. Every last jerry can had been tipped over and emptied! "I don't. . . ." He couldn't finish.

Still holding on to the cans they had just arrived with, the three men squatted down on the ridge of soft soil piled high above the trench. They were studying the toppled cans in the pit when a peculiar noise made them frown and turn to one another. It sounded like rain on a tin roof. At first they couldn't tell where it was coming from. Then they realized it was coming from them! Something was striking at the jerry cans in their hands like a storm of buckshot in an open field. When they looked down at the cans they were still holding, they froze. *Batches* of mean-looking water moccasins were hurtling themselves at the cans like a hissing downpour of spiked rain. But they weren't striking with their fangs. It took the men only one horror-filled moment to figure it out. When they did, they dropped the cans and bolted up off their haunches in a flash, attempting to get out of there. But the freshly turned-out earth on which they stood was slippery, and they skidded into the pit, along with the cans they had dropped.

What had caused the men to panic was that the snakes carried stones in their jaws. As they struck the jerry cans, sparks flew. In the trench, where the gasoline fumes were thick, it only took one cherry-red speck of fire, no bigger in size than a grain of rice, to set it all off.

Flames roared through the trench like a dozen flamethrowers gone wild. The cans buckled, exploded, and came hurtling out of the pit like blazing meteorites. And so, too, did the three men. They were knocked right out of the hole like rag dolls—all arms and legs going every which way as they blazed. They were dead before they hit the ground, but something kept their bodies running like fiery globs of light toward the pond. It was a silent run, and a very speedy one. But they never made it to the water. They collapsed, in one luminous heap of intense flame, on the outcropping of smooth stone that overlooked the water.

Behind them, like a grinning scar in the earth, the crescent-shaped trench that they had all dug with backhoe and shovels blazed like a broad smile that had been cut into the hillside.

There was a strange glow in the sky, but that wasn't what woke Lettie up—the shades and drapes covering the windows of her bedroom had been drawn too tightly for that. It was that hollow-clocking noise again. As though something was rubbing or knocking on the bare wooden floor. Only this time it didn't go away when she focused on it. After a while the hammering noise began to sound like something out of control . . . and it was coming from Ginny's room.

Lettie quickly rose from her bed and didn't bother with a robe as she hurried across the hall to the girl's room. The noise grew louder and louder with each cautious step she took toward the child's door, where she now stood for a moment and listened. There was no mistake about it. The girl was moving furniture in there again! But *why?* Lettie thought as she seized the doorknob and twisted it in her hand. Why!?

Her mouth opened wordlessly as she stepped into the girl's bedroom. Whatever she had imagined to be the cause of those strange noises had nothing to do with the sight that met her eyes.

Every piece of furniture in the room—the bed, tables, a desk, the dresser, *everything*—was shifting back and forth and around as though it were a doll's house; a doll's house whose demented owner was shaking it to pieces. Books were flying off their shelves and papers were sailing all about; a small braided floor-rug spanked the air as though someone were shaking the dust out of it.

She was about to scream, but it froze in her throat when she saw that the floor was moving. It was alive with a twisting blackness that glistened in the dark like something wet and . . . *snakes!* That was what it was. The floor was covered with knots of weaving moccasins! And Ginny, who she now saw for the first time, was sitting in the old sofa chair by the window. It was spinning and thumping on the floor in sporadic movements of jerks and slides—like a bumper car at a county fair. A curious redness filled the sky behind her, and its shadows dappled the girl with shimmering fingers of the blood-red glow. It was as though the child was on fire!

When Ginny saw the old woman at the door, the chair came to rest with a great thump and the room fell still. Her eyes were filled with the glow of the sky, and in her lap was a pile of water moccasins. They coiled about in the bowl of her nightdress like a litter of kittens. She pointed at Lettie and screamed something at her in a language the old woman did not understand.

Lettie was too horrified to analyze what was going on. It all suddenly became some sort of an abstraction to her, like a bad dream. Even as she stood there in the doorway, drinking it all in with her hand still on the doorknob, the horror seemed to fade—and she grew curiously drowsy. All she wanted to do was quietly close the door and go back to bed, as though nothing had happened. She closed her eyes. And in so doing, she blocked from her mind everything she had seen; as effectively as she had blocked the agony of her own father's death.

Lettie gently closed the door to Ginny's room and returned to her own bedroom across the hall. She was asleep before her head touched the pillow. If darkness could keep things from reaching out at you in the night, so, too, could sleep. Deep . . . deep . . . forgetful sleep. And as she drifted further and further into a void of dreams she would never remember, something soft and cold touched the side of her neck like a gentle kiss. There was a playfulness to it, like when she was a child and her father sometimes nibbled at her, pretending he was eating at the freckles that then dotted the side of her rosy cheeks.

Curiously, one word stuck in Lettie's rapidly fading mind. She moved her lips and silently pronounced it with the last breath she was ever to draw. "Baby," was the word. And she died with it on her lips.

PART THREE

CHAPTER THIRTY-ONE

It was in the middle of the same night—the night that Winkie Bols, Judd Winslow, and Jerry Knox met their fiery deaths at the pond—that Edna Malikoff couldn't sleep. She tossed and turned half the night away, thinking about the child she had seen "slithering" about on the smooth outcropping of rock that overlooked the pond. It wasn't until after she had seen the hawk tumble out of the sky, as though it had been struck by cannon shot, and fall dead into the pond, that Edna had felt the chill—the same chill that had coursed through her veins at the Wilderness School in Wiltshire, outside of London. It was there, many years before, that she had experienced the terror that had caused her to give up the study of parapsychology forever—the terror of the poltergeist child, the same child she and her husband had later adopted and grown to love.

Perhaps it was the story Sara Garrett had told her, about all the snake-related deaths in town, that now made Edna get dressed in the middle of the night and cut across the college campus to her husband's astronomy lab. She knew it was foolish, but she was simply too frightened to be alone. It wasn't the first time she had sat through the night with her husband, while he studied the stars and made those scrawling calculations of his in a log that was as thick as a ream of paper.

"I thought you might like some tea," she said, entering the cavernous lab. It was lit very dimly. The only light an astronomer craves is the light that falls from the distant stars. "Seems the older I get, the less sleep I need." Edna shrugged.

Sir Jimmy, as she called him, because of his boyish face and bright blue eyes, looked down at her from his mount at the large telescope and smiled. Above him, the stars blinked in a field of velvet blackness through the slitlike opening of the telescope dome. "You read my mind," he said, running his fingers through the shock of uncombed white hair on his head. "I was about to climb down and fix a pot myself." Which wasn't the truth. The truth was that she had interrupted him in the middle of a dazzling bit of mental number crunching. And now it was all lost. To pick up where he had left off, he would have to start all the way back at the beginning, which was . . . which was? Gone, he told himself. Simply gone. Whenever such a thing happened, he liked to think of himself as some sort of superentity, capable of wandering out into the vast canopy of stars above his head, searching for whatever it was his memory had locked up and refused to give back. It's out there somewhere, he thought, scratching his head. Nothing is ever lost.

It wasn't until after the tea had been made, and set on a lab table—along with a tin of dry soda biscuits and a pot of the crystallized alfalfa honey he loved so much—that the knighted astronomer saw the trouble in his wife's eyes, even though the lab was very dark. "There's something wrong," he said. "What is it?" And he smiled that familiar boyish grin that was as warm and assuring as it had been when they had first met at a school dance.

Edna returned the smile, as warmly as she could muster it. "I was going to be terribly British about the whole thing," she said, elongating her vowels for emphasis—a thing that signified to Sir Jimmy that there was indeed something terribly wrong—"but thought I'd rather not." She cleared her throat. "Shall I put the honey in for you?" she asked, passing the freshly poured cup of tea across the table to her husband.

He took the cup from her, and after placing it down, reached for her hand and held it. "What is it?" he asked. "Something's gotten you very upset."

Edna slid her hand from his, as though his holding on to it any longer would betray the unidentifiable terror she felt gnawing away at her.

"Can we have some brighter lights on?" she asked. There was only one small desk lamp lit in the cavernous lab. The spill of its light resembled the faint glow of a candle at the other end of the long table at which they sat. Sir Jimmy didn't need light for his work. A small nightlight-type of lamp was clipped to a mount on his telescope, so he could see to take notes and make calculations. He had turned that off when he climbed down to be with Edna. A broad shaft of moonlight poured in through the opening of the telescope dome and cast eerie shadows among the steel beams and metal platforms on which the instruments were mounted.

Sir Jimmy looked at Edna as though he was considering the possibilities of her request for more light with the same full-minded precision that he crunched pages and pages of numbers to arrive at a mathematically feasible conclusion. "I can't," he finally said. "Not unless I place a call into maintenance, and wake all of them up. It has something to do with fuses and circuit breakers. Since I never use the overhead lamps, they close them off for the night." He thought for another moment. "I'll call them," he said, beginning to rise.

"No, no," Edna said, holding him back with a broad, almost helpless, gesture of her hands. "There's no need to go and wake anyone up in the middle of the night for a silly little thing like that. I'll be all right."

"Are you sure?" Sir Jimmy asked. He was about to suggest that they go elsewhere, where the light was perhaps better, when he thought of something else. "Why don't I lift the shades," he said. "That will bring in more moonlight." And he did just that, without the slightest equivocation from Edna. "There, that's better," he said, after raising nine tall and narrow shades that covered a wall of nine equally tall and narrow windows that faced the pond down the hill. "It's now bright enough to read by." And indeed it was, but the luminous glow of the moon made Edna look as pale as death.

"Now," Sir Jimmy said, once again seated opposite Edna at the table. "What was it that *really* brought you here?"

"I thought I saw a ghost," she said, so simply that it startled even her.

"A *ghost?*"

Edna looked away. Her eyes searched the emptiness outside one of the tall windows, the one through which she had seen the little girl cause a circling hawk to tumble lifelessly out of the sky and hit the pond. The spotting scope she had witnessed it through was now mounted to the giant telescope that was poked through the dome of the lab. They both felt the peculiar wind that swept in through the opening.

"You saw a ghost?" Sir Jimmy pressed. His long fingers worked about the edge of a soda biscuit, as though he were absent-mindedly attempting to Braille-read the edge lettering of a rare coin.

Edna's mood changed swiftly. Her dimly lit features sparkled with mirth. "You see ghosts all the time, Jimmy. So why on earth can't I see one?"

He was puzzled. It showed itself in the sudden halt of his fingers about the edge of the soda biscuit. "I don't follow," he said, dipping the biscuit into the pot of crystallized honey and then, with a dollop clinging to it, into his tea. He was placing it to his lips when Edna responded.

"Stars. You know." She leaned forward as though sharing a secret. "They're the ghosts of the universe. You told me so yourself."

Indeed he had. They could not have been much older than twenty-one when he had once taken her to a friend's astronomy lab, where they had spent the night looking at the sky—he, attempting to teach her the names of certain stars in certain constellations (Schedar and Caph in Cassiopeia, Sirus in Canis Major, Alioth and Dubhe in the Big Dipper), and she, forgetting them just as quickly as he spoke their names. He remembered explaining that many stars were probably "ghosts," their central fires having gone out perhaps billions of years ago—but that their light was still visible because it took that long for it to reach the earth from the great distances of the solar system.

"Eddie," he said, uttering her pet name with a gentleness that was reserved for very special, almost tender, moments. "You didn't come all the way over here tonight just to tell me you were out looking at the stars."

Edna wrapped the fingers of one hand about the knuckles of the other until she almost stopped the flow of blood in it. "I had a dream, Jimmy," she finally said. "I don't know if it was caused by something I saw earlier this afternoon, or if. . . ."

"Or if?" Sir Jimmy gently prodded. It was the first time in their long relationship with each other that he considered the possibility that her mind might be showing signs of age. It made him suddenly aware of the frailty of life itself, and what that life might mean without her. He placed his uneaten biscuit in the saucer of the teacup and reached out for both her hands. She brought them up from her lap and welcomed the warmth that flowed back into her from him. "Or if?" he asked in a whisper.

Her hazel eyes were filled with moonlight when she spoke. "Or if it was . . . Melissa," she finally said. "Our daughter. I think she's dead."

The chair he was sitting on creaked like a broken heart when he released her hands and sat back into it. "How?" he asked. There was a sorrowful medley of controlled emotions in his one-word question.

"I saw her," Edna answered, and her eyes glistened in the moonlight. "She was smiling and waving to . . .

to us. She was calling to us from a . . . I don't remember it now, but I think it was a boat of some sort. There was water, that I remember clearly. *The water of life,* I said to myself in the dream. *If the living have life, so, too, do the dead—like the stars.* I remember saying that, too, to you."

Sir Jimmy was never as chilled as when Edna told him of her dreams. "And the meaning?" he cautiously asked.

Edna's shoulders sagged and she took a deep breath, as though to reinflate herself with the breath of life. "I think it simply means that we are either going to live forever," she said, "or that we are going to die together."

Sir Jimmy couldn't help it, his mind automatically calculated the odds of their dying together—of natural causes. Life without Edna would be as barren for him as it would be for her without him.

"My God!" Edna screamed, rising to her feet and facing the wall of windows. Sir Jimmy quickly turned and saw what she was looking at. His eyes widened.

Outside the windows, down toward the pond, the sky flashed red. The explosion rattled the wall of windows in front of them, and they both heard the sound of falling debris entering the lab through the telescope opening in the dome. Flames shot up from down the hill and spewed out into the darkness like jets of spiraling fireworks. And through it, they both saw the unmistakable hurtling of three blazing men frantically attempting to climb an invisible ladder back up into the sky as they disjointedly tumbled back to earth.

"It's that girl!" Edna said, raising her hand to her lips. "She's doing this!"

Sir Jimmy couldn't take his eyes from the windows.

As quickly as the ball of light had reddened the sky, it now subsided, leaving the blazing men scuttling toward the water—which they never made. He watched in horror as they collapsed on the broad outcropping of rock that overlooked the pond.

"I have to tell someone," Edna babbled. "Something must be done to stop that child. I'll tell Sara! Sara will know what to do!"

Sir Jimmy turned and gasped at the "debris" the explosion had blown into the lab through the telescope opening in the dome. Great splotches of blackness clung to the telescope, the metal platforms and beams of the mountings. Bits of the same blackness caught in coils on the edges of the dome's opening and dangled down like thick sets of ropes. They all seemed alive, flexing and coiling and dropping to the platform and floor like . . . like shiny black *snakes!*

Edna stopped when she saw the look in her husband's eyes. It wasn't terror. It was more like the look he sometimes had when he was in the midst of a complicated number crunch. His mind was lost in an infinite maze of mathematical equations! Or was it? Maybe he was. . . .

Edna turned to see what her husband was looking at. "My God!" she gasped. "We *are* going to die together." The floor was covered with snakes, as were the tabletops, chairs, and file cabinets.

And in that one, long, terrible silent moment it took the water moccasins to reach them, Edna and Sir Jimmy clung to each other in a desperate attempt to be . . . to be British about the whole thing.

"You know, I've always loved you," she said.

Sir Jimmy couldn't help the boyish grin that spread

across his face. “Thank you,” he responded. “And I, you.”

In almost sixty years of marriage they had never said such a thing to each other. The only regret they read in each other’s eyes as they faced death together was that they had never said it before.

CHAPTER THIRTY-TWO

During the course of the next few days, the dead were buried. Their freshly dug graves baked like soft mounds of red clay in the sunny green lushness of the old cemetery that overlooked the town. Winkie Bols and Judd Winslow were interred with their wives—their names hastily engraved on the same tombstones they had themselves purchased when their wives had passed away. The final resting place of Jerry Knox, who had never married, was indicated by a temporary wooden marker; as were the graves of Harvey and Nancy Ocean. When permanent tombstones arrived, they would replace the temporary markers. Edna and Sir James Malikoff were there, too, since the college could not locate any next of kin, nor a will that would indicate how their remains were to be disposed. The college promised the town it would continue to look into the matter. The temporary marker that was placed above their common grave looked the same as all the others—cut-out wooden letters, glued and nailed to a flat pine board, stained and varnished. The

Malikoffs' grave was not far from where the Reverend Watkins had been buried. He and his long-dead wife did not share a common grave. She had been cremated in Africa and her ashes had been deposited there beneath a tabletoplike slab of heavy slate. Her name and the dates of her birth and death, along with the fact that she had died in childbirth, were engraved about a raised carving of the African continent on which she had died. Lettie was there, too, the only natural death among them. Her final place of rest was beside the small stone marker that read BABY. She had bought and paid for her own grave and tombstone at about the same time as she had buried the child. The granite marker had been in place ever since she was in her twenties. Her name and year of birth had already been carved into it, too. All that needed to be done was to fill in the date of her death. That, too, had now been done, by the son of the same man who had sold her the tombstone. Loren Mitchell had persuaded Sara Garrett—and it didn't take much for her to agree—to take care of Ginny until something could be worked out, something that would not involve the state authorities stepping in and placing the child in an orphanage for adoption. And, while there had not been any more snake-related deaths since the night the town was awakened by the explosion at the pond, there was an uneasiness in the air that smelled as though another disaster was on its way. But no one wanted to think about it. No one even wanted to talk about it—no one but Bobby Jennings, the radio announcer whose doberman pinscher had been killed by snakes the same afternoon that Reverend Watkins was attacked and killed by a water moccasin. He was pushing as hard as he could for a town meeting to settle the issue of the deadly vipers, once and for all. But with each day that passed, without anyone's reporting a snake anywhere in sight, his argument fell on increasingly deaf ears. "Let the dead bury the dead," he had been told more than once. And, more than once, he had retorted: "They will have to. No one else will be left alive to do it!"

It was in the middle of all this that Ginny found herself up at the graveyard after school one day. She stood atop her mother's slablike tombstone and surveyed the graveyard as though she were standing at the prow of an oceangoing vessel cutting through the freshly turned humps of red earth that covered the recent dead. She didn't know who all of them were. She had never met the Malikoffs and had known the guidance counselor's wife only by sight, having seen her once or twice at school or about town. Yet . . . yet she was *relieved* they were all dead—even, in a very odd sort of way, Lettie. Somehow, they had all posed a threat to her, and to the snakes at the pond. Every threat had to be eliminated. She would miss Lettie, but there was Sara to take her place. And, for some curious reason, she liked that better.

Clouds formed on the distant horizon and slowly moved in toward the graveyard like a raging sea. But where she stood the sun was still bright and the sky a brilliant blue. She knelt down on her mother's tombstone and traced her fingers along the carving of the African continent. There was a tiny star etched into the lower central portion of it, signifying where her mother had died, and where she herself had been born. She leaned back a bit and trailed her middle finger through the grooves that spelled out her mother's name and the words that told of her death in childbirth. She squinted at the date of her mother's death, which she knew to be her own birthday—but she had wanted to check it anyway.

A fresh breeze picked up the scent of flowers that had been placed on the new graves, and tiny birds chirped and swooped through the branches of the old trees that surrounded the place. She filled herself with the deliciousness of the sunny afternoon and gazed through the sea of tombstones, obelisks, and crosses that engulfed her. The smile faded from her lips when her eyes came upon Lettie's grave. She sat back on her heels.

She had loved the old woman, but there was something inside of her that commanded her not to love—not ever to love anyone, only the snakes. It wasn't the first time she had felt such a thing. Ever since she had called the water moccasin down upon her father in the church, she was beginning to feel more and more like . . . *herself* . . . more and more of the *thing* she really was, deep down inside. Maybe she shouldn't love anyone again. If she didn't, she would never feel the pain she now felt at having lost the kind old woman.

She'd have to forget, the thing within her insisted. It also whispered how bad it would be for her ever to love Sara, too. But she knew that was already beginning to happen; she couldn't help it. The lady from the college, who Sheriff Mitchell had brought over to Lettie's house to stay with her for a while, was becoming more and more like what she had always imagined a mother to be.

Ginny had never known what it felt like to have a mother, and, for the past few days she had enjoyed pretending that she was Sara's daughter. Sara was the same age as her mother would have been had she not died a dozen years ago. That was the reason why the girl had gone to the graveyard that day, to compare the date of birth that Sara had given for herself with her mother's, which was carved into the tombstone. They had both been born in the same year, within days of each other, thirty-six-years ago!

Ginny turned over on her back. The clothes she wore constricted her. Why, she wondered, did people have to wear clothes? Why couldn't they be more like . . . like . . . and she thought of how the water moccasins at the pond liked to bask in the sun on a smooth, flat rock, the way she herself had done a few days back. She stood up and looked around. There was no one in sight. The only trail that led up to the graveyard from the town was clearly visible from where she stood. She would do it. She took off all her clothes and laid herself out on the thick slab of slate that covered her mother's grave. The raised carving of the African continent fit snugly into the small of her back as she stretched her arms above her head and then slowly lowered them across her breasts, letting the fingers of each hand touch the opposite shoulder—like an Egyptian mummy she had once seen in a picture book. She closed her eyes, and in so doing, all the doubts and fears she felt about the snakes' not wanting her to love anyone but them vanished into the warmth that radiated from the thick gravestone on which she basked.

When she opened her eyes again, the dark clouds that had been off on the distant horizon had moved in closer. But that wasn't it—that wasn't what had caused her to open her eyes. There had been a noise. Someone was coming, not from the path that led up from the town. Someone was already there, and had been there all along, watching her!

Before Ginny could get back into all her clothes, that someone revealed herself. It was Betty Bird Johnson. And the moment she stood in full view of Ginny, a flash of lightning licked out of the deep grey storm clouds that were coming in fast.

"Looks like there's a storm coming," Betty Bird said. "Better get your clothes back on."

Ginny's eyes filled with fire, as intense as the gathering storm. Whatever clothes she had managed to slip back into, she now removed again—tearing them from her body and hurling them to the ground with such force that they raised a cloud of dust about her. When she was naked again, she climbed back up on her mother's grave and glared at the busybody who had come to spy on her. Betty Bird looked like a startled gnome. Ginny laughed.

Betty Bird looked at her as though Ginny were something other than an ordinary girl like herself. Ginny was older, taller, and more developed than herself, but that wasn't it. Betty Bird had been watching her sunbathing naked on the gravestone ever since she had followed her up there after school that afternoon. There was something about the whole scene that was scary, and the laughter that now came from Ginny sounded as though it echoed from the depths of a dark cave. Betty Bird straightened her spine and finally said: "Shouldn't you be getting back to town? There's a storm coming, you know." She looked at her wristwatch with its pretty pink and red plastic band, and tapped its crystal with a painted fingernail. "It's getting late, too."

"Why did you follow me here!?" Ginny demanded, completely ignoring what her classmate had just said. Her voice was cold and icy.

"I . . . I came up here to . . . to tell you . . . tell you. . . ."

"Tell me, what!?"

Betty Bird swallowed hard. She looked behind her to the trail that led back down to the town. From where she stood she could almost see the roof of her house. Running, at full speed, she could probably reach home in under five minutes. Ginny wouldn't dare follow her, naked as she was.

Ginny shrieked at her as though she had read her mind: "You're not going anyplace until you tell me why you followed me here!"

Betty Bird broke out in a sweat. A wind came up from the approaching storm and made the dust cling to her arms and the back of her neck. She wanted more than anything to get out of there, but it was as though her legs couldn't move. She decided she'd better tell Ginny the truth. *The truth will always set you free.* Hadn't her mother been telling her that ever since she was old enough to remember?

"There's talk 'n town 'bout how you might have to be put in a home, now that your dad and Miss Lettie are gone." (So far, so good, she told herself, taking a deep breath before going on.) "They say, too, that the lady from the college won't be carin' for you very much longer, either."

The agony that Betty Bird's words caused in Ginny's heart didn't show itself on her face. Her expression remained as contorted and glaring as when she first discovered that the girl had been spying on her. And the flashes of lightning that played in the background above her shoulders gave her face a demonic cast. Betty Bird shivered. She had sat next to Ginny in the same classroom for almost a whole year, and suddenly she didn't look like the same person anymore. . . .

Thunder barreled out of the sky, sounding like a heard of stampeding stallions. Betty Bird's heart raced as the rain began to pour down like spikes of shiny steel. Ginny's body glistened as the rain cascaded down her body and onto her mother's grave. She laughed again. This time it was drowned in the roar of thunder that filled the dense black sky. Even though Betty Bird couldn't hear the laugh, the menace of it was clear. She bolted for the path that led back to town.

Ginny sprang from the stone slab on which she had been standing and picked up one of the smooth round rocks that were abundant in the graveyard. She hurled it at the fleeing child with such force that it seemed to hiss through the drenching downpour. One moment it was a smooth, round stone traveling at a speed she couldn't imagine having produced, and in the next instant, just before it struck the girl, it was a snake—a long black water moccasin with gaping jaws, ready to sink its sparkling white fangs into the back of Betty Bird's neck.

The girl tumbled when she fell, and rolled into a thicket beside the path that led down to the town.

There was not the slightest doubt in Ginny's mind that she was dead. She climbed back up on the slab of stone that covered her mother's grave and raised both her arms into a boiling sky that shot lightning all about her. Her laughter was a sound that matched the terror of the sky itself.

know."

It all seemed so incongruous and out of place, that for a moment Sara thought she might be dreaming. But she knew she wasn't. Yet, she found herself accepting everything as though it was a dream. A part of her knew that under normal circumstances her analytical mind would be racing with questions—*Aren't you warm in that heavy clothing? Where was it made? How did you get here? How did you hear of your parents' death? How did you know my name?*

"That's right," Melissa said, as though she could read Sara's mind. "There's little need for questions." She motioned Sara into the main part of the cottage, and she followed.

The room had changed in the few days since Sara had been staying at Lettie's house with Ginny. The mattress on the bed had been stripped and folded to the top, so that half of the springs were exposed. The chair by the desk at the window had been placed, upside down, on top of the desk. The window shades were rolled all the way to the top, exposing the full force of the storm as rain pelted the windowpanes like handfuls of tiny stones. And the kitchenette had been cleaned and made tidy again.

Sara decided against removing the chair from the desk and offering it to Melissa to sit in. Instead, she turned to face her. She was eager to find out what was going on.

It seemed the woman was lost in thought, and had no desire to sit, even if the chair had been offered her. And when she finally began to speak, it was as though she were still in the middle of the same thought. *"There is a part of everyone for which there can be description, no words, no names, no feelings, and no knowledge,"* she said. The familiar words had been spoken plainly, without emphasis or emotion to detract from their meaning. "Do you remember that?" she asked.

Of course, Sara did. She had used the quote from Castaneda's sorcerer, don Juan, in her talk before the National Parapsychological Association, about two weeks ago. It illustrated the similarities of concepts, of cultural myths, between the Sotho witch doctors with whom she had studied and the doctrine that the famed anthropologist had expanded upon.

A shudder suddenly ran through Sara's body as she remembered the ink stain that had ruined the note card she had been preparing for the talk. Red ink had spilled from her old-fashioned fountain pen and the ink blot had formed the shape of a serpent's head complete with gaping jaws and blood-dripping fangs. She hadn't thought of it before, but she now wondered if that could possibly have anything to do with. . . .

"There is not very much time," Melissa said, cutting into Sara's thoughts. "To be truthful, I didn't know what to expect when I arrived here." Her eyes focused steadily on Sara's astonished gaze before she went on. "The snake killings that have occurred will continue," she said flatly, again without emotion or emphasis. "No one can stop them but you."

Sara stiffened. The tide of questions Melissa's appearance and remarks had caused were almost to her lips—ready to flood out at her. But the woman sent them back to the core of her being when she lifted her hand and began to speak again.

"You have spent some time with sorcerers," Melissa said. "Therefore, you should know that there *is* a part of us for which there can be no explanation. You have within you all that is necessary, all you will ever need, to combat this . . . this *evil* thing that has occurred. But there is risk involved. Great risk. Your life is in peril. And that is what I have come to tell you. My mother implored me to do so. She said you would know what to do next. I cannot be of any further assistance."

And with that, Melissa broke off. Sara's bewildered eyes followed her movements intently as she turned and paced in a small circle on the bare wooden floor. There were puddles from Sara's own footprints leading into the room from the vestibule. But none from Melissa.

"Do you mind if I use the other room?" Melissa asked, pointing to the bathroom door. The request was so commonplace, so ordinary, that Sara nodded. "Sure," she said with a shrug, just as simply as if she had been speaking to a college roommate. "Be my guest."

Before Melissa opened the bathroom door, she stopped and turned to face Sara again. "Don't forget your cosmetics bag when you leave," she said. Then she smiled and went inside, closing the door softly behind her.

Sara immediately sprang to her feet when she realized what was happening. It was as though she had come awake in the middle of a bizarre dream. She raced to the bathroom door and began pounding on it. "No!" she screamed. "Don't!"

But when the door slowly opened, Sara was swept with a sudden wave of embarrassment and confusion. "Melissa?" she called out in a small, almost apologetic voice. "Are you there?"

When there was no response, Sara stormed into the room. There was no sign of the woman anywhere. The only sign that remained of her presence was the peculiar aroma of her musklike perfume. Her body slowed itself way down, the way it sometimes happens to people involved in a disaster. What was she doing here? she wondered. Then she saw the cosmetics bag conspicuously perched at the edge of the washstand, right where she couldn't miss it. When she hesitantly reached for it, something made her glance at her wristwatch. It was three-forty-five—the exact time she had noted upon her arrival at the cottage.

CHAPTER THIRTY-FOUR

One of the cleaning women thought she heard a noise coming from the cottage, right next to the one she was working in, and went to investigate. When she arrived, Sara was starting out the door, pale and looking somewhat disoriented.

"You okay, ma'am?" the woman asked. " 'cause if you not, I kin get a doctor at the infirmary."

It was the same black cleaning woman Sara had seen about the campus several times in the past two weeks. She wore the familiar blue and white uniform of the campus maintenance staff, and carried an umbrella that was still open, even though she had stepped up onto the narrow porch to stand beneath the eaves of the roof beside Sara.

Sara crossed her arms and clutched the cosmetics bag to her breast with both hands. The faint aroma of musk that still clung to it was the only tangible evidence of the encounter she had just had with. . . .

"I asks you lady, do you need a doctor?" the cleaning woman pressed when there was no response to her first offer.

"Do you have a car?" Sara suddenly asked, her eyes

now fully focused on the cleaning woman's velvety black eyes. "I'd give anything for a lift home in ail this rain. It's less than a mile."

The woman took a step back and studied her for a moment. "You got yo'self good 'n wet, comin' here without an umbrella," she said, examining Sara more closely. "Didn't I see you here before?"

"Yes," Sara said. "I just came back to pick up something I'd forgotten."

"I can take you home." The cleaning woman said, pointing to a rusted yellow Volkswagen that was parked outside of the cabin next door. "You jes wait here 'n I'll get the bug. You be home in no time."

And when she let Sara off in the driveway of Lettie's house, the cleaning woman said, "Excuse me for sayin' so, ma'am. But, you know, it's kinda funny."

"What is?" Sara asked.

"Funny 'bout that cosmetic bag you say you forgot. I been all over that cottage six times in the past two or three days. You know somethin'? I never seen it. Not one single time."

When Sara came into the house, Ginny was upstairs drying her hair and changing her clothes. She had arrived only moments before. She now called over the handrail of the second-floor landing and told Sara she would be down in a few minutes.

A few minutes, or a few hours, it didn't matter to Sara. Her mind was still reeling from her experience at the cottage.

There is not very much time. The killings will continue. You are the only one who can stop them.

Sara sat down heavily on one of the ladderback chairs at the round oak table in the kitchen. Her clothes were still wet, yet she didn't feel the discomfort of them. She slid her shoes off beneath the table and raised her feet off the floor and placed them on one of the legs of the pedestal that protruded from the single column that supported the tabletop. What did she mean, she wondered, that I'm the only one who can stop the snake killings?

Why am I even *thinking* about it? It was obviously some sort of a seizure, she told herself. Like the one that had stopped her in the middle of her presentation before the conference that day. She'd see a neurologist first chance she had, she thought. There'd be tests done and medication prescribed.

"What's the matter?" Ginny asked. "You look like you've just seen a ghost."

Sara looked up. For the first time since she'd arrived home she assessed her appearance. She laughed realizing what she looked like sitting there. Her hair, in spite of the "combing" she had given it with her fingers in the cleaning woman's Volkswagen, was a mess. Her clothes, although somewhat dryer, were still wet and wrinkled. And she was clutching the cosmetics bag to her breast again, as though the fading scent of the musklike perfume was the only link to her own vanishing sense of reality. She'd have to hold on—hold on for as long as it took to figure things out. The laughter that now rose from her was natural, and as strong a hook to reality as there was.

"Come here, you little skunk," she said to the girl. "And I'll show you how hard a hug someone who's just seen a ghost can give."

Ginny melted into her arms. The fondness that had so unexpectedly sprung up between them over the past few days could only be described as magical. Sara thought it had something to do with needs—the need (both biological and emotional) she herself had to be a mother, and the need of the child to identify (probably for the first time in her entire life) with a woman who so closely fit the image of the mother she had never known.

They squeezed each other tightly, and drew apart only when it was realized that Ginny's clothes were getting wet against Sara.

"Yikes," Ginny said, laughing. "Now I'll have to change all over again."

"Oh, sweetheart, I'm so sorry," Sara began. "I didn't. . . ."

Her words momentarily vanished, and so too did her smile. For the first time since the child entered the room, Sara now focused on the bright yellow ribbon that was tied to her hair. It reminded her of the child she had seen from the astronomy lab that day she stayed behind to tidy up after having had tea with Edna—the child who appeared to be skipping so merrily up the trail that led from the pond. It was the day before the three men had been killed there—the same night that Edna and Sir James had been killed by snakes in the lab. She brushed her thoughts aside.

". . . I didn't mean to get you so wet," Sara finally finished saying. "Why don't we both go upstairs and change before starting dinner."

As they made their way to the stairs that led to their rooms above, Sara playfully fluffed the yellow ribbon in Ginny's hair. "I love the color," she said. "Have you worn it before?"

"Sure," Ginny said. "Lots of times."

After dinner they sat in the parlor. Against the sound of rain hammering on the house like fistsful of buckshot being hurled from the sky, they spoke of things no ordinary child would have dreamed of discussing. Yet, to Ginny, the questions she asked seemed to arise from an inner need to know, as though the answers might somehow untangle the curious knots that had begun to twist deep within her—ever since the killings had begun, ever since she had killed Betty Bird Johnson that very same afternoon.

"What are witch doctors?" she asked. "What do they do?"

Sara looked across the coffee table to the sofa where Ginny sat in the milky spill of an old Victorian floor lamp. Beside her was the homework Sara had helped her complete some time before. Sara was not surprised at the child's questions. Once Ginny knew of the two years she had spent in Africa, there had been many such questions. It seemed only natural. After all, she told herself, the child was born there.

"The witch doctors I knew did a great many things," Sara began. "They prepared herbs for the sick, predicted whether or not the child a pregnant woman carried would be a boy or girl, settled disputes over land, cattle, water rights, and performed rituals—which, in many ways, are similar to what. . ." She was about to conclude by saying that rituals were similar to what clergymen do in church, when she remembered that Ginny's father had been a minister.

She didn't want to awaken any memories of that. ". . . .similar to what goes on in witchcraft."

"Witchcraft?" the child pressed.

"Black magic. Sorcery. Things like that."

Ginny studied her, as though seeing her for the first time. "You *lived* with such people?" she asked, disguising the feelings that rattled her insides, as the storm outside was rattling every window in the house.

"Well," Sara said with a smile. "It's not as bad as it sounds. Most—no, I'll correct that to *all*—of the witch doctors I knew were men of honor. They all thought of themselves as having been born with a special gift, a gift to be used for the purpose of helping others. Their main magic was in helping to heal the sick."

Ginny thought of the rounded black stone she had hurled at Betty Bird Johnson that afternoon at the graveyard, and how it had left a streak through the rain as it hurtled toward the fleeing child's neck. Then, moments before it struck, it had turned into a water moccasin—just like the one she had called down on her father in church. A dark chill crept up her arms as she remembered standing above the dead body of her classmate in the pouring rain . . . then kicking Betty Bird, until she began to roll farther and farther into the thicket, where, hopefully, no one would ever find her. There was a gaping bite wound in her neck—right where the snake had grabbed her.

"Suppose a witch doctor was bad," the girl asked. "Suppose there was nothing he could do about it—like he couldn't help himself? Suppose the only thing he was good for was to make bad magic?"

Sara couldn't help but wonder at the nature of the Ginny's questions. They helped to place her own "magical" encounter of the afternoon in the background for a while.

"There are bad sorcerers," Sara finally responded. "They're usually people who discover their *gift* late in life—by that I mean . . . about your age, Ginny. Eleven or twelve."

Ginny wrinkled her nose. "That's not late in life," she said. "That's young."

Sara nodded. "Not in the African veldt," she responded. "There, everyone grows up real fast." She sat back and studied the child for a moment before going on. "I never met a bad sorcerer myself," she said. "But the way the bad magic is put under control, so I've been told, is when the other witch doctors—the good ones—get together and take the sorcerer off to a place where his magic is somehow neutralized." There was more to it than that, but Sara didn't feel comfortable in going any further with what that was. "Do you know what that means, Ginny . . . to *neutralize?*"

Ginny nodded. "Like a car?" she guessed. "When it's in neutral, it can't go anyplace?"

"That's right!" Sara said, beaming at the child's ability to absorb and incorporate knowledge. "It's the same as stopping the magic cold—stalling it out."

Ginny pursed her lips and drew them tightly to one side of her mouth. Her nostrils flared from the pressure of it. She almost looked like a smug little kitten. "Do you believe in magic?" she asked.

Something about the question made Sara feel less sure of herself than she had ever been. It was the same feeling teachers sometimes have when they are asked a question by a pupil they feel might be one-up on them. She didn't know how to respond. *Did she believe in magic?* The answer to that, if truthful, had to be yes, she did. Yet, there was magic, and there was *magic.* Sara had never been one to believe in hocus-pocus. But, in healing, and, sometimes, in determining the sex of a child before it was born—well, yes, that *was* magic. What she finally answered, though, was: "I don't really know." And, truthfully, that covered her belief in magic, thoroughly.

"I think my mother believed in magic," Ginny said brightly, folding her knees up to her chin and circling them with her arms. "I think she was doing a book about it when she died."

Sara sat back and stared at her. The questions in her emerald-colored eyes made them sparkle in the lamplight.

"The book she was writing when she died is in the college library," Ginny continued. "She never finished it. My father put it there—donated it—when I was very small. He said I should go and have a look at it some day. But I don't want to." A frown formed on Ginny's brow. "I don't ever want to lay eyes on it."

The finality of Ginny's statement startled Sara. There was an edge of unspoken anger beneath the child's soft-spoken words.

"Well," Sara said, injecting a note of motherly authority into her voice. "Enough of all *that* for tonight. It's up to bed with you now. Tomorrow's another day." It was the same way her own mother used to whisk *her* off to bed on a school night. Using the words somehow made her feel better, more secure, less chilled by the workings of her own imagination.

After Ginny had gone to bed, Sara went to sit on the screened-in porch outside of the kitchen. The violence of the storm was just the thing she needed to still the inner turmoil of her thoughts—which she likened to the storm itself. She didn't know how long she had been sitting there, gazing out at the blackness beyond the screening, being occasionally dazzled by a sudden flash of lightning, and startled in return by the explosive blast of the thunder that followed.

She sat in a large old wicker chair that was close to one of the screened walls, and when the wind gusted, rain splattered in at her. She didn't mind. It was like sitting at the top of a dark, rain-swept mountain. She closed her eyes and tried to imagine the open grasslands of the African veldt being washed by such a torrential downpour. But, try as she might, she couldn't hold the image. It kept retreating and transposing itself into an image of the snow-capped ranges of Tibet—where Edna Malikoff's daughter had run off to with her lover. Tibetan magic and African sorcery blended into the nightmarish storm that boiled in her mind. *There is a part of us for which there can be no name, no description, no knowledge.* Sara suddenly sat back in the creaky old chair and laughed at the oddity of her own runaway imagination. She knew she'd have to take care, lest she lose a full night's sleep. Lightning glistened on her rain-soaked face as she tried to smile away her grim thoughts.

With her cold hands she wiped the rain away from her face and shook her head. She wondered what on earth was keeping Mitchell. The sheriff had called earlier to see how everything was going and had said he would stop by to see her on his way home—as he had been doing ever since she'd first agreed to stay with Ginny. She was suddenly aware of the fact that she . . . missed him. She knew his presence there that night would help dispel the feeling of gloom she had allowed herself to be swept into. What's keeping him? she wondered. She didn't know what time it was, but she had the feeling it was already too late for him to stop by. He must have been stopped by the storm, she thought, and she pulled her knees up to her chin—just as Ginny had done earlier—and circled them with her arms.

The tension that ran through her spinal column was relieved by the pull of her shoulders as she tightened her arms about her knees. It felt good. She thought she might sit that way for a while and have the spool of her thoughts run out like the skein of a loom, shuttling through the warp of her troubled mind until the tapestry that was hidden beneath her thoughts was fully revealed. But nothing came of it. All she could think of were the words: *There is not very much time. The killings will continue. You are the only one who can stop them.*

How? How can I do anything about it?

And, as though in response, she heard a thumping noise against the screen opposite her. Then another, and another—until the sound multiplied, built, and surrounded her like the frantic beat of a racing heart. She quickly rose to switch on the outside light. She took a step back and gasped. Outside, seemingly falling from the sky and hitting the ground like smoldering lumps of coal, was a sea of shiny little frogs. They leaped at the screening before her as if to find sanctuary from the storm. Thick black water moccasins leaped up to the screens after them, swallowing them whole and leaping for more, and more, and more. . . .

And mingled into the coiling, slithering terror of the storm, there came another sound. At first she was too horror-stricken to know what it was. Then, as the sound continued, she was able to identify it. It was the familiar sound of innocent laughter. She looked up at the ceiling of the porch as though she could see right through it. Upstairs, in the bedroom that was just above her head, she heard Ginny, laughing in her sleep.

CHAPTER THIRTY-FIVE

They could hardly hear each other above the roar of the storm. Loren Mitchell and Bobby Jennings, the radio announcer whose doberman had been attacked and killed by water moccasins behind the church, were out looking for little Betty Bird Johnson. The child's parents had called to inform Mitchell about their missing daughter just as he'd been about to leave the office and go on over to see Sara about how things were going with Ginny. Bobby Jennings had been with him when the call came in from Betty Bird's parents. He had stopped by earlier to speak with Mitchell about the possibility of convening a town meeting to persuade the selectmen to do something about the snake-infested pond—or get them voted out of office if they refused.

Now, dressed in their yellow storm slickers and wide-brimmed hats, he and Mitchell stared down at the pond from up the hill. So much rain had fallen that it was filling up, overflowing its shores and growing larger by the minute. If it weren't for the fact that the pond was so far downhill, it would by now have flooded the town. Like the problem with the water moccasins, Bobby Jennings thought, the pond was growing larger, too.

"It's one of the places we haven't checked yet," Mitchell shouted, one hand cupped to his lips like a megaphone, while, with his other hand, he pointed the beam of his powerful police lantern down toward the pond. "I don't know where else she might have gone to."

Bobby Jennings didn't think the child had gone down to the pond. No one in their right mind, even a child, would do such a fool thing. The news of the snake killings was all over town. He had even put together a special radio program designed for children, describing the dangers of water moccasins. *They're the meanest varmints of all God's creations,* he had read on the air. *They have no fear of anything. If you happen to come across one, don't expect it to run away from you. The darn critter hasn't sense enough to do a thing like that. What you can expect is that it'll chase after you! Folks tell me they have actually seen a water moccasin come right up out of a lake or river and chase after someone. So, if you happen up on one, and it sees you, run like the dickens. And whatever you do, kids, don't go anywhere near the pond . . . the one folks in these parts call "Snake Pond."*

Bobby Jennings bit into the side of his mouth as he followed Mitchell down the hill. He tried with all his might to control the fear he felt in the darkness. Them moccasins can jump clean over a full-grown man! Yes sir, they'd have no trouble, no trouble at all, in getting you anywhere they wanted. He wormed his empty hand, the one he wasn't holding his flashlight in, through the slitlike opening inside the pocket of his yellow slicker and cupped his groin. When he had been in Korea, he'd once seen a soldier brought in, spreadeagled, in the back of an army pickup. The soldier had been screaming in bloody agony, and had been doing so, he later found out, for the entire seventy-five-mile trip in to the base hospital. The soldier had dug a shallow latrine near the frontline to do his business in. It was too shallow. A poisonous spider, no bigger than a flea, had jumped up and bit his scrotum. By the time they'd got him to the hospital his testicles were the size of two major league footballs! Jennings now slid his hand deeper into the slitlike opening inside his slicker's pocket and got a good hold of himself. If one little ol' Korean spider could do a thing like that, he told himself, imagine what the heck a water moccasin can do!

Keeping as close behind Mitchell as he could possibly get, and trying to walk right into the sheriff's own footsteps as his boots left the soggy ground, Bobby Jennings found himself holding his breath every time he stepped on a rock or twig. The vision he had of a thick black water snake coiling up out of the darkness and striking his privates was a hard one to shake. And when Mitchell suddenly stopped cold in his tracks, Jennings bopped right up into him.

"What's that!?" Jennings asked. The uneasiness he felt etched itself into the hissing downpour like a knife. "You see something?" he quickly asked, attempting to regain his composure.

Mitchell lowered his shoulder so Jennings could see what he was playing the beam of his lantern across. The radio announcer, who wasn't nearly as tall as the sheriff, was standing uphill, which was the only way he could see over Mitchell's shoulder. In the beam of the lantern, Jennings saw the spot where Winkie Bols, Judd Winslow, and Jerry Knox had perished as they carried out their ill-fated plan to rid the pond of snakes. The deep gash they had cut into the hillside with the backhoe, to keep the fire from spreading up to the town, was filling in with the same soil that had been dug out of it. The rain had almost completely washed it all back in.

A thought hit both men at the same time—*What if the child they were looking for was buried in the trench?*—but neither man spoke his mind. If it came to that, there was no way Betty Bird Johnson could still be alive.

Almost every big city paper they had come across lately told how child abductions were on the rise. The number of missing children reported annually was staggering. It far exceeded the population of almost every major city in the entire state. Some fiend passing through a small town pulls over in a fancy car and asks a little child a seemingly innocent question—like if they know where the church is, or if they could tell them where the school might be—and that's the end of it. The child's gone. Period. The agony the parents then go through from not knowing whether or not their child is alive or dead kills *them,* over and over again—every day for the rest of their lives.

While both men would gladly have killed a child abductor with their own bare hands, neither of them really believed that that was what had happened to the little girl they were searching for. It was the snakes. They both knew it, *felt* it right down in the marrow of their bones. They knew they would eventually find her body—riddled with snakebite punctures like all the rest—yet neither of them could say the words. They had silently searched through every part of town they could think of. Yards and alleyways were not ignored. They had even looked through the schoolhouse, and later searched the grounds about it. They were going to go up to the old graveyard, too, but they thought that would be the *last* place a child would wander off to alone. That left the pond. If they didn't find the missing child there, then they'd finish up at the graveyard. By then it would be dawn.

It was now almost four A.M., about the same time it had been when the town was awakened by the explosion that had killed the three men several days ago. Something about its being so close to the same time gave Bobby Jennings the creeps. It went into him like the rain that slithered down the back of his collar every time he forgot to tilt his head forward and empty the brim of his hat. He shivered.

"You're not catching yourself a cold?" Mitchell asked.

"No," Jennings responded in a flat, almost toneless, voice. "How long do you reckon we keep up this search?" he asked, turning the conversation around a corner and away from the dread of his own true feelings. He was shivering so much that the loose bridge at the side of his lower jaw rattled. He had to suck his cheek in to keep it still.

"Why don't you go on back home," Mitchell said. "I can finish down here on my own."

Bobby Jennings didn't even have to think about it. "No," he said, simply. "I guess another hour or so won't harm me any." And he drew his lips back tight, showing that it would be useless for Mitchell to try and persuade him otherwise.

Mitchell was too tired and too worn out to smile, otherwise he would have. Bobby Jennings was a good man. A shade past sixty, and a bit on the lean side, he was the kind of man Mitchell would like to have on his side if things got tough. "Well, let's get on down there," he said, pointing the beam of his lantern toward the pond. "The closer we get, the easier it'll be to tell if she's there."

Bobby Jennings knew that was true. He also knew that the closer they got to the pond, the closer they would be getting to the water moccasins that infested it. But he never thought of himself as the type of man who turned back on something once he set out to do it. Neither of them thought that way.

Had Mitchell and Jennings gone first up to the old graveyard on the hill above the church, they would have found a stranger there. He had arrived in an old 1952 Packard sedan right after Ginny fled the place that afternoon, just when the storm started to boil in earnest. He had driven there directly from West Virginia, a tall man in his sixties, looking like a backhill scrub farmer—faded Oshkosh overalls and all. His name was Garry Sorter, and he was the son of Jeremiah Sorter, a long-ago friend of Lettie's.

She had met Jeremiah when she was a little girl. She had been no more than eleven or twelve years old at the time, and he had been a young man in his twenties. Lettie's father had brought her to West Virginia one summer to have a look-see at a curious group of folks he had read about. They handled dangerous snakes for some kind of religious purpose he never *did* understand well enough to explain to her. But that wasn't the reason for their going there. Scripture had never held any value for Lettie's father. He had brought himself and his young daughter to the snake handlers so they could see for themselves how those people picked up copperheads, rattlers, and cottonmouths—and any other poisonous viper they could lay their hands on. Somehow, Lettie's father thought it would help him with the work of milking snakes, which was a task he had just begun to get interested in. There were a lot of rattlers and cottonmouths in Texas, and he might just get himself rich at it. Lettie was fascinated by one particular snake handler her father got to speaking with. That was Jeremiah Sorter, and he was the leader of the snake handlers. One night, after her father had fallen asleep, Lettie climbed out to the canvas tent her father had pitched up for them over the bed of their old Ford pickup. She couldn't sleep. There seemed to be some sort of a celebration going on near where the snake handlers had congregated. When she walked to where they were—in a small clearing that had been closed in by piles of boxes, boards, and pails, to form a closed pen—she saw the most incredible sight of her whole life. Standing in the center of the pen, *covered* from head to foot with every sort of poisonous viper anyone could imagine, stood Jeremiah Sorter. All around him, people were saying things from the Bible, about picking up serpents and being not harmed, and how the Lord had sent serpents among the peoples of the earth, serpents that could not be charmed. When Jeremiah spotted little Lettie staring at him in amazement, he smiled and summoned her with a nod of his head to join him in the pen. The crowd opened up for the little girl who had traveled with her father all the way from Texas just to see them. Lettie was seized by the most powerful emotion she had ever felt. She walked directly through the crowd and toward the pen, never once looking back or being hesitant in any way. When she stepped into the center of the pen with Jeremiah, he lifted one viper after the other from his body and placed them on the child, until she was covered with them. The crowd gasped. Shouts of Hallelujah! and Amen! rang out into the night. It was the most beautiful sight they had ever seen. There was this little, unafraid child from Texas, standing in the center of the pen with their leader, Jeremiah—sidewinders, diamond backs, adders, timber rattlers and copperheads, they all moved across her body as though they were a part of her living being. The glow on her face was as radiant as the light of the full moon that poured down on her through the fragrant pines. She was an inspiration to them all.

In the crowd that night there was a little boy. He could not have been any more than four or five years old. He was Garry Sorter—the man who now sat in the Packard sedan up by the old graveyard—Jeremiah's only son. He would remember what he had seen that night for the rest of his entire life. During the course of his growing up, he had read every letter his father ever received from the little girl from Texas—and he had fallen in love with her. He had never spoken to her, nor had he ever written to her, and never once—in all the years since he had seen her, that one and only time—had he spoken a single word to anyone about his feelings for her. And that was why he had come to Texas that night to visit her grave. Not so much as to whisper the words that had been locked up in his heart ever since he first laid eyes on her, but to bury with her the shoebox full of letters she had once written to his father—letters he had learned to read by, letters he had learned to love by.

It was dawn, and it had stopped raining for almost an hour before Bobby Jennings and Loren Mitchell slowly began to climb back up the hill from the pond to where the sheriff had parked his old Peugeot. They were worn out and not sure if they had what it took to carry the search for the missing child up to the old graveyard on the hill behind the church. The fact that they had not found the child at the pond was a relief—and the fact that they had not seen any water moccasins around was a puzzle. It was as though the snakes had gone into hiding. Or were they waiting for something, something special? Jennings wondered as he trailed up the hill behind Mitchell.

Both men had removed their long yellow rain slickers and carried them in their arms, along with their wide-brimmed hats and flashlights and lanterns. Mitchell didn't know what he was going to tell the little girl's parents. They had probably been up all night, calling his office every twenty minutes. He didn't blame them for that. If it weren't for the fact that he had firmly asked the child's father to remain at home, where he could be a comfort to his wife, he would have been out all night with them, too. He didn't want that. Betty Bird's father was a sparrow of a man, always chirping off about something—for that matter, so was his wife. Mitchell didn't know the little girl very well, but had heard she was a chirper, too. But that didn't affect his desire, in any way, to find her—and find her alive.

The men stopped for a moment to catch their breath and turned back to look at the pond. The rain had caused it to swell, and its shoreline now ran right up to, and in some parts slightly past, the trench that the three men had dug. The tall willows that surrounded the pond now looked like shrubs, with long spiderlike tentacles floating away from them on the unruffled surface of the water. The fire-scourged earth was covered beneath the mirrorlike calm of it all. One would never suspect the great tragedy that had occurred there only a few days back.

As vapors rose from the surface of the pond, like a veil lifting into the sunlight that was just beginning to fill the sky, the two men turned to continue their climb up the hill to the sheriff's car. They had only taken a few steps when they looked up and stopped dead in their tracks. Both men saw it at the same time. They were high enough away from the pond by now to see the hill behind the church—the hill upon which the old graveyard stood. Out of the swirling mist that rose from the ground surrounding it, they saw the indistinct form of a tall man emerge, as though he was being created right before their eyes. The rising sun, which was coming up behind Mitchell and Jennings, cast a line of light on the ground that raced toward the figure. When it reached him it moved up along his Oshkosh overalls like a shade being raised. it clearly revealed the man and the burden he carried in his arms. Jennings and Mitchell quickly realized what it was. In his arms was the little girl they had been searching for.

Garry Sorter had fallen asleep in his Packard while waiting for the storm to subside. When the pelting on the roof of his car had finally stopped, he woke up and went out to bury the box of letters beside Lettie. Somehow, he hoped the simple act of doing so would relieve the deep feelings he still had for her. He knew it would take time, possibly the rest of his life, but the despair he felt would eventually disappear, he thought—now that he no longer had the letters to touch and read.

He had been about to climb back into his car when something out of the corner of his eye caught his attention. Halfway down the hill, toward the back of the church, he saw what he thought was the arm of a doll sticking straight up out of the ground. The rain had washed away a small clump of bushes and there, in the center of a shallow pocket of wet mud, was this arm. When he took a second look, he kind of realized it was too big to belong to a doll. Then—and he wasn't too sure about it, since the sun was only just beginning to light the sky with a hazy greyness—he could have sworn it had a wristwatch on it.

Garry Sorter hurried over to it and immediately saw what it was. There was a *child* under there! He knew it was a girl because of the painted fingernails and the pink and red plastic strap on the wristwatch—the second hand on the dial was still going! That gave him a chill, even more of a chill than when he got down on his knees to dig into the mud and pull out the body of the little girl who was buried there. It only took an instant for him to see that she had been bitten in the neck by a snake. What in blazes was going on in this town! Snakes seemed to be killing everybody! He knew of the killings from stories he had read in a local newspaper that served Lettie's area. She had once sent his father a clipping from it, and he'd copied down the address and sent for a subscription. That was a long time ago. He's watched it grow from a monthly four-page tabloid to the twenty-one-page weekly that it now was. Reading it had always made him feel closer to Lettie. Once, there was even a picture of her in it—when she had won a national contest for her home-made barbecue sauce. He'd clipped it, made it himself, and thought it was good—almost like planting a bashful kiss on Lettie's very own lips. It was in the last issue of the same paper that he had learned of her death.

Now, standing in the road beside the sheriff's car, he gently laid the body of Betty Bird Johnson on the hood of Mitchell's old Peugeot. "I'm Garry Sorter," he said, wiping his hands on his overalls. "My father was a friend of Miss Lettie," he said. "We're from West Virginia. He's gone now, but I know he would have wanted me to come by and pay the last respects." He looked back up the hill to where the graveyard was. "I was about to get in my car and head on back home when I saw . . ."

He didn't have to finish what he was saying. His eyes, along with those of Mitchell and Jennings, were focused on the child's body. The mud had impregnated her clothing so that the natural color of the fabrics could not be discerned. The same was true of her hair. her flesh, except for the arm on which she still wore her ticking wristwatch, was the color of it, too. When Gary Sorter had first lifted her out of the muddy grave, her head had fallen lower than the rest of her body and gravity carried a small quantity of crimson blood to the gaping wound in her neck. It looked like a crater of molten red in the child's mud-caked neck.

Even Mitchell did not know what to say. The sun was higher now and the light from it was brighter. Without saying a word he bent over the child and lifted her arm to feel for a pulse. He knew there would be none. Plainly the child had been dead for many hours, but the simple, routinelike act helped him come to terms with his inner feelings of grief. He studied the movement of the second hand on the child's wristwatch for what seemed like an endless moment. Something about its going on like that made him feel the urgency of finally dealing with the water moccasins at the pond. Something surely had to be done, and soon—just as Winkie Bols had said all along. Winkie was right, and the town selectmen were wrong! When he looked back up and saw Bobby Jennings gazing blankly at him, he knew the radio announcer was thinking the very same thing.

It suddenly occurred to Mitchell that he hadn't spoken a single word to the man who had carried Betty Bird down the hill from the graveyard.

"What made you bring her to us?" Mitchell asked, having had to first clear his throat to do so. "Why didn't you just get her in your car and drive on into town or something?"

Garry Sorter pointed to the roof of Mitchell's old Peugeot. "Saw the red bulb," he said. "I was about to do what you just said when some light came up from down the hill and caught on it. I figured you were the police. I already had the child in my arms, so I just carried her on down. I hope I didn't cause any harm," he concluded. From having read the town newspaper regularly, Garry Sorter knew the two men he was talking to. They were the sheriff, who had seen duty in Vietnam, and who drove a 1964 Peugeot that he'd serviced himself ever since he bought it new (Garry Sorter like that. He had worked on his own 1952 Packard ever since he'd bought it new, too!), and the radio announcer, who sometimes served as the sheriff's deputy, and who'd seen his military duty in Korea. As for himself, well, Garry Sorter had seen his own duty in the Philippines at the start of WW II—one whole week of it before he took a hit in the head by some flying shrapnel and had to spend the rest of the war in a psychiatric hospital. Yessir, he thought, we're all veterans of one war or another. Garry Sorter wouldn't have dreamed of going into the details of exactly how he knew all he did about Mitchell and Jennings. Folks where he came from thought he was strange enough. He didn't want to let on to the two men before him just how strange he really was.

Bobby Jennings looked at the man. He was a farmer, he thought. His thinning grey hair, which revealed a well healed, dentlike scar at the hairline above the left ear (which Jennings wrongly guessed might be the result of a farming accident), as well as the man's honest eyes and hardworking hands showed what he was made of—and it was all good. "How'd you say you knew Miss Lettie?" he questioned.

"Didn't say," Sorter responded. "Said my daddy knew her. I . . . I just met her once, a long time ago. She and her dad came onover to West Virginia to. . . ."

"I remember now," Bobby Jennings interrupted. "Your daddy was a . . . a snake handler. Wasn't he?"

Garry Sorter nodded. "Yessir," he said, swallowing against the dryness that had begun to swell his throat.

"Lettie *did* mention something about that once," Jennings came back.

Something made Mitchell and Jennings now look at the pond as though the dead little girl on the hood of the car was no longer there. A thought more vast than the child's death had suddenly seized them. Bobby Jennings was the one to voice it.

"What, exactly, is a snake handler?" he asked. "Can they really make snakes do what they want—control them?"

In one instant Garry Sorter saw the width and breadth of the question. It made prickles stand up on the backs of his arms. "I'm afraid I can't help you with what you might be thinking," he said. "My father was a snake handler. I'm not. Never have been." Which was the truth—although, ever since having seen Lettie that one time, he had always wished he had the faith and courage it took to be one. "I can't charm the snakes away from here, if that's what you're thinking," he said, as though he had read Jenning's mind. "Don't know anyone who can, for that matter. That's not what snake handling is."

It seemed like all the hope had come out of Jennings when Sorter said that. It was blind hope, but Mitchell had felt it too. They *were* looking for a miracle, and they n ow felt a bit foolish that they'd thought they might have actually stumbled upon one.

It was Garry Sorter who now gazed at the pond as though nothing else in the whole world mattered.

Mitchell and Jennings didn't notice. They were busy wrapping the body of the dead little girl in a blanket, and finally placing her on the rear seat of the sheriff's car. When they finished, Gary Sorter was gone, as though he had just vanished into thin air. They looked up the hill to the graveyard and saw that he couldn't have headed in that direction. That much time hadn't elapsed for him to have made it all the way up to the graveyard without their seeing him on the narrow footpath that led to it. Then they looked up and down the road on which they were standing. The man was nowhere to be seen. That left only one other place. The pond. But when they looked down the hill toward it, he wasn't there, either.

"Where in *tar*-nation did he go off to?" Bobby Jennings wondered out loud, astonished that the man appeared to have evaporated into thin air—just as the morning mist was beginning to. "One minute he's standing right here beside us, and the next he's gone." He scratched the top of his head as though doing so would provide him with the answer.

Mitchell couldn't figure it, either. "He said he drove here," he finally said. "That means there's a car, probably parked on the other side of the cemetery we can't see from here." He thought for a moment. "Let's get the girl on over to Estelle's funeral parlor and call the coroner. On the way I can put out a call on the radio for a car bearing West Virginia plates. The man's no crook, thief, or murderer," he concluded with a frown. "But *something* sure made him go off like that!"

Bobby Jennings shrugged. "Maybe he's afraid of snakes," he said climbing into the car beside Mitchell—who was already reaching for the radio phone. "Maybe he's just plain and simple afraid of snakes," he repeated, staring blankly ahead through the windshield.

Maybe it was because they had been so tired from being out all night, or because of all the wondering they were doing about how they were going to tell the town meeting that night—but, had they just looked down at their feet before climbing into the car, they would have seen where the man from West Virginia had disappeared to. Right off the edge of the road, beneath the lip of a culvert that carried water down the hill from the other side of the road behind them, Garry Sorter crouched beneath a crystal-clear fan of cascading water. He was now waiting for them to leave—waiting to do something he had all his life dreamed of doing, but had never had, until now, the courage or the conviction it took to try.

CHAPTER THIRTY-SIX

This forbidden mountain range is a place of whispers. One can, at times, feel the hushed silence of the caves come alive with voices of the dead. They murmur out over the barren plane on which these mountains rise in a voice that is indistinguishable from the woeful cries of wildlife being trapped and killed by the natives. Tortured sounds. Sounds of whispered longings to be free. They fill the infrequent visitor with a sense of dread that goes to the core of one's soul. It is a terrible place. A place where aberrant sorcerers were once banished, centuries and centuries before anyone can remember. A place that offered them no means of escape, their magic was so evil. Here, they lived out their lives in isolation, unloved and unloving, in caves chewed out of granite rock through millenniums of biting time. When all is still, it is a place of inspiration. When the wind howls, awakening the cries and whispers of those who had been left here to die, it is a place more terrifying than the thought of hell.

Sara Garrett looked up from the handwritten manuscript that Ginny's mother had been writing when she died. There was a neatly typed note card clipped to it. It told the reader that Mrs. Watkins, then only twenty-four, had died in one of those caves while giving birth to her only child, a daughter. The manuscript had been recovered by native guides when she'd failed to return to camp the following day. She had also made a number of pen and ink drawings of the wall paintings in the cave in which she'd died. These were meant to accompany the text of her manuscript. "Unfortunately," so the neatly typed note card continued—as though some nice lady librarian were apologizing for an obvious blunder that was beyond her control—"the drawings are now to be found in the art annex."

"Where's the art annex?" Sara asked a young woman student who was seated behind a librarian's desk. She was reading Proust and had to look up slowly in order not to lose the thread of the author's thought—which up to that point had run to almost three hundred pages.

"Art annex?" She squinted at Sara. Then something in her eyes focused. "Oh, the art annex," she said, removing her John Lennon eyeglasses. "It's closed, but we can get you something from it if you fill out this call slip." She offered Sara a small pink slip of paper.

"How long will it take?"

The young woman thought. "You can probably have it by tomorrow. First thing in the morning," she amended after checking a laminated index card that was taped to the desktop.

"Tomorrow's Saturday," Sara said. "How late does the library stay open?"

"Until noon," the woman answered. "But if you fill out the slip, the book you want can be here first thing in the morning. We open at nine."

Sara thanked the woman and filled out the call slip and left.

She had had a terrible night. First there were the

snakes at the porch, coiling and leaping into the air after what had seemed to be a downpour of toads. Then there was that chilling laughter she was sure had come from the room above the porch, the room in which Ginny was supposed to be asleep.

Outside the college library she drew in a deep breath of fresh air. It helped ease her tension. She looked up into the clear blue sky and shielded her eyes from the sun. The storm of the night before seemed a distant memory, one easily forgotton in the brilliance of the endless azure that filled the cloudless sky. It matched anything she had ever seen in Africa.

Something made her look down the hill toward the pond. It looked much larger than she had remembered seeing it that day from the window of the cottage. She had wanted to go down and have a better look at it before she left town, and this now seemed like a good time to do it. Ginny was at school and wouldn't be home until much later that afternoon. It wasn't even lunchtime yet . . . and . . . there were her own abstract thoughts to be contended with. She had a feeling she'd be able to sort things out if she took a few minutes off, right now, to find someplace where she could be alone—someplace where she could sit peacefully and gaze at the pond for a while, without getting too close. She remembered such a place. It was over toward town. There was a paved road from which an unobstructed view of the water could be had. She remembered passing the spot, several times, on the way to the graveyard.

Garry Sorter really didn't know what he was thinking about when he hid beneath the lip of the culvert, where Mitchell and Jennings couldn't see him from the road. His mind had been a jumbled mass of images and words—Scripture words he had often heard his father recite, and images of his daddy picking up and handling all sorts of poisonous snakes. Sometimes the old man would pick up a copperhead along the road and put it inside his shirt and bring it home with him. Then he'd pull it out at dinner and stick it in a sack. *Plum forgot about that one!* he'd say, closing the burlap sack full of vipers he'd use for his services in the woods—a sack that was always kept out on the back porch.

Little Garry Sorter was the only one in the whole family who never used the back porch to get into the house. He always used the front way in, even though the teasing he had to endure over it was almost more than he could bear. He swore to himself that he would someday overcome that fear. His only regret, right now, as he waded out into the shallows of the pond, was that his father wasn't still alive to see him.

"Yiii-*eeeee*!" he shouted, holding a water moccasin high into the air above his head. He had a good grip on the thing, too. Right in the circle of his tightened fist, the viper was caught as though a trapper's snare had been looped around its neck. "Got me another one! You see that, Father?" he asked the sky. "I'm not afraid of them anymore. I'm gonna be a hero! Gonna get me every snake in this here town and . . . "

To demonstrate what he meant, he reenacted a scene he had been performing for the greater part of that morning: He carefully slipped his pointing finger up along the back of the snake's head, while maneuvering his thumb beneath its slippery chin—thus clasping the viper's jaws tightly shut. Then he cautiously brought the head to his own mouth . . . and crushed its skull between his teeth—taking care not to break the skin lest the serpent's venom might gush into his mouth. Each time he heard the crunching noise of the snake's skull shattering in his mouth, he held the lifeless, twitching thing high in the air and smiled a crooked smile. "See that, Daddy?" he again addressed the sky. Then he stuffed the dead water moccasin into a makeshift sack he had already made by tying bulky knots at the ends of each leg of his Oshkosh. It was looped in the crook of one of his arms by the overalls' wide straps and brass-plated buckles. "See how easy it is to catch 'em and kill 'em?" he said, still speaking to the memory of his dead father. "Bet you could never do a thing like that! And I ain't using no Scripture talk, either. Snakes is varmints! Never to be worshiped, like you did. Like you wanted me to!"

Ever since he had taken that shot of shrapnel in the head, and spent the rest of the war in a lunatic asylum, even *he* knew he was not altogether right in the head. But it didn't seem to matter anymore. He had killed some thirty water moccasins that morning, and he was aiming to get himself a whole lot more.

On her way to the pond Sara thought of the breakfast she had had with Ginny before the girl went off to school that morning:

"Did you have a funny dream last night?" she had asked Ginny.

Ginny looked at her and frowned. "No," she said. "I

don't think so. Why?"

Sara shrugged, not wanting to betray the chill she'd felt the night before when she'd thought she had heard Ginny laugh as the snakes leaped up at the frogs outside the screened-in porch.

"I guess it must have been all that rain last night," Sara replied. "But I thought I heard you laughing in your sleep."

Ginny quietly laughed. It was as warm and bright and as innocent as the sunlight that streamed into Lettie's comfortable old kitchen.

Sara had been buttering a piece of toast when Ginny reacted to her remark with that bubble laughter of hers. There was something about the sound of it that was totally different from what she had heard the night before. It reminded Sara of when she herself was a child. She and her mother used to sit in the cozy kitchen of their New England home and giggle and laugh about all sorts of things. It was in that kitchen that there was also some very serious talk. She looked at Ginny across the table and felt the void that would someday swell within the child. It was a void she knew something about. She hoped to help Ginny bridge it.

"I have a secret I've never told anyone," Sara said when she stopped buttering her toast.

Ginny looked up and squinted. "What's that?" she asked. She had never had an adult confide in her. It made her eyes widen with anticipation.

Sara placed her toast on the napkin beside her plate and looked directly into Ginny's large blue eyes. "I never knew my father," she said. "He died before I was born. My mother raised me until I was about your age. Then she died. But that's not the secret," Sara said. She picked up the piece of toast and nibbled at the corner of it. When she swallowed, she said. "The secret, that I've always kept deep down inside of me, is that if I live to be a thousand years old, I'll never get over being angry that my parents died and left me all alone in the world. It's a terrible feeling."

For a long moment they both looked into each other's eyes with an understanding warmth that hadn't been there before.

"How about you, Ginny?" Sara finally asked. "Do you have any secrets?"

It was a while before Ginny was able to speak. When she finally did, she lowered her eyes to her breakfast plate. "I don't think I'm going to miss my father very much," she said softly. "But I always wished my mother was here."

The direct and total honesty of Ginny's response had startled Sara. As the girl lowered her eyes to her plate, Sara thought she was searching for a way to avoid answering. She had been about to tell the girl how sorry she had been about asking such a question—sorry that she had even brought the subject up in the first place. But before she could say so, Ginny had looked up and said something Sara would remember for the rest of her life.

"Don't worry," Ginny had told her as they hugged each other. "I don't care anymore. Now that you're here."

He looked like some sort of a sea creature out there in the water, reaching down and so effortlessly scooping up moccasin after moccasin, snapping their heads in his strong jaws, then stuffing them into the Oshkosh sack he had rigged up. He didn't know what he was going to do with all the dead snakes when he finished. He didn't care. What he was doing was better that all of WW II. He had the enemy now, and they were his!

"Yiii-*eeeee!*" he screamed, grasping another one behind the neck and gingerly crushing its skull between his teeth. "Yiii-*eeeee*!"

Sara head the shrieks coming from the direction of the pond long before she ever arrived at the point along the graveyard road where she could get a clear look at it. When she did, she stared down the hill in complete bewilderment. There was a man standing in the water up to his waist, grappling up one water moccasin after the other in his bare hand, and . . . when she suddenly realized what he was doing to them, before stuffing them into the sack that was looped to one of his arms, she recoiled in horror. The man must be insane!

Garry Sorter turned at that instant and saw Sara standing at the top of the hill, holding the back of one hand to her mouth. He smiled and waved a dead water moccasin at her, as though it were the ear of a killed bull in an arena. Had he not broken his concentration, focusing all his attention on showing her how much of a hero he was, he might have seen what was happening behind him. Sara saw it, but she couldn't get the words out of her mouth fast enough to warn him.

Behind Garry Sorter, with their heads poked up out of the water so that they left long V-like channels on the calm surface of the pond, a squadron of moccasins was headed his way. He saw the horrified expression in

Sara's eyes, and heard the words of her warning too late. By the time he turned, they were right up on him. They hit with such force that it tumbled him over. There must have been a hundred of them.

He never screamed, not once. Sara did that, when she saw him being carried out to the center of the pond and dragged beneath the bubbling water. As she watched in horror, Garry Sorter's blood rose to the top of the pond and spilled across its boiling surface like an oil slick from a sunken war boat.

Loren Mitchell held his hand down on the receiver of the phone for a long time after hanging up, as though the pressure of his hand upon it would also serve to cut the connection with the grief he was feeling. He had just informed Betty Bird's parents that she was over at the funeral home, and that the coroner had just confirmed she had died of a snakebite. He left out all the other details.

Jennings stood beside him, too embarrassed to look at the sheriff, too embarrassed about his own feelings of grief to have Mitchell see what he looked like. He turned himself slightly and stared out the window, looking down the road as though it would carry him somewhere else—someplace where the past two weeks hadn't happened. When the silence finally got to him, he cleared his throat.

"So it's settled then," he finally said, clearing his throat a second time.

Mitchell looked up at him. His mind had been a long ways off, too. "What's that?" he asked, finally lifting his hand from the telephone receiver.

"Town meeting," Jennings responded with some firmness returning to his voice. "All I have to do is mention this thing about the little Johnson girl on the air and follow it with a call for a meeting. There'll be no resistance to getting something done about them mocs this time, I can tell you that!"

As Mitchell went to a locker for some coffee, Jennings rehearsed some of the impromptu lines he would use to persuade the selectmen to convene an emergency meeting on the matter. He wouldn't use the word *election* at all, but they would hear it all right, nice and clear.

"By the time I finish with them," Jennings thought out loud, "them young pups are gonna wish they had me up there with them, on *their* side!"

Mitchell smiled and opened the tall metal locker for the jar of instant coffee he kept there. His smile faded when he looked up and saw his reflection in the fly-specked mirror that was hanging on the inside of the door. Having been out in the storm all night, he looked like a wreck—so did Jennings. "Let's have ourselves a cup of coffee and wash up," he said. "Then we can take us a look up at the graveyard and see if that fellow left his car there. No one's responded to my call for a man driving a car with West Virginia plates—so maybe he's still around. And if he is, we want to know why he disappeared like he did."

It wasn't that he wanted to take one last look at himself in the locker mirror before closing the door, but something in the spotted and age-stained glass caught his attention. It wasn't his image, either. He saw, reflected in the mirror, something moving very rapidly outside the window behind him. When he turned, he saw that Jennings was staring at it, too. There, racing up to the office, in what seemed like a fit of hysteria, was Sara Garrett. Her arms were flying every which way and she was screaming something that neither of them could make out. Both men were seized with the notion that something terrible had just happened to little Ginny Watkins. And it was with something close to relief that they learned, when they rushed out to meet her on the road, that they were wrong. A man, probably the same man who had found the body of Betty Bird Johnson, had just been killed by snakes at the pond.

"They . . . they dragged him under," Sara gasped. "I . . . I watched. His body's still out there. Floating. They're . . . they're *eating* him!"

CHAPTER THIRTY-SEVEN

The sixth grade had been rehearsing the African play, "The Spear," in the school gymnasium when the news came in that the body of Betty Bird Johnson had just been found. Louise Walden, the principal, was so upset that she called the superintendent of schools and petitioned him for permission to dismiss classes for the rest of the day. It was Friday, a cold-lunch day, and the sandwiches could be saved in the school's refrigerators. By midmorning, after the superintendent had had a brief telephone conversation with the president of the local school board, permission to do so was granted, and it was easy to see why. Almost everyone, from the school board president on down to the principal and several of the teachers, had children attending the school. On the day when news arrives that a child has been killed by a snake, everyone wanted to be at home with their own.

Those children who had been rehearsing were still in their costumes when the news of the school closing arrived. The boys, in loincloths made of terry cloth towels that had been watercolored to resemble leopard skins and zebra pelts, hurried to their lockers and changed; while the girls, in hand-painted terry togas that resembled giraffe skin, did the same thing.

Ginny, still wearing her costume, didn't leave the girl's locker room with the rest of her classmates. As the other girls were changing and gathering up their books to go home, Ginny, when no one was looking, squeezed herself into her locker and waited for everyone to leave. Even her teacher, Mrs. Peabody, didn't notice she was missing when she led the rest of the class out of the school.

It was hot in the locker, and when Ginny finally heard the school grow silent, she emerged from it dripping with perspiration. Mrs. Walden, the principal, was always quick to cut the air conditioning off when it was not needed. The dank locker room was almost as hot as the inside of Ginny's locker had been. And the gymnasium, which was right through the double set of swinging doors, was even hotter.

She now stood in her bare feet and stared at the African stage set of the play her grade had been rehearsing. Somehow the painted scenery had taken on an aura of reality for her. During the rehearsal she had become lost in the painted mountains, rivers and streams that engulfed more than half of the entire gym. It had been a final dress rehearsal, with everything in place, just as it was going to be presented the first thing Monday morning. Everyone was supposed to know their lines, and those who didn't have speaking parts—like the dancers—had to know their cues.

Ginny was the main dancer, though she hadn't always been. She had started out, at first, in the last row. Then, with each successive rehearsal, she was directed to a more prominent position—until she now dominated the center of the stage. It was in the dance that she had somehow become lost and the set about her had become real. When she had glanced at the painted sky as she moved to the throbbing drumbeat vibrating from the phonograph, the clouds and brightly painted birds had appeared to move. In the mountains, rivers and streams flowed. And at her feet, the polished wooden floor became a trampled plain. It was while they were in the middle of the dance routine that the news of Betty Bird's death had arrived.

Ginny was now in the center of the set. About her were the papier-maché trees, bushes, hills, and rocks that represented Africa. Her body was smoldering, aching to begin; she was aching to immerse herself once again in the reality of the dance and become lost in its heated beat. She stepped out of the uncomfortable terry "giraffe skin" toga that had always constricted her movements. The only thing she then had on were her cotton panties. She slipped them off and went to the prop box, where she knew there was a short skirt made from the spiked leaves of a palm tree. She tied it about her waist and listened to its rustle as she snapped her hips—it fit her perfectly. There would be plenty of room for her to move about in it, she thought. Then she picked up the spear that figured so importantly in the play. It was made from the slender branch of a young fruit tree, peeled clean of its bark and tipped with a pointed stone that was tied to a notch at one of its ends. Ginny had made it herself—just like the real thing, which she had seen in and copied from a book. Mrs. Peabody, her teacher, had wanted her to paint the tip-stone silver. Ginny had resisted, strongly arguing for authenticity, and had won. She now walked with it to the large phonograph that was off to the side of the set. It was on a classroom desk, atop a thickly folded blanket that had cushioned it against the vibrations of the children's pounding feet. Over half a dozen speakers were hidden behind the sprawling semicircle of trees and shrubbery that ran in front of the painted backdrop of mountains at the rear of the set. The record was still on the turntable, right where it was when everyone left. She now turned it on and placed the needle in the first groove. There would be at least thirty minutes of uninterrupted drumming to dance to. More than she had ever danced to before. Her body glistened with rivulets of perspiration as she raced back to the center of the set, spear in hand, ready to start the moment the drums began—ready to lose herself once again in the rhythm of the tribal beat.

Louise Walden was in the principal's office down the hall from the gym, speaking on the telephone with the superintendent of schools again—about how orderly the dismissal had gone—while her son, Tommy, a first grader at the same school, leafed through the copy of *National Geographic* he had taken from his mother's book rack beside her desk. For a six-year-old, he was being very patient about waiting for her to take him home—where he could watch television. Tommy wore a hearing aid in his right ear. There was no use bothering with his left ear. In that, he was completely deaf—all an accident of birth. He was also dumb, having been born with a paralyzed larynx. He heard well enough with the aid, but had developed a permanent squint in his eyes, the result of trying to read the words as they left someone's lips. He also knew how to sign with his fingers and hands. His mother had taught him how—insurance against the day when, so the doctors had told her, he would lose whatever little hearing he had left. He didn't bother keeping his hearing aid turned on all the time, either. If no one was talking right at you, he thought, what was the sense of keeping it turned on all the time?

Right now, Tommy's hearing aid was off. But, it was *as though* he could hear something. He looked up from the *National Geographic* and squinted first at his mother. Her lips were moving noiselessly against the receiver of the phone. No, he thought. It wasn't her. Then he squinted at the closed door of her office, reached up behind his right ear and turned the aid up high. He still didn't hear anything. It must be that he . . . felt the noise. Like the storm last night, it had made such a racket he could "hear" it, even though he hadn't even been wearing the aid. It was the same way he could also hear things like heavy footsteps, or the "sound" heavy objects made when they dropped to the floor.

Tommy caught his mother's attention for a moment

and signed to her that he was going to the bathroom. Without interrupting the telephone conversation she was having, she signed back that he should be quick about it because they would shortly be leaving for home.

The gymnasium throbbed like the beating of a thousand racing hearts as Ginny swirled, jumped, and stamped about the set. Her breasts were swollen and red, the tiny nipples erect. The sweat evaporated from her undulating body and lifted from her shoulders in a fine mistlike vapor. She wasn't herself anymore. Something deep within her had taken over, abandoning itself to the rhythmic surge of the incessant drumbeat that reverberated through the papier-maché set of the African landscape.

She was a Goddess, a God, a Demon! She didn't know which. She didn't care. Her eyes were closed and she was in the midst of creation itself. She swung her spear, and in its wake, the sky came into existence. Poking at its azure blankness with the stone point created the clouds, the stars, the moon, and all the tiny creatures that flew with brightly colored wings. Her palm-leaf skirt clattered like a field of locusts as her pelvis trembled, and the earth was born. Stamping her feet rapidly up and down cooled the fires and created mountains, rolling hills, and lush green valleys. Slicing the air with the bottom edge of one hand, as though it were a knife cutting pieces of bread, created streams and rivers. Point and point and point, and point again, the spear created trees and shrubs and grassy plains.

It was a world that was as vivid in her mind as was the sight that greeted little Tommy Walden's startled eyes when he gingerly opened the heavy door of the gym a crack, just to see what he thought he might have "heard" coming from it. He gasped at Ginny's nudity, at the wild dancing-prancing-leaping frenzy she was in. The beat vibrated into his small body. Every cell in his body jumped with the abstract, almost nightmarish quality of the scene he had so unexpectedly stumbled upon.

Once Louise Walden got off the phone with the superintendent she had heard the drumming, too. Her first thought before leaving the office to investigate, was that her son had wandered into the gymnasium and turned on the phonograph. Then, as she stepped out into the corridor she saw him charging down the hallway, signing wildly at her. Something was wrong. The open palm of his right hand repeatedly lifted the closed fist of the other. The sign meant *aid, assist, help!* She thought he must have broken the phonograph and couldn't get the thing turned off. But he was too frantic for something as innocent as that. There were even tears streaming down his hot cheeks.

What is it? She signed before he reached her. *What's wrong?*

Tommy clung to her tightly and noiselessly sobbed.

Her hair dripped with sweat, and beadlets shot from its wispy ends as she swirled and twisted through the gym. The voice had gotten into her again. It told her not to love Sara—only the snakes. If she did, they would be angry with her—It, the voice, would be angry with her. She tried to balance the inner urgings against the throbbing beat of her feet on the wooden floor. They hammered to the rhythm of the drums as though they were one. Her feet moved up and down so rapidly it was as though she hovered in the air, suspended in a magic that was as real to her as the sight that befell Louise Walden's eyes when she entered the gym with Tommy clutched to her side.

"What is this!?" the principal demanded. "What in the name of God is going on?"

Ginny continued to prance in an apparent state of ecstasy, she pointed the spear at the principal. Words poured from her lips in a cadence that matched the rapid flutter of her feet upon the floor. Staggering words. Surprising sounds. Grunts and echoes from the hollow vastness of a darkened vault. Louise Walden didn't understand. Neither did Tommy, who squinted at Ginny's lips. Though neither he nor his mother understood the dark language that Ginny spewed at them, they felt the dread of it—the forbidden terror that was locked up behind the unknown sound.

Instinctively, Louise Walden reached for Tommy's hand. Something had gone terribly wrong with Ginny. It probably had something to do with her father's recent death, she thought. But with that spear pointed directly at her, Louise Walden wasn't about to attempt an instant therapy session with the naked child—not with her Tommy there, not with the feeling of dread that was now trickling into her veins like drops of stinging acid, spreading itself through her body as rapidly as the vibrant voice of the drums.

As she reached for the door, something made her turn to take one last look at the spear in Ginny's hand. There was something about it that . . . .

The spear! It was now twisted about Ginny's arm. It wasn't a spear—it was a snake! A huge water moccasin with gaping jaws!

An audible gasp came from Tommy's paralyzed larynx. It was the first clearly distinguishable sound he had ever uttered. But his mother hardly noticed. She was paralyzed in a shroud of frozen terror as she watched the snake uncoil from Ginny's arm and race toward them with a jerky quickness that could only occur in a dream. And for one fleeting moment she thought it might be a dream, but the notion immediately faded as the serpent shot up from the floor and sank its fangs deeply into her throat.

Louise Walden struggled and finally fell backward with the snake coiled to her neck. It struck her repeatedly between the chin and throat until it opened a flapping, blood-gushing wound. Blood spurted out in a pumping rhythm before her heart finally stopped beating. Tommy was covered with the crimson sliminess of it. He did the only thing he knew to save his mother. As the snake was chewing its way into his mother's throat, he fell upon the serpent and began to bite it. But it didn't work. The six-year-old's teeth were too small, too young to penetrate the serpent's scaly hide. It merely ignored him until it was through with his mother. Then it turned on him.

Ginny laughed, not so much for the carnage that had just taken place before her eyes, but for something else as well. From between her legs, blood dripped onto the highly polished wooden floor.

Blood! She was a *woman!*

The laugh she now laughed came from the inner madness of her own dark power—a power, now that she was a woman, that was on its way to becoming fully realized.

CHAPTER THIRTY-EIGHT

While Mitchell and the local rescue team were fishing out what remained of Garry Sorter's body from the pond, Sara sat out on the back porch of the house. She was in a daze. The image of the man at the pond being eaten alive by what appeared to be hundreds of water moccasins had etched itself so deeply into the cellular structure of her retinal matter that every time she blinked, a picture of the whole scene would once again flash before her mind. Why hadn't the snakes attacked him before she got there? she wondered. Judging by the sackful of them he had looped to his arm, he had been there, doing that dreadful thing to kill them, for some time. It almost seemed as though the water moccasins had waited for her to arrive—as though the attack upon the man had been some sort of a warning. To *her.*

The thought of Melissa Malikoff's words—that the snake killings would continue, and that she was the only one who could stop them—now caused her an anguish she had never known before. Behind it all there had to be the reason she had accepted the invitation to speak at the college. She had never before given a paper, and had never had the desire to do so. So why? she probed. Why this particular conference, in this particular town?

Sara had never believed that life was simply a set of unrelated circumstances. Everything had a place. Everything had to fit. There *was* meaning to it all. She simply had to piece it together. That she had knowledge of African sorcery, and that she was now taking care of a child who had been born in Africa, a child whose mother had died there while working on a book that touched on sorcery, were not, in her mind mere coincidences.

Ginny had been standing in the kitchen looking out at Sara on the porch for a long time. When she'd first arrived she had wanted to burst in and tell her the news about her period starting. But something held her back. She was thinking of Sara, again, as she might have thought of her own mother. If only she could tell Sara about the snakes, she thought. She would understand. She would know. And maybe, together, they could. . . .

That's what it's like to have a mother, she thought, someone she could tell anything to, and be loved, even though what she was doing was bad. The only thing that really loved her was the dark thing inside of her—and it told her so. Told her in such a way that she clearly understood she must never love Sara, or anyone else. If she ever did, there would be a terrible price to pay.

Without saying a word, Ginny quietly left the kitchen and went upstairs to her room. She would slip out of her sweaty clothes and take a bath—wash away her childhood, and welcome the birth of her womanhood.

CHAPTER THIRTY-NINE

Once the news about the deaths of Betty Bird Johnson, Louise Walden, and her son Tommy got around (to say nothing of the bizarre stranger who had been half-eaten alive by the water moccasins at the pond) Bobby Jennings didn't even have to ask for an emergency town meeting. All he had to do was read off, over the air, the names of everyone the snakes had killed so far.

REVEREND WATKINS
HARVEY and NANCY OCEAN
WINKIE BOLS
JUDD WINSLOW
JERRY KNOX
JAMES and EDNA MALIKOFF
BETTY BIRD JOHNSON
GARRY SORTER
LOUISE and TOMMY WALDEN

There were twelve of them in all, including the stranger—but not including Sally, his pet doberman. That was too personal.

By the time Jennings was through reading the names of the snakebite victims, the telephone in his tiny broadcast shack had begun to ring off the wall. The first call was from Jeffrey Hollister, spokesman for the board of selectmen. He said the board had already met earlier that day and wanted him to announce a meeting for that very night. There was now an urgent need to get something done about that snake-infested pond—once and for all.

(Funny, Bobby Jennings had felt like saying over the air, *but those were the exact same words that Winkie Bols used just about a week ago.)*

There had been too much procrastination, Jeffrey Hollister continued, and too many people were now dead. When Winkie Bols had first asked that the town put its whole mind to the problem, there had only been the death of Reverend Watkins to consider. Now, in the ten days since the minister was gone, there were a dozen more—half of them occurring within the past forty-eight hours! It seemed obvious that the problem was growing and speeding up, all at the same time. That was why, Hollister concluded, the selectmen were urging as many people as possible to attend tonight's emergency meeting at the grange hall.

Seventy-five people showed up for the meeting, in forty-nine cars, station wagons, pickups, and one blue van that carried the license plate sticker of the state capital. The gathering represented almost ten percent of the total population of the town—the largest turnout for any town meeting that most folks there could recollect. There were so many of them, in fact, that the grange hall (above the three-table billiard parlor in the center of town) was too small to hold them. So, all seventy-five citizens, plus seven selectmen, climbed into the vehicles that had carried them to the meeting and silently drove through the center of town to the church—which was one of the structures, other than the school and Estelle Whidden's funeral parlor, that could accommodate such a large group.

As Jennings now looked about the inside of the white clapboard structure where the Reverend Watkins had been killed less than two weeks before, he studied the faces of the people who were still entering and gathering in the pews. Even the selectmen, who were taking their places on the hardwood folding chairs they had carried from the rectory, were craning their necks up toward the rafters to make sure there were no snakes getting ready to drop down on them. He turned to Mitchell, who was seated beside him, and in whose car he had shared a ride to the meeting, and his tired eyes smiled a very faint smile. Mitchell nodded, and looked up toward the exposed rafters to indicate he knew what Jennings was thinking: One, it would be a quick meeting, and, two, it would be resolved that something would finally be done about the snakes—just as Winkie had suggested several days ago.

Once everyone was seated and quiet, Jeffrey Hollister, tall and lanky, stood up and called the meeting to order. There was no table to separate the selectmen from the townsfolk, and there was no gavel to strike. He simply stood up, involuntarily shot a glance up toward the rafters as he cleared his throat, and then began earnestly to address the townspeople.

"To get right with it," he said. "The first thing we did this morning, after the news of the most recent deaths came in, was to call the state capital and ask them for some emergency assistance."

There was a rustle among the gathering. Nobody needed the state to do anything for them. All they had to do was to burn the pond down (as Winkie Bols had suggested—only don't set out to do it when you're dead drunk!), or drain the pond, or spill poison into the pond, or pour concrete into the darn thing, paint it green and make a useful playing field for the children. There was no end to the ideas people now popped up with. They didn't need any assistance from the state. Every time the state did anything for you they wanted to raise your taxes, anyway.

"I know. I know," Jeffrey Hollister said, raising his hands in an attempt to restore order. "But we thought," he continued once it grew reasonably quiet again, "that if we had only called the state to begin with, right after Reverend Watkins was killed. . . ." (Almost everyone there looked up toward the roof of the church and tucked their necks in a bit.) ". . . a good many people who are gone today would still be here!"

Well, folks weren't so sure about that. If the selectmen had approved Winkie's plan in the first place, it could have been carried out in a more clear-headed way. Take every man in town, set him in a specific task, insure that the proper safety precautions will be taken, and go to it!

That caught the selectmen staring at their shoes for

a moment or two. One of them rippled his shoulders, as though he was about to say something, but he was restrained by another selectman at his side. The gesture wasn't lost on anyone—especially Jennings. "Them fools are real guilty about it all," he whispered to Mitchell. The sheriff looked at him and whispered back, "Wouldn't you be?"

Jennings sat back. That was the thing about Mitchell, he thought. He never liked to fault anyone—anyone but his own self, like *he* was responsible for the snakes all going crazy like they were. When Mitchell had come home from the army he could have had any big city job he'd wanted. But he'd chosen to stay right there where he was raised, to do a job he'd have been paid ten times as much for in any city. Except for feeling guilty every time something bad happened in town, it seemed he was content. But something was missing. If he would only go out and find himself a wife, maybe that would complete him, Jennings thought. Maybe then he'd quit faulting himself about everything.

Jeffrey Hollister drew the edges of his lips in tightly. Whenever the selectmen were in a jam, he was the one who could pull them out. His voice was as smooth as honey, and his heart was just as pure. Folks knew it, respected him for it. "I can't say that we didn't make a mistake by not listening to Winkie," he said, leveling his chin. And he didn't have to say any more. It was an apology that everyone there could understand. How would they have acted if a drinking man had made such a proposal to them? At the time there had been only that one death of the minister, and that had looked as though it might have been some sort of freak accident. But not anymore.

"As I said before," Hollister continued, "we asked the state for some emergency assistance, and this is what they sent." He pointed toward the rear of the church. "If you stand up and look toward the doors you can see what I'm talking about."

When the gathering did as they had been asked, what they saw in the strong beam of the outside light that was mounted above the wide-open doors of the church puzzled them. It was the blue van that had followed them from the grange, the one with the sticker of the state capital on its license plate. Two men in orange coveralls were unloading a stack of long wooden crates that had rope handles on each end. They looked like coffins.

They came up easily over the lip of the roadway across from the church. Many of them had taken part in the feast that had taken place at the pond that afternoon. They had attacked and eaten most of the man they had pulled out into the center of it, all but the chunk of meat—all that was left of his body—that was fished out of the water by the town rescue team. The scales on their bellies dug deeply into the soft earth as they hastily made their separate ways toward the flock of cars that were parked all about the church-grounds. They lifted their heads and focused their hard black eyes on the undersides of all the vehicles.

Teams of them tested coils, springs, pans and rods. Mufflers and pipes were still hot, so they were avoided as the moccasins raised themselves up into the blackness at the bottoms of all the cars, station wagons and pickups.

When the men in the orange coveralls had stacked all the boxes in frcnt of the selectmen, they left without a word. The townspeople, who had for some curious reason remained standing while the unloading was going on, now sat back down.

"This," said Jeffrey Hollister, spreading his hands across the stack of twelve coffinlike boxes, "is what the state has sent us in the meantime." He paused, dramatically.

"In the meantime," Hollister repeated. "We can use what's in these boxes until the national guard gets here tomorrow, or the next day at the latest. They have a special unit of about a hundred men who've been training with some kind of new electronic device—used in clearing jungles. It's supposed to drive snakes off in a hurry. They think they can get this whole mess cleaned up in one day—no chemicals, no trenches, no chopping down trees, and no fires. They promise to do it all with this new electronic. . ."

"If the mocs don't do it to them first!" someone called out. And, for the first time in that grim night, there was laughter. Even Hollister had to repress a quiet chuckle. A loosening of tension was felt by everyone.

"What's in them boxes?" someone else asked.

Hollister looked at the pile of them where he stood and said, "Well, why don't we just have ourselves a look."

The two men in orange coveralls drove carefully along the dark and unfamiliar road. They hardly spoke a word. Not that they were angry with each other; but they were angry that they had to make the long drive from Austin to this town, a distance of almost three hundred miles. Four hours one way. Allow one or two hours for loading and unloading. And that came out to be somewhere between nine and ten hours—not counting stops to eat. When they had reported for work at the state supply depot that morning, they had never expected the day would be that long. They hadn't even had a chance to go to the bathroom before leaving Wilston, and they were hungry, too. But every eating place they now passed along the road was closed.

"Shee-it!" one of them said. "Let's stop here for a minute before I bust."

The driver, a soft, fat, balding man, pulled the van to a gentle stop along the side of the pitch-black road. "Me, too!" he said. He left the lights on as they both stepped out to relieve themselves in the darkness on the side of the van that faced away from the road.

They didn't know what they had delivered to the town. They didn't even know what the problem there had been. And they didn't know what hit them. All they heard, in the split second before they clutched their throats in stinging pain, was something that sounded like the ruffling of a cloth sheet being unfurled in a stiff breeze. They were dead before their bladders were fully emptied.

It had taken a while to get that first box opened. But when it was, the selectmen gathered about it and frowned. Jeffrey Hollister thought there must have been some sort of a mistake. He went back to his chair and picked up the large brown envelope that the men had handed him before leaving. It was a packing manifest for the contents of the boxes. He began to read it out loud: "Seven hundred and fifty pair of snakeproof leg gaiters . . . adjustable to fit any size. Seven hundred and fifty pair of heavy duty gloves . . . broken down into two hundred and fifty pair each of the following sizes—small, medium and large. One hundred and fifty snakebite kits . . . reusable. Emergency medication, tourniquets, and seven hundred and fifty snake catching poles!"

The last item caused a lot of frowns. Hollister lifted one out of the open box and showed it around. It was an aluminum pole, about three feet long, and had a slotted handle like a shovel's, while the other end was forked like a Y. A leather thong was attached near the Y and hung down loosely from several inches above the fork, where it could easily be looped over a snake's head once it was pinned to the ground beneath the fork.

Even Jeffrey Hollister was disappointed, as well as puzzled. "What do they expect us to do?" he wondered out loud. "Go out and hunt the darn things down ourselves?"

"The state isn't sending in any national guard unit," someone in the crowd said. "Them boxes is their way of telling us to go do it on our own!"

And a surge of anger shot through the crowd like a sudden jolt of electricity. Everyone was on their feet, shouting something or other that couldn't be made out because of the roar. It seemed everyone wanted blood. It almost seemed as though they were ready to do something, too, something that would probably be as irrational and as ill-thought-out as what Winkie Bols and his two pals had done. That was when Loren Mitchell pushed himself through the swirling knot of people at the boxes and called for order. When he didn't get it, he removed his .45 Smith and Wesson from his holster. That quieted most of them right away. When he then removed the clip, so it wouldn't go off and shoot anyone, and hammered its butt on the lid of one of the wooden boxes, the noise of it quieted down the rest.

"I appreciate your not having to have me put a rain hole in the roof of this church," he said when he had everyone's attention. "But you all heard what Jeffrey said. The state will be here tomorrow, or the day after at the very latest. If we go out tonight and try to get everything done ourselves, a lot of people are going to get hurt. It would take us from now till dawn to get ourselves a safe plan that would work, anyway. There would be tools needed, trucks, tractors, and God only knows what else. Not only that, but we would first have to come to terms with what it is that has to be done. Everything that was suggested earlier had the taste of something wrong with it. Burning the pond with gasoline, like Winkie wanted, can wreck the whole town—spread right on up the hill and take the college, too. Draining the pond sounds good. But does anyone here know how to drain a down-the-hill pond? The water would have to be pumped out and carried away. It would probably take a couple of thousand trips. And where on earth do we get the pump trucks to do it? Even then I'm not sure the snakes would go away. Poison the pond and you poison everything else—the trees, the fish, even the birds that feed on the insects will disappear. And whoever it was that said we should pour concrete into the pond and paint it over, well, I'm not even going to comment on that."

People relaxed a little after that. No, they certainly didn't want to go off and do some fool thing in the middle of the night, possibly get themselves killed.

"Then what should we do, sheriff?" somebody questioned.

Mitchell looked at the man who asked. He was a farmer, just like his own father had been—just like he himself would have been if he hadn't been elected sheriff over twenty years ago. "Wait," he answered simply. "Wait the two days, just like Jeffrey suggested. I don't know what these new electronic devices are that the national guard has, but it might just be the answer we've all been looking for. If they're not here in two days—and if they can't solve the problem if and when they do come—then we'll get ourselves a plan of our own that *will* work. It seems we don't have any other choice. If there is, now's the time for somebody here to speak up." He looked out to the townsfolk and searched their silent eyes, and then twisted from side to side to see if any of the selectmen gathered about him had anything to offer. None of them did. No one in the entire assembly did.

"So, what I'm suggesting now," Mitchell went on, pointing to the boxes, "is that we take as much of this as we can carry, for ourselves, our friends, and neighbors, and go home. In the morning, those of you who are inclined to can come on over to my office and we'll begin to plan something out—just in case the national guard *doesn't* come in."

Someone toward the rear of the church said, "Amen!" It was Bobby Jennings. People turned as he continued to speak. "I guess there's a little bit of the preacher in me," he said with a quiet chuckle in his voice. But . . . didn't you all notice something about being here tonight?"

No one had, not even Mitchell.

"Well, a dozen of our friends and neighbors are gone. Family, too. I know there's been more services for the dead over the past two weeks than there has been for a long time. But I thought . . . since we're all gathered here, in a church, that we should, probably, end this meeting with a prayer—not only for those that are gone from us, but to ask the Lord for help, for ourselves and for our families. We may all need it before any of this is through."

The cruelest sound in all creation was made later that night. It wasn't something that anyone could hear, unless they happened to be right up close to the source of it. It was a soft, muffled, thumping sound—not too unlike the sound a cow makes when it drops a pie on the grass. That was what it sounded like when the water moccasins plopped themselves down from the bottoms of the vehicles they had hitched a ride on. They landed in the driveways and backyards of everyone who had gone to the meeting that night. It was a fearsome, eerie, and unnatural thump against the earth—a hushed sound that quickly turned to whispered slitherings of motion toward the shadows of the sleeping houses.

CHAPTER FORTY

After the meeting, Mitchell let Bobby Jennings borrow his car to get home while he himself walked the short distance over to Lettie's house to see how Sara was doing. Except for the brief and hysterical meeting that morning, when she had come running up to his office with the news that snakes had attacked a stranger at the pond, Mitchell hadn't seen her in almost two days. Not only did he want to find out how she was feeling, but he was wondering what effect the death of Ginny's classmate, Betty Bird Johnson, might have had on the girl.

As he approached the front door, he began to have second thoughts about going in. Although it was only ten o'clock, he was tired, not having had any sleep the whole night before, when he and Bobby Jennings had been out looking for the missing child. He needed to shave, and a good scrubbing, too. He stopped in the walkway. Yes, he thought, looking at the familiar old house, with its reassuring lights on in the parlor and the curtains softly billowing in the gentle breeze—yes, everything's all right. He didn't think there was a need to stop in, not tonight. A better idea would be to get himself on home to a good night's sleep. Tomorrow promised to be a very hectic day. He swallowed a deep yawn.

He was about to turn and leave when he saw a shadow pass in front of the living room window. It was Sara. She was carrying a wine glass in one hand and a book in the other. It looked as though she were about to settle down in the comfortable old chair by the window and relax with a book. That decided it. He'd just get himself on home and into a hot tub. Then go to bed.

"Loren? Is that you?"

The outside light went on. Sara stood at the open door. "Where are you going?" she called.

Mitchell, who had almost reached the road, turned. The sound of her voice pronouncing his name had awakened something in him. It wasn't desire. It was something else—something that hung before him in the fragrant night air like the glimmer of some hopeful glow. She was lonely, and so was he.

He turned to walk back toward the house. "I was thinking of ringing the doorbell a minute ago," he said when he got to the door. "But . . . well, the truth of it is, I just didn't realize how tired I was. I decided it would be best if I just got on home instead."

"Why don't you come in," Sara said. "I can fix you a cup of coffee."

It had been a long time since a pretty woman had offered to fix anything for him. It almost made him forget how tired he was. He had lived alone ever since he was home from the army and his father passed away. Fixing for himself was mostly all of what he had ever known. He shyly accepted the invitation. It was as though he was about to embark upon a unique and pleasurable event—one that was filled with certain aspects of the unknown. He had never had occasion to sit with a woman who possessed a Ph.D. before. She was also the most beautiful woman he had ever had occasion to visit with.

"How are you feeling?" he asked walking diffidently into the house. "After what you went through this morning, I was worried about you."

"I'm fine now," she said, noting the concern in his kind brown eyes. "I was just about to curl up with a book and a glass of wine. Would you rather have some wine, instead of coffee?"

Mitchell smiled. "I'm afraid that would put me right to sleep," he said. "If it's too much bother, I can fix the coffee my. . . ."

"Oh, it's no bother at all," Sara interrupted. "It's already made. A fresh pot, left over from dinner. All I have to do is heat it up."

While Sara went to the kitchen for the coffee, Mitchell went upstairs to the bathroom to wash up. In all the time he had known Lettie, he had only been upstairs once—and it wasn't to the bathroom. It was when Ginny had called him on the telephone to tell him there was something wrong with the old woman. She had been knocking on her door all morning and Lettie didn't answer. When she went in to find out what was wrong, so she had told Mitchell, she thought Lettie might have had a heart attack. Her face was all white. Mitchell had wasted no time in getting himself over there.

Mitchell looked down the hallway to the girl's room. From the absence of light beneath the closed door, he assumed she was asleep—which meant she probably hadn't taken the death of her classmate as badly as some of the other children in town. As a matter of fact, he thought, she hadn't taken the death of Lettie, or her own father, all that badly. Some kids are very resilient, he thought.

From where he stood he could also see into the old woman's room. There was a small light on by the bed, and from the looks of it, it appeared as though the entire room had been rearranged. He though Sara had probably done that to make the room seem more of her own, and not one in which an old woman had died in her sleep. That she could even bring herself to sleep in the same bed made him shake his head in wonder. He wasn't sure he could ever do a thing like that.

The bathroom didn't look anything like he'd expected. With Sara and Ginny living there now, the bathroom looked as though it belonged to a pair of college roommates. There were towels on the floor, cabinets had been left open, soap had been left out of its dish and was drying on the windowsill above the bathtub—which had a grimy ring about it—and dirty clothes were piled on top of the wicker hamper, not inside of it. Yet, somehow, there was a comfortable feel to it. Not only did it remind him of his own place, but it showed that Sara was not the type to get on a little girl's back about being tidy. Neatness will come with time, he thought—and, in amusement, wondered when it would come to him, to Sara. He smiled into the mirror above the sink as he toweled his face dry. The whole of it had the feel of comfort, of peace, of welcome familiarity.

"Did you ever find out who that man was at the

pond this morning?" Sara asked, pouring Mitchell's coffee into a mug in the living room.

Mitchell took the mug and leaned back into the sofa opposite her. "Somebody visiting the graveyard found his car up there," he said, allowing the coffee to cool down a bit before he had some. "We had the license plate traced and put in a call to a Texas Ranger I know at the capital. He got in touch with someone in West Virginia, where the man came from, and found that he had spent the past thirty years in and out of a variety of psychiatric institutions. He was an old army veteran who got wounded in the head during World War II and was on one hundred percent disability ever since."

"What was he doing *here*?" Sara asked. "In Wilston?"

"Bobby Jennings and I spoke to him right after he found Betty Bird up at the graveyard. He said he came to visit Lettie's grave. He didn't know her, but his father had. He came to pay his father's respects. The man's father was a snake handler."

Sara looked at him. She had once read a study about the West Virginia snake handlers. A chill passed into her. She knew it was foolish, but she suddenly wanted to tell Mitchell about the book Ginny's mother had been working on when she died. She wanted to tell him everything—about the rain of frogs at the back porch last night, about how the snakes had leaped up into the air after them, swallowing them in one quick gulp. She also wanted to tell him about Melissa Malikoff. But he would probably think she was crazy. She didn't want that.

"How did Ginny take the news about Betty Bird?" Mitchell asked.

The chill again. It was seeping deeper and deeper into her bones. "She didn't react at all." Sara answered. "It seems, by the time she got home from school, the news had already been dealt with. Children are much stronger than we give them credit for." She didn't totally believe the last thing she'd said. She knew what psychological blocking in adolescents was all about—which brought her thoughts back to the poltergeist story of the little girl from the Wilderness School that Edna Malikoff had later adopted, the same little girl who grew up to be the woman she had met in the college cabin two days ago.

"What happened at the meeting?" she asked as she lifted her glass of white wine to her lips. "Did the town come up with a plan?"

As she listened to him talk about the militia, snake-bite kits, gloves, snakeproof gaiters, and the aluminum snake catchers, she thought about how much she liked him. She hadn't felt anything for a man in years. It wasn't just that he was handsome. Beneath his rugged, unshaven, and currently unkempt appearance, she could tell that he was a caring, gentle, and deeply sensitive man. And it wasn't buried too far beneath the surface, either. His being with her was helping to ease the desperate feeling of hopeless confusion she had about being in that small American town, taking care of a child she was beginning to love and mistrust at the same time—to say nothing of the other mysteries that plagued her. If she could only bring herself to tell him what she was thinking. Tell him that. . . .

She had been so absorbed in her own wandering thoughts, thoughts that filtered in and out of Mitchell's words, that, at first, she hadn't noticed how his speech was becoming slurred, how it was slowing down.

"First thing . . . in the morning . . . just in case the . . . militia doesn't get here. . . ."

Mitchell's head slumped to the side and he began to breathe deeply. Sara got up and walked about the table to where he was sitting on the sofa. She sat beside him for a moment and studied him. There was a deep rhythm to his breathing and the muscles in his face relaxed. He had fallen asleep.

Sara almost laughed. She contemplated leaving him there and going upstairs to bed, but there was something so comfortable about sitting there beside him that she decided to stay a while longer. Perhaps he'd wake up soon. She picked up her book and began to read—remaining beside him on the couch, where there was a better light. It was a book her mother had given her when she was only thirteen years old. She had read it many times before, and would probably read it as many times again. It was a book written by a European lady who had once lived in Africa. Isak Dinesen's *Out of Africa.*

Ginny had started at the top of the staircase landing, listening to Sara and Mitchell quietly talking in the living room. She was now sitting on a step near the bottom of the stairs, staring through the balusters as they both slept, deeply and soundly. She had been watching them for a long time. Neither of them had moved very much—except for Sara. Her head had come down on Mitchell's shoulder and was now resting there as though it was a comfortable pillow. It looked as though the two had known each other for the whole of their lives. Ginny was touched by the idea of going over to sit beside them. The sheriff's other shoulder was there for her to rest her own head against.

Some deep and forgotten thing stirred within her as she watched them sleeping. It struggled against a murky tide of darkness to lift itself to the surface. When it did, it arrived as a swell of tears in her eyes. She quietly went back upstairs to her bedroom. There, she threw herself on the bed and pulled the pillow tightly over her head.

CHAPTER FORTY-ONE

When Bobby Jennings was driving home in Mitchell's old Peugeot, a thought came over him. It wasn't a new one, but one that hadn't occurred to him so strongly before. He missed Sally, his pet doberman that had been killed by the snakes. Maybe it was because she had always been right with him whenever he was out alone driving at night. He didn't know. All he knew was that he now felt so sick over the loss of her that he didn't want to go home—not just yet.

He passed the turn-off to his house and kept right on going, straight toward his broadcast shack just outside of town. He knew his wife, Martha, would be waiting for him at home, but he just couldn't bear to have to answer all the questions she was sure to have ready for him about what had happened at the meeting. She was a good woman, and as kind as they ever come, but she never seemed to know when he was too tired, or upset about something, to answer a long string of questions. Like the questions she had asked the moment he'd returned home that morning from helping Mitchell grapple the stranger's body out of the pond—while he and a couple of other men from the town's rescue team kept a sharp look-out for moccasins. He didn't feel like talking to anyone that night—especially since he'd got to missing his Sally so much. He thought he'd just get himself on over to the studio for a while, and drive back home after his wife was sure to be asleep. In the morning, he'd be able to answer her questions.

Tiredness had something to do with the way he was feeling, too. He could feel the sting of it burning his eyes as he tried to focus on the dirt road that now began when the paved one ran out. At the broadcast shack, where he could be alone—where he could miss his doberman all he wanted—he'd prepare a script for tomorrow's broadcast. There was juice enough there for a whole *series* of radio programs, he thought. The town had never had the national guard to be called in before. There might even be some high-ranking official he could interview. He hadn't done many of those in the years since he first started the show. By gum, he thought, waking up a bit, if only he wasn't so dagblasted worn out, he could . . . he could. . . .

Bobby's mind was wandering all over the place, just like his car along the dirt road. Wouldn't it tickle ol' Martha if he walked away with a Peabody Award, for the best radio coverage of a local event!? It could lead to a lot of things. Maybe one of the majors—NBC, CBS—or God knows who, might even like his flare for the spoken word. That show he had put together for the town's children, about the dangers of the water moccasins at the pond—well, that was one heck of a show. That alone should have won him some kind of a prize, he thought.

The shot of adrenaline that the thought of winning awards pumped into his veins didn't make it all the way to the rest of his body. Piece by piece, it began to fall asleep. His hands, which he liked to carry at six o'clock on the steering wheel, as though he were holding the reins of a galloping horse between his legs, were going numb from the vibration of the unfamiliar car he was driving. Then, there was the trouble with the circulation in his legs. And if he had bothered to notice, he would have discovered that his feet were falling asleep, too. As for his legs, which were all tired out from having climbed up and down the hill to the pond, they were already dead behind the knees. And his head, well, that was rolling and pitching about on his shoulders as though it weighed a hundred pounds. Images of his wife, his doberman, and his Peabody Award, were all rolled up in a scroll that now unraveled itself out along the darkened roadway like a stack of pictures being flipped in an old-fashioned moviebook, one thumb-bent picture at a time: camels and Turkish dancers, baseball players and fishes going round and round in a fishbowl, a man wearing a handlebar moustache, puffing on a baseball bat cigar and blowing billowing clouds of soft white smoke out of his mouth—for page after page after page of moviebook stills.

His chin was almost touching his chest. If it weren't

for the fact that the road he was on was as straight as an arrow, he'd have gone off it a long time ago. And maybe that was why the water moccasins—which had slithered up through a rusted-out hole in the floorboard of the old car—grew impatient. Coiled up on the back of the driver's seat, right behind his head, they saw the woman standing at the door of the radio shack as the car whizzed by. They had no way of knowing that the woman was the man's wife, and that—having grown tired of waiting for him at home, she had decided he might have gone to the studio and gone there to see if she was right. She'd tried calling, but she knew that he sometimes did not answer late-night calls. There were a lot of questions she had to know the answers to before she could get herself some rest that night. The expression on her face as he went past her, doing seventy, went well beyond astonishment. She screeched as loudly as the wind that whistled up the front of her cotton dress when the car roared by.

And, maybe, that was what woke Bobby up.

His head snapped up with a jerk that was so sudden it loosened his upper plate and made it rattle about in his mouth as though he had nearly swallowed a slippery harmonica. The first thing he tried to do was get the thing settled back in place before he really *did* swallow it. But when he tried to lift his hands from the steering wheel, he discovered they wouldn't move—not only had they fallen asleep, but something like coils of thick, icy rope were holding them down!

It was too dark to see the bottom of the steering

wheel down between his legs, and the car was now moving too fast for him to take his eyes off the road. He needed both hands on the wheel, and both eyes on the road. In the side-view mirror he could see a spume of dirt rooster-tailing out behind the car as though he was driving a speed boat across a lake. He tried lifting his foot off the accelerator, but that wouldn't work, either. Something was holding it tightly to the floor—as though it were tied there—just like his hands were tied to the wheel.

Martha watched it all as though it were a scene from a TV movie. Her momentary fit of terror when she saw her husband's head tipped down as though he was asleep at the wheel gave way to a curious, completely out-of-place sense of amusement. He was obviously playing some sort of a joke on her, she thought. It was just like him to do a darn fool thing like that—especially if there was a new situation at hand, like driving a car that didn't belong to him. She knew he was getting a lift in Mitchell's car, he had told her so before the meeting. He'd wanted to leave her with their own car because she had to visit a sick cousin. It was only down the road about half a mile from where they lived, and she usually walked the distance, but with all that had happened lately, he had insisted she drive. He didn't want want her to be walking out alone on a dark road that night.

Martha looked up at the sheriff's old car disappearing into the darkness, expecting the taillights to brighten and the car to stop at any moment—just as soon as her husband decided the joke had gone far enough, and reverse back. He probably had wanted her to believe he was the sheriff on his way to an emergency. And, sure enough, the car did appear to be coming to a rolling halt. But the taillights didn't brighten, as they should have if the breaks were applied. That began to bring the worry in her back up to the surface again. What if he got himself to laughing so hard he went and caught himself a heart attack, she thought.

It was a thought that appeared to confirm itself by the manner in which the car then slowly rolled to a full stop. The dirt it had lifted from the road settled about it in a cloud of distant silence that was as eerie as anything she had ever seen along a dark and deserted stretch of roadway. She waited a full minute and a half for Bobby to throw the car into reverse and come on back to her, smiling his familiar little grin to show he was only fooling. But something told her it wasn't going to happen. He would never keep her in suspense for that long a period of time.

Martha Jennings didn't even think of getting into their own car and driving down the road to where the sheriff's car had come to rest. She walked at first, hoping that *if* he was fooling, he would see her coming and do the right thing and reverse back in a hurry. When, after she had taken a few dozen steps toward it, she saw that nothing was happening in or about the car, she broke into a slow trot. That, she thought, would surely get him moving on back to her. When it did not, she immediately broke into a full screaming run.

Inside the car, the three water moccasins darted their tongues out over Bobby Jennings' dead body. Their bloodied fangs glistened as they hissed.

And this was only the beginning of a night of terror for Wilston.

CHAPTER FORTY-TWO

Mitchell's eyes opened when the first light of the sun coming in through the living room window touched his face. He felt a weight on his shoulder, and before he had a chance to wonder where he was, he reached out to rub his aching arm—but touched something else instead. He quickly pulled his hand away and turned to see what it was. It was Sara. She was sleeping soundly beside him, her head on his shoulder. It slowly came back to him that he had probably fallen asleep while talking to her last night. A wave of embarrassment swept through him. He hadn't done anything like that since he was in the army. But what was she doing there, beside him?

Maybe she was growing fond of him. If not, he reasoned, she would either have awakened him and sent him home, or he would have awakened alone—possibly with a thin blanket draped over him. That she had spent the night beside him on the couch touched him in a way he had not felt in a very long time. It was almost enough to make him forget the hectic day he had ahead of him. He looked at the clock across the room. It was almost six A.M. He would go on over to his office first, get a shower and shave there. By the time he was through with that, he was sure the phones would start ringing. He knew his invitation for anyone to stop by and discuss a plan to rid the pond of snakes—just in case the national guard reneged on its promise to come in—was sure to be taken very seriously. He expected he'd be tied up at the office all morning, until the national guard arrived. If they arrived.

He stretched his legs out in front of him and supported Sara by the shoulders as he lifted himself up from beside her. Then he gently lowered her until her head was resting on one of the pillows. She showed no sign of awakening, so he lifted her legs onto the couch as well. There was something close to a smile on his unshaved and scruffy face as he then turned to leave. It was a Saturday, and Ginny would probably be sleeping late too, like almost everyone else in town.

At first there didn't seem to be anything unusual taking place in the quiet streets of the town—which was usual for six A.M. on Saturdays. But then, as he approached the center of town, things started to register differently. There was a knot of people out in front of Estelle Whidden's funeral home, and over a dozen vehicles were parked about the sprawling old Victorian mansion like chaff before the wind. From the haphazard arrangement of cars and pickups, it looked as though they had been driven up to the front door of the funeral home and abandoned. Some of the vehicles still had their doors open.

Word must have gotten to Estelle that Mitchell was on his way, because the grey-haired sixty-two-year-old woman came out the front door of the home and walked toward him with a briskness of pace that was usually reserved for a person much younger than she was. It seemed she wanted to speak to him before people started to gather about.

"I've been trying to reach you all night," she said breathlessly. "Tried ringing your house every fifteen minutes, the office, too. Even had someone go on over to see if the telephones had gone out or something."

He appreciated the fact that she had not asked where he had been. Then he realized she would never do a thing like that. She, like all funeral directors, was among the most discreet persons on earth.

"What's happened?" he asked.

It was a question that Estelle hadn't wanted to hear. She wanted him to tell *her* what had happened, that he knew all about the deaths that had taken place during the night, and that everything was now under control—that all she had to do was get the thirty-six people (who had so far been reported dead) into the ground and the nightmare would be over.

Estelle Whidden looked at him. In all her forty years of being the county's principal funeral director, she had never had to report such a tragedy to anyone. She opened her mouth to speak, but the words escaped her. "You'd better come and find out for yourself," she finally said, indicating the receiving entrance of the funeral home. "I can't find the words to tell it."

Estelle Whidden's grandfather had been the inventor of Whidden's Egyptian Embalming Fluid, a product that was still on the market and had amassed a fortune for her when he had passed away and left her everything. When she had been sixteen, she had been the only one in the family who had wanted to go into the same business as her grandad, so he'd sent her to one of the finest schools of mortuary science in the country. She had rebuilt the facial features of more traumatically killed victims—with Whidden's Restorative Elastic Wax, another of her grandfather's products that still generated income for her—and drained the blood from more dead bodies, made them up, given them permanents, clipped their nostril-hairs, and scrubbed more nicotine-stained teeth and dentures with Bon Ami than most people would care to recount. And once a week, though she would never admit it to a soul, she slept in the prize model of her favorite casket—a Batesville Mahogany with a brushed metal finish—while "Amazing Grace" played itself over and over again on the old reel-to-reel Philco tape recorder she had set up in her private chapel. It was the same type and model casket that her grandfather had gone to his reward in, and which her casket company—Whidden's Classic Coffins—now reproduced. While most people were forced to deal with death a relatively few times in their entire lives, Estelle had lived with it for over half a century. Death seemed to be the only thing she had ever known. But even she couldn't find the words to describe to Mitchell what had happened last night.

Mitchell paled when Estelle led him down the ramp at the side of the house and into the cellar—or "receiving room," as she called it—of her mortuary parlor. It was as white and as bright as a hospital's operating room, and as broad in width and as wide in girth as the house itself. She prided herself on having the most technically advanced preparation room in the whole state. Very few people, while they were still alive, had ever been there. Only her assistants, from the mortuary school she had founded in Austin, were given access to it. Mitchell himself had only been there two or three times before—a couple of road accidents and one suicide—but on those occasions there had only been one light illuminated above the preparation table. Now, with all the fluorescent lights turned on, he saw how big the place really was, and how ghastly a scene the funeral director had just led him into.

There were bodies all over the place, most of them in body bags. Only their faces were exposed. Every table held two bodies, head to foot, and folding chairs had been brought down from the chapels upstairs and placed together to form rows and rows of makeshift tables. There were even some bodies stacked up on two of the broad stainless steel sinks over by the wall. When Estelle had run out of body bags, her assistants had wrapped the rest in linens, which she had instructed them to "borrow" from friends or family of the recently deceased. She always had three assistants there at a time, but she had already put a call in to her mortuary school at the capital to send the whole graduating class on up to help—all twenty-eight of them.

Mitchell studied as many of the faces of the dead as he could see—those that weren't blocked from view by other bodies or the backs of the folding chairs. The people he saw had all been at the meeting the night before. It gave him the sinking feeling that there would be more coming in—the rest of the people who'd been there. But that was foolish, he thought. That would have to mean that the snakes somehow *knew* who had gone to the meeting.

"Does Bobby Jennings know about this, Estelle?"

The woman looked down at her wrinkled hands for

a moment. They were like ice and almost looked the same shade of blue as some of the dead bodies were beginning to turn. Seeing as how there were so many of them, she had turned the air conditioning up as high as it would go. It must have been between forty and fifty degrees down there—the same temperature as the inside of a refrigerator. Even Mitchell felt the shiver of it as he waited for her to respond to his question.

"He's here too," Estelle Whidden finally said, looking back up at him. She knew how close he and Jennings had been, and at first she wanted to console Mitchell the same as she would have consoled a member of the dead man's own family. But she knew he would rather have the news as straight as she could possibly tell it. She broke her professional code of being the sensitive care-giver to the living and told it to him plainly. She had known Mitchell for a long time, buried his own mother and father while he was still a young man. She could tell by his steady eyes that he appreciated her telling him the news that way. But in the silence that followed, she thought she might have made a mistake. Mitchell was obviously fighting back his emotions.

"Where is he?" he finally managed at ask.

"Back over on one of the tables." She pointed.

Mitchell slowly walked over to the other end of the cellar and saw that Jennings's wife, Martha, was there, too. He shook his head. The sour lump he thought he had swallowed was still well embedded in his throat. Had he tried to talk, his voice would have faltered.

* * *

When Mitchell got to his office the telephone was

ringing.

"What in *the* hell is going on up there, Mitch? First you had that escaped lunatic up there, trying to eat the water moccasins at the pond. And now, I just heard from a highway patrol report that your deputy was killed in your old car, by snakes—his wife, too! What's going on?" It was Mitchell's old friend, Jed Mailey, the Texas Ranger at the state capital.

Mitchell wished there was something he could say that would help him forget the grief he had just experienced in Estelle Whidden's icy cold cellar. Why? he wondered, visualizing the rows and rows of snake-bite victims. *Why?*

"That's not the half of it, Jed," Mitchell finally responded, swallowing hard. He was glad no one else was at the office. There might have been if they hadn't all been killed! From the way it was beginning to look, he was the only survivor among those who had gone to last night's meeting. Was that because he had not driven home in his own car? he wondered as Jed repeatedly asked for an explanation of what he had just said about Jennings's death not being the half of it. Was that what the snakes had done? he continued to wonder. Gotten into the cars and been driven home by the people who were killed!? The implications of *that* idea left him momentarily stunned, and silent—before he rejected it. It was too absurd a notion even to consider.

Mitchell took a deep breath and finally responded to Jed's request for an explanation. He then filled Jed in on all the rest—about how the dead were still being brought in to Estelle Whidden's funeral home, and how—so it appeared—the snakes had attacked only those people who had been to the meeting last night—a meeting that had been called to get something done about the snakes.

He heard Jed's silence at the other end of the line. "You don't mean to tell me you think the snakes *knew* about the purpose of the meeting?" he finally asked. The skepticism in his voice was deeply etched.

"Hell no," Mitchell answered. "What the heck do you take me for?"

"Hold it, hold it, Mitch. I didn't mean anything by what I just said. It's just that you put emphasis on it, like it might have had some sort of meaning. You know, as well as I do, that snakes are among the dumbest creatures on earth."

"Dumb enough to have killed forty-nine men, women, and children—at the last count," Mitchell couldn't help but add. He didn't know why he'd said that. Deep down inside he felt the same about the creatures' lack of intelligence as Jed did. "Pay no mind to it, Jed. I'm just . . . just *confused* about it. That's all." He looked out the window and saw that the road leading up to his office was deserted. He sure would have liked to see Bobby Jennings walking up to it that morning.

"Have you heard anything about the national guard yet?" he asked. "They said they'd be here today, or tomorrow at the very latest. Over a hundred men. They're supposed to have training with some sort of new electronic device that can clear snakes away in a hurry. From the looks of what happened here last night, we're going to need all the help we can get."

No, Jed hadn't heard anything about any national guard, not yet. But he was going to make sure and check on it and get back to Mitchell as soon as he could. He would also spread the news of what had happened, hoping it would help push things along if they had gotten stuck anywhere.

Mitchell placed the receiver back on its hook after the call. He had never felt so afraid and lonely in his entire life. Out there, throughout the town, whole families, friends and neighbors, had been brutally attacked and killed by water moccasins. Yet, none of the snakes were still around. It seemed as though the slimy creatures *did* have an intelligence of sorts—or at least a purpose. And now they were in hiding—waiting to take over the town.

CHAPTER FORTY-THREE

Ginny sat in the midst of a sea of sails—sheets hung out on the clothesline in the backyard of the house. During the night she had bled, well beyond anything she had ever expected. And, somehow, that didn't make her feel any better about becoming a woman. She had never had such feelings of conflict before.

During the night she had had a dream. She was a snake—a huge, slithering black water moccasin at the pond. She swept beneath the surface of the icy water and was impregnated by a coolness that seeped into every pore of her body. It felt good. She coiled and circled and headed for the deepest part of the water's murky darkness. There was something to be discovered way down there . . . something she had to be reunited with . . . something that would bring her lasting joy, forever and ever . . . something she was driven to become at one with. She couldn't see through the darkness of the water to discover what it was that called her down into the deepest part of it. But it didn't matter. She had already embarked on a course that would, now that she was a woman, carry her there. All she had to do was explore the depths, and she would find whatever it was that had driven her to kill.

She was still swimming deeper and deeper when

something woke her. She was in a sea of sweat—and sticky blood! Her sheets were drenched with both, her clinging nightgown, too. She looked at the clock beside her bed. It was almost ten A.M. The house appeared to be perfectly still. She quickly rose and removed her nightgown and the sheets from the bed. When she returned from cleaning and changing herself in the bathroom, she slipped into a fresh blouse and a pair of jeans. She then stuffed the soiled linens into a pillow case and went down to the kitchen.

Ginny found a note on the table telling her that Sara had to go somewhere and that she would be back in about an hour. Judging from the stillness of the house when she first woke up, Ginny figured Sara would be back anytime now—she had probably gone down to get some groceries for breakfast. Ginny had to be quick. For some curious reason she didn't want Sara to know about the bleeding—her womanhood. She went back upstairs for the sheets and dirty nightgown and carried the pillow case to the washing machine. It was now only a little after ten A.M.

After washing the bloodstains from the sheets and hanging them out on the line in the yard, she sat on an overturned metal wash pail between the sails that billowed in the warm breeze. In her mind she was at sea, as deeply into the uncharted ocean of her thoughts as the sails would carry her. That morning, as she had been waiting for the sheets to finish spinning in the washing machine, something extraordinary had happened to her.

There was a mirror in the old pantry-laundry room between the kitchen and the porch, and it had a beveled edge. As the sheets were in their final spin,

Ginny had been looking at her reflection in it. When she twisted her head slightly, and focused on the beveled border of the mirror, her image became distorted. Going along with it, she screwed up her face and poked out her tongue. The humorous portrait she had expected to result from such a momentary flight of distraction filled her with something else. The image had split her face and made it appear hatchet-shaped and narrow. If she jutted her chin toward the glass, her eyes grew wider apart and her normally full lips became a tight slit. That was when she'd decided to poke her tongue out to see what that would make her look like. The tongue came out forked, distorting the image of herself into a serpent!

At first, she took a step backward and the image quickly returned to her normal appearance. By stepping forward again, and aligning herself in relation to the beveled edge of the mirror, she once more became the serpent, and she forked her tongue rapidly in and out of her mouth to amuse herself. That was when a bright green-blue horsefly landed on the edge of her upper lip. She carefully studied it for a moment, then, with a gesture that was as instinctive and natural as anything she had ever done before, she flicked her tongue out and drew the fly into her mouth. It had seemed as ordinary an act for her as licking a scrap of toast from the corner of her lips. But the event unsettled her. That was why she was now sitting out in the backyard, between the billowing sheets, pretending she was aboard an old-fashioned ship at sea—where she could be alone with her conflicting thoughts.

Ginny examined the sheet in front of her to see if the washing had completely removed the bloodstain. It had, but something else now replaced the stain. It was a silhouette of the row of pickets atop the fence behind the sailing sheet. The sun had not yet fully risen into the sky, and its low angle caused it to cast the shadow. As the sheet puckered in the warm breeze, the pickets moved and swelled, reminding her of the heads of a row of water moccasins. She knew the terror that had been inflicted on the town during the night, but didn't know exactly how many people had been killed. She didn't care. They were a threat to the water moccasins at the pond and they had to be taken care of. If she wanted to, she could wipe out the rest of the town in one night!

But what would then happen to Sara, and to the sheriff, too? she wondered, only now remembering the inner warmth that seeing the two of them asleep on the living room couch had caused her. There was something about Sara that she had never felt with anyone else before. It was a feeling that somehow managed to fill up all the dark and lonely spaces in her heart—the spaces that were left empty by the fact that she had never had a mother to. . . .

Something hit the galvanized bucket she was sitting on. It struck the metal with the force of a stone that had been picked up by the blade of a high-powered lawnmower and shot out. Had it hit her, it would have knocked a hole right through her. She stood up and looked down to see what it was. The biggest water moccasin she had ever seen rose up before her until it was almost as tall as she was. It hissed angrily in her face!

But Ginny didn't run. "I don't," she said to the hissing viper. "I don't love her."

And it was as though the air had been let out of a bicycle tube. The water moccasin shrank and slithered away, out through the slats of the picket fence at the back of the yard. She followed it with her unblinking eyes. And with her unblinking eyes she now studied the silhouettes of the pickets that were cast on the flapping sheet before her. The pointed, swelling, moving shadows looked as real as the water moccasin that had just departed. She took it to be a warning—a warning from the thing that was deep within her, the thing she was powerless to do anything about. And for the first time since the killings had begun, she was terrified.

CHAPTER FORTY-FOUR

It seemed as though Mitchell's office had turned itself into a bus depot in the heart of a major city. He had never seen so many people—mostly sheriffs and deputies from other counties—stopping by to offer their assistance. The phone rang so often that the receiver was hardly let down into its cradle when it rang again, right in Mitchell's hand. This time it was from his friend, Jed Mailey, at the state capital. The Texas Ranger had just received the full news of the total number of people killed by the water moccasins the night before.

"Jesus," he said to Mitchell over the telephone wire. "Over *seventy* people killed in one night! That makes it a total of eighty-seven dead in just two weeks! There must be something going on over there that's . . . *unnatural.* Like toxic waste or something. Are there any factories or plants. . . ."

Mitchell cut him short. There wasn't a nuclear plant for over a thousand miles, and no factory for over fifty miles.

"Well, maybe it's that college you got over there," Jed suggested, continuing to pursue his theory that a pollutant of some sort might have caused an aberration in the behavior of the water moccasins. "Who *knows* what kinds of experiments might be going on up there. Have you ever thought of that?"

No, Mitchell hadn't thought of that, and he wasn't about to think much of it now. He had the feeling that if anything of that sort were going on he'd have known about it a long time ago—Sara might even have told him about it, too. No, he thought. The college wasn't responsible for what was happening. "Look," he said, his voice sounding tired and strained, "this is the biggest disaster we've ever faced here in Wilston. Estelle's funeral parlor is packed to the roof with dead bodies and the coroner is so taxed he's about to slip into one of her caskets himself. . . ." Mitchell almost lost himself in what he was saying and momentarily forgot the point of it. "The point of it all," he said, regaining his hold, "is . . . have you spoken to anyone yet about getting the national guard here today?"

There was a long pause on the other end. When Jed began to talk, his voice darkened with hesitation. It was almost noon and he had had five or six hours, since he had first spoken to Mitchell that morning, to muster all the special favors he needed to help push things along for his friend. But it hadn't been enough. He had friends in the military, but they tended to do things their own way. He had to accept that. "They're getting ready now," he said, trying to force a note of hopefulness into his voice. "But don't expect them to be there until later tonight. Seems it takes something like eight or nine hours to charge those electronic things they have. If I hadn't gotten to them with the severity of the news about what happened in Wilston last night, the darn things would still be in their boxes." There was another long pause. "The best thing would be for you to suggest that everyone stay indoors tonight, and that they keep a sharp lookout for the snakes. Make sure everyone wears those gaiters you told me about, and that everyone has some sort of a weapon—like a knife or a stick, or those snake-catcher poles that were delivered over there. It's the only thing you can do."

As much as Mitchell's insides disagreed with what Jed had told him, his mind told him that it probably *was* the only thing he could do. There were twenty-five sheriffs and deputies from nearby counties in town, helping with the dead and waiting for instructions from him on what to do next. But the pure truth of the matter was that he didn't know what to do next. He had already asked anyone who owned a set of binoculars to get up on their roof to see if any snakes could be spotted. If they were, it was to be reported to him immediately. By now there must have been over fifty people perched up on their roofs all over town, and no one had yet reported a single water moccasin. Going after them, like Winkie, Judd, and Jerry had done, as well as the lunatic from West Virginia, had only backfired—drastically. Mitchell didn't want to run the risk of getting any more people killed. The only hope seemed to be to sit tight, and hope—now that everyone was fully alerted to the danger of the situation—that the townspeople would be better able to protect themselves. Whenever the snakes got someone, it seemed they had taken that person by surprise—like Harvey

Ocean, the guidance counselor, in his study; like . . . like all the rest—like everyone who'd been killed last night! He had already donned a pair of gaiters and was keeping his own eyes sharp. He was ready to respond to the slightest movement out of the corner of his eye. He knew many of the townsfolk were now ready to do the same thing. Yes, he thought. The only thing to do while waiting for the national guard was to remain alert.

"Agkistrodon piscivorus," Lieutenant Colonel Darling said. He had to speak above the beating sound of military choppers coming in from a practice run along the Rio Grande. "The cottonmouth," he explained to the men of the special unit of national guardsmen seated before him. "The water moccasin."

Funny how those three phrases, all meaning the same thing, stiffened their spines, the colonel thought as he watched the men shift their backs against the metal folding chairs they were sitting in. He was a soft man in his early sixties with soft, warm eyes, soft wrinkled face, and a soft waistline. The type of man who reminded many of the men of a favorite uncle they might have had somewhere along the line. One who would unexpectedly show up for supper and have a great deal of fuss made over him. He'd tell jokes and tall tales, and sometimes he'd even reach into his pocket and hand you a coin of some sort—then tell you a long and wonderful story about where it came from and how he had gotten it. By the time he was through, it was a coin you would never lose—and if you did, you'd remember it and regret losing it for the rest of your life. The young men gathered before him in the crowded assembly room at Fort Wayne loved listening to him talk. The sound of his voice was reassuring. It told them that no matter what the assignment, whether it was to suppress a riot in downtown Houston or to patrol a dangerous narcotics crossing along the Rio Grande, you'd be okay. All you had to do was follow what "The Old Man" said and everything would turn out just fine. What most of the young men there could not understand was why he looked so haggard. They didn't have to wait long for an answer.

"About seventy people were killed last night," he said. "It happened in a little town some three hundred miles down the road. All of them, men, women, and children, killed by water moccasins."

He watched from the platform as the men once again drew their spines up along the backs of the uncomfortable metal chairs.

"So far, close to ninety people have been killed by the snakes during the past two weeks. We just got news about it yesterday, before what happened last night."

Some of the men thought they saw the colonel wince. And indeed he might have. The total number of dead was higher than some of the kills his famous unit strikes had earned him a chestful of decorations for—at Okinawa, south of the 38th parallel in Korea, and in Vietnam. He had taken so many bullet wounds that his wife—before she was killed in a private plane crash—used jokingly to call him "a hunk of Swiss cheese." He had been coaxed out of retirement after the loss of his wife to keep him from going mad, and had been "helping" with the national guard for the past fifteen years. Being with the young men sometimes helped him more than it did them. They thought of him as "The Old Man," and he thought of them as family—for indeed they were all he had left in the world.

The unit he now headed was made up of about a hundred bright-looking men. Accountants, teachers, ranchers, artists, and even a writer or two. The unit had been code-named Pied Piper. No one there, except the colonel, had ever seen action of any kind. They were in an experimental unit, in the process of taking a two-week training session in the use of a newly created device that was supposed to sweep away poisonous snakes in the advance of a foot army. South America, so the military believed, was the next big battle zone, and the Amazon was filled with some of the nastiest creatures on earth. If a foot army ever had to push its way through that, it would need something like the experimental unit to lead the way.

"You will be issued your equipment, briefed, and flown into the area tonight. We'll be using three of the new Sikorsky choppers. They have a ground speed of over three hundred miles per hour. That'll put us there in under an hour. The point of concentration will be a pond, just outside the center of town. It's the place from which the water moccasins appear to be emanating. This will be the first time we will actually have a chance to test our equipment under real conditions. When we get there, we will destroy every last water moccasin we find."

"Piece of cake, sir!" one of the men called out. Some cheered at that, some laughed, and a sprinkling of applause scattered about the assembly room.

With the top edge of his pointing finger, Lieutenant

Colonel Darling brushed a speck of perspiration away from his upper lip before concluding. "And we'll all be back home for early breakfast tomorrow." It sounded like a promise that everything was going to run as smooth as silk. He wondered why he didn't believe it.

Sara didn't learn of the deaths that had occurred during the night until she stepped into Mitchell's office and he told her—above the hubbub of activity that filled the cramped office area of the small jailhouse. Her first instinct was to forget about why she had gone to him and return home immediately, where she could be with Ginny. Then she looked down at the pale grey envelope she carried in her arm. It contained a stack of photocopies she had made in the college library that morning—of the manuscript that Ginny's mother had been working on when she died.

"I have something to tell you," she said. "Can we speak privately?"

Mitchell looked at her. There were almost a dozen people in the seemingly airless office, mostly deputies and sheriffs from other counties who had come to be of assistance. Some were busy with reports, while others were on the phone and taking messages; still others attempted to locate next of kin of the dead by going through old town records. And, at any one time, three or four men walked out the door as another three or four entered. The ceiling fan was on high, but the air conditioner was barely whispering, never having been designed to do the job that was necessary for that morning.

"Can it wait?" Mitchell finally responded. His forehead was slick with perspiration and his shirt was stuck to his chest. He knew he smelled of not having had a shower in almost three full days.

Sara lowered her eyes for a moment and wondered if what she wanted to tell him would make any sense in the midst of everything that was going on. If she opened the envelope she carried, to show him what was inside, it would be the same as opening Pandora's box—its revelations of evil would swamp an unprepared mind.

She looked past him to the cell in the next room. Three men sat opposite one another on the cots. Between them, spread out on a low table, was a map of some sort. One of them was making markings on it while he spoke to the other two. She then looked to the cubby of what passed for the jailhouse kitchen. There were people in there, too. Through the window she saw several more people headed up the path to the office. And one of the men inside was gesturing Mitchell to pick up the telephone—it was important.

"What time can you come by the house?" she asked.

"If it's important you can tell me now," Mitchell responded. "I can kick them fellers out of the kitchen if you want."

Sara looked. It didn't have a door. "It's okay," she said, attempting to lessen the urgency of what she had to say with a feeble smile. "I can talk to you later."

The man who had been gesturing to Mitchell to pick up the phone now gestured more strongly. *It's the capital.* His lips formed the words.

Still, Mitchell couldn't let it go at that. He felt there must have been a great urgency for her to have come to his office. "What's in the envelope?" he asked.

Sara clutched it tightly to her breast. "I can tell you about it later," she said. "What time can you stop by?"

Mitchell rubbed his fingers across the stubble on his chin. Three days without a shave and his face was beginning to itch. "In an hour, two at the very most," he said. "Just as soon as I can get things quieted down over here."

That wasn't a long time, Sara thought. She could wait that long.

CHAPTER FORTY-FIVE

There is not very much time. The killings will continue. You are the only one who can stop them.

Sara looked down at the pile of photocopies in her lap. She had gone to the library that morning to see the drawings that Ginny's mother had made of the wall-paintings inside the cave where she died. Serpents! Hundreds and hundreds of them. Page after page of angry, hissing vengeful-looking serpents. They were so lifelike it appeared they could leap from the sheets of paper and attack her. And the handwritten text that accompanied them was a real shocker, too.

When Sara had returned to the house after briefly speaking to Mitchell at his office, it had been a relief for her to hear Ginny upstairs in the bathroom, taking a bath. She hadn't wanted to see the child—not just then. But now, after having read through the manuscript one more time, and expecting Mitchell to arrive at any moment, she thought she would try something. Pandora's box, she thought. Open it up. It's the only way.

Sara spread out the photocopies of the vipers on the living room table. They were no match for the ochre-colored originals that Ginny's mother had copied from—but there was a life to them that was absolutely eerie. It sent shivers through the tips of her fingers just to touch them.

Pandora had opened a box the gods had given her, and every kind of evil had escaped from it and spread throughout the land. It was only through hope, through love, that the lid was able to be replaced. Sara hoped it would work.

"Ginny," she called from the bottom of the stairs. "Can you come down a minute? I have something to show you."

Upstairs, in her room, Ginny heard. But she was too mesmerized by the reflection of her naked body in the full-length mirror behind the locked bedroom door to respond. The strong sun had quickly dried the sheets and Ginny had remade the bed and taken a bath. As she now finished drying herself she noticed something about her body that she had never seen before. She delicately traced her fingers across the tight flesh of her abdomen, then up and away from her rib cage until she had her hands cupped about her breasts. She frowned at herself in the mirror. The feel of her skin was no longer smooth. It had a cold, leathery quality to it now—and dozens of little crescent-shaped ridges were beginning to form, too. They were faintly outlined in a tone that was slightly pinker than the rest of her body. She turned to see if they were on her back, too. They were. In the hollow of her spine, and spreading down across her buttocks like a camisole of clinging lace, there were row after row of barely discernible crescents. They looked like the overlapping shingles of a roof, only more rounded along the bottom edges, like . . . like what the scales of a snake looked like!

"Ginny? Are you in there?" Sara knocked on the closed door.

Sara pounded on the door more strongly when she discovered that it was locked from the inside. Still, Ginny didn't answer. She continued to examine her arms and legs. There were none of the markings on them like the ones that spread up from her abdomen to the bottoms of her breasts and cascaded down the small of her back and spilled across her rounded buttocks. She quickly reached for a robe and pulled it on.

"I'm here," she called out to Sara, opening the door. "Is something the matter?" she asked innocently. "I was taking a nap."

Sara looked at the bed. It was freshly made and unwrinkled.

"In the chair," Ginny said brightly, in response to the question in Sara's alert eyes. "I was reading by the window and must have fallen asleep or something. What time is it?"

Sara knew she was lying. There wasn't any book by the chair, and she had heard her getting out of the bathtub a little while ago. The girl's hair was still damp. She looked at her watch. It was almost four o'clock. Mitchell should have been there about two hours ago. She told Ginny what time it was, and, as casually as she could manage it, invited her downstairs.

"There's something I'd like you to see," she said.

"Okay," Ginny responded, tightening the robe about her waist. "Let's go."

Downstairs, in the living room, the innocent tone of Ginny's voice changed the moment she saw the photocopies on the coffee table.

"Where did you get those?" she asked.

Sara remained silent.

"I said where did you get these!?" Ginny demanded, rushing over to the low table and grappling a handful of photocopies up into each of her hands. "WHERE!?" she shrieked in the face of Sara's silence.

The girl rushed at her like a charging bull and caught her just above the abdomen with both of her extended fists. Sara had the wind knocked out of her and went toppling to the floor. "WHERE!" Ginny screamed, climbing up on top of Sara's chest and hammering her face with her balled-up hands, making it bleed with razorlike paper cuts from the edges of the copies she still clutched.

Sara struggled to get the child off her. The girl's attack had occurred so unexpectedly it seemed unreal, as though it were happening to someone else. It wasn't until the pain and the shortness of breath caught up to her that she realized what was happening to her. She could hardly breathe, and the bashing she was taking across the face was making her see flashes of light shooting about like rockets in the darkness behind her eyes. When it cleared, and she could focus again, she discovered she had Ginny's wrists locked tightly in her hands. The photocopies the girl had been clutching were now scuttling across the bare wooden floor like crumpled leaves in an autumn storm. But the child was strong. Like a slippery eel, she writhed and twisted free. Sara leaped after her. "Stop," she said. "Ginny, please stop!"

Sara froze. In their struggle several pieces of furniture had been overturned. The pictures of the vipers that had been on the coffee table were now scattered all over the floor. Some of them had begun to move in the strong breeze that suddenly gushed in through the open windows. For a moment Sara thought the violent-looking serpents were real.

As she stood gaping at the shifting sheets of paper, Ginny attacked her again, this time with a force that was greater than before. Sara was bowled off her feet and landed with the back of her head sharply striking the bottom step of the hardwood staircase. She blacked out for a moment. When she opened her eyes Ginny was sitting on her chest, holding her by the hair and smashing her head against the edge of the step.

"Ginny . . ." she moaned. Through the darkness and shooting flares of Sara's fading consciousness, she felt a terror—not of Ginny, but for her. Instead of fighting back, Sara reached out to Ginny.

Sara's lips touched the side of her face. "Ginny, stop this," she whispered weakly against the child's ear. "Everything's going to be all right, I promise. As long as we love each other."

Ginny collapsed against her and sobbed. Hot tears streamed from the girl's eyes and bathed Sara's face, causing needle points of fire to sting as the salted tears flowed into the cuts on her cheeks.

Ginny lowered her lips against Sara's neck and kissed her there. It was no ordinary kiss. When she pulled away, dangling from between her teeth was a piece of Sara's flesh.

Sara's last conscious thought was that she had been bitten by a huge black snake. It seemed to be confirmed in the fleeting image of the slimy, toothed thing that then moved away from her body and twisted up the stairs.

Lieutenant Colonel Darling slapped the palm of his hand over the side of his neck. He had felt a sharp sting. When he lowered his hand to the reading lamp beside his chair, he carefully examined it, expecting to find something quite larger than a mosquito in his palm. There was nothing there. Nevertheless, the experience gave him a chill. He didn't like things like that. He had been reading through a pile of instruction manuals for the equipment that was being loaded into the helicopters for the short flight to Wilston. It reminded him of the time he had been looking through an album of family pictures and for some reason had focused on a portrait of his wife and son. They were standing in front of his seventeen-year-old son's single engine Cessna-150—the plane they were then off in at that very moment. They were smiling and had their arms about each other. He had been thinking of them, soaring above the clouds at sunset—just as they had done a hundred times before—when something had touched the side of his neck. It was as though someone had come along beside him and squeezed the side of his neck with an icy hand. It was at that moment that the knock had come on the door to his study. His wife and son had just been killed. He had still had the photo album with the picture of them smiling up at him in his hands.

He laid the instruction manuals to the side and rubbed the side of his neck until it grew warm again. He didn't like it, not one bit.

CHAPTER FORTY-SIX

The central nervous system works neuron by neuron. When it is assaulted, as Sara's had been, it takes a while before the mind can recover—but first it must forget. The electrical misfiring of the complicated circuitry that connects the spinal column to the base of the brain had been severely battered against the bottom step of the hardwood staircase, but the memory of the event was lost in the dimness of the inner workings of her mind. Eventually, the memory of what had happened would begin to filter back to her like flakes of light drifting down through a sky full of heavy clouds. But for now, she could not remember.

When she found herself at the bottom of the staircase—with a thick clot of dried blood at the back of her head—she thought she must have tripped and fallen. It seemed she had been lying there for a long time, unconscious. Perhaps she had had another seizure, like the one she'd had when she had first arrived at the college a couple of weeks ago. What she did not understand, at first, were the abstract furies that assaulted her consciousness like a horrible nightmare. Every time she blinked her eyes, the image of a giant viper glistened out of the darkness of her mind to attack her. There were also fragmented sounds of struggle and laughter, and noxious smells. It all seemed so real that her body trembled—and was still trembling.

The first thing she did was to restore order to the living room, without ever once questioning what had happened there. She calmly gathered up the photocopies of the serpents from the floor and replaced them in the pale grey envelope from the college library.

No wonder she was having those awful mind-flashes of being attacked by serpents, she thought. The pictures of the serpents were so real. The wind coming in through the window must have blown them off the coffee table and scattered them on the floor. She had no way to account for the ones that Ginny had crumpled up in her fists and battered against her face. Some of those had traces of blood along the sharp edges of the paper. Those, she merely picked up and laid out on the coffee table so they could be smoothed with the flat of her hand. Then she placed them into the library envelope along with the others.

Sara then went to the kitchen to clean the caked blood from the back of her head with a towel she soaked in cold water at the sink. It had grown dark outside and she could see her reflection in the window above the sink as though it were a mirror. Her hair was disheveled and there were tiny scratches on her face. Probably from her own fingernails, as she tried to protect her face in the fall, she thought. She wiped at them with a clean part of the towel. They didn't look bad. A little makeup and no one would ever notice them, she told herself. It was then that she saw, for the first time, the irregular patch of flesh that had been torn from the side of her neck. The wound was not very deep, about the size of a quarter, and looked more like a burn than anything else. She touched it with a freshly moistened corner of the towel and it stung. She leaned closer to the window and gingerly traced her finger along the jagged edges of the wound. Her eyes widened. Something was now coming back to her.

As she continued to stare at her reflection in the window, images of the horrifying events of the afternoon gradually began to assemble themselves together like the irregular pieces of a jigsaw puzzle. One frozen abstraction after the other was carefully matched and placed against the edge of another until it fell into place. When the whole of it was assembled before her inner mind she dropped the cloth she had been holding and gasped. Ginny! she thought. Ginny had done this!

She looked about the kitchen as though someone had suddenly entered and was standing there beside her. She felt the cold of it, the prickling sensation of a magnetic charge that is sometimes exchanged between two people. Her insides were quivering, and she now realized they had been quivering ever since she had first come to at the foot of the stairs. Ginny! she thought, this time feeling another piece of the puzzle fall into place. She had to find out for sure.

Sara raced out of the kitchen and was headed for the stairs to the girl's room when a pair of arms reached out and grasped her. They held on to her tightly and wouldn't let go until she focused her full attention on who was holding her. It was Mitchell. He had been informed that the national guard was on its way and he wanted to see how things were with Sara and Ginny before they arrived. He had entered through the front door of the house when no one answered the doorbell. He saw the small pool of blood at the foot of the stairs and was about to charge upstairs himself when he heard Sara's hurried footsteps coming toward him from the kitchen. She had landed right in his arms.

"What's wrong?" he asked once he saw Sara's startled eyes focus on his.

Sara, who had once—on a dare from an African witch doctor—snatched prey away from a feasting lion, clung to him like a frightened sparrow. "Oh, God," she said against his chest. "I'm so glad you're here!"

When he slid his hand around to the back of her neck, to calm her, he felt the spongy clot of blood at the base of her skull. He removed his hand and examined it. There was blood on his palm. "What happened?" he asked. "Did you fall?" He looked down at the bloodied first step of the staircase.

Sara didn't answer. She began to cry. It was as uncontrollable and as unexpected as anything she had ever done. She continued for a short time, as he held her in his arms, until the tears subsided like the passing of a sudden storm—a storm that could not be diverted and had to run its course. "I'm all right," she finally said, pulling herself away from him. "Yes. I fell down the stairs."

She didn't know why she had lied to him. Maybe it was because she had wanted to tell him the truth, but felt he wouldn't believe her. Or perhaps she was afraid . . . for Ginny. "I was coming down from my room and I guess I must have stumbled," she said. "I have something to show you," she said, seemingly oblivious of the past several moments when she had cried in his arms like a demented hysteric. "It's in that envelope on the coffee table." She pointed to the living room.

Mitchell didn't know what to make of it all. The house was quiet, and because it was so late he knew Ginny would be asleep. She probably had not heard Sara's fall down the stairs. But there was something about the way Sara was acting that made him feel as though she was trying to conceal something from him. As he followed her over to the coffee table he thought he now understood what that might be. The spongy clot of blood at the back of her neck was almost hidden by the fluffy bun her hair was pulled back into. But on the side of her neck there was a wound he had not seen before. It looked as though a swatch of flesh had been ripped from the area just below the ear.

"What happened to the side of your neck?" he asked, reaching out in an attempt to examine it more closely. "It looks as though. . . ."

Sara quickly pulled a hairpin from the bun and her long blond hair cascaded down across her shoulders, concealing the wound from further scrutiny. "Nothing," she said. "It happened when I fell. Then she turned to pick up the envelope from the coffee table.

"You're hiding something," he said. "What's going on? Where's Ginny?"

The envelope in Sara's hand quivered as though it had a life of its own. She dropped it to the floor. Several copies of the serpent pictures spilled out when one side of the envelope split apart from the impact.

Mitchell bent down and slowly gathered them up. "What are these?" he asked, shuffling through the leaves of angry-looking vipers. "They look so *real!*"

It was a moment before she could say anything. When she finally did, her eyes glowed in the lamplight like polished jade.

"They're photocopies of cave paintings," she said, holding her cold hands together to keep them from trembling. "Ginny's mother made the drawings for a book she was doing while she was in Africa." She took a deep breath before going on. Her voice was now as even as it had ever been. "She copied them from the walls of the cave in which she died while giving birth to Ginny." It was as though she were reading a paper before an academic gathering. "The paintings were originally made by a sorcerer who had been condemned to die in that particular cave. It was said he possessed a power to control serpents."

Darkness covered the graves at the old cemetery on the hill like a shroud, allowing only an occasional wisp of vapor from the warm earth to escape into the cool night air. Locked and secure behind doors that had been stuffed along the bottom edges with strands of rope, or carpeting, or a bunch of old towels or discarded scraps of clothing—to keep snakes out—most of the town was asleep. Forty-five volunteer deputies, sheriffs, and constables patrolled the main streets of the town, as well as those streets and roads that were less frequented. They couldn't be everywhere, but they tried their best. They covered the backyards of moonlit houses and anywhere else they thought the snakes might be. Mitchell had strictly forbidden them to go anywhere near the pond. He didn't want their innocent blood on his hands. The men were all on foot, wore leg gaiters, and had strapped to their backs a snake pole that was issued to them by Mitchell. In their hands they all carried a lantern of some sort, and some of them had their weapons ready, too. In a little while they would gather at the grange and most of them would turn in for the night, waiting for the arrival of the national guard. They were the volunteers from neighboring counties, and they had brought with them their own sleeping bags, blankets, and food. Earlier that night, before Mitchell had gone over to see Sara, he had told the men how relieved he was to have them there. They knew he meant every word of it.

There was a sound so faint and distant that none of the men patrolling the town paid any attention to it. But closer to its source, at the old graveyard on the hill outside of town, it sounded like the footfall of a giant. A tombstone had just toppled over, and from the grave beneath it a group of serpents rose from the ground. They poked their heads from the earth as though they were newly born—as though the dead who had been buried there had somehow given birth to them. As their cold black eyes scanned the quiet cemetery, another tombstone toppled over. Coiling black vipers arose from that grave, too. They were quickly greeted by the others. It wasn't long before more and more stones and markers were toppled. And it wasn't long before more and more serpents appeared. Their thick black scaly bodies glistened with moonlight. They resembled teams of armored warriors, summoned from the bowels of the earth to engage in some dark combat.

And there were others, too.

In the basement of Estelle Whidden's funeral home, where the bodies of the recently killed had been stored, hundreds of them appeared. They rose from the body bags and other wrappings in which the dead had been stored. They came slithering out of lifeless eye sockets, gaping mouths and other orifices in the lower parts of the body—as well as through the putrefying flesh itself. Men and women, children too. They were rent through with jagged holes before the last of the serpents emerged.

And more.

They gathered about and in the waters of the pond, in the darkened crevices of low stone walls, in the shadows of foundations, in rooftop rain gutters, about the roots and in the branches of trees and shrubs, and in gardens everywhere. Some had already penetrated the flimsy barriers that had been stuffed and taped—or even glued and nailed—beneath doors and broken cellar windows, in nooks and crannies and any other fissure or chink that a house might have. Their infiltration of the town was complete.

They saw the teams of men patrolling the darkened streets. It was easy to avoid the beam of their lights—as easy as it would be for them to strike out and kill them, too. But they waited, patiently, as though some signal had yet to arrive. They were as one, united, waiting for the call that would unleash them on the sleeping town.

Lieutenant Colonel Darling was on the tarmac earlier than any of his men. Although he had the primary responsibility for the Pied Piper unit, he had never actually seen one of the experimental electronic devices in operation. He wanted to understand it more fully than the information he had been able to glean from the operating manuals he had just gone through. Arrangements had been made for a demonstration in one of the hangars where three army helicopters waited for the men to arrive for the hop to Wilston.

"I don't know the exact science of it, sir. But it works on the same sort of principle as a gofer chaser."

Darling looked at the officer in charge and smiled his familiar warm smile. The man had a pack on his back that was no larger than a small knapsack. From it a thick plug-in cable ran to the handle of the device that was gripped firmly in his hand. It looked like an ordinary metal detector with a circular sweep at the bottom.

"When the switch is turned on," the O.I.C. continued, "a vibration is sent out into the ground at a frequency that annoys every snake for miles around, so. . . ."

"Sort of to let them know you're coming, I suppose," Darling interjected, hoping to get a rise out of the young man.

The O.I.C. smiled, but did not comment. In a short while the men from the colonel's unit would be swarming all over the place, looking for and asking for everything that was right in front of their noses. He wanted to be back in his bunk and fast asleep long before that happened. He pointed to what looked like a long box that was covered by an old army blanket. Two men in olive drab stood at either end of it. They were regular army, like he was. "Okay," the O.I.C. finally said, nodding to his two subordinates. "Take it off."

When they removed the blanket the colonel's eyes narrowed and focused. Although there was a bright overhead light shining directly on it, he couldn't see the point of such a dramatic presentation. Beneath the blanket there had been a long, stainless steel wire cage, which was now fully revealed. Inside, running the full length of the nine-foot cage, there rested a thick green tree branch lying on its side. Clusters of heart-shaped leaves, which were greener than the twisted bark itself, jutted from it in all directions. Clumps of violet-colored flowers protruded from a number of places along the contorted branch like the splayed tops of tropical pineapples. Darling looked at the young officer and shrugged. "I don't see anything," he said.

"Look closer, colonel," the O.I.C. replied.

Darling stepped up to the cage and was about to touch it when one of the soldiers standing to the side shouted, "NO!"

Darling's warm eyes turned to chunks of blue ice. He had never been shouted at by an enlisted man before. His eyes demanded an explanation.

"Sorry, sir," the soldier said, looking first to the colonel, then to the O.I.C. who was now at the colonel's side.

"I should have explained, sir," the O.I.C. took over and apologized. "But there's something inside that will probably take your fingers off if you lean on the cage."

Darling took a step back and squinted through the half-inch squares of the wire mesh cage. When he finally saw what it was, he took a full step back from it. Inside was the longest, greenest, thickest, meanest-looking snake he had ever seen in real life. It had twisted itself about the branch in such a way that it appeared to be part of the branch itself. That was why he hadn't seen it before.

"Put a sign on the goddamn thing!" he said.

"Yessir!" the officer snapped. "I'm sorry, sir!"

Darling softened again. "So what is it?" he asked.

"A South American Mamba, sir. It's. . . ."

"Quit calling me *sir*, and get on with it," the colonel interrupted. "I don't care what the snake's name is. I just want to know how that blasted thing you're holding operates."

Careful not to call the colonel *sir,* the O.I.C. simply said, "Yes," reached over his shoulder to turn the device on, and aimed the round pan at the end of the handle directly at the cage. Inside the Mamba leaped from the branch and scuttled about in three or four different directions at once, looking for a way to escape the confines of the long cage. When it discovered it could not, it bunched itself together and struck at the wire mesh as lightning-fast as machine gun fire. Between its bright green scales, the skin was black, and the angrier the snake became, the more it puffed itself up, making its scales look more and more like bright green feathers. By the time it was through the thing looked as though it could fly. It was one of the weirdest displays of animal behavior the colonel had ever seen.

"That's enough!" Darling commanded. "Turn that stupid thing off!"

The O.I.C. didn't bother reaching over his shoulder to turn it off. He simply disconnected it by pulling the cable from the polelike handle of the thing—it was quicker. The demonstration had obviously upset the old man.

"How in the name of all that's merciful," Darling began, "is that thing supposed to clear a snake-infested area, when all you have to do is turn the dumb thing on and the snake *attacks* whoever's pointing that device at it!?"

"It doesn't happen that way. . . ." The O.I.C. had been about to end with *sir,* but caught himself. "When the device is turned on in an open area like a field or jungle, which this unit was designed for, the snakes waste no time in getting *away* from the vibrations it sets up in the ground. The last thing a snake will do is attack it."

Lieutenant Colonel Darling pulled the corners of his lips back tight. "Well, let me tell you one simple little thing," he said. "Did you ever see a water moccasin run away from *anything?*" He didn't wait for an answer. "I'm just a poor old country boy who happened to make good in the army," he went on. "When I was growing up I had the occasion to witness what water moccasins are capable of, and, let me tell you one thing, if you go and disturb one, it'll come clean up out of the water and chase you halfway to hell before it gives up! Have you ever been bit in the ass by one?" he asked. Not waiting for an answer he undid the highly polished buckle of his belt. "Well, I have!" And he lowered his pants to show them the scar. It was right next to that of an old bullet wound . . . but that was another story.

The two soldiers on either side of the cage stared straight off into space. They were career men, and, while they would have a good chuckle about this later, they both knew this was not the time to see, hear, or say anything. As for the O.I.C., he didn't know *what* to say. His two men had begun to cover the cage before the colonel had a chance to turn on them. When they finished they both stood at full military attention on either side of the cage, each of them secretly wishing they had the power to turn themselves invisible.

The colonel was almost finished buckling his pants back up and was going to tell them the story of how it was that a water moccasin happened to bite him on the ass, when he heard the arrival of his men for assembly. In under ten minutes the men of the Pied Piper unit would come swarming toward the hangar, ready to be briefed before boarding the waiting helicopters.

"Get that God-awful thing out of here," he said to the two soldiers, indicating the cage. Then, twisting his head slightly to the side, so that he made contact with the O.I.C.'s eyes, he added, "You are *all* to forget anything you might have thought you just saw or heard." He snapped his buckle closed so that it made a noise that sounded very much like the empty casing of an M-1 shell hitting the ground after a round of fire. "Is that understood?" he asked in his familiar soft tone of voice.

The O.I.C. and his two soldiers saluted at the same time. It was a struggle, but all three of them managed to avoid saying *sir!* as they snapped their hands to their foreheads in the prescribed military gesture.

In a little under an hour, Lieutenant Colonel Darling and his men would be at the pond in Wilston.

"Inside The Serpent's cave one can still feel the presence of the sorcerer who was once banished here. His name remains unknown, but the natives call him 'The Serpent.' He is still here. The Sotho curse, which is said to bind him here for all of time, is carved deeply into every wall of the cave where it cannot be missed: 'May you perish in pain!' it reads. 'And may you know it horribly!' He was said to have been more evil than Satan himself. You can feel his vile breath hissing from the

mouths of the hideous vipers he so skillfully painted over the deeply carved curse of his everlasting home, in an obvious attempt to obliterate it. There are thousands of them. I can only sketch a few at a time, they are so real, so terrifying to behold. His skull and bones are scattered like sticks of bleached driftwood to the far reaches of this dark and lonely place. It conjures in my mind the image of a defiled graveyard. I have never seen such a thing. My fire, ablaze with the glow of the sun itself, offers little warmth. His magic is said to have been more terrible than anything I can possibly imagine. The oral myth, which still survives, tells how he had slaughtered whole villages, ravaged innocent women and children, and tortured the warriors who were sent to kill him. He had a power over serpents. They were his allies, and were said to obey his unspoken will as though it were the voice of their own consciousness. Toward the end, so it is said, he was able to transform himself into a serpent of any kind. That was his downfall. While in such a state, so the legend tells, he was captured by a group of men who tricked him into becoming a small and harmless viper. They had first intoxicated him with drink before challenging him to show the world how powerful he really was. They argued that everyone was aware of the awesomeness of his ability to transform himself into a serpent of tremendous size, but there was a rumor spreading throughout the land (so they said) which proclaimed he could only do that one thing. Just this once, they entreated him, couldn't he show how great he really was, and change himself into a tiny viper? He couldn't resist. When he awoke, he found himself in the forbidden mountain range of evildoers. Sorcerers who had been born with a special ability to heal, but who chose to use their gift badly, were banished to this sacredly protected realm from which I write these words. Here, the evildoers were forced to seek the refuge of a cave and live out the rest of their lives in isolation, where they could no longer cause bad magic to occur. When they died, their magic was said to remain locked within this forbidden range forever and ever. No sorcerer has ever been known to escape, either in body or spirit."

Sara looked up from the manuscript and stared into Mitchell's eyes. They were rimmed with red. She had been reading to him for over an hour and wasn't sure he understood what it was all about. "Do you know what this means?" she asked, indicating the photocopy of the handwritten text that Ginny's mother had written to accompany the serpent drawings. "It tells us that Ginny is somehow responsible for what's happened!"

Mitchell shook his head. "I'm sorry," he said. "But I don't follow. I can't see how Ginny has anything to do with any of this."

Sara knew it was time to confide in Mitchell. She needed him to understand. She rose from the couch where she had been sitting and walked around the coffee table to his chair. She pulled her hair away from the wound on her neck and knelt down beside him so he could study it in the light from the floor lamp beside the chair.

"Ginny did this," she said as he stared incredulously at the bite wound. "Can you see the teeth marks?"

He certainly could. There were two sets of indentations about the swollen wound, like crescent-shaped brackets. "How did it happen?" he asked.

"I showed her the pictures of the serpents her mother had made and she attacked me," she said. "I didn't fall down the stairs. I was knocked off my feet when she charged me like a bull. I landed against the bottom step with the back of my head. Then she jumped on me and tried to bash my skull in. If I hadn't gotten a good hold of her, and. . . ."

Sara couldn't finish. She didn't know how to explain the protective feeling she had for the child, and how she had tried to help her by holding on to her tightly and whispering that everything was going to be all right.

"And . . . ?" Mitchell prompted her.

Sara stood up again and stared at him. Her eyes blinked angrily.

"Don't you see!?" she blurted out, her eyes brimming with tears. "The sorcerer! He did escape! Through Ginny! While she was still in her mother's womb! It was the only way out! And she's . . . she's possessed!"

Mitchell wondered if Sara was having some sort of a nervous breakdown. Before she had begun to read from the diary notes that Ginny's mother had made, she had told him some of the most bizarre tales he had ever heard—about something called *poltergeists,* about adolescent little girls, and about a hallucination she had had in her cottage at the college. And now this—about Ginny being possessed by a sorcerer who had died hundreds of years ago! He had never heard anything like it in his entire life. It all sounded like a bunch of nonsense.

"I think you need to get some rest," he said gently. "Taking care of Ginny while all this business with the snakes has been going on has probably been too much for you."

"NO!" Sara shouted. "I'm not a lunatic! I know what I'm talking about! It's just that. . . ."

Lieutenant Colonel Darling and his men had landed in a field outside of town and were now on their way to the pond. As the equipment was being strapped to the backs of his men, he had told them that it was to be a quick operation—a quick march to the pond, and an even quicker disposal of the water moccasins. He wondered why the local sheriff was not there to greet him, as he should have been. Instead, a flock of about fifty other sheriffs, deputies, and constables had appeared to direct him and his men to the pond—and they were all from other jurisdictions. There was something about it that made him feel . . . uneasy. He didn't like it one single bit.

Darling wasn't the only one to feel the uneasiness of the night spilling into his veins. Estelle Whidden felt it, too. She pulled aside the curtains of her bedroom window and stared down into the street to find out what all the commotion was. She saw Darling and his men jogging off in lock step through the center of town, toward the pond. There was something about the look of Estelle's old Victorian mansion that gave Darling the willies as he passed, and he shot a glance up toward her bedroom window as though someone had called his name. Estelle quickly dropped the curtain back in place and took a deep breath. She felt as though she had been kicked in the stomach. She reached for the telephone beside her bed.

"Hello?" she said into the ivory-colored receiver in her hand. "This is Estelle." She had dialed the number of Whidden's Classic Coffins, the casket company she owned. She knew someone would be there, filling the emergency order she had placed earlier that day for the bodies being stored in the basement of her funeral home. She now ordered a hundred more of the plain pine boxes. Then she hurriedly dialed a second number. This time it was to her mortuary school. Her director—a frail, balding man with perpetual dark rings beneath his eyes—was always there. He lived in a small apartment on the top floor of the building.

"I want you to send me every student you've got left," she said after she was sure he was awake. Then she listened attentively to what the director had to say from the other end of the line. "Yes, yes," she responded, on the edge of impatience. "The whole darn freshman class, too. Everyone you haven't already sent. And you come, too!" Then, before she could give the confused man a chance to ask any questions, she let the receiver fall back into place against its cradle.

Estelle Whidden already had the entire senior class on hand—eight students who were sleeping exhaustedly in an attic dormitory they had hastily rigged up for themselves—to help with the snakebite victims who had come in that day. What she had felt after her eyes met those of Darling from her window, was that she was soon going to be needing all the extra help she could get. She had a sense about such things. It was one of the reasons why she was so successful in the business she was in—and she was hardly ever wrong.

Something like a pause in the beat of the universe stirred the serpents. Somehow they responded to it as though it were the will of their own inner consciousness. They were being called back to the pond. Something was wrong. Without hesitation they quickly slithered from their nooks and crannies about the town and headed directly to the pond.

A scream came from Ginny's room. At first Mitchell thought Sara had awakened the girl with her shouting about not being a lunatic. But it wasn't only Ginny's scream they had heard, there was a hollow, thumping noise that sounded like bare feet hurriedly scampering about on the wooden floor directly above their heads. Mitchell shot to his feet. "You stay here," he said to Sara.

Sara wasn't about to wait anywhere; she beat him to the staircase and together they raced to the locked door of Ginny's bedroom. Sara rattled the knob as Mitchell hammered the door with his fist. When Ginny screamed again they shouldered their way through the door, knocking it right off its frail old hinges. Sara tried to enter first but Mitchell managed to step in before her. Together they froze in their tracks. A peculiar stench assailed them. It reminded Mitchell of a pit of decaying corpses he had once come upon in Vietnam. He almost gagged.

The room was as still as a morgue. The only thing that moved was the thin bedsheet that covered Ginny's body. The moonlight slanting in on it from the window beside her made it appear as though the child was sleeping beneath the vaporous cover of a slightly rolling sea.

Curled up on the floor at the foot of her bed, there was something else that rolled and undulated in the moonlight. At first neither of them could imagine what it was. The mere motion of the thing sent shivers through their scalps. It moved like the hull of a sunken ship—its timbered ribs broken and curled after centuries of torturous currents, its walls worn thin, almost transparent, by the sea in which it had gone down. Then, as their eyes grew more accustomed to the dark, they began to recognize it for what it really was—though they could hardly believe it. They were staring at the shed skin of an enormous snake. From the size of it, the serpent had to have been over fifteen feet long—and as thick around as a fat man's thigh. It rocked like a cradle in a draft of wind that swept into the room from the window. They now knew where the stench was coming from.

Ginny's eyes suddenly popped open, like those of a mechanical doll. She screamed. Her body twisted and shuddered on the bed as though she were being lashed by a rod of steel. "No!" she cried, clutching herself as though she was trying to keep her body from coming apart. Her flesh stung the same way it had that morning Gary Sorter was at the pond, biting into the heads of the water moccasins with his teeth. Only this time it wasn't only her head that ached, it was her whole body. "They're trying to kill me!" she shrieked.

As Sara and Mitchell raced to comfort her, Ginny suddenly pulled herself up in the bed and stared at them. They stopped in their tracks. There was a movement from beneath her thin nightdress that was disturbingly familiar. It was as though a serpent were inside of it. The girl laughed, a pained and tortured laughter that seemed centuries old. She began to speak, but what came out of her mouth sounded to Mitchell like gibberish. But Sara understood it immediately. It took only a moment for her to recognize it as the first part of the Sotho curse—the curse that had been carved into the walls of the cave in which Ginny had been born. *May you perish in pain.*

Ginny threw the covers aside and glided from the edge of the bed as though she had somehow overcome the force of gravity. In the deep shadows of the room, her movements were swift and graceful—having an animal-like dignity to them that were disturbingly unnatural. On her way to the window she passed through the moonlight. The silhouette of her body inside the nightdress looked somewhat thicker than it should have—and there was a reflective, almost iridescent, quality to it too, as though her skin were composed of something other than ordinary flesh. At the window she turned to them. Her face was lined with the agony of a wounded animal. *May you perish in pain!*

she said again in the dialect of a Sotho sorcerer. *And may you know it horribly!*

Ginny then slipped out the window. Sara and Mitchell reached the other end of the room almost as quickly as the train of her nightdress disappeared outside along the edge of the wooden windowsill.

What they saw, or thought they saw, caused them to step back. On the tin roof of the back porch, just beneath the window, was a slimy path of gummy ooze. Moonlight falling through the surrounding trees cast its swaying shadows on it like hordes of scampering tarantulas. Yet, through all that, there seemed to be the unmistakable signature of a serpent's scales—a serpent of considerable size—or was it something else? Something conjured up from the darkness of their troubled imaginations? The ooze faded into the darkness at the end of the roof, where there was a drain pipe leading down to the yard. Beside it, toward the very edge of the darkness itself, their eyes strained at something that was far more real and familiar than anything they had encountered in the few moments they had been in the girl's room. It was a footprint, the footprint of a child.

"Let's go," Sara said. "I know where she's gone."

Things were going well for Darling and his men. He had stationed a perimeter of the volunteer law enforcement officers near the top of the hill with guns, machetes, and powerful night lamps. Everyone wore thick snake-leggings. In between each of the civilians stood an unarmed national guardsman with one of the electronic "snake chasers." He then sent the remaining half of his men down to the pond. When all was set, he gave the order for the men at the pond to turn on their equipment. In an instant, the water moccasins leaped into the air as though they had been stung by lightning and attempted to escape up the hill. Darling then gave the order for the guardsmen who remained uphill—where he stood to the side beneath a huge umbrella tree—to turn on *their* equipment. It caught the snakes in the middle. They twisted and knotted in an agonized maze of pain and confusion as the civilians then advanced and began to shoot and hack the stunned moccasins to pieces. Darling smiled. Like shooting fish in a barrel, he thought.

Segments of the snakes' bodies twisted blood-red in the strong beams of light. The popping sound of guns and the slicing ring of machetes was reassuring to Darling. He loosened his grip on the tree he had been prepared to climb if all did not go well. It looked as though the men were winning fast and the guard would indeed be back home for breakfast, just as he had told them they would. A huge grin spread itself across his face. He wondered why he had felt so darn uneasy about getting this job done in the first place. Like one of his men had said at the briefing that morning, it was going to be a piece of cake.

The men cheered and joked when they saw how easy it was. All they had to do was keep shooting and chopping, and it would be over with in no time. The civilian law enforcement officers had enough of the guards' weapons and ammunition to handle another couple of thousand serpents if they needed to. Darling was about to pick up a machete and chop a few for himself when the broad grin on his face suddenly vanished. A little girl had just raced out of nowhere into the midst of all the shooting and chopping. She was as pale as death.

"Cease fire!" Darling commanded. "There's a child out there!"

The weapons were instantly stilled. But the guardsmen down the hill, about fifty of them at the pond, hadn't heard the command. They continued to train their equipment at the bushes and rocks that surrounded the water. Hundreds of snakes continued to race up the hill, not toward the men, but to Ginny. It seemed their number had multiplied, not diminished. Darling blinked his eyes in disbelief. Caught in the vortex of blinding beams of light, the girl appeared to be some sort of a demented spirit. Her mouth was blood-red and her disheveled hair hung from her twisting head like thickly matted ropes of dancing snakes. And her eyes . . . when she rolled her head the piercing lights made them look like endless pools of night set into the chalk-white firmament of her contorted face. She clutched herself as though in pain. There was something else that chilled everyone who saw it—the silhouette of the girl's body writhing inside of the thin nightdress she wore. As she twisted and hunched herself over in convulsive shudders of pain, she appeared to be one of the very creatures that swarmed at her feet! Some of the men dropped their lamps and began to run. Others leveled their rifles at the child and began to fire. But with most of the lamps on the ground, their beams crossed in all directions, it was too dark. Some of the men thought they saw a cloak of snakes rise up to engulf and protect the girl.

"STOP!" Darling commanded. "It's only a child."

The gunfire continued, but without the lights focused directly on her, it was useless. The bullets went astray and began hitting some of the guardsmen farther down the hill. As they shouted and ran for cover, they dropped their equipment. Had they been armed they would have returned the fire.

"I said, cease the goddamn shooting!" Darling roared above the din. "I have men down there and they're being hit!" He pulled his own gun out, ready to turn on the civilians if they did not stop their firing. They stopped immediately; they also dropped their guns and lamps and joined the other men who had already fled before them. In absolute and utter frustration at the sudden chaos that he found himself engulfed in, Darling fired his own .45 into the air until he used up the clip. All it did was knock a shower of leaves off the tree he was beneath. "Goddamn sons of bitches!" he shouted after the fleeing civilians. "You killed some of my men!" He now knew he had committed a grave tactical error in turning his men's weapons over to the volunteer law enforcement officers. Stupid! he cursed himself. Stupid old fool!

Something made him spin about. It was the sound of laughter, not of the guardsmen who swarmed up the hill past him, but . . . he focused on the girl through the shadowy, smoke-filled air. With most of the electronic devices broken or discarded, Ginny was feeling much better. So were the snakes. No more needles of agonizing fire pierced their bodies. They huddled about Ginny's feet like a rejoicing army. The joy of it showed in their cold black eyes, which sparkled like jewels in the few remaining lights that raked along the ground to where they were.

Ginny gazed down at the moccasins and laughed again—that same bubbling laughter that had, moments before, caught Darling so unaware in the midst of his own personal chaos. His eyes now widened: She appeared to be *conversing* with the snakes! She spread her arms above them in a loving gesture and slowly brought her hands to indicate the men who scampered toward the top of the hill. Darling could have sworn the girl's lips then formed the word *go*.

And the snakes did indeed go. They slithered up after the men like blades of light. Their bodies sounded like a refrain of snapping bullwhips as they quickly caught up with and lashed the men in a frenzy of glistening fangs and spewed venom. As the men trampled the lights, sparks showered the dark like shooting stars. Some of the men caught fire. The scent of burning flesh and gunsmoke filled the air. It seemed to drive the snakes wild.

Screams and the feeble crying for help of dying men rose up about Darling like a chorus of agony lifting from a darkened battlefield. He had heard it too many times before. In Guam, Saipan, and the Caroline Islands—where he had come close to losing his own life. Coming to him now, just minutes after thinking he and his men would be home for early breakfast, it did something to him. A grotesque montage of horror spilled into his mind as the sounds of gunfire and men calling to one another in the blackness blended with the darkness that filled his own heart. He turned to the little girl and slowly shoved a fresh clip into his automatic. "You little bitch!" he shouted, pointing the .45 directly at her head. "You . . ."

He got no further. A violent clattering of leaves in the tree above his head caused him to look up. When he did, a shower of moccasins cascaded down upon his face like a stinging rain of icy whips. They sank their venomous fangs into his throat and chewed his face while clinging to his shoulders, arms, and chest. He went down, not only to the ground, but into the deepest part of himself—where all things end. With his last belabored breath of life, he cursed himself through a bubbling pool of blood that erupted in his throat. He was a fool, he told himself. And he had committed the worst possible sin of any commander: He had taken the enemy for granted. Some of the finest men he had ever known were meeting a brutal death. It was a sin, he felt, that even an eternity of fire could not absolve.

Sara had led Mitchell directly to the pond after leaving the house. They went the back way through town, the way Sara had discovered the day she went over to the college in that rainstorm. It was shorter and they missed running into the guardsmen and civilian volunteers being attacked by the moccasins as they tried to escape. By the time Sara and Mitchell got to the pond the national guard had been decimated. So, too, had the civilian volunteers. All the lights had gone out and small clumps of burning men smoldered in the darkness. A thin veil of smoke clung to the surface of the moonlit pond like a cold shroud. But it couldn't conceal the tragedy that had occurred there. The shouts of dying men and the rifle fire Sara and Mitchell had heard on their way to the pond were now completely stilled. They knew there could only be one reason for such a silence, and they felt it in the pit of their hearts as though they had themselves been dealt a devastating blow.

Sara almost doubled over with the stench, not only of the burning flesh but of something else, as well. It was the same putrid odor that had earlier filled Ginny's darkened bedroom. They looked at the pond. Its surface was alive with moccasins that leaped into the air and lashed about like hundreds of glistening whips, cracking and snapping against the choppy surface of the water as they fell back into it. On the broad outcropping of stone that overlooked the pond, the moon lit the girl as though she was a luminous creature of the night.

Sara and Mitchell stared at her. Having taken the back route, they had come down on the part of the pond that was closer to the college. Ginny was across a narrow inlet from them, not more than thirty yards away—less than a hundred feet of water that was choked with leaping moccasins. There was no way they could reach her by land, either. The ground was covered with teams of twisting vipers that slithered about, over and between the fallen bodies of the guardsmen and civilians like sentries, blocking every possible path that led to the stone ledge on which she stood. It was the same jutting ledge on which the bodies of Winkie Bols and his two friends had burned to ashes not very long before.

Ginny laughed when she saw Sara and Mitchell gaping at her. She reached down and slowly began to lift the nightdress she was wearing. When its hem was at the level of her knees, she gave it a quick jerk over her head and watched it sail into the darkness behind her.

Standing naked in the moonlight, she reminded Sara and Mitchell of something from another world. They didn't know if it was because of the dark or the distance that separated them from her, but the girl looked like a serpent as she undulated about the ledge as though performing a ritual dance. Her arms flailed the night air while her hands, fingers together and fully extended from the cup of her slightly curled palms, struck out at the darkness like two angry cobras. The pond boiled with moccasins. Their splashing and lashing sounded like the ocean crashing against a rocky shore. At her feet there was movement, too, that of slithering young moccasins. They coiled upon her feet and ankles and climbed her naked body until they covered her in a coat that was indistinguishable from her own flesh. Her eyes were alive. It was as though she were transformed into something else—

something that had been sleeping within her since the day she was born. It had finally broken loose of the bonds that had imprisoned it to claim the inner darkness of her mind, and now she glowed with the ultimate recognition of it. What she was, what she had always been, was real at last!

Ginny laughed.

The sound of it went into Sara like the chill of a tomb that had been sealed for centuries. At first a pencil-thin shaft of light, then, as the air gushes in to fill the void, the centuries sigh. Sara now knew in an instant that she *was* the only one who could stop the child. Pandora's box! she thought. It had to be closed again. If not, the serpents would go on to kill everyone in town.

Sara took a deep breath and stepped away from Mitchell, toward the snakes, toward the waters of the pond. The snakes opened a path for her but kept their cotton-white mouths agape with sets of sparkling fangs. It didn't matter. In Africa she had learned there were many ways to die. The best way was not to mind it.

Mitchell was so bewildered by what was happening that all he could do was stand there, surrounded on all sides by the moccasins, with his gun in his hand. What he was going to do with it, he didn't know. Eight rounds in the clip and one in the chamber, nine shots in all. And there appeared to be over a hundred snakes about him—every one of them poised to strike. At that moment, he also gave himself up for dead. It didn't matter; yet, he somehow had the feeling that if he didn't move from the spot where he was standing, the vipers would leave him alone. And as though to confirm his thoughts, Sara turned to him when she reached the water and motioned with her hands that he should remain where he was.

Sara quickly stepped out of her clothes and walked into the water until it lapped about her knees. She called to the girl, "Ginny, I know what's happening. I want to help you. But first you must stop all this." She spread her hands apart to indicate the batch of thick black moccasins that splashed about her legs. "Make them stop," she asked. "I know you have the power to do it."

"No!" Ginny cried. "I can't!"

"You can!" Sara insisted. And she waded further out into the water until it reached her waist.

"Go back!" Ginny entreated her. This time there was terror in her voice, as though she were slipping from a crumbling hand-hold above a treacherous cliff. "You can't swim!" she screamed.

Sara pushed off into the midst of the swarming moccasins, doing her best to swim toward the outcropping where Ginny stood. The girl circled in a frenzy. The young vipers that had been clinging to her body were hurtled off into the darkness. "What are you doing?" she shrieked at the larger moccasins that now clung to Sara's body, weighting her down and carrying her beneath the surface of the water. "DON'T!" When they didn't release themselves, Ginny dove into the water and headed toward Sara. When she reached the churning spot where Sara had been dragged under, she turned herself up and slipped beneath the ink-black surface like an eel.

Mitchell watched in horror as the water boiled. Its surface erupted as though it had been struck by a meteorite. Every snake that had been at his feet, every snake that had been protecting the girl while she was on the ledge, was now in the water, racing toward the spot where Sara and the girl had disappeared. He ran to the water's edge and emptied his gun. Nine rounds. It didn't make the slightest difference. The .45 caliber bullets had struck like a handful of pebbles lost in an avalanche. He looked about for something to hurl into the water, in case . . . in case Sara was still alive. A short distance behind him there were the remains of several trees that had been cut down the night the three men had tried to set the pond on fire. The rainstorm a couple of nights back had carried some of the logs closer to the pond. He hurried to find the biggest one he could drag back.

When he returned he was so winded from having dragged such a heavy load that he didn't at first notice. It wasn't until after he had managed to slide the trunk into the water that he looked up and saw that the surface of the moonlit pond was as calm and smooth as a black mirror. He could even see the moon and stars reflected in it. The trunk slipped from his hands and glided out into the water, leaving rows of gently rolling ripples in its wake. As he focused on the spot where Sara and the girl had disappeared, his heart sank. They were gone. And it was his own damn fault! He should have shot the girl and carried Sara away. But what would have happened if he had? Hadn't Sara somehow managed to . . . to *what?* he suddenly wondered. Rid the pond of snakes?

He stared at the water as though attempting to read the message of the violence that had so unexpectedly erupted there. He didn't realize that he was now up to his knees in the water, heading toward the spot where Sara and the girl had gone down. When he felt the wetness climbing up his thighs he stopped and looked down. The water circled his legs in ripples that caught the moon and broke it into a thousand glittering diamonds. For a moment he lost himself in the vortex of it, as though he were a space traveler falling through a dazzling field of stars. He thought he saw something coming up at him through the void of it, something as pale and ghostly as the moon itself. At first he suspected it was merely another aspect of the reflected light of the moon. But as it drew closer and closer to the surface he began to recognize its shape. He couldn't move. And when it finally broke the surface and touched his leg, the shock made him feel as though the skin had been peeled right off his face. It was a hand. An outstretched open hand. Sara's hand.

Mitchell quickly yanked it out of the water until the arm appeared, then the shoulder. When he lifted Sara's head he almost dropped her. She looked like a corpse. But as he grappled her up into his arms and headed for the shore, her body shivered against his chest. She was alive.

"Sara," he cried on the grassy embankment as he rested her down. "Sara!" He repeated her name again and again as he rhythmically pushed the heel of his hand upward against the bottom of her rib cage, trying desperately to restore the rhythm of her breathing. There wasn't a mark on her body. The snakes hadn't gotten to her! "Sara!" He was about to press his lips to hers in an attempt to force his breath into her lungs when she finally opened her eyes. The cool air gushing into her from the pond filled her with its chill. Mitchell reached for her dress, which was lying nearby, and covered her with it.

"What happened?" she murmured, weakly lifting her head to look about. She saw the water. A vale of vapor lifted from its mirrorlike calm. She turned to Mitchell who was still kneeling beside her. A sudden radiance filled her eyes. "I . . . I *swam!*" she gasped. "I . . ."

She suddenly bolted to her feet, clutching the dress about her shivering body. "Ginny!" she cried, frantically searching the pond for any sign of the girl. "What have I done!?"

Mitchell didn't know what to say. From what he had seen there that night he wasn't sure he would ever know what to say. All he could do was help her back into her clothes and hold her in his arms to keep her from trembling. Sara cried against his breast as freely and as unashamedly as a woman who has just lost her own child. There was no question in his mind that she would gladly have sacrificed her own life to have Ginny back again.

"I wanted her," Sara said weakly. "I wanted her to love me."

They stood there silently clutching each other as their eyes hopelessly scanned the water for any sign of life. There was none. The snakes appeared to have vanished.

"What happened out there?" Mitchell finally asked. From what she had told him earlier, about sorcerers and snakes, the cave, and Ginny's mother—and from what he had himself just witnessed—there seemed little reason to doubt anything she would ever tell him again.

"I tricked her," Sara said. Her voice was faint and somewhat choked. "By going into the water with the moccasins I forced her to help me. I knew she would. And it destroyed her. I didn't expect that."

"The moccasins turned on her?" Mitchell asked.

Sara couldn't answer. Neither could she answer his next question about why the moccasins had apparently vanished.

"I wanted to help her," Sara wept. "I thought I could save her."

They stayed there for a very long time after that, alternately gazing out over the rows and rows of dead men, then at the pond—as though the answers to the many questions they still had would somehow rise from the quiet surface of the dark water. The log Mitchell had earlier thought of using to rescue Sara and Ginny had drifted to the center of the pond and now turned in a lazy circle, sending quiet ripples out from it until they reached the shore.

When the first pale light of dawn touched the water, Mitchell placed his arm about Sara's waist and began to lead her back up the hill toward home. The town was still asleep and the snakes were gone. All he wanted now was to get Sara back home. Feeling the weight of her against his shoulder as she leaned against him, he found himself wanting her. It was crazy, he told himself, and there was hardly an earthly reason for it, but he had the feeling she wanted him, too. As they slowly made their way further and further up the hill, unseen by them, the ink-black surface of the water was broken by a bubble emerging from beneath its silky calm. It was followed by another, then another, until there were dozens and dozens of them sailing out on the mirrored surface of the pond like shiny capsules from an unknown world. And when they broke into sparkling beadlets of splashing light, it was like the bubbling laughter of a child escaping into the dawn.